#1 *New York Times* bests

KRESLEY CO

PLEASURE OF A DARK PRINCE

"Consistent excellence is a Cole standard!"

—*Romantic Times* (4½ stars)

"There are few authors that can move me to tears. Kresley Cole is one of them."

—Book Binge

"Kresley Cole's Immortals After Dark series does not cease to amaze me."

—Love Vampires

KISS OF A DEMON KING

"Perennial favorite Cole continues to round out her Immortals After Dark world with kick-butt action and scorching passion!"

—*Romantic Times*

"Kresley Cole knows what paranormal romance readers crave and superbly delivers on every page."

—Single Titles

"Full of magic, mayhem, sorcery, and sensuality. Readers will not want to miss one word of this memorable and enchanting tale. The closer to the end I got the slower I read because I knew once the story ended I would be left craving more of this brilliant and emotionally gripping saga. . . . It is truly one of the most amazing tales Kresley Cole has ever released."

—Wild On Books

***Dreams of a Dark Warrior* is also available as an eBook**

"Cole deftly blends danger and desire into a brilliantly original contemporary paranormal romance. She neatly tempers the scorchingly sexy romance between Sabine and Rydstrom with a generous measure of sharp humor, and the combination of a cleverly constructed plot and an inventive cast of characters in *Kiss of a Demon King* is simply irresistible."

—Reader To Reader

DARK DESIRES AFTER DUSK

"*New York Times* bestseller Cole outdoes herself. . . . A gem."

—*Romantic Times*

"Kresley Cole is a gifted author with a knack for witty dialogue, smart heroines, fantastic alpha males, and yes, it has to be said, some of the hottest love scenes you'll read in mainstream romance. . . . You're in for a treat if you've never read a Kresley Cole book."

—RomanceNovel.tv

"A wonderfully romantic tale of two people from the opposite sides of their immortal world. . . . Everything I had hoped it to be and so much more!"

—Queue My Review

DARK NEEDS AT NIGHT'S EDGE

"Poignant and daring. You can trust Cole to always deliver sizzling sexy interludes within a darkly passionate romance."

—*Romantic Times*

"The evolution of this romance is among the most believable and engrossing I've ever read. Cole's Immortals After Dark series continues stronger than ever with this latest installment."

—Fresh Fiction

WICKED DEEDS ON A WINTER'S NIGHT

"Leave it to the awe-inspiring Cole to dish up a combustible mix of sorcery and passion. One for the keeper shelf!"

—*Romantic Times* (4½ stars)

"Kresley Cole . . . effortlessly delivers heart-wringing romance, likable heroines, hot heroes, and hotter sex . . . set against an original and exciting paranormal mythology that keeps the both the story and reader speeding along from one high point to another."

—Love Vampires

NO REST FOR THE WICKED

"Sizzling sex and high-stakes adventure are what's on tap in mega-talented Cole's sensational new paranormal release. . . . One nonstop thrill ride. Brava!"

—*Romantic Times* (Top Pick)

"Oh, wow! Kresley Cole writes another spine-tingling, adventurous, and passionate romance. . . . I recommend readers grab a copy of Kresley Cole's *No Rest for the Wicked* today. It's a definite keeper."

—Romance Reviews Today

A HUNGER LIKE NO OTHER

"Intense action, devilishly passionate sex, and fascinating characters . . . leads readers into an amazing and inventive alternate reality. . . . Hot stuff!"

—*Romantic Times* (Top Pick)

"Rich mythology, a fresh approach, and excellent writing make this vampire tale superb."

—Fresh Fiction

Books by Kresley Cole

The Sutherland Series

The Captain of All Pleasures
The Price of Pleasure

The MacCarrick Brothers Series

If You Dare
If You Desire
If You Deceive

The Immortals After Dark Series

A Hunger Like No Other
No Rest for the Wicked
Wicked Deeds on a Winter's Night
Dark Needs at Night's Edge
Dark Desires After Dusk
Kiss of a Demon King
Pleasure of a Dark Prince
Demon from the Dark
Dreams of a Dark Warrior

Anthologies

Playing Easy to Get
Deep Kiss of Winter

KRESLEY COLE

DREAMS OF A DARK WARRIOR

London · New York · Sydney · Toronto

A CBS COMPANY

First published in Great Britain by Simon & Schuster, 2011
A division of Simon & Schuster UK Ltd
A CBS COMPANY

3 5 7 9 10 8 6 4 2

Simon & Schuster UK Ltd
1st Floor
222 Gray's Inn Road
London WC1X 8HB

www.simonandschuster.co.uk

Simon & Schuster Australia
Sydney

A CIP catalogue record for this book is available
from the British Library

Paperback B ISBN: 978-1-84983-038-6
Paperback A ISBN: 978-1-84739-780-5

Printed by CPI Cox & Wyman, Reading, Berkshire RG1 8EX

Dedicated with much love
to the amazing Roxanne St. Claire,
a bright shining star of a writer and dear friend.

Glossary of Terms
from
The Living Book of Lore

THE LORE

". . . and those sentient creatures that are not human shall be united in one stratum, coexisting with, yet secret from, man's."

- Most are immortal and can regenerate from injuries. The stronger breeds can only be killed by mystical fire or beheading.
- Their eyes change with intense emotion, often to a breed-specific color.

THE VALKYRIE

"When a maiden warrior screams for courage as she dies in battle, Wóden and Freya heed her call. The two gods give up lightning to strike her, rescuing her to their hall and preserving her courage forever in the form of the maiden's immortal Valkyrie daughter."

- They take sustenance from the electrical energy of the earth, sharing it in one collective power, and give it back with their emotions in the form of lightning.
- They possess preternatural strength, speed, and senses.
- Without training, most can be mesmerized by shining objects.

THE BERSERKERS

"A berserker's lonely life is filled with naught but battle rage and bloodlust. . . ."

- A cadre of human warriors, known for their merciless brutality, who swear allegiance to Wóden.
- Stronger and faster than mere mortals, they carry within them the spirit of the bear and can channel its ferocity into a *berserkrage,* temporarily becoming as powerful as an immortal.
- When a berserker wins his two hundredth battle in Wóden's name, the god will grant him *ohalla*—immortality with untold strength.

THE ORDER

"The immortal takers. Once captured by the Order, immortals do not return. . . ."

- A multinational mortal operation created to study—and exterminate—nonhumans.
- Thought to be an urban legend.

THE VAMPIRES

- *The Fallen* are vampires who have killed by drinking a victim to death. Distinguished by their red eyes.
- *Tracing* is teleporting, the vampires' means of travel. A vampire can only trace to destinations he's previously been or to those he can see.

THE TURNING

"Only through death can one become an 'other.'"

- Some beings can turn a human or even other Lore creatures into their kind through differing means, but the catalyst for change is always death, and success is not guaranteed.

THE ACCESSION

"And a time shall come to pass when all immortal beings in the Lore, from the Valkyrie, vampire, Lykae, and demon factions to the witches, shifters, fey, and sirens . . . must fight and destroy each other."

- A kind of mystical checks-and-balances system for an ever-growing population of immortals.
- Occurs every five hundred years. Or right now . . .

PROLOGUE

Hark! Hear this tale, the legend of Aidan the Fierce and Reginleit the Radiant One, a pair of lovers both bound and cursed by fate.

It begins, as many legends do, with a destined meeting—this one between an immortal girl who would never know death and a jaded mortal man who lived only to kill.

Theirs is a story of woe and warning. Take heed and listen well. . . .

– i –

The Northlands
In ages long past

"So this is debauchery," Reginleit murmured as two guards led her into the mead hall of the notorious warlord Aidan the Fierce.

At twelve years of age, and newly quit of the paradise of Valhalla, Regin was certainly getting an eyeful.

As she and the guards wound through the crowd of hundreds of berserkers, she gaped at drunken warriors sparring in naught but loincloths while half-clad whores served ale, trenchers of meat, and . . . other needs.

Luckily Regin's disguise would conceal her expression—and her glow. She rechecked her cloak with gloved hands. The hood was deep, falling far over her face.

By the light of the fire pits smoking up to the thatched roof, she glimpsed kissing, fondling, and some acts her young mind couldn't yet attach names to.

Yet none within this battlefront encampment laughed; no jaunty music could be heard.

Though they'd seized a bloody victory today—from the cliffs above the field, she'd observed their clash against an army of vampires—all the many warriors here seemed to be simmering, snarling even. Much like the bears these mortals revered.

Mounted bear heads with ominous fangs lined the walls. Viking glyphs of ravening bears decorated the rafters and doors.

Everything she'd ever heard about the uncivilized berserkers was apparently true. Her favorite half sister, Lucia, had once told her, "Berserkers are grim, covetous, and possessive, savage when faced with the loss of something that belongs to them. They are obsessed with war and intercourse—they think of nothing else. Even our older sisters avoid them."

Regin had known the risk in coming here, but she wasn't fearful. As Lucia had also told her, "Sometimes I don't think you have the sense to be afraid when you should." Regin had interpreted that to mean, "You have no sense of fear, oh, great Reginleit."

Besides, she had no choice. She needed the aid of these mortals. She was horseless and had barely escaped a vampire ambush just days ago. Her belly was empty—the trenchers of stew and haunches of venison atop laden tables made her mouth water.

And Lucia was in danger.

Reminded of her purpose, she straightened her shoulders. Since the berserkers were her father's guard, surely they'd be duty-bound to serve her as well. But if she met with trouble here, she wouldn't hesitate to use the long sword holstered across her back or even her claws. They extended through slits in the fingers of her gloves, concealed by her draping sleeves—

Two nearly naked warriors locked in combat lurched past her. Fights continued all around, brawls over women, wine, and weapons. These men fell into their berserkrage, with their eyes glowing and muscles burgeoning, at the smallest slight.

Fitting that this encampment had been built at the edge of a war zone. For decades, these berserkers had defended this strategic pass against an immortal menace, protecting the villages in the valley below; she began to see that anything keeping these men here on the battlefront—and out of civilization—was a boon.

As she and the guards wended deeper within, Regin stopped abruptly. A short distance away, seated atop a throne on the hall's dais, was a male she'd seen in frenzied combat earlier. One she'd watched raptly.

Considering his unmatched speed and power as he'd wielded his war ax, she'd suspected he was their leader Aidan.

A buxom brunette sat on the arm of his throne,

serving him a tankard of drink and murmuring in his ear.

The wench's eyes were excited, her breath shallow. *She thinks the warlord handsome?* Regin's gaze flicked over him. *Then the wench and I are in accord.*

He had broad shoulders and muscular arms, his build as massive as a bear's. His blond hair was thick, some hanks plaited in ravels to keep them from his field of vision. He possessed all his teeth, and they were even and white. His sun-darkened skin made his wintry gray eyes stand out.

Today, when he'd been in his berserkrage, those eyes had glowed like storm clouds ablaze with lightning.

Now he pulled the woman onto his lap, no doubt to join in the debauchery. *And lo, there he goes. . . .* He began to unlace her straining bodice.

"My liege, a moment," one of the guards hastened to say. To catch the warlord before 'twas too late?

"What is it?" Aidan didn't look up from his task of freeing the female's ponderous breasts. Once he'd loosened her bodice, his big hand dipped down to grasp one.

"This boy demanded to see you."

Boy. Males always assumed she was of their sex, simply because she wore trews and carried a sword.

Aidan turned, his gaze falling on Regin. "Who are you?" he asked, his deep voice booming. Throughout the hall, the enthusiastic skirmishes and fornicating slowed.

She answered honestly, "I am a weary traveler in need of assistance."

At her words, his brows drew together. "You sound . . . familiar." He removed his hand from the woman's bodice and sat up straighter, his demeanor now tense. As if her very voice had set him on edge. "Though your accent is strange."

"Yours is not my first tongue." She spoke the ancient language of the immortals first, his Norse mortal language second.

"Come forward."

Though it nettled to take orders from a mere human, Regin stepped forth.

His gaze grew alert, assessing. She knew he was scrutinizing everything about her—her walk, the uncommonly fine material of her cloak, the gold brooch that clasped the hood in place.

The wench tried to reclaim his attention by cupping his face, but Aidan brushed her hand away. When she wriggled suggestively in his lap, he scowled at her and said something in her ear that sent her flouncing away with a huff.

But the woman couldn't prevent a longing glance over her shoulder.

For some reason, his dismissal of the buxom brunette gladdened Regin. She supposed she was merely relieved to have his full attention. "I saw you on the battlefield today, warlord. You fought well." As ever, her thoughts left her lips without any mediation. Lucia's words repeated in her mind: *You have to learn to hold your tongue. You could try even a glacier's patience.*

He leaned forward. "Boy, we are berserkers—we *all* fight well."

'Twas not true. She jerked her thumb at a young black-haired man to Aidan's right. "Not him. His guard's too low." *Hold your tongue, Regin!*

After a stunned silence, a few awkward chuckles sounded. Even Aidan grinned, then seemed startled by his reaction.

The man she'd insulted shot to his feet and stalked closer, his green eyes narrowed. "I'll show you a low guard."

At once, Regin dragged her long sword from its sheath, raising it between them.

He gave her a look of disgust. "That sword's bigger than you are, cur."

"The better to teach you to raise your guard, mongrel."

As more chuckles sounded, the man's fists clenched, his muscles tensing, growing. . . . Already on the verge of berserkrage.

"Stay your hand, Brandr," Aidan ordered.

Perhaps coming here was a mistake. These men were too violent and quick-tempered to aid her. And that was something for a Valkyrie to suppose!

Even Aidan, who had appeared to possess more control of himself than the others, now seemed to seethe with . . . *something.*

And though the berserkers were Wóden's guards, perhaps they would hurt her if they found out she was female. What would Lucia do? She'd leave this place anon without revealing herself as a woman.

"Boy, you are either very brave or very stupid to goad one of my strongest warriors," Aidan remarked. "Now, tell me why you've come to my hall." He tilted his head at her. "And why you've covered your skin like an aged druid."

Brandr grated, "The whelp probably had the pox."

Pox? She'd just stifled a hiss at him when Aidan said, "Enough." He rubbed the blond stubble on his chin. "Were you ill, then? Mayhap you haven't the strength needed to wield that long blade—or to taunt men bigger than you."

Regin's eyes went wide. "Haven't the strength?" She might only be twelve, and still vulnerable to harm, and 'twas true her blasted sword was far too big for her, but she could massacre all these mortals with tooth and claw if need be—

Brandr struck without warning, lunging for her. Before she could defend herself, he'd delivered two punishing blows to her wrist, knocking the sword from her grip.

When he straightened with a smirk, she gladly dismissed the weapon as her instincts took over. She leapt atop a table to her right, then bounded back to the left in front of him, raking her claws across his chest.

Gods, the feel of rending flesh . . . what need have I for a sword?

Landing softly, she hunched low, ready to spring again as the towering warrior bellowed, "He carries hidden daggers?" He gaped at the deep furrows in his skin, slashes that had severed even his leather scabbard. "Aidan, his death is mine! Any taller, and he'd have slit my throat."

Regin said, "I *chose* not to slit your throat. Thank me with ale."

Suddenly a huge palm closed over her nape. Another hand captured her wrists behind her. Hissing with fury, she twisted around and sank her small fangs into a brawny forearm.

'Twas the warlord! Aidan had her. How had he moved so quickly?

Lightning struck outside, thunderclaps rattling the hall. *If only the bolt would hit me!*

"Cease this!" He roughly jostled her until she had to release her bite. Before she could blink, he had her cloak clutched in his fist.

"Nay! Do not!"

He ripped it back. Sucked in a breath. Promptly dropped her.

All around her, wide-eyed men closed in. She hissed again, pivoting to keep the threats in sight, baring her claws and her fangs.

One of them asked, "What *is* she?"

Aidan frowned down at her. "She is merely a little . . . girl."

Brandr said, "By Wóden's beard, she glows!"

Regin spat, "He does not wear a beard!"

At her words, recognition flashed in Aidan's expression. His gaze lit on her pointed ears, then her eyes. By the way he stared, she knew they were wavering from amber to silver. "You are a Valkyrie. The one whose skin lights up the night. We've heard tales of you."

"You know nothing of me!"

Raising his brows in challenge, he quoted a recent edda: "'Eyes like amber cast in sun, skin and hair of firelit gold. Formed to war, courage as none, beauty to behold.' You are Reginleit the Radiant."

Now several of the men murmured, "*Reginleit,*" in awed tones.

But not Aidan. He shook his head. "Brightling, you are a very long way from home."

Of course that ass Brandr said, "*She* is one of Wóden's treasured daughters?"

Shoulders back, Regin said, "Most treasured. Above all my sisters." Except for Lucia. And Nïx. Likely Kaderin. No need for these mortals to know that perhaps she was not a favorite of his. *At present.*

"Then why are you in the middle of a war, instead of the safety of Valhalla?" Aidan seemed angry about this. "You're so small." He'd begun to look at her with a peculiar intensity, different from the other men's, more . . . protective.

"What concern is it of yours where I might be?" She shoved her braids from her forehead, lifting her chin. "And I'm not *that* small."

"You are"—he ran a hand over his face—"*young.*"

Beside him, Brandr asked, "What is it, friend? Your eyes grow fierce."

Aidan opened his mouth, closed it. Then he gazed around the scene as if seeing it anew. "Gods." He reached for her with a hand raised, as if to shield her vision. "Come with me, little one. 'Tis no place for you."

She backed up a step.

He cast her a disapproving frown. "I have pledged my life to serve your father; you were born of his lightning.

I could no more harm you than I could myself." When she relaxed not one whit, he said, "Come. You must be hungry. You can dine in my quarters." He gathered her sword, offering it to her hilt first. "There will be plenty to eat."

They *would* have plenty of food. His army had scavenged this countryside like locusts. All the game that she could have hunted had been slain.

She peered up, regarding his face. The mortal did seem to have an honest visage. And mayhap he'd do as she bade, or at least give her a horse and enough food for her journey.

Regin accepted her sword, sheathing it. But when he wrapped his arm around her shoulders protectively, she stiffened. "I can walk on my own, berserker."

Under his breath, he said, "'Tis a display of favor I offer you before all."

"A display of favor," she said in a dry tone. "From a *mortal*. Then how can I possibly continue without it?" She allowed him to usher her through the crowds of staring warriors and wenches.

A few berserkers sought to touch her "fair locks" or "alight skin," but Aidan's hand tightened over her shoulder, his eyes blazing even brighter. He cast the men a baleful look and they all retreated without another word, their faces paling.

Once she and Aidan had navigated the hall's gauntlet and exited into the summer night, he visibly relaxed, though he still seemed preoccupied. She took the opportunity to study him up close.

His towering frame was even more imposing, his

height at least six and a half feet. His white tunic was of a fine weave, fitted over those wide shoulders. Black trews of soft leather outlined his powerful legs. When a breeze blew up from the valley below, carrying the scent of summer wheat and stirring the blond hair around his face, she had the urge to sigh.

The midnight sun had finally set, and as they walked, he gazed up at the stars, as if for some kind of guidance. For the last week, as she'd searched for Lucia in this strange world of mortals, she'd often done the same. "Whatever is your question, warlord, the stars will not answer you."

He peered down at her with those intense gray eyes, rekindling her ridiculous urge to sigh. "Mayhap they already have."

Before she could question his words, he stopped before the largest longhouse in the camp, opening the door for her. The interior was rich, with woven rugs on the packed dirt floor. A gleaming table with two chairs sat at one end and a thick pallet of furs covered the opposite end. A fire burned in a center pit.

He took a pair of candles from a generous supply of them and lit the wicks in the fire, then placed them in holders flanking a polished bear skull.

"Are you wealthy?" she asked. "For a mortal?"

"I've won spoils enough. But what do you know of coin? You are the daughter of gods."

"I know I have none, and I need it for food."

He strode to the doorway, ordering some servant outside to bring their dinner, then sat at the table. He waved her to the other chair.

When she removed her gloves and cloak, her boy's clothes beneath—trews and a tunic—earned another disapproving frown. She shrugged and joined him, feeling like an adult to be sharing a lord's table. Even if he was only a warlord.

"This world is a dangerous place for a girl, Reginleit. And you are not invulnerable to harm."

She shook her head. No, she'd not reached her immortality yet. She could still be injured, grow sickened, even die. Though she wouldn't need food as an adult Valkyrie, now she required it to grow.

"Then what possessed you to leave the safety of your home, child?"

"I am no child! And I've been safe enough." *Except for the bloodthirsty foes I had to face to reach this side of the conflict.* "I've slain vampires." But it'd been close. *I lost my sword early in that skirmish, too.*

He waved away her words as if they were mere fables. "Reginleit, answer me."

Though she suspected she should be secretive and cautious with a stranger like this, she'd never learned to be either. And she needed his help. Out spilled the truth: "I followed my favorite sister when she followed a man. He promised to wed Lucia, yet I am uneasy. She is everything to me, and I believe she is in danger." Regin couldn't explain how she knew, but she felt as if time was running out for her sister.

"You left heaven for her? Though you can never go back?"

"'Tis forbidden for a Valkyrie to return."

"Then I applaud your loyalty."

"She would do the same for me." As exasperated as Regin made her—indeed, all her sisters—she knew Lucia loved her.

"You sought me this night," he said. "What would you have me do?"

"I need assistance to find Lucia."

"Done," he said with a shrug. "I will do everything possible to reunite her with you."

Regin blinked up at him. "Because you serve Wóden?"

"Nay." He rose to pace, running his hand over his mouth. "I do this because we will serve each other."

"I do not take your meaning."

"There is no easy way to say this. Reginleit, when you are grown, you will become my wife."

"Are you mad, mortal?" she cried, her skin glowing brighter. "Like my sister Nïx?"

"Nïx the Ever-Knowing, the soothsayer?"

"She's touched with visions. What is your explanation?"

He looked to stifle a grin. "You are direct, a good trait. But I'm not mad. I'm a berserker. Do you understand what the men of my people are?"

"I've heard tales of your kind. You're stronger than other mortals, faster. And you're all possessed by the spirit of a beast. The snarling, the fighting, the possessiveness—all the traits of a lean bear in winter."

"'Tis true. And the beast in me sensed its mate, rousing inside me from your very first words. I thought you would be older when we met, but I feel fortunate just to have found you."

He said this as if it was an understatement. She was speechless. A rarity.

"In the morn, I will take you to my family's holdings in the north," he continued. "My parents will complete your upbringing and keep you safe until I return for you. I will bring your sister there to join you."

An actual madman stood before her! This situation grew interesting. Regin found she might like to play with mad mortals. Feigning an earnest tone, she asked, "And how long would it be until you returned for me?"

"Mayhap in five or six years. When you are grown, and I have warred enough to earn my own immortality. Then we would wed."

Ah, she remembered now. Berserkers could earn *ohalla,* deathlessness, from Wóden once they'd won two hundred battles in his name. They tattooed his mark—dual ravens in flight—upon their chests.

She wondered if the battles had come before the rule, or if the rule had spurred the battles. "I'm to sit there and wait for you? What if another mortal decides I'm to be his chattel instead?"

His hands clenched. "You are meant for *me* alone," he said in a strange tone. "Do you understand what I am saying?"

"I'm not ignorant of such things." She was almost completely ignorant of such things—of men, of coupling. She couldn't comprehend why her sister would ever voluntarily leave the paradise of Valhalla to follow a man.

One I do not trust.

"Reginleit, you will not know another male." His gaze held hers. "I consider us wed from this moment on."

What a crazed mortal; how touched in the head. Her father would turn this berserker to ash if he dared kidnap her and force her to wed him. Perhaps she oughtn't toy with Aidan anymore? "Reconsider. You're far too old for me. One foot in the grave and the other doddering at the edge."

He glowered. "I am not that old! I've only thirty winters."

She began to fear that he wouldn't be dissuaded, so she said, "I might look upon your suit, but only if you help me save Lucia first."

He shook his head firmly. "You will tell me where to find her. And I will do so only once I've conveyed you safely to my people."

"You can never locate her without me." As a sister Valkyrie, Regin could sense her if she got close enough. "And we haven't time to dally."

"You came to me for guidance, and this is my decision—"

"Guidance! You *are* mad. And arrogant. I am the daughter of *gods*. I came to you for a horse, food, and mayhap a pair of outriders. So I could be on my way!"

"'Tis a done thing, brightling. In this realm, my word is *final*."

They were interrupted by the brunette from the hall, now carrying in a tray of food and drink. As she served two trenchers of some kind of savory stew, she made sure her ample bosom was displayed for Aidan.

Regin thought of her own barely budding chest. For the first time in her life, she felt lacking.

And mayhap jealous. Ah, but 'twas Regin who sat at the warlord's table like a woman grown. 'Twas Regin the stubborn, mad mortal wanted to wed. She cast the wench a smirk.

"No ale for the girl, Birgit," Aidan said to the woman. "Do we not have milk?"

Regin's face heated. And all the worse, because she would dearly love some milk.

When Birgit returned with some, Aidan dismissed her so absently that the worst of Regin's pique was soothed.

The rich scent of game stew called to her hunger, and she eagerly dug in. The meat melted in her mouth. Gods, mortals did know how to cook.

"Tell me of your home," he said, breaking a piece of flatbread for her trencher.

"'Tis a beautiful land of mists," she said around bites. "Slow and peaceful." Usually. Unless Loki descended upon them, or someone released Fenris, the giant wolf.

"What was your life like?"

Regin swallowed a mouthful of bread. "You truly wish me to . . . talk?" Most of the time, her sisters bade her be quiet, serious.

"I am curious about you."

She shrugged, deciding that she might as well enjoy this short time with this stubborn, immovable warlord—because unless he could be made to change his mind, she planned to slip away in the night and continue her search.

At least now she'd have food in her belly and likely a stolen horse.

So she regaled him with stories of Valhalla and the silliness of the demigods. He laughed at all of the tales, seeming genuinely amused.

At one point, his expression seemed even . . . *proud*, earning another frown from her. "You do not mind my humor?"

"Not at all. I've not laughed like this . . ." His brows drew together. "I think I've never laughed like this."

"Usually I exasperate people. And I jest at inappropriate times. Such as during executions. Freya says 'tis my gift and my bane to frustrate others."

"I like your manner, Reginleit. Life is long without humor."

She felt like preening in the face of this steely-eyed warrior's praise—until he added, "We will suit well, brightling."

She sighed. "Still you believe we will be together." Though she sensed that Aidan was an honorable male, he was misled in this. Wóden would never allow Regin to wed a mortal berserker.

And the ohalla Aidan sought? She'd only ever heard of one berserker in all of history who'd earned it. The rest died in battles long before their two hundredth one.

A fact that the cunning Wóden well knew.

"I am certain we will, little wife." Finished with his meal, Aidan rose and crossed to his bed, dividing the furs into two pallets on opposite walls. He waved her to one, then took the other. Easing to his side, he propped his head in his hand. "When you are older you'll come to see that every woman needs a man, even a Valkyrie."

"Why?" She plopped down across from him.

"You'll understand when you go through the change."

"You mean when I become immortal?" When she would change from a growing, vulnerable girl to a nigh invincible woman. Her sisters spoke of this time in whispers, but Regin didn't know why. Mayhap this male would tell her.

"Those months will be sweet." He lay on his back, his hands behind his head. In a knowing tone, he said, "You'll definitely want me around then."

"Why? What happens?"

"You'll become a woman. And you'll need me as much as I will surely be needing you."

"Would you try to kiss me?" she asked slyly.

"Depend on it."

"And?"

"And now you should go to sleep. We've a long journey ahead of us."

"Warlord, tell me!" She crossed her arms over her chest and lightning struck outside.

He *chuckled*.

"Why should I choose *you* to kiss, then?"

He turned on his side again, his gaze holding hers. "Why *not* me?"

"All you do is war."

"True, and I'm damned skilled at my trade. Which means I'll always be able to protect you. And by the time you're grown, I'll have accumulated enough loot to spoil you."

"You're not noble or refined."

He nodded easily. "I possess no refinement. But that also means I've no guile—you will always know what I'm thinking."

"And you believe *you* are entitled to a Valkyrie for your bride?"

"I am the most powerful berserker *ever* to live," he said, not with conceit but as if he merely stated an indisputable fact. "So if not me, then who?"

She shrugged. "I remain unconvinced of your charms, Aidan." Also an indisputable fact.

"There is another reason. . . ."

"Tell me."

His voice gone gruff, he added, "You should choose me because . . . I will love you, Reginleit."

Her heart seemed to skip a beat. "How can you say that? You cannot know the future!"

"I know because, at twelve years of age, you've won me with your wit and bravery. Your staunch loyalty, too." He leaned back once more, grinning up at the roof of the longhouse. "When you have your wiles about you, I'll be no match. I concede defeat well in advance."

"When I'm grown, others will vie for my hand."

"Undoubtedly. But you belong only to me."

Lightning struck again from her frustration. He truly believed he had the right to take away her freedom, to keep her as his untouched prize while he continued his debauched lifestyle. Perhaps that was the way of things with mortals. *But such is not good enough for the likes of me.*

"Berserker, hear my words," she said. "I vow to you that I will stay as true to you as you do to me." That would shut his mouth. He couldn't go a week without a Birgit. "Every wench upon your lap means I sit upon a warrior's. Every woman's mouth you kiss is a man's lips upon my own."

His fierce gaze met hers, his eyes ablaze once more—as if the mere thought of her with another sent his ire spiraling. Seeming to struggle for control, he grated, "Then I give you my oath that I'll not touch another. Now are you satisfied, little wife? Any more demands?"

"I have to go with you to find Lucia."

"In this I will not bend, Reginleit. You are vulnerable. You can be harmed. And that I could not abide."

Before he doused the candles, he leaned over to press a quick kiss against her hair, then chucked her under the chin. "Brightling, the time till you're grown will pass slowly for me. Every night, I will dream of the woman you'll become."

He returned to his pallet, and in the dark she saw his eyes closed and his lips curled, as if with anticipation.

She inwardly sighed. *You will never see me grown, warlord. But from time to time, I might think of the stubborn mortal who was kind to me.*

– *ii* –

Nine years later

"What are you doing, sister?" Lucia the Archer demanded as she barged into Regin's room.

Though Regin had hoped to slip away this night from the manor house she shared with Lucia, her sister's huntress senses were too acute.

I should probably lie. Yet out spilled the truth: "I am deciding which garments will best please a warlord."

Lucia gasped, her hands falling to the bow she always wore strapped over her body. As her fingers nervously plucked the string, she said, "You are seeking out that berserker?"

She nodded. Regin would become a full immortal soon and, as she'd finally been warned, her desires were growing overwhelming.

When she imagined fulfilling them, only one man's face arose in her mind. Just as Aidan had predicted, she needed him now. "He's near. His army is camped within the dark woods."

Over the years, as she and Lucia had sought out other Valkyrie on this plane and others, Regin had often heard tales of her berserker. He was little closer to his gift of immortality, having spent more time searching for her than for battles to win. And already he had forty winters.

He was said to be *changed*—his beastlike nature even more dominant. He was quick to conflict, letting his berserkrage free at the earliest provocation.

And yet she couldn't stop thinking of him.

"Now, shall I wear the nigh-transparent skirt"—Regin tapped her chin—"or the trews that encase me like a second skin?"

Lucia sputtered.

"Yes, well said, Lucia. Males *do* ogle me more when I wear the trews." She pulled them on over her generous backside—with effort—then lay on the bed to tie the tight laces. Next she donned a sleeveless leather vest with a plunging neckline. Though it covered her breasts, the vest bared her midriff.

Lucia had begun to pace. "We've talked of this."

"*You* talked of this," Regin said as she braided her hair into a dozen haphazard plaits around her face. The rest she left flowing. "I averred nothing."

Lucia wanted her to join the Skathians—the celibate archeress order she herself had entered—but Regin was too curious about coupling, too eager to discover what the warlord's secretive smile that night had promised.

Yet that wasn't the only reason she would seek him out. Though he'd been so stubborn and arrogant, he'd also laughed with her and enjoyed her humor. Over these years, men had gazed at her with lust, reverence, and even, on occasion, respect—but Aidan had looked at her as no man had since.

With *appreciation.* He'd appreciated her exactly as she was.

"To seek him out is madness, Regin. He believes that he alone will possess you. Like some . . . some *thing,* some object. He will never let you go!"

"Then he will not have me to begin with. We will

make a bargain for three months, or for nothing." She would explore her attraction to him, slake these drives, and loosen the hold he had over her.

Regin dug into her copious chest of jewels—containing no glittering stones, of course. She decided on adornments of polished gold. Males grew fascinated with how she made it glow. She donned serpentine bands of it around her upper arms and a circlet crown with strands to dip over her forehead.

"If you must do this, choose another male, any but a berserker! They're animals, and I do not use that word lightly," Lucia said, her eyes still haunted by her own encounter with a male nine years ago.

The man she'd thought she loved had been a monster in disguise, one who'd turned on her, harming her in unspeakable ways.

Regin had been right to worry—and to leave Aidan behind. *If I'd been but a single day later . . .*

"I cannot choose another male. Else break an oath." It seemed her brash words from all those years ago had come back to haunt her. "I vowed to Aidan that I would be as faithful to him as he was to me. Lucia, rumors hold that he's forsaken all others. If 'tis true . . ."

Yet this only alarmed Lucia. "An insatiable beast lurks within him, one that wants only to rut and conquer and possess. I hope to the gods, for your sake, he's not tried to leash it for nearly a decade."

"I am going to him," Regin said simply as she turned toward the stairs. Her mind was made up. She wasn't one to debate things with herself. She rarely pondered, never mulled. She acted.

Lucia sighed, following her down to the front entrance. "Then for once, be circumspect." At the door, she handed Regin her hooded cloak. "Survey the situation before you stride into his army's camp as if you own it. Promise me."

"Very well." Regin shrugged into the cloak, then stepped outside, glancing at the darkening sky. A spring storm neared. "Wish me luck," she said cheerily, leaving Lucia to pluck her bowstring with disapproval.

Regin set off across the countryside, hurrying through melting ice fields into the forest. She was so eager that she easily outpaced the oncoming storm.

As she neared Aidan's encampment, she heard women's voices among the men's. Camp wenches, as usual. What bawdy scenes would she come across this time?

Perhaps Aidan had a bedmate this very night.

The thought made her claws straighten with aggression. *He vowed to me.* Yet though she would feel betrayed, her desires were growing so intense that she might just toss the woman away and take her place.

Nay. If he'd broken his oath, she would not gift him with her innocence.

I have to know. . . . At the edge of a central clearing, she leapt into a tree, adjusting her cloak to keep her glow concealed. Around a great fire sat berserkers of every stripe, all with women or jugs of mead or both clasped in their meaty fists.

Except for one.

Aidan.

He sat off to one side on a long bench, his blond head

in his hands. He looked to be squeezing his temples.

Brandr, that cur, sat beside him with a wench in his lap and one hand up her skirt, fondling her backside. With his other hand, he clapped Aidan on the shoulder. "There will be other leads, friend."

"I felt so certain." He raised his head, revealing a miserable expression. "Last night, I dreamed I'd found her."

Regin stifled a gasp at his appearance. Aidan's striking face was weary, his mien defeated. Yet underneath the signs of the ongoing years, he was still the most beautiful male she'd ever seen.

Brandr handed him a jug. "Here. Drink this."

Aidan pushed it away. "I need a clear head. We ride north tomorrow."

"Forget for one night," Brandr said with an exaggerated slap of the whore's bottom.

Aidan scowled at that, then all around at the men groping and the women writhing. He took the jug, turned it up. When he'd emptied it, he swiped his tunic sleeve over his mouth. "Gods, what was that? It burns my throat."

"That was the choice spirits! Now follow them with a choice woman."

Nay, do not!

"For once, Aidan."

For once? He truly had kept his vow?

When Aidan cast him another scowl, Brandr sighed. He lifted the woman to her feet, telling her, "Go pleasure others for this hour. I'll find you for the next."

Once the two men were alone, Brandr said, "This

cannot go on, Aidan. I am your friend, and I cannot see you like this any longer."

"What would you have me do?"

"Return to being the leader you used to be. For all the gods' sakes, Aidan, *I* am closer to ohalla than you are, and you've half a dozen years of age on me. Forget this obsession. You think of nothing but her."

"And can you blame me? Imagine the woman she would be." He gazed up at the cloudy sky as if picturing her at that moment, and Regin's heart clenched again. Then Aidan faced Brandr. "Nay, do *not* imagine her."

Brandr exhaled. "There are women aplenty in this camp. Women who burn to bed you. Surely you can replace her."

"The idea is laughable. As well you know."

"I'd take a warm woman in my hands over a cold Valkyrie in my mind."

I am not cold!

"By the way," Brandr added, "that was enough drink to put down a horse. You'll be on your face soon. Mayhap you'll actually sleep a night through."

With a snarl, Aidan shot to his feet, then lurched toward a nearby tent.

"Go to your lonely bed, old man!" Brandr called.

Brandr and I are going to cross swords one day, Regin decided. Then she leapt from one limb to another, settling in a tree outside Aidan's tent. From there, she could spy the dimly lit interior through the outer flap.

Inside, he angrily ripped off his tunic, displaying broad shoulders and a brawny back that tapered down to narrow hips. As he moved, his muscles flexed beneath smooth tanned skin.

Magnificent male. She hissed out a shaky breath at the sight.

He kicked a shield on the ground, then knocked a tankard from a table. He was like the approaching storm, his ire building as he began to smash his belongings—weapons clanging, wood splintering.

Regin tilted her head in wonder, frowning at the mortal's rampage.

When the storm gave up its first bolt above, he froze. She thought she heard him mutter, "Lightning. *Lightning*?" Out of the tent he staggered, clearly the worse for the liquor, and headed away from the camp.

Regin dropped down and silently followed as he made his way out of the forest into a nearby field. He stopped before an ancient rune stone—an upright slab of rock more than ten feet tall, carved with glyphs. They were numerous in these Northlands, each created to be a direct path to Wóden's ear.

He faced the stone. "You give me lightning this eve?" With every word, his voice grew louder, until he was shouting: *"To remind me of what I have lost?"* He launched his mighty fist against the rock.

Regin's jaw dropped at the blasphemy.

Aidan punched it again, bloodying his hand. *"To remind me of what I cannot find?"*

With his every word, she felt his pain. It washed over her like a flood, temporarily numbing her desires. She'd never known hurt like this—a torment not of the body but of the mind.

Of the heart?

She'd never known he would come to this.

As if pulled to him by an invisible force, she eased closer. When he drew back his bloodied fist again, she stayed his arm with a touch.

He went still, but his whole body seemed to be thrumming. Regin's was as well; her own lightning lit the sky from her turbulent emotions.

Slowly, he turned to her. With a shaking hand, he reached for her cloak. She didn't think he even realized he spoke aloud: "*Be her, be her, gods, let it be* her."

He unfastened the garment, let it drop to her feet, then sucked in a breath at her uncovered face. His bloodshot eyes now glowed gray as they flickered over her features. Brows drawn together as if he were pained, he held up a lock of her hair, threading his fingers through it. "So fair."

A light rain began to fall, misting their skin, but he seemed not to notice as his gaze dipped to her body. Rocking on his feet, he rasped, "Gods, *ängel*. I dreamed of you like this. Every night." Then he frowned, muttering to himself, "Still in reverie. That *was* the choicest spirits."

"'Tis no dream, warlord—"

One strapping arm shot out to circle her shoulders; the other was a band around her arms and torso, dragging her against him. She felt him groan from deep in his chest as their bodies met.

The closest she'd ever been to a man.

"You've returned to me. No longer must I worry for

you, out in the world alone," he said, his voice breaking lower with emotion. "You were just a little girl. Without my protection." He nuzzled her hair, inhaling with another groan. "But you're a woman now." His erection pressed against her belly as he growled, "*My* woman."

The bare skin of his chest was smooth against her cheek and felt so hot in the rain. His scent surrounded her, enticing her as much as his muscles rippling all around her. When he rubbed his chin over the sensitive tip of her pointed ear, her claws curled, readying to sink into his body and pull him ever closer.

Yet then he drew his head back, suspicion in his expression. "Have you lain with another?"

She frowned, genuinely curious when she asked, "Would you not want me if I had?"

A muscle ticked in his jaw. He ignored her question. "Has there been another, Valkyrie?" His wild eyes were seething gray. "Tell me! The beast in me stirs. It can't share its mate. *I* can't share my mate."

Regin swallowed at the intensity of his gaze. He would never give her up, would never accept the mere months she'd intended to give him. "Th-this was a mistake."

"There *has* been." He threw back his head and roared like an animal in pain, crushing her against him with one arm as he pounded his fist into the wet stone over and over. "You were meant for me, meant only for me!"

"Aidan, wait," she cried, grappling to free herself, but he'd pinned her arms to her sides. "Listen to me!"

He didn't. "I was true to you, Valkyrie!" The rune

stone began to crack under his assault. "I will slaughter any who've touched you. . . ."

Seeing no other recourse, she sank her fangs into one of the thick muscles of his chest.

He seemed not to feel it. She bit harder until she'd drawn blood.

Finally he slowed. "You're biting me?" he slurred.

With a roll of her eyes, she released him.

"If you mean to pain me, you will have to do better than that. I've had nine years of perfect misery."

"I had to do something to make you listen. Aidan, I've never been touched. Not that it should matter—since *you* are certainly no innocent."

He sagged against her in relief.

She added sarcastically, "My virgin's blood is still yours to spill."

He took her words seriously. "'Tis *mine* by right. You belong to *me*! If there'd been another, I would make him eat his own entrails."

She blinked up at him. "And these are your words of sentiment?"

"There's no poetry in me, Reginleit. No fine words." He stared down at her, his gaze seeming to consume her. "I come to you as a man unfinished."

Raw, grim male.

He took her hands in his bloodied, callused ones. "Accept me?" His eyes glowed, his lashes spiked from rain.

Lightning struck then and her breath caught—he had a face made even more beautiful in the blaze of lightning. "Warlord, you once told me I'd always know what you're thinking. What are your thoughts now?"

"Partly, I'm thinking that I might shame myself in my trews, just from the feel of you next to me." One of his hands snaked around to cover her backside, gripping her there.

"Oh!"

"And partly, I'm fearing I will frighten you away again."

"You did not *frighten* me away before. Nothing frightens me."

"Then why did you leave me?"

"Because you would not listen to me. You sought to take away my freedom."

"And give you mine in turn, woman! Then why've you come to me now?"

"Mostly because of . . . the change. When beset by these needs, I came to you to have them eased."

Again, he went still. "You came to me," he repeated hoarsely. "To your man. Reginleit, you make my chest bow with pride." His lips curled. "And my shaft swell. I'm greedy to sample these generous new curves you've brought me."

"My looks please you?" She straightened her shoulders self-consciously. "I fear I did not grow tall."

"Please me?" He laughed from deep in his chest. "You stun me. Ah, little wife, if you did not grow up, you certainly grew out." One of his hands dropped to cover a breast, giving it a tender squeeze. When he shuddered with delight, she felt a thrill down to her toes.

"And you came to me to ease you here?" His

other hand trailed down between them to gently cup her sex.

She gasped. "Y-yes."

His eyes burned with excitement, with possession, with pride. "I'm going to make your lightning rain down." He pressed the heel of his palm harder, and her head fell back.

"Ah, yes! Make love to me, warlord."

"Words from fantasy. But I cannot. I need more time."

She lifted her head. "I do not understand."

"I want more of you. I want eternity."

"What are you speaking of?"

"If I deflower a Valkyrie before wedding her, I will never earn ohalla. Wóden would never gift me with it."

"Wed?" She yanked his hand from her. "Immortals cannot wed mortals! It's unnatural." To watch him die a little each day, until he withered with age . . .

"Precisely. So I must be of your kind. And even were it not forbidden, I still would not wed you without ohalla. I know of no warrior older than sixty winters. I've forty. Two decades should be but a taste of life with you."

In a crestfallen tone, she said, "You want me to . . . wait?" Her plan was foiled, utterly. Not only would she *not* get what she came for, she'd be punished for trying.

"Only to be claimed. Rest assured, I'll sate you in other ways till then."

But she wanted to know everything, to experience it all. "How many battles do you have left?"

He lifted his chin. "A mere six dozen or so."

"Are there even that many wars?" she cried.

"Between the vampires and the unallied demonarchies, a lifetime of war awaits."

"Seventy battles could take years! I came here because I wanted you to be my first lover."

"By all the gods, I will be, woman. But not yet. You wait for me, Reginleit. I will seize ohalla for you, for us."

"And what would you expect me to do while you are out fighting? My Valkyrie nature hungers for war as much as yours does. And I hold no love for vampires." Her mother's people, the Radiant Ones, had been exterminated by them.

"You will remain behind—"

Eyes widening, she opened her mouth to give him a blistering reply.

"—to train, as all my men do before they go to battle," he finished.

"Train?" she scoffed. "I've readied for war all my life."

"Using the wrong weapon. You still wield your long sword?"

"Yes."

"With your small height and Valkyrie speed, you should be fighting with two short swords. I could teach you how."

She pursed her lips, reluctantly intrigued by that idea. "And once I am trained . . ." she prompted.

As if the words were pulled from him, he said, "You can join me at the front. But only after I deem you ready."

She dug one fang into her bottom lip, actually considering his offer.

He must have taken her silence as acceptance, because he leaned down to kiss her neck, his mouth so hot in the rain. Against her skin, he rasped, "And, brightling, know this . . ." His tongue flicked out to lick drops from her. "I vow to you now, I will be your *last* lover."

She couldn't think when he was doing that! "I-I haven't agreed to this. Am I to have no say? Again?"

He inhaled as if for control, then raised his head. "Give me a chance, and I *will* claim your heart. All I need is time."

She didn't believe that could happen. An immortal like her could never fully love a mortal. Her instincts would rebel against tender feelings like that.

After all, she could never give her heart to a man who would take it to the grave with him, leaving her broken and yearning for eternity.

Still, there was something captivating about Aidan's utter confidence. As if he knew something about her that she didn't even know herself. And her out-of-control desires were making it difficult to deny him. "I will give you three months, warlord. You have three months to win me."

"Ah, Valkyrie"—he curled his finger under her chin—"your heart will be mine in two."

– iii –

Seven months later

Where is he? I'm going mad without him here.

Regin paced their longhouse as a blizzard raged outside. Aidan was a week overdue from a campaign. She'd ridden the countryside searching for him for days, but found no sign.

There was rumor of a capture.

Did he even live?

Aidan. The bear of a warrior she could never allow herself to love, but the one she *wanted* above all others.

Even though she was a full immortal now—her appetite for food had disappeared, her need for war burgeoning—she lingered with him here at his camp.

I am better for being here, for being with him. She was a better swordswoman—though he hadn't deemed her ready for war yet, and she secretly feared he never would.

She was a better lover. Though he hadn't coupled with her.

Seven months ago, she had tried repeatedly to seduce him, coaxing him to take her completely. Yet in time she'd come to want more of him, too. No, he couldn't win her heart, but he'd won her desires. He'd pleasured her relentlessly, teaching her to slake him as well.

Each time he set off to battle, she demanded, "Take me with you, warrior." His ploy to keep her in camp? He left her sexually sated and sprawled on the furs, exhausted but glowing with bliss. Already pining for him to return.

As he'd done so long ago, Regin had begun to ask herself, why *not* him?

Because once she'd learned how to handle her stormy berserker—knowing when to tease him, when to claw him, when to draw him into her arms and murmur, *"Shh, be at ease, warlord"*—life with him had been surprisingly gratifying.

He treated her like a goddess, spoiling her with gifts and surprises. And they laughed constantly. She savored the sound of his laughter coming from his big barrel chest—as well as his gruff words of affection: "Remember those years ago when I vowed I would love you one day? I told you true."

Could any male make her feel as he had the night he'd lightly rasped his blond stubble over her stomach and murmured, "I want babes with you—berserker sons and Valkyrie daughters." He'd raised his head, gazing at her with clear gray eyes. "Give them to me one day?"

Having a Valkyrie for his mate had done nothing to curb his arrogance. He behaved like an immortal already—even more arrogant and lordly—thrilling her. "Wóden will look upon me with favor," he'd told her. "No male could treasure his daughter more than I do you."

'Twas simple enough. Regin desired him above all males and knew she always would, which meant two decades was far too short—

He stumbled through the door.

She gave a cry, leaping to her feet. "Thank gods, you've returned! Where have you . . ." She trailed off at the wild look on his face. "Aidan?"

His eyes ablaze, he dropped his bloody ax, then ripped off his sword belt and crimson-stained tunic. His tattooed chest heaved as he stalked toward her, his expression warning her to take a step back. Then another.

"Aidan, say something."

"They tried to keep me from you." He backed her into the table, cornering her, predatory.

"Who? The vampires?"

"*No one* keeps me from you. Not immortals, not men, not a god. *Nothing* can keep me from you."

"Aidan, wh-what are you doing? You're on the very edge. You must calm yourself."

"My life passed before me, Reginleit. I'd rushed to battle because I want you forever—only to fall without a single night inside you? The idea sent me into a frenzy!"

She'd never seen him this far gone when not fighting. They both worked to keep him from reaching his berserkrage, knowing he'd lose control to the beast within.

The beast that roared inside him to claim its mate.

"I left a wake of death to return to you"—his hand shot out to cup her nape, yanking her close—"to make you mine in all ways." He dipped his head to nip her breast, making her gasp. "Tonight I'll ride your little body till you scream with pleasure."

"Have you fever? Are you maddened?" She shoved him away, but again, he stalked closer. "You know why we can't!"

"We can! You are *mine* to claim. Ohalla is mine to take! I demand it all—mine by right."

"This is the berserkrage speaking . . . speaking *nonsense.* Think about what you are saying! We've set our course, and we will be steadfast."

Regin knew that the hotter his rage, the faster and stronger he'd be. If she didn't make it out of here with a burst of speed, all would be lost. She feinted left, then ducked to the right, sprinting past him—

He caught her dress, snatching her back.

"Aidan, nay!"

He seized her in the cage of his arms, carrying her to their bed, dragging her down with him. "'Tis unnatural to deny this fated need. You know this—you feel it too!"

Before she could escape, his hands fisted in the front of her dress. With a roar, he rent the material clean from her body, his smoldering gaze raking over her breasts and lower to her sex.

He was going into that mindless state, his muscles bulging even more. "You wanted me to claim you before. Is that no longer true?"

"Of course I want you to, but not yet!"

He tore off his boots and breeches, rising up above her. His mighty shaft swelled with lust, moisture beading the proud crown.

Raw male. Against her will, the flesh between her legs dampened, her breasts growing heavy.

Whenever the spirit of the bear quickened inside him, she responded—as if he'd imparted some of his beast, imprinted it upon her.

Because once it rose, she grew desperate to answer its call.

Now she fought the growing need. "Nay! Do not do this!" She pummeled his chest, but when he was like this, she was no match for his strength. He caught her wrists, easily pinning them over her head.

"Aidan, I-I am pleading, just wait—" The words caught in her throat when he dipped his head to one of her breasts, his lips closing over her nipple.

As he sucked, his finger slid into her core. "Wet for me," he growled around the peak. A second finger delved as he moved his hot mouth to her other breast, suckling with greedy lips, his tongue swirling.

Her nipples were damp and throbbing, her sex quivering to his touch. "Aidan!"

"You're ready, nigh coming." But he slipped his fingers from her. She whimpered, undulating for them.

With her arms still captured over her head, he covered her body with his own. "You are mine, Reginleit!" He rocked his hips between her thighs.

She felt his thick manhood pulsing, seeking . . .

And gods help her, she tilted her hips so it could surge home.

"Mine!" he roared.

"'Tis done now, brightling," Aidan said, his voice hoarse from his bellows of pleasure, his body warm and relaxed over her. "No going back." He put his forehead to hers.

She could hardly stem her tears. Over the last few

hours, she'd experienced more ecstasy than she'd ever imagined. But now sand in the hourglass had begun to flow. Only so much remained. "Do you have regrets, warlord?"

"That I was not doing this every hour for the last several months."

Somehow she forced herself to smile. "You had better make this the best twenty years of my life."

"You think I've given up on eternity with you?" He stood, rising before her, naked, big and bold. So beautiful she wanted to weep. "If you knew my feats, the clashes I won to escape those vampires. Don't you understand? *Nothing* can keep me from you! Nothing could touch me. With you as my woman, I *feel* immortal already."

And gods, he *looked* it.

"Wóden should be honored to have me as a son."

"Aidan!"

"Will he deny me when I win a thousand battles bearing his mark?" He pounded his tattooed chest. "I will win the entire world in his name if I have to!"

The power of this warlord's body. The strength of his will. The might of his sword . . .

He was so confident that even she began to believe it. If they were together, why couldn't they do anything?

He rejoined her, covering her once more. "And you will wait for me. I do not ask this of you. I demand it." His lips descended on hers, his rough kiss brooking no refusal.

As she arched up to him, she knew she would wait

forever. Something about this male had always drawn her, captivated her. She couldn't explain it, but she was through fighting it. Love or not—this was her man and always would be. . . .

More hours of blissful coupling followed, more unimaginable pleasure.

And afterward, as she began drifting to sleep with their bodies still joined, he cradled her face with his callused palms, brushing kisses over her forehead, her cheeks. "I promise you eternity, Reginleit. And each day I will love you more than the one before—"

Suddenly pain stabbed in her torso like fire. "Aidan!" A blade had sunk into her? How? In a panic, she pushed up against him. Blood poured as she disentangled them.

"Reginleit?" he bit out in confusion. A sword tip jutted from his chest.

"Aidan!" she shrieked. *"Ah, gods, no!"*

A vampire loomed behind him; the assassin had traced into their home and stabbed Aidan from behind.

The vampire wrenched the sword free, raising it to finish Regin as well. "For the lives you took yesterday, berserker! For your wars . . . now you and your woman die!" He swung; Aidan shielded her with his body, taking the blow across his back.

Just as the vampire readied to strike once more, Brandr burst inside, cleaving through its neck with his ax. The vampire collapsed.

Brandr cast one look at Aidan and fell to his knees. *"Nay, Aidan,"* he rasped. "The fiend must have followed you back."

Still struggling to protect her, Aidan rolled onto his lacerated back, reaching for his sword.

Brandr hastened to hand it to him, but said, "There are no more, my friend. R-rest easy."

When Aidan turned his head to her, shock threatened to engulf her. Even as she numbly curled up beside him, in her mind she was still shrieking, still hungering to slaughter the thing that had done this.

Aidan's mighty chest labored for breath. "Brandr will earn ohalla and watch over you." He faced his friend. "Vow it."

His voice ragged, Brandr said, "I vow it."

Seeming relieved, Aidan turned back to her. "I love you, Reginleit."

She swallowed back a sob. *This cannot be happening.* "I-I love you, too."

"Nay. Your heart is . . . still your own." He raised a bloody hand to her face, and she knew he'd lost sight in his eyes. "*I but needed more time.*"

She seized his hand in both of hers, squeezing hard. "Then *take* it, warlord. Take more time—you fight for us! You heal so quickly, you can recover from this!"

But his lids slid shut, his breaths rattling. Brandr roared with grief.

"*Aidan, come back to me.*" She wept over him, tears spilling onto his skin. "Come back to me, come back to me!"

Just before his breaths ceased, he vowed, "*Somehow, love . . . I will find you.*"

* * *

And Aidan did.

Yearning for Regin endlessly, he was reborn again and again for the next thousand years, re-embodied in different guises and lives, with no memory of his past. Yet each borrowed lifetime ended more tragically than the last.

A pair of lovers—bound and cursed by fate.

Some say 'tis Wóden who punishes Aidan for his hubris, dooming him to perish just when he's found Reginleit and remembers his love for her.

Some say Aidan's indomitable will proves so strong that, at times, he can escape the Reaper's gaol; but no man can elude that dark scythe forever.

Others say that the Valkyrie's kiss was so sweet that it enchanted the mortal, who finds her through eternity by following a mad longing within his heart.

Whatever may be the case, to this day, Reginleit awaits.

To this day, Aidan returns. . . .

"Check yourself before you wreck yourself?"
*If I hear that one more *$#&%@! time . . .*
—Regin the Radiant, Valkyrie,
prankster, modern-day swordswoman

The only good immortal is a dead immortal.
—Declan Chase, magister of the Order

ONE

Outside of New Orleans
Present day

Declan Chase eased his Humvee down a winding bayou drive leading to Val Hall, the estate where a notorious coven of Valkyrie lived.

My target will be within.

Regin the Radiant.

Though his head was splitting from lack of sleep and his usual tension plagued him, he felt a measure of excitement about his mission. Ever since he'd received her dossier two weeks ago, Declan had been impatient to seize this female.

Perhaps because no other magister had ever captured a Valkyrie?

Yet he reminded himself that tonight's target would be merely another capture, yet another prisoner he delivered to the Order—the mortal army to which he'd pledged his life.

When he spied lightning in the distance, he pulled off into the thick brush, deep enough to conceal his truck. After turning off the ignition, he readied for the night with a swift efficiency born of years of combat.

He strapped his sword to his side, then checked the pistols in his dual holster and the extra cartridges in his dark flak jacket. More cartridges filled the pockets of his camo pants. He was well aware that a gun couldn't kill an immortal, but an armor-piercing round between the eyes at close range could bring one to the ground.

He opened a briefcase filled with sensitive electronics, retrieving a minuscule GPS beacon/listening device. After carefully stowing the bug in another pocket, he tested his radio earpiece.

Despite the lateness of the hour, the bayou heat was intense, assailing the truck's cab. With the jacket, his customary gloves and high-necked shirt, he began to sweat. Drops of perspiration trickled down his chest, over the countless scars covering his torso.

His never-ending reminders of a time spent in hell. . . .

Tamping down those memories, he focused on the mission. Tonight's was one of only two remaining. Then he could return to his island, to his sanctum. *To my medicine . . .*

With that thought in mind, he stepped out into the humid air, then began jogging along the dirt driveway.

Under a canopy of oaks, he ran through muddy ruts until he reached the estate's opened entranceway: a pair of battered stone columns, each with a rusted gate clinging by a hinge.

He turned a corner and slowed, taken aback by the sight before him.

The Valkyrie's antebellum mansion was draped in

a dense fog that didn't stir, not even with the breeze. Lightning struck all around the building; the grounds bristled with metal lightning rods. Spectral wraiths flew around the manor, defend-ing it against intruders.

An incongruous row of luxury cars lined the drive. Inside, loud music boomed and raucous women's laughter sounded. Intermittent Valkyrie shrieks pierced the night.

So this was where Regin the Radiant lived.

Though the Order possessed much information about other species of immortals—such as the vampires and demons—they had acquired only basic facts about her kind.

Valkyrie had little need for sleep and didn't eat or drink, instead taking nourishment from some unknown mystical source. Though they varied in looks and abilities, they all possessed superhuman strength, speed, and regenerative powers.

Declan knew of only one way to destroy her kind: beheading.

The Order had garnered a few specific details about Regin. *History: Thought to be over one millennium in age. Description: Five foot three, slight build with small claws and fangs. Pointed ears. Waist-length blond hair and amber eyes.*

But her most notable feature was her skin. She'd been named the Radiant One because she purportedly had skin that *glowed*.

The file had contained no clear photos of her. The exposure would show only a bright light where she was supposed to be.

Glowing skin. Another freak of nature. Yet she went out freely among civilians.

She customarily wore two short swords crisscrossed over her back—even in public—and was rumored to be an exceptional swordswoman.

That skill wouldn't save her tonight.

If Declan had been put in charge of this immortal's capture, then she was a priority to the Order. He'd never failed to bring in a target. He had backup troops awaiting in the city, ready to mobilize in an instant.

Initially, he'd considered storming this place, inflicting as much damage and destruction as possible. But there were other Valkyrie inside, and though their species was uniformly female, they were among the strongest and most vicious in the Lore.

Regin might be slight, but she could likely lift a car by herself.

To bring in a team would risk his soldiers' lives unnecessarily, and he'd already lost men at a recent capture. A powerful, older vampire had put up a fight as few others ever had.

Plus, Declan had no idea how to battle those wraiths guarding the house. No, he'd wait until Regin the Radiant was separated from her kindred. Then he'd strike.

He approached the row of cars, pulling the bug from his jacket. Determining which one was hers proved simple enough. The *RegRad* license plate on a red Aston Martin was a dead giveaway.

The field notes in his dossier had described her as ostentatious, prone to flaunting her uniqueness in public. No wonder she'd been targeted. One of the

Order's objectives was to prevent civilians from ever discovering the deathless beings living in their midst.

He eased open the door and affixed the bug under the driver's side headrest. After testing the sound with his earpiece, he gingerly shut the door and turned to leave—

Out of the corner of his eye, he spied a light, turned to it.

Through one of the mansion's front windows, he spotted her, or at least the radiance she emanated.

She does truly glow. . . .

He silently moved in, camouflaged behind a tree about two hundred feet from the front porch. He couldn't see her face, but from the back, her figure was curvaceous. She wore a pair of indecently low-cut hip-hugger jeans and a cropped red T-shirt that revealed her midriff.

Indeed, two swords in black leather sheaths crisscrossed her back.

Her blond hair cascaded all the way to her waist, except where it was braided into haphazard plaits that jutted out all over the top and sides of her head.

Declan suspected she would be as attractive from the front; Lorean females often were. He detested all immortals but especially the females. They used their seductive looks as a weapon, a tool to rob mortal men of their senses.

They will separate you from your purpose, lure you to your doom. How many times had his superior told him that?

A row of bushes between him and the house rustled.

Another enemy lying in wait? The Valkyrie had plenty of adversaries. And they had no idea danger lurked so close—

The front doors burst open; a woman stormed outside.

Regin.

He released a sharp breath.

Those wild braids held her hair back from her face, revealing all her delicate features. Her cheekbones were high and defined, her nose pert. Blond brows drew together over her vivid amber eyes, and her full lips were parted.

She radiated a pure golden light.

A feeling of recognition swept over him. At once, the near crippling tension he'd endured for decades began to ebb. Why? How?

She wasn't the first unearthly beauty they'd tracked—the Order's island compound was filled with them—so he would've thought himself prepared for her comeliness. But he feared she might be the *most* beautiful.

At least to me.

"Make a hole, bitches!" she yelled to the wraiths, tossing one of them . . . a braid of hair? When the red-robed beings parted, she strode down the steps, her thick-heeled boots clicking.

Out on the lawn, she stopped and cocked her head, drawing those swords with a lethal grace. One of her pointed ears was visible and clearly twitching as she scanned the night. She would see Declan . . . would *sense* him.

He was about to slip back when the bushes nearby rustled once more.

Without a second's thought she dove into them, pouncing on whatever skulked there. A moment later, a ghoul's severed head came flying out. When she bounded from the shrubs, her swords were already sheathed and twigs protruded from those haphazard braids. She reached up, felt them, then left them there with a shrug.

When a trio of other women staggered out onto the front porch, Regin held up the head and made an exaggerated curtsy. They cheered drunkenly. Witches, no doubt. They were the Valkyrie's allies and notorious drunks.

One laughed, tripped over her own feet into a pratfall, then laughed again.

Regin turned back to face his direction. With her skin glowing brighter and her expression animated, she punted the ghoul's head like a football, then shaded her eyes melodramatically. As it sailed far above him toward a nearby swamp, she cried, "It. Might. Go. All. The. . . . Way!"

She cannot *be one thousand years old.*

The witches cheered again.

That task completed, she plucked a sat-phone from a holster on her belt. She texted something, her fingers so fast they were a blur, then strolled over to her car and hopped inside. The engine purred when she started it. She pulled up in front of the house, honking the horn and rolling down the windows.

"Nïx!" she called. "Get your ass out here!" She

said something to the witches in a lower voice, and they howled with laughter. But when Regin turned from them, her easy grin faltered, her demeanor preoccupied.

Another Valkyrie sauntered from that madhouse, a black-haired one with vacant eyes, cradling what looked like a paralyzed bat in one arm like a babe.

She had to be Nïx the Ever-Knowing, a powerful soothsayer. Though she looked to be in her mid-twenties, she was one of the oldest—and most crazed—immortals on record.

She wore a long, flowing skirt, cowboy boots, and a T-shirt that read VALKYRIE in big block letters with an arrow pointing up at her face.

Flaunting themselves. The arrogance. Christ, how he hated them.

She too proffered a braid to the wraiths—*a toll of some sort?*—then joined Regin in the car, blowing a kiss to the witches. The two Valkyrie pulled out, some asinine song blaring from the car stereo—the only lyrics were "Da-da-da." They bobbed their heads in unison to the music.

As they passed, he drew back into the brush, his heart thundering. But the dark-haired one turned, looking directly at him with eerie golden eyes.

Just as the hair on the back of his neck stood up, the soothsayer mouthed, *You're late.*

Regin the Radiant sensed some enemy was hot on her ass as she sped down dark country roads.

But she simply didn't have *time* for a fight to the

death just now. Regin had to reach Lucia before it was too late.

She adjusted the rearview mirror. "Are we being followed?"

Nïx nodded happily. "Usually." She tapped her chin with her free hand. "You know, you think you don't like it, but actually you'll miss it when it's gone."

Regin scowled at her sister, doing her damnedest to ignore Bertil—the bat Nïx carried. It'd been a gift from a *secret admirer.* "Seeing as we're on our way to the Loreport, you probably should tell me where I'm flying out to tonight." Nïx's last report on Lucia had her in the Amazon, of all places.

"Hmm. Should I remember?"

"Me. Meeting up with Lucia. Who's gearing up to slay Cruach, her worst nightmare." Crom Cruach was the ancient horned god of human sacrifices and cannibalism—and the monster who'd tricked Lucia into leaving Valhalla. Every five hundred years, he tried to escape his prison. For the last two times, Lucia—with Regin as her trusty wingman—had forcibly denied his parole. "Any of this ringing a bell, Nïx?"

Blankness.

"Gods, I don't have time for this!" Lucia was out there alone; Cruach was rising nowish. And Nïx was *spacing*?

"Don't shriek," Nïx chided. "You'll hurt Bertil's ears, and he needs them for echolocation." As she stroked her new pet in a love-him-and-pet-him-and-call-him-George kind of way, her eyes were even more vacant than usual. Her visions of the future had been hitting her rapid-fire lately, and they were taking a toll.

Assholes were laying odds in the Lore betting book that Nucking Futs Nïx wouldn't make it through this Accession with any remaining sanity intact. And there wasn't a whole lot remaining.

"Don't fret, love," Nïx said reassuringly.

"How can I not fret . . ." Regin trailed off. "You're talking to the freaking bat!"

She tickled its belly with a claw. "Coochy-coo." Regin swore the bat smacked its lips with contentment, snuggling into her arm.

Had Nïx been feeding that little winged rat her blood? "Don't you know that those things spread Cujos? Damn, Nïxie, you're getting worse. Even more cray-cray than usual."

She briefly glanced up. "That's fair."

"Uh-huh." Regin downshifted, tires squealing as she swerved to dodge a roadkill-bound possum.

"But what about your own cray-crayness, Regin? You've been behaving very badly of late. Getting high on intoxispells and picking fights. You are acting out, and it simply must stop unless you invite me to join in."

Also fair. But what else was Regin supposed to do? A year ago, she and Lucia had undertaken a badass mission to discover a way to defeat the unkillable Cruach forever. Instead of merely imprisoning him. They'd traveled all over the world together, risking their lives.

In other words, good times. But then Prince Garreth MacRieve, Lucia's werewolf admirer, had started following her everywhere, sticking his nose where it didn't belong. Regin's solution? Euthanasia.

Lucia's solution to Regin's solution? Leave her behind when she was nursing a hangover.

Abandoned me like last year's wardrobe. Regin's claws dug into the steering wheel. After a millennium of never leaving each other's side. *But last year's wardrobe is determined to make a comeback.*

"Nïx, you promised you'd tell me where Luce is if I did everything you asked me. I cleaned your room. I took your Bentley to the shop after you went off-roading again. And I put in hours at the Lore foundling house with those little punks." Regin had begun to call it the Lorphanage and predicted it'd stick. "I *need* to keep moving anyway. You know he's returning soon."

Aidan. With his heart-stopping smile and big, possessive hands. Though she longed to see her Viking in any reincarnation, she'd decided that he might actually live a full life if he never found her.

Nïx sighed. "Have you truly given up all hope of finding a way to be with him?"

Regin glanced over at her, trying not to feel even a sliver of hope. "Any reason not to give up?"

"I believe my advice to you was 'Go find and bang your berserker.'"

"Huh. Well, see, I tried that, and it didn't quite work out for me." *The last four times!* "I just can't . . . I'm not doing it again." The guilt got worse with each reincarnation. She was his doom, might as well deal the deathblow herself.

Aidan had been sword-struck in his first life, poisoned

in his second, crushed during a shipwreck in his third. In his fourth, he'd been shot. All directly after she and his reincarnation had made love for the first time.

"Unless you can tell me things might be different this time?" Regin added. Damn, could she sound more desperate? But Nïx helped other immortals with things like this. *Why not me?*

"What would you do to be with him, hmm? What would you sacrifice?"

"To break this curse, I would do just about anything."

"Just about?" After long, tense moments, Nïx said, "I have no resolution to tell you." She couldn't foresee everything, wasn't *all*-knowing. Instead, she'd been dubbed the Ever-Knowing, because her visions had appeared without fail for three millennia.

"No resolution?" She hadn't expected Nïx to pony up the answer to a thousand-year-old curse before Regin ran her next red light, but a crumb of hope would've been nice.

"No matter," Nïx said. "You must find something to occupy yourself. There's more to life than destroying vampires."

"Right. Like destroying evil cannibal gods with Lucia," Regin said, proud of her segue.

"Always back to Lucia. You're exceedingly loyal to all your friends—even to your own detriment."

"Whatever. Loyalty's not a bad thing."

"It is when you leave heaven for it. It is when you have nothing to show for it. For instance, your some-some meter is reading empty. What about that nice leopard-shifter pack that wanted to date you? The benefits of a variety pack of males cannot be overstated."

If the rest of her sisters—or, gods forbid, her witch buddies—found out Regin hadn't been laid in nearly two hundred years, she'd never live it down. But like some stupid, sappy tool, she stayed faithful to Aidan and his reincarnates.

"Are you happy, Regin?"

She gave Nïx the look her question deserved. "I'm the prankster, remember? The happy-go-lucky one. Ask anyone—they'll tell you I'm the cheeriest Valkyrie." She studied Nïx's expression, this time noticing the shadows under her sister's eyes. "Why? Are you happy? You seem tired all the time." She didn't mention Nïx's shrieking fits or disappearances, the bizarre eccentricities that only grew worse.

"I'm actively involved in steering the lives of thousands of beings. Which directly affects hundreds of thousands, which indirectly affects millions, with a ripple effect reaching billions. If someone said, 'It ain't easy being Nïxie,' I wouldn't call him a liar."

Regin never really thought about the pressure Nïx might be under. If the bat made her happy and calmed her, then . . . *Welcome to the family, Bertil.*

In a prickly tone, Nïx said, "And yet all anyone talks about is how the Enemy of Old is making power plays in the Lore. His power plays are *child's play* compared to mine."

Like Nïx, Lothaire the Enemy of Old was one of the oldest and most powerful beings in the Lore. But the vampire was pure evil.

Nïx sniffed, "Lothaire's no saner than I am."

As Regin opened her mouth to correct her, Nïx amended, "Not *much* saner."

"There, now." Regin reached over to pat Nïx's shoulder, but that bat hissed at her. "Why don't you hook up with someone, cozy away with a male for a few weeks? Weren't you seeing Mike Rowe?"

"I do miss that baritone-voiced rapscallion." Nïx sighed. "But above all else, I'm a career woman. I've no time to dally."

"You could take just a short vacay, you know? See some sights." *This might be one of the most lucid conversations I've ever had with Nïx.*

"I'm three thousand and three years old." Nïx turned her vacant gaze out the window. "I've seen *everything*—" She sat up, eyes wild. "Squirrel!"

Strike *lucid*. "Hey, I know, you could come with me to find Lucia!"

"Maybe she doesn't want to be found just yet. You know she'll call you before the final showcase showdown with Cruach. For now, I've told you she's with MacRieve."

"*With* with? 'Cause I refuse to believe that yet another Valkyrie is making time with a werewolf." Much less the prim and proper Lucia.

The earthy Lykae revered sex and matehood; Lucia's magical skill with a bow was celibacy-based. If she got horizontal with a guy, she'd get kicked out of the Skathians, losing her archery forever. Which she needed to fight Cruach.

Hence the fleeing from MacRieve and all.

"Refuse or accept, I call 'em like I see 'em," Nïx said. "Now, I have just one final task for you in the Quarter. I need you to go take out some adversaries. Make it an example killing."

"Example killing? Must be Tuesday. And you're not going to get in on the action?"

Nïx blinked at her, aghast. "Who will sit Bertil?"

Regin groaned.

"Besides, I'm going to visit Loa's voodoo shop. She's having an Accession sale. Everything must go." She snickered.

"If I do this, will you finally tell me how to find Lucia?"

Another pet of the bat. "Don't worry, dearling. You'll fly out tonight. I promise."

"Are you talking to me or Bertil? Oh, me? Then, fine." She gunned the car even faster, speeding toward the Quarter. *Lucia, I'm on my way . . . just hold tight.* "Tell me where my victims are."

TWO

Late for what? What the hell had the soothsayer meant? Declan was half-tempted to confront Nïx, but she was not to be engaged, by his commander's order.

So for now he bided his time, pursuing the pair of Valkyrie. Since his Humvee stood no chance of keeping up with Regin's sports car and maniacal driving, he'd tracked her vehicle while he listened to their conversation—or what he could make out over the static. It was as if an electrical field had interrupted the relay.

What he'd heard had made little sense to Declan—talk of berserkers and cannibals and some absent sister. All he knew for certain was that Regin had been dispatched to kill.

Not who, not where, only why.

An example killing.

Historically her enemies were the vampires and certain species of demons. She might lead him to an entire nest of their kinds.

Once he'd reached the Quarter, he quickly spotted Regin's car, parked half on the street, half on the curb. A three-hundred-thousand-dollar car treated like junk. He'd throttle her just for abusing a car that fine.

He parked a couple of blocks away, then hurried into the crowd, searching for the two. Though he was several minutes behind, he swiftly reencountered Regin sauntering down Bourbon Street alone.

Easy enough to track her. She left a trail of slack-jawed men in her wake.

And they reacted not only to her glowing skin. The Valkyrie walked with an otherworldly sensuality, her hips swishing in those low-cut jeans, her plump arse attracting male gazes like moths to a flame. Some men adjusted obvious erections or rubbed cheeks recently slapped by outraged girlfriends.

As Declan trailed her, even he felt his shaft twitch, as if trying to stir for her—though his "medicine" would make that impossible.

To be aroused by a revolting detrus? When nothing else could tempt his deadened, scarred body?

While others in the Order called the immortals *miscreats,* short for miscreations, Declan often used the term *detrus,* the coarsest word they had for them.

It meant "vilest abomination."

That was how he saw them. How he'd always seen them, ever since he'd learned of their existence twenty years ago. . . .

As the Valkyrie covered blocks, several beings approached her. More witches tried to coax her to go out with them. Two pointed-eared females—likely more Valkyrie—twirled swords, looking like they were primed for a battle and inviting Regin to come along.

She turned them all down with a grin, which promptly faded as she moved on.

Even more beings avoided her. Declan noticed several large males striding in the opposite direction when she came into sight; all wore hats of some type. No doubt behorned demons.

The field notes in her dossier reported that she was notoriously hard on demons. Whereas she simply *ended* vampires.

When she paused to text something on her cell phone, he drew back behind the cover of a nearby building. Then she gazed up with a peculiar look of sadness. That expression didn't fit her glowing, animated face, seeming as foreign as joy on a dying man's visage.

She stowed her phone back on her belt, then crossed to a back alley behind a five-story hotel. Without warning, she leapt to a balcony on the fourth floor, easily jogging along the rail before scaling to the roof. There he saw her hunch down at the edge, her ears twitching once more as she searched for her prey.

A perfect killer.

If it weren't for the Order, immortals would likely rule the earth.

Recently, several had made strikes against well-known human leaders around the world. His commander, Preston Webb, had told him, "Even the more moderate species are aggressing on us, son. Any tenuous truce has fallen by the wayside."

There truly was to be war between the species. As ever, Webb was right—

Declan lost sight of her. He hastened around to the front of the building, then cased the next, but he didn't see her on any of the roofs. Where the hell was she? He tore up and down streets, head craning.

In the distance, he heard what sounded like an explosion. Seconds later, he got a call on his earpiece from the leader of his backup unit. When Declan answered, he heard a war zone on the other end.

Yelling. Gunfire. Was that groaning metal?

"Magister, the target . . ."

"You weren't ordered to engage her!"

"Sir, she found us!"

His men were the prey. The example killing.

Fuck! He raced toward the sounds, turning a corner. He spotted her maybe half a mile away along a riverside quay downtown.

Never had he seen anything like the scene there.

One of their three black vans was on the bank of the river, upended on its grill. A second lay on its side in the street, with claw marks carved down its length. Bodies of slain soldiers sprawled all around it.

Declan sprinted, unable to reach her before she struck out, swirling with those swords like a tornado, slicing down men with unfathomable speed.

A dozen more soldiers had opened fire on her with their laserlike charge throwers. But those powerful weapons weren't slowing her.

Hair whipping all around her face, she took the electricity, seeming to consume it. Lips curling, she stabbed her swords back into their sheaths and opened her arms wide.

Her lids briefly slid shut in pleasure.

As he ran, he inexplicably shuddered in reaction.

Thoughts arose that never should, impulses long denied. . . .

"That all you got, muthafuckas?" She glowed brighter, illuminating the street. "I *like* electricity, you dumbasses! Hit me with another."

They did. She sucked it in. The streetlights surrounding her began to flare from her radiant energy.

"Know what else? I'm a freaking conduit." She caught a jolt in one hand, and channeled it back with her other. She hit one soldier, exploding him into the air, killing him instantly.

Rage erupted within Declan. The strength and speed he fought so hard to hide rose to the fore. Blood pumped to his muscles, his thoughts dimming. Like a blur, he closed in on her, unsheathing his sword as he ran.

"You want some of this?" She turned to another soldier, shooting again. "How 'bout you?" And again.

Declan stole behind her, wrapping one arm around her neck to yank her back into him. He inhaled her scent, felt her body, hesitated. *Stab her, incapacitate her.*

When she thrashed against his chest with inconceivable strength, his training took over and he planted his sword into her side, twisting the blade within her.

Lightning struck nearby. She gasped at the pain. A debilitating wound, even for an immortal.

Blood bubbled from her lips and poured from the gash. Her little body trembled against him, her skin cooling as her light *dimmed*.

Wrong! his mind screamed. Dizziness hit him as that familiar tension multiplied, knotting every one of his muscles, nearly crippling him. He swayed, quickly withdrawing his blade.

Without him supporting her, she collapsed, curling up on the filthy street. As blood streamed from her side, she narrowed her eyes up at him. They were bright silver, brilliant. Her blond lashes seemed to glitter all around them. Two tears spilled.

Wrong.

He clenched the hilt of his bloody sword, his gut churning until he almost vomited.

"*You,*" she bit out. She gazed at him with recognition, brows drawing together as if with . . . betrayal. "You'll *pay.*"

Some of the remaining soldiers stared at the exchange in confusion. Reminded of his mission, Declan grated, "Bag her."

Disabled by her wound, she couldn't defend herself as two soldiers bound her wrists behind her back. She drew a breath to shriek, but they slapped a special tape over her mouth. Another pair descended on her, one with a black sack for her head and another with a sedative-filled syringe. She struggled wildly as they tightened the sack over her.

Once they'd administered the sedative, her body twitched twice, then fell limp. Utterly defenseless.

This creature had demonstrated monstrous power. Now she lay as if dead.

His men disarmed her, then tossed her into the sole functioning van. Her shirt rode up, revealing the bloody wound Declan had given her.

Why was he sickened? He raked his hand through

his hair, then squeezed his forehead. His skull felt like it was splitting.

A thousand times he'd struck, collecting enemies to be taken back to the Order's compound. What was different about this one?

"Magister?" a soldier said. "Are you all right, sir?"

Declan gazed at their captive, then down at his gloved hands, noting how they shook. *No, I'm not fuckin' all right!* He'd almost wished his hands had been bare when he'd taken her. To feel a woman's flesh after so long . . .

He'd craved touching her even as he'd stabbed her.

Sick.

Declan peered at the soldier. As he coldly said, "Of course, I'm all right," he thought, *They're being led by a madman.*

THREE

In the transport plane's cabin, Declan scuffed to the bed, only partially dried off from his recent shower. He shed the towel around his hips, then fell back on the foam mattress. Shoving the heels of his palms against his eyes, he rubbed till his lids stung.

His fatigue wasn't surprising. Whenever he unleashed his abilities, he suffered acute exhaustion, which was one of the reasons he took medicine to diminish them. Plus, he seldom slept on these hunting trips.

Just hours after the Valkyrie, he and his remaining men had set back out and bagged an easily captured witch. Now, at last, he could return home.

He should be out cold, but the tension within him wound even tighter. For as long as he could remember, he'd felt a constant pain in his chest coupled with a punishing anxiety that ate at the pit of his gut. To this, he added frequent nightmares about a fiend at his back, his body gored by steel, and a woman's screams.

That harrowing sense of loss . . .

He called it *the strain*. Because even as a lad, he'd known it would break him one day.

His medicine helped, but those nightly injections

couldn't quell it completely. It proved too strong, too pervasive.

Right now, the strain was grueling, and he'd depleted his travel supply yesterday. They were still hours away from their isolated destination—a secret installation in the stormy southern Pacific. Which meant hours before he could score more.

Declan supposed it was his fate always to be injecting something.

The ride was jarring, the weather turbulent. He didn't mind flying, had trained as a pilot, but this nauseated even him.

Or maybe it was the aftereffects of this night's work.

The betrayed look in the Valkyrie's eyes still confounded him. When capturing immortals, he'd been critically injured, even bespelled once; but never had one looked at him with recognition and then . . . hurt. As if he'd broken the gravest promise.

Never had he nearly vomited in the midst of a capture.

He lifted the rubber-edged dog tags hanging around his neck. Behind one, he'd soldered a small medallion, an old Irish charm for luck. His da had bought it for him when Declan was a lad. At times like this, Declan would rub his thumb over it, though no luck had ever come of it.

It was a reminder of what her kind had cost him, what they were capable of.

The Valkyrie had killed ten of his men.

And yet he couldn't stop himself from glancing at

his cabin door. She was in the transport bay. He could reach it easily from here.

What is this? Why did Declan feel like he'd die if he didn't see her that second?

He recalled that expression of ecstasy on her face—and the way he'd responded. He remembered his thoughts at that moment, was shamed by the ideas that had arisen.

To touch that glowing skin, to be burned by it . . .

When he'd seized her in his arms, he'd nearly groaned. That had been the most his body had touched a female's in years. Her scent and curves had tantalized him.

But in the end, his training had taken over, and he'd stabbed her.

He reached beside the bed, collecting the sword he always kept close. He unsheathed it, turning it back and forth in the muted cabin light. Crimson still stained the blade near the hilt.

How much blood it has spilled. Immortal blood.

Just two nights ago, he'd used it to capture an ancient vampire, one that had killed thousands of humans over its unending lifetime, like a silent plague.

Preston Webb had given Declan the blade for his Order initiation, telling him, "Your family would have been proud, son."

If they hadn't been tortured by detrus creatures right before my eyes.

Right alongside me . . .

Best that they hadn't survived. Else they'd be as fucked in the head as Declan was. And his brother,

Colm? Who'd had his throat slit at fifteen years old?

Colm had been the lucky one.

With an inward shake, Declan sheathed the sword. *Why am I thinking about that night now?* He'd buried those memories deep; his medicine helped keep them there.

He'd been considering doubling up on his doses for months. Now he decided it was time. Which meant he'd need to see his "pusher" upon returning to the island. For now, he could do nothing but wait.

Another glance at the door . . .

When Regin woke, she was bound and gagged, with a hood over her head and her body strapped to a gurney of some sort. She could tell she was on a plane, could scent saltwater miles beneath them.

Can this night get any worse?

Memories flooded her consciousness: shadowy men shooting her with electricity . . . her bliss from said electricity . . . a large male with uncanny speed getting the drop on her. . . .

He'd stabbed her in the side? The pain still throbbing there confirmed her injury—

Ah, gods! He'd been Aidan, returned once more.

She felt crazed, almost laughing hysterically. Had she thought this night couldn't get any worse? *Aidan, have you come to perish gruesomely? Then I'm your girl!*

But never in his other lifetimes had he harmed her. If he was truly Aidan, then surely those other men were evil, and he'd had to play along.

By twisting the knife?

He'd been so fast, powerful. No surprise there. In each reincarnation, he'd been a berserker, even if he hadn't known it.

No matter what, she had to get away from him. She strained against the bindings securing her wrists behind her back. Nothing. Likely unbreakable. And that injection had probably weakened her.

Forced to lie here, bound, in pitch darkness.

Regin didn't have Zen, wasn't insane like Nïx or laser-focused like Lucia. Each second like this, in a plane taking her farther from where she needed to be, was maddening. "Oh, you'll fly out tonight," Nïx had told her. *Yuk it up. You're* so *going to pay.*

But why would Nïx do this? Especially after the bomb she'd dropped on Regin right before they'd separated on Bourbon Street: "When Cruach rises this time, he'll ring in the apocalypse. Every sentient being on earth will become infected with the need to sacrifice whoever they love most."

Uh, man down here, Nïx. One fewer apocalypse aversion associate. *Whiskey Tango Foxtrot, soothsayer—*

The click of a door sounded. Then footsteps. Someone sat next to her. She could feel tension rolling off him, knew it was Aidan.

Who for some reason had gutted her in a dirty street.

He rose, paced, then sat once more. He said nothing, didn't move, but she knew his gaze was raking over her.

When she remembered to breathe, he said, "Awake already." A faint accent tinged his deep voice, but she couldn't place it. He pulled her hood off.

She blinked against the low light, noting details as he came into focus. Dear gods, he was big, as tall as the original warlord she'd almost fallen in love with.

He was dressed all in black, from his jacket and combat pants to his gloves. His skin was pale, stark against the pitch-black hair that hung down past his forehead, partially concealing scars on one cheek. He was middle-aged, probably upper thirties, with a strong jaw, broad cheekbones—and Aidan's eyes. In this face, they looked cold.

Though for one brief moment tonight, they'd glowed with a berserker's light—the telltale sign she'd spied while bleeding out in the street.

Aidan. She hadn't imagined it. Hell, she'd been sensing his reincarnation for three decades, had been warned by Nïx for just as long.

"I have questions for you, Valkyrie."

Oh, I've got some for you, too. Like why you did a blender on my insides.

"Answer them truthfully, and you won't be harmed more this night."

This night? Finally, she nodded. With one gloved hand, he reached for her mouth. With his other, he shoved a cocked pistol against her temple. "I know a gunshot won't kill you. But it'll shut you up. Try one of your Valkyrie shrieks, and I'll put a bullet in your brain."

Definitely not an act. Great. Her Viking had come back wrong. She'd figured it would have to happen sooner or later. *Hello, later.*

All the effort she'd gone through to flee from him

these past decades, to spare his current life, was for nothing.

So why had he captured her? And who were those men with him?

"Do you understand me, female?"

When she nodded again, he snatched the tape off, leaving her lips stinging like fire. She bit back a foul curse, growing less freaked and more pissed with each second. Regin's temper was legendary for a reason.

"How did your sister Nïx know we'd been following you? And why did she dispatch you to attack my men?"

"Dispatch?" He must've bugged her car! What exactly had he heard? "You know, it was more of a suggestion, like try the prime rib."

His pale lips curved into an evil sneer. "Have you ever been shot in the head before? I've often wondered what the pain would be like."

"I have been, and it hurts," she answered honestly. "I'll answer your questions, if you tell me who you are and why I've been captured."

His eyes narrowed. "I'm Declan Chase."

He thought his name was Declan. *But not for long.*

"I work for the Order, a mortal army at war with your kind."

"Never heard of 'em." *I'm screwed.* "Then why have you taken me prisoner? Why not just kill me?" Maybe she was to be a war prize? Then history would repeat itself. She had to bite back a hysterical laugh. "You were coming for me anyway, weren't you?"

"You were selected for capture. We also . . . study unique immortals."

Something about the way he said that last part gave her chills. "You mean experiment?"

"Correct."

Yep. Screwed. Her eyes darted around the cargo hold. How the hell could she escape? "And that's where you're taking me now? To a jail? Or probably a lab?"

"We call it a *facility*. Now answer my questions," he said, his accent growing thicker.

It was either Irish or lowlands Scot. This Aidan version was Celtic. Before, he'd been a French knight, a Spanish privateer, and an English cavalryman.

"Nïx knows just about everything," Regin said. "She's a soothsayer. In fact, I'm sure she's already foreseen where you're taking me. I don't know why she wanted me to attack your men." *Unless she* planned *for me to get captured.* Knowing Nïx, she probably considered all this a date that she'd set up between Regin and Aidan. "With her, I usually don't ask."

"We'll discover it on our own anyway." The muzzle pressed harder against her temple. "Tell me, then, did you enjoy killing my men?"

Regin rolled her eyes. "Of course I enjoyed offing them. You guys came to *our* turf, remember?" *Filter, Regin!*

"I should *off* you right here." He began unconsciously running the muzzle up and down her cheek.

She could shriek before he could shoot her, blowing out the glass of this aircraft. She might survive a crash. Aidan would be done for.

Even now she hesitated to harm him. "I can't tell you how much you would regret that."

"Because your kind will exact revenge on me?" He cast her that cruel sneer, a twisting of his lips. "And I can't tell you how many times I've heard that."

She shook her head. "No, not because of revenge. You'll regret hurting me."

"Regret? I despise your kind. I savored hurting you, anticipate the next time I can."

Once he remembered, his actions would put him to his knees with misery.

"Why did you act as if you know me?" he asked.

How to answer that? The sooner he remembered, the sooner he died. In the past, she'd done everything she could to keep him from remembering. *I can't tell him.* "I thought you were someone else." When she shrugged as best as she could, the wound in her side erupted in fresh pain. Between gritted teeth, she said, "Since you've brought it up, my kind *will* exact revenge. They'll unleash hell on you for this."

He leaned in as if imparting a secret. "Then they had best do it fast. Because we're going to interrogate you, and examine you, and then we'll behead you. You'll beg for mercy, but I'll grant you none."

Icy dread shivered over her. "What the hell," Regin whispered, "did I ever do to you?"

He shoved the tape back over her mouth and yanked the hood down. At her ear, he rasped, "You exist."

Another shot in her arm, and unconsciousness took her once more.

FOUR

Back at the facility, Declan signed over his unconscious prisoners to the warden, a stout, beady-eyed arsehole named Fegley.

The man hated Declan. The feeling was mutual.

Fegley was in charge of processing the inmates, removing their effects and any hidden weapons, formally ID'ing them, and collaring them. While he worked, a physician from the research arm would take biological samples for an initial workup, then the prisoner would be transferred to one of the three hundred cells spread out over two containment wards.

"Which cell are you putting the Valkyrie in?" Declan asked.

"Seventy."

"Why there?" Two inmates already occupied that cell. Yes, the facility was overcrowded, and they'd been doubling up, but prisoners were usually placed with much forethought.

So why put the Valkyrie with a female fey assassin and a semi-catatonic male halfling?

"More prisoners came in while you were gone." Fegley shrugged. "Webb ordered her into that one. And I don't question orders," he said pointedly.

Stifling his long-denied urge to strike the man, Declan turned toward the research ward and his own suite of rooms.

Though he didn't understand Webb's reasoning at times, it wasn't his place to question an order either. Or to question *anything.* Even when he itched to know how Webb acquired new information about their foes. Or how this island was kept hidden from their detrus soothsayers and oracles. . . .

When Declan reached his suite, he unlocked the executive office he used as a reception area. From that room, two corridors branched off behind concealed panels. One led to a storage warehouse—with an emergency escape tunnel—the other to his private quarters. There he had a sizable multilevel space with a gym, a kitchen, a work and sleep area, and an adjoining bath.

The only home he'd known for nearly a decade.

Inside his inner chamber, he removed his gloves and jacket. There were only two places in the world he felt comfortable enough to shed the layer of clothes that kept his ruined skin hidden: here within this sanctum, and out in the desolate forests on the island.

Releasing a weary exhalation, he sank into the chair at his control console. Above the curved desk and computer keyboard stretched a ninety-six-inch LCD screen. Across that extended monitor, he could pull up multiple broadcast feeds from the facility's cameras.

With the click of a button, he could view—and hear—the occupants in any of the holding cells, could deploy security measures against them.

From this console he could run the entire base. In fact, he often did.

This military installation had once been used only to secure and interrogate prisoners. Now the facility also housed a research arm in a dedicated ward. A team of scientists lived on-site, investigating the immortals' innate defenses, their physical strengths—and especially their weaknesses.

Webb had turned over control of the base to Declan a decade ago. Since then, Declan's life had fallen into a routine: work out in the morning to deaden his abnormal strength, oversee operations, interrogate some of the higher-priority captives.

Now he reviewed several backlogged cases as he mindlessly ate a military MRE—and awaited a doctor's house call.

After finishing his meal, he pulled up the feed from cell seventy to front and center on the monitor. Fegley and a guard were just tossing the Valkyrie to the floor inside. She was still unconscious with her head bagged.

"New roommate, fey," the warden said to the female assassin already in the cell. "She's a Valkyrie. Maybe this prisoner will actually talk to you."

The fey didn't move to assist her, merely stared at Regin with cold indifference.

Odd. From what he understood, the fey and Valkyrie were ancient allies. Of course, the assassin wasn't completely fey.

The other inmate—a teenaged halfling—continued banging his head against the wall. The boy hadn't known he was a detrus, hadn't known they'd existed, until he'd been dispatched here by one of the four other magisters. Apparently, he'd committed no crime other than setting his sights on the wrong girl—a magister's daughter.

Upon arriving here and seeing living, breathing monsters, the boy had gone nearly catatonic.

Declan hadn't even been eighteen when he'd faced these beings for the first time. He had survived the encounter.

But not intact. . . .

For long moments, Declan watched the even rise and fall of the Valkyrie's chest. Her T-shirt was hiked up, revealing her flat belly and her wound. The skin there had already closed.

Typical immortal resilience. How many times had he cursed it? With their ability to regenerate, they were nightmare adversaries.

Not to mention when they possessed other powers. Like the vampires' and demons' teleporting or the witches' spellcasting. Without the Order controlling their number, there'd be no stopping them.

He drummed his fingers on his desk. The Valkyrie was fresh from ten murders, and still he was curious about her, wanting to know more than the limited details in her file.

What is wrong with me? Of all the immortals he'd been sent to capture, Declan might hate her the most—for flaunting what she was, for being proud to have *offed* his men.

And Declan wasn't *supposed* to be curious; he was simply supposed to act—under orders. For nearly twenty years, he'd followed commands, had been the weapon the Order wielded.

He wasn't content in his life, but at least his sense of purpose warred with the strain. He owed everything to Webb—his life, his career, whatever sanity he still possessed.

Someone buzzed his inner chambers. Only three people would dare: Calder Vincente, a former Ranger and his right-hand man, Webb on his infrequent visits, and Dr. Kelli Dixon, the physician in charge of prisoner research.

He glanced at the video of the outer hallway. Dixon, with a familiar metal case in hand.

Though he wanted only to observe the Valkyrie—to relish her reaction when she awakened and comprehended her position—he had business with the doctor. He donned his gloves, then buzzed her in.

She entered, her smile fawning. Which he despised. Sometimes Dixon acted like a schoolgirl fan of his. He knew she was attracted to him, but then for some reason women usually were. The more coldly he treated them, the more they seemed to desire him.

Yet even if there were any aspect about Dixon to tempt him—her looks were forgettable, her figure boardlike—she of all people should know why anything more was impossible.

She waited for him to ask her to sit. Since the only place in this corner of his chambers was his bed, he didn't.

"How was your trip?"

"The hunting was plentiful."

"That's what we've heard." She pushed her large glasses up on her nose, casting him an MD's assessing glance. "You look exhausted. Were you able to sleep?"

"I'll catch up over the next week." Normally, he slept just four hours a night, yet that got shaved down to two on these hunts. And he'd been gone for two weeks, completing lengthy preparations for his three captures.

"How was your heart rate? Any palpitations? Any adverse effects of the medicine?" Dixon had been supplying him with his injections for more than a decade—ever since she'd begun giving Declan his yearly physicals.

She'd been keeping his secrets and keeping him dosed for all that time.

"No adverse effects. I've decided I need to double up."

She set the case on his console. Inside, he'd find two weeks' worth of vials and syringes, a convenient doping kit. "Chase, what you're injecting should knock out a horse. It's going to start affecting your mind, with potentially permanent complications."

He'd long suspected that at some point, she'd begun to add an opiate to the mix, increasing it gradually. Now he felt certain of it. "Then I must be building up a tolerance, because it's not working."

When capturing the vampire and even the Valkyrie, he'd suffered that familiar rage, and with it had come the customary physical symptoms.

Thought left his brain, while his heart felt like it would explode. His muscles twitched and swelled as if they couldn't handle all the blood pumping to them. He would experience a marked surge in strength and speed, yet afterward, he would be nearly feeble with exhaustion.

Dixon squinted behind her glasses. "If I hadn't tested you myself, I'd swear you were one of them."

"I am no bloody detrus."

She flinched at the coarse term.

"And you did test me, finding *nothing,*" he reminded her. Though he did heal faster than most, his cells were still vulnerable to contagion and death. His skin scarred. His broken bones mended with calcium remodeling; an immortal's bone would set as if never broken.

Of course, he'd felt no need to tell her that he possessed animal-like senses, could see in the dark or hear a whisper from half a klick away. "Dixon, you're the one who came *to me* with the idea of injections. Now you're pulling back?"

"I need to do new workups on you, run more tests," she said. "Then we could finally get to the bottom of this."

His attention was back on the Valkyrie. "No more tests. You've subjects enough." Besides, he feared he knew why his strength was burgeoning.

Blood that wasn't my own . . .

"If we could find the root cause," she said, "then we wouldn't have to systemically suppress everything."

They'd gone over this before. In addition to deadening his abilities, his doses suppressed his emotions and any appetites, whether for food—or for sex.

She couldn't seem to believe that he was ecstatic about that particular side effect.

"Chase, we have been friends for a decade."

Of a sort. *I use you.* She was his source, his dealer, providing him a bimonthly stash.

From one drug to the next. *Just a couple of quid's worth, I'm beggin'.* He shoved away the stray thought.

She leaned against the console—in front of the screen. "You're a male in your prime. Don't you . . . *miss* it?"

No. No, he didn't. Even if he didn't suffer that punishing anxiety with each sexual encounter, his body had been ruined.

"Listen, Chase, there's something I need to discuss with you."

"Can it not wait until tomorrow?" Had the Valkyrie stirred?

"It will only take a second. It's important to me. To us," she added significantly.

To us? He cast her a menacing look, the message clear—*you do not want to fuck with me tonight.*

She blanched. "We c-can talk later, then, of course. I'll let you get some rest." She almost laid her hand on his shoulder, but a chilling glare made her recoil, backing to the door. "And I'll have additional vials prepped for now, if you want to start doubling up. Just till I can formulate the stronger doses for you."

Be quick about it. "Very good, Doctor."

As the door closed behind her, he realized Dixon

would not be easily dissuaded. The daft bitch thought she was in love with him. How could she want a man she innately feared?

He exhaled with irritation. Damn it, he just wanted to watch his monitor, to see his new capture—

The Valkyrie was rousing.

Because her deadly cell mate was kicking her.

FIVE

"Where am I?" Regin mumbled groggily, fighting to wake. Was somebody kicking her hip? "Who are you? Why's it dark in here?"

"Take the bag off your head, you tosser," a female said in a British accent.

Bag. Abduction. Not a dream. "Don't kick me again," Regin warned.

The next time a boot connected with her hip, her hands shot out to seize it, twisting until the owner went spinning to the ground. The move had Regin wincing from the pain in her side, but she swiftly snatched the bag off her head as she labored to stand.

Her eyes darted around. *I'm in a cell?* So this was the Order's facility?

A black-haired female was bounding back to her feet, her purplish eyes narrowed. She wore tight club shorts, a leather halter, fishnet stockings with ripped holes, and the stiletto boots Regin had already been acquainted with.

"I recognize you," Regin said. "Yeah, you're Natalya the Shadow. Dark fey assassin." She remembered the female's onyx-colored lips and claws. Her *poisonous* claws. Rumor had it that her very blood was black.

"And you're the glowing Valkyrie."

They'd had a contentious relationship in the past. Regin and her sisters used to snicker and call Natalya the Killer Fairy. Until she'd flung poisoned knives at them. Now Regin defensively reached for her swords—

"No swords for you." Natalya swept back her mane of stick-straight jet hair and began stalking around her, claws bared.

"And no daggers to throw for you."

As they circled each other, Regin flared her own claws as she tried to get her bearings.

Within this small cell, there were two sets of bunks, a toilet, and a sink. Three of the walls were made of solid metal, while the front was a wall of thick glass. In the corner was a second inmate, a young male, maybe late teens. *Don't know what kind.* He was knocking his head against the metal wall, his eyes glazed.

Down a long corridor were even more cells.

Attention back to Natalya. "Aren't you s'posed to be dead?" Regin asked as they each assessed the other for weaknesses. Natalya's gaze flickered over the remnants of her wound, Regin's over the weird collar Natalya wore.

Regin reached up to her neck. What the— *I do too?* She yanked on the metal band, but couldn't break it.

"Not dead," Natalya said. "Just put on involuntary hiatus."

"So are we fighting again, or do you always kick people in greeting?"

"Your m.o. is to attack first and ask questions later. Mine is the same. Seems to me that we don't have that luxury if we're going to escape this place." She lowered her hands. "I think we might need to join forces."

Normally the fey and Valkyrie allied. But Natalya was a dark fey—half fey overlord, half demon slave. "I'll agree to a truce, but I'll escape this place with or without your help," Regin said, lowering her hands as well.

She didn't need any dark-fey deadweight slowing her down. As soon as Regin knew the lay of the land, the schedules, and the security protocols, she'd devise something. "In any case, my sisters will come for me soon."

"That's what everyone else keeps saying, but no one has ever mounted a rescue. We think this installation is hidden from the outside."

In a smug tone, Regin said, "Everyone else doesn't have Nïx the Ever-Knowing in their corner." *Though Nïx might be the one who put me here!*

"Seems the most powerful oracle alive could have given you a heads-up about your capture."

"She does everything for a reason," Regin answered truthfully. Her every stray glance or offbeat Nïxism could be pivotal in shaping the future. But deciphering these portents took more patience than Regin possessed.

"I've got information you need," Natalya said. "The immortals have a grapevine of gossip passed from cell to cell. In the two weeks that I've been here, I've learned much about this place. And about our captors.

For instance, I know the magister took you down personally."

"Magister?"

"Declan Chase. Tall, pale face, soulless eyes."

"Completely soulless." This time. "How did you know?" Regin spied a camera above, placed to capture everything within. She'd bet he was watching her right now. *Creepy.*

"Because he stabbed you in the side. He's also known as the Blademan. Sometimes the Order catches us in sweeps, and sometimes they target us specifically. Appears that you were on the magister's shopping list."

"And magister means *in charge*?" Great. Aidan was the bossman of these mortals—the ones insane enough to provoke immortals.

"I believe a magister is one step below a commander."

Behind them, the young guy's head banging increased tempo. "Uh, you wanna to tell me what his drama is?"

He was handsome and dark-haired, built like an athlete, but he couldn't be more than seventeen or eighteen. He looked disconcertingly human, wearing some high-school football T-shirt, broken-in jeans, and weathered cowboy boots. "'Cause I can see this getting old in a hurry." The hair on his right temple was matted with blood.

"He's been like this ever since they threw him in here four days ago. He doesn't eat or drink, just stares and bangs."

"What is he?"

"I can't puzzle it out. He doesn't have horns, pointed ears—or apparently a need to eat. He does have small fangs, but he also sports a tan line."

"You *checked*? Natalya, you durrrty bitch."

"Hey, I had to determine if he was a blood sucker or not. Now I don't know what to think."

Doing her best to ignore the banging, Regin asked, "Who else have they taken prisoner?"

"It's a who's-who list of the Lore."

Regin gave the fey the look her comment deserved. "As evidenced by the fact that *I* am here."

"Volós the centaur king and the Lykae Uilleam MacRieve have been here for a couple of weeks. They brought Carrow Graie in just before you."

Carrow? Regin was good friends with the witch. *My man is responsible for all this?*

"They've got scads of ghouls, Wendigos, some high-powered Sorceri. Numerous succubae and vampires . . ."

Out of the corner of her eye, Regin spied two guards dragging by a towering prisoner. She turned, gasped.

Lothaire the Enemy of Old.

The vampire was drugged, his head lolling, his pale blond hair stained with blood. His clothes were unmistakably moneyed—his muscular legs encased in leather pants, his shirt tailored to fit his lean build.

But the shirt had a bloody slit in the side. Natalya murmured, "The Blademan took *Lothaire* down?"

The Russian Horde vampire was diabolical. If these humans could capture and contain *him* . . .

With difficulty, he raised his head, his hooded

eyes flashing to Regin, his reddened irises darkening. Without a word, he bared bloody fangs at her.

Once he and the guards passed, Regin bit out, "Those two with Lothaire . . . they're truly *human*? I think I finally understand what a mindfuck is."

"It's the collars. The mortals call them torques. They weaken us, dim our powers through some mystical means."

Regin yanked at hers again. "So how do you get it off?"

"They can't be broken. Only the warden or magister can unlock them—with a thumbprint."

Oh, yeah, I'm screwed. "All righty, then. About that alliance." Regin shot a look up at the camera, rubbing her hand over her nape. "How old are you?" she asked the fey.

"Why?"

"'Cause you could use a little work." She switched to the old immortal language to say, "Because you might understand this tongue."

Natalya answered in the same, "I know it."

"Has there *never* been a successful escape?" Regin asked, but she feared she knew the answer. There was a reason Regin had never heard of the Order.

"The fox shifter next door has been here for years—she hears *everything,* conversations even in other wards. No one has gotten free."

"There's got to be a way."

"It's said we're on an island, far from any coast and surrounded by shark-filled waters. The cell is inescapable, the glass unbreakable. To have any chance at freedom, you'd have to get out of the cell first. They only take us out for three things—torture, experimentations, and executions."

"Mark my words, fey. I will escape this place. And if you get me up to speed and keep me there, I'll take you with me."

Natalya tapped her chin with a black claw. "If I didn't know better, I'd say you have a card up your sleeve."

"Maybe I do." Regin had knowledge of an upcoming event.

Declan Chase's imminent demise.

SIX

What the hell are they speaking?

Declan had observed the Valkyrie and fey's tense interaction with interest. He was fascinated with the hierarchies and alliances in the Lore, the usual predictability of their castes and classes.

But once their initial discord had faded, they'd begun calmly speaking to each other in a different tongue, one that seemed familiar to Declan.

Over the years, he'd studied on his own to learn the languages of his enemies—the vampires' Russian, the Lykae's Gaelic, the rough Demonish of the various demonarchies—but he couldn't place this.

With the click of a button, he started a program to translate their words, confident that he'd soon have a transcript of everything.

Input invalid.

What the hell? His program couldn't pin down the language. He rang a technician. "I want a translation from cell seventy. *Now.*"

"They're speaking no known language, sir."

Declan hung up, tamping down his frustration. He'd heard tales of an omnilingual fey—an elven creature who somehow knew all languages. He put her on his capture list.

The phone rang. Webb was the only one who called his personal line. Declan had no friends or family.

When he answered, Webb said, "You completed all of your captures! Good work, son."

Even after all this time, Declan savored the praise. He knew he'd cast Webb in a father's role, but Webb had been just as quick to put Declan into a son's. They'd both lost loved ones in this war. "Thank you, sir. But we sustained casualties when taking both the vampire and the Valkyrie."

"I saw the videos of the captures. Of course, we knew taking Lothaire wouldn't be easy. You confiscated a ring of his?"

"A plain gold band. He was incensed to lose it, even more homicidal."

"It must have mystical powers. Find out what it does. And what about the Valkyrie? How did she know we were closing in?"

"Her soothsayer sister dispatched her to attack my men."

"Nïx the Ever-Knowing did this?" Webb asked, his tone peculiar. "When is the glowing one in the exam schedule?"

Declan pulled up the rotation on his screen. "Dixon won't have her until next week." The facility was backlogged with inmates, and still Webb insisted on bringing in more, no matter how much Declan protested.

"Question the Valkyrie before then. Dig for as much intel as you can get before the docs get through with her. We need to discover how she produces energy, how she channels it—"

"You knew she could channel electricity?" *That intel would've saved lives tonight.*

"Not until we watched her capture," Webb said. "Think, Declan, she doesn't eat or drink, but she produces continuous, uninterrupted power. She's like a walking reactor. Tapping into her energy source could solve the limitations inherent in the TEP-C."

The Order's charge throwers, or tactical electroshock pulse cannons, were incredibly effective against detrus—at least, against most of them besides Regin the Radiant—but they had limited firing power.

"If you can discover what fuels her, we can use it against her own kind. . . ."

Turning their strengths into weaknesses. Dixon's team of scientists would cut the Valkyrie open on the operating table to get to the truth. Since they'd need measurable, duplicable results, they'd do it repeatedly.

Declan gazed at the monitor, regarding the female with puzzlement.

"In any case, now that we finally have a Valkyrie, we need to learn everything we can about her species, and what sets this one apart."

Whenever the Order had been close to capturing a Valkyrie in the past, the target had grown spooked, as if she'd been tipped off. Likely by Nïx the Ever-Knowing.

So why had Nïx allowed Regin to be captured?

Why tell him he was *late*?

"And we need to know about the vampire's ring," Webb said. "I understand how difficult it is to get miscreats to talk, but I'm confident you can get me these answers."

Though Declan had become an expert at torture, the immortals were astonishingly closemouthed, even withholding information about their natural enemies. The only way to get results was by tormenting a loved one or mate, but Declan had no leverage like that over either the Valkyrie or the vampire.

No matter. Somehow he would break them. "Yes, sir," he said absently.

"Son?" Webb sighed. "You're not feeling mercy for the Valkyrie? Because you had to harm a female?"

Thirty-five years of *something* had rushed to the fore.

"Remember, their beauty is a weapon. This one will not hesitate to wield it on you." A pause. "Has she compromised your judgment? Tempted you in anyway?"

Declan grated, "No, sir!" The Order would mind-wipe and cast out any member who became involved with a detrus. Even an involuntary entrancement was enough to have one's memory erased.

Unless it happens to me.

Two years ago, a witch had entranced Declan, cursing him to relive every terror and agony he'd ever experienced.

Webb had procured a countercurse before Declan had been driven insane—or at least *noticeably* insane. Then the commander had covered up the whole ordeal.

How many more rules would the old man break for him? Would he fix any more transgressions?

On this night, Declan had savored the feel of a captive's body in his arms. *And I'm . . . changing.* His doses could barely control it.

Cast out.

At the idea, sweat beaded on his upper lip. The Order was all Declan had. He'd rather die than lose it. "I'll get the results, sir."

"Maybe I'll come out and check on things next month or so. Might be a good time, with so many developments on the horizon."

"Very good, sir. And perhaps we can talk then about culling some of these prisoners."

Declan didn't want them contained, or, God forbid, created. He wanted them all exterminated. "This facility is well over capacity."

"We'll talk about that when I get there."

Once they'd hung up, Declan called for Vincente. The former Ranger was as trustworthy as any, he supposed, though Declan could never fully trust another, no one but Webb.

In moments, the burly guard arrived. Not for the first time, Declan wondered if the man ever slept.

He handed Vincente the protective box guarding the vampire's ring. "I want you to get this ring analyzed. Have the metallurgist test for any mystical properties. The usual precautions—no one touches it. Return it before I question Lothaire."

With a nod, the man took the box and exited.

Even after the warning that Webb's call had

provided, Declan turned back to the monitor for another look at the Valkyrie. She was sitting on the floor of her cell in front of the glass, resting her forehead and hands against it, as if she expected the door to open at any time.

Instead of feeling satisfaction to see her like this, he suffered more of that inexplicable conflict within him.

He'd done his duty with her. So why this . . . guilt? He clasped his aching forehead.

Why do I feel like I'm going mad? If so, then it'd been a long time coming.

He'd always known he wasn't a perfect soldier, had known he was fucked up. How could he not be? His days of torment had left him emotionally stunted, unclean. But he got the bloody job done, controlling his eccentricities and deviations with exhausting training regimens.

Every day, he worked out in his room, lifting weights with a punishing intensity, then he ran at least forty miles—half the width of the island. He ate only enough food to stave off the worst of his hunger.

Anything to weaken himself, to help him appear normal.

And for years, his injections had rendered him an automaton, mindlessly carrying out the Order's agenda. Those years had been the most satisfying in his entire life.

Clearly, he just needed stronger doses to get back to that state. Tonight he'd begin doubling up. It would help him ignore his new prisoner and finally get some sleep.

Decided, he stripped off his clothes, then snagged the case. Sitting on the edge of the bed, he plucked a needle from its cradle, using it to extract the clear contents from two glass vials.

He rested his elbow on his knee and squeezed his right fist, readying one track-marked inner arm.

A hungry vein answered the call. *Kill the tension and pain, let me rest.* He pressed the plunger . . . exhaling with pleasure as his heartbeat grew plodding, his breaths slowing. The higher dosage confirmed his suspicions.

Oh, aye, Dixon had been adding something illicit. *Bless her.*

The strain eased, the pain of old battle wounds lessening until he could lie back—but he kept the monitor in sight.

His lids grew heavy as he watched the Valkyrie, until he eventually fell asleep.

Yet instead of the oblivion he'd expected, he dreamed of a night in Belfast when he was just seventeen, the night his life changed forever.

SEVEN

Declan rolled off the chit onto his back, staring up at the rotting warehouse ceiling above his mattress.

Maybe he wouldn't have it this time. *That feelin' in the pit of me gut, in me chest.*

Waiting . . .

The girl—he didn't remember her name—slurred, "Ah, Dekko, that was just grand."

Bullshite.

She was some loose bird who hung with the junkie gang he'd fallen in with three years ago. Their city was unforgiving. Since then, half had died. The other half were like him: hankering for the next score, fleecing anything and anyone.

"Though for a spell," she muttered, "I thought ye weren't to come a'tall. . . ." Then she passed out.

Declan yanked off his empty condom. *I didn't.* Already anticipating the misery to follow, he'd gnashed his teeth, struggling to finish like a man. And couldn't.

He gazed over at her, feeling the strain build. *Wrong.* Wrong girl beside him, wrong time, wrong place. He rubbed the medallion hanging from his neck, frantically circling his thumb over it—

He shot upright, shoving his fist against his mouth to hold down whatever meager slop he'd forced himself to eat during the day. Chills seized him, his muscles shaking.

He felt this way every time he was with a woman.

Hell, he felt a measure of the strain constantly. Whenever Declan woke, his anxiety was worse than the day before, as if acid seethed in his belly and barbed wire cinched around his heart.

Tracks lined his arms; he could take or leave food even though he was still growing like a weed; bouts of nightmares plagued him.

For as long as he could remember, he'd had a frenzied sense that he was supposed to be *doing* something. No matter where he was, he felt like he was supposed to be *somewhere else.*

And that strain was killing him.

After sex, it grew stronger, like a beast lived inside him, clawing at his insides to get free. Though only seventeen, he was ready to give up women altogether.

For now, he'd numb the feeling the only way he knew how. He reached toward the battered crate beside his mattress on the floor and plucked up the syringe that lay ready.

Why did he always expect to feel different after sex? When he knew better?

Because, Dekko, ye're not ready to admit ye're done as a man.

He frowned at the weight of the syringe in his hand. He'd been shooting heroin for three years, and knew it was too light. Dread seized him as he gazed down. Empty.

Rage building, he hurled the syringe across the room, then turned on the girl. Jostling her awake, he yelled, “Ye feckin’ slag! Ye stoled it?” That was all he’d had. No money to buy more.

She woke, mumbling, “Needed a wee bump—”

“Get out!” he roared, shoving her up and out on her arse, tossing her clothes at her before slamming the door in her face.

He punched the wall, moldy plaster exploding. Tonight he’d have the nightmares again. A monster at his back. Burning pain slicing through his chest. A woman’s grief-stricken screams.

Those screams . . .

Desperate to avoid those dreams, to numb the strain, he yanked on his pants and threw on a jacket, readying to leave. On his way out, he passed the bitch in the hallway, spat in her direction.

Half an hour later, he pleaded his case to his dealer: “Just a couple of quid’s worth. Give me the shite now, and I’ll fleece ye some of me mam’s jewelry if I have to.” Would he actually steal from his own mother?

Oh, aye. But it’d take time to get to his parents’ house and back.

The verdict: “Cash first, Dekko.”

Declan would need even more time to fence the jewelry. Might take him a day to get back here with the scratch. He didn’t have that long.

“I’m beggin’.” He was about to vomit. The dealer

clearly thought it was from withdrawal. *No, from madness, more like.* He'd do anything to avoid what awaited him. Anything. Others in his gang had no problem giving to get. With that in mind, he said, "There's got to be *something* I can give ye?"

His dealer's eyes widened with surprise. He hadn't known Declan Chase would suck for it.

I hadn't either. Could anything be worse than this feeling?

"Hie yer arse out o' me sight, Dekko." The man booted him in the back, sending him reeling out the door.

Unsure whether he was relieved or not, Declan scuffed back out into the streets.

When a biting wind blew in from the sea, his chills worsened until his teeth chattered. With a despairing eye, he gazed around, tempted to break into a house right off the main strip, but everywhere he turned, bars covered the windows.

No choice but to set off for his parents' place. They were working-class; any jewelry of his mother's had been either handed down from her own mam or hard-earned by his da.

But she can't need it like I do.

An hour into his journey, Declan passed the run-down cathedral where he'd been an altar boy. At fourteen, he'd confessed his constant gut pains and tensions to the parish priest—a stern old codger who'd told him to keep his ailment to himself and find a vocation.

Declan had found heroin instead. He'd never told

another what he grappled with every day. Not even his brother, Colm—not even before their falling-out.

His mam wouldn't be the first family member Declan had stolen from.

By the time he reached his parents' at three in the morning, he was quaking so hard his vision blurred. He'd already vomited twice, laden with strain. *Those screams . . .*

The front door was open, the house quiet. He eased inside, going straightaway to the kitchen, to the bottle of whiskey he knew he'd find in one of the cabinets. Might help him get through the next couple of hours. He lifted it, chugging—

He lowered the bottle, peering into the dark. In a murky corner of the kitchen, someone lay on the floor. Was his brother passed out? "Jaysus, Colm. Ye're too young. Ye want to end up like me?" Declan would beat his arse for this. "Colm?" he demanded, striding over. "What the bloody—"

His brother's sightless eyes were opened wide, fixed on the ceiling. His throat was slashed down to the spine.

"C-Colm?" he rasped. *Dead?* Someone had murdered his little brother? He stared dumbly, tears welling. Until muffled screams sounded from the living room.

Somebody's hurting me parents too! Fury ignited within him, burning away the tears. In a daze, Declan slipped into his parents' bedroom, grabbed the bat propped by his da's side of the bed.

When he entered the living room, he faltered, barely able to comprehend what he saw. Red-eyed beings with fangs and claws filled the area. And those were the creatures with humanlike bodies. Others were winged monsters with bulging eyes and limbs jutting out all over.

The winged ones had gagged and tied up his parents on the floor so they could . . . slowly feed. Their deformed mouths peeled away one strip of flesh at a time—while his mam and da still lived, screaming in agony against their gags.

Me mind's going to break, can't do this, can't believe this is happening. But just when Declan thought he'd pass out from the crazy pounding of his heart, one monster's head rose up from his da, and blood dribbled from its mouth.

Da's blood.

A mindless wrath overwhelmed Declan, and he attacked them. All he could hear was his thundering heart, his bellows, the bat connecting with bone over and over. He didn't know where this frantic strength was coming from, but he crumpled the metal bat against their skulls.

Yet as powerful as he was, they were more so. They kept coming and coming until they overpowered him, pinning his thrashing body to the floor. Even as he flailed, he spied a glimpse of some eerie kind of intelligence in the hideous eyes of a winged monster, and Declan had an instant of clarity.

Colm was the lucky one. . . .

As ever, Declan's mind wasn't ready to relive what those creatures had done to him—the unimaginable torment until he'd blacked out; twenty years later, his dream easily flickered past, picking up at the time when consciousness had trickled in once more. From outside his parents' house, he'd heard voices, and finally the blackness wavered.

He felt the biting tension on his bound wrists and ankles ease, nearly screaming as circulation coursed to his hands and feet once more. How long ago had he been tied up?

Days. . . .

He was aware of a man's voice telling him that he would live, that help was here. "Those things have been slaughtered, son. They'll never hurt anyone again."

"Da?" Declan rasped before the blackness took him once more.

In a kind of twilight, he felt his bones being set, his skin pierced again and again as his numerous wounds were stitched.

When he woke, he was in a hospital, covered in bandages and casts. A tall, dark-haired man sat beside his bed.

"I'm Commander Webb," he said, his Yank accent marked. "You're in a private hospital. You're safe now."

Declan recognized the voice of the man who'd saved his life. He was middle-aged, his hair closely cropped. He wore what looked like a military uniform, but Declan had never seen one like it. "Wh-what happened?"

"I'm sure you're in a state of shock right now. The docs are amazed you survived—"

"And me family?" He hated the way his voice broke.

"I'm sorry, Declan, but they're all dead."

He'd known, but he'd still held out hope. "You're the one who got me out of there?"

"My team and I did. I belong to an organization called the Order, and it's our job to protect people from those miscreats. Unfortunately, our scouts didn't locate this pack until too late."

"Miscreats? *Pack?*" Declan pinched his forehead, wincing as the skin on the back of his hand pulled tight under a bandage.

Webb nodded. "Miscreations. They're immortal beings. Just about anything you thought was a myth is out there walking the streets. Sometimes various species band together in leagues."

Declan's lips parted. He'd also held out hope that they hadn't been real. That he'd gone crazy. Now someone, a man with authority, was staring him in the face, confirming what his eyes had seen. Declan's mind reluctantly accepted it. "You killed them?"

"Yes, a complete extermination. Again, too late for your parents and brother and . . ."

And you, the man hadn't needed to say.

The things those monsters had done to him, to his skin. *The blood in my mouth, blood that wasn't my own . . .*

Declan looked away in shame, his face flushing. "They . . . they fed."

"Those were the Neoptera, some of the most nightmarish of them all."

"Why *us*?" Declan's voice was raw with bitterness. He realized he'd never grasped what bitterness was until this exact moment. *Hatred that burns cold.*

"As near as we can tell, you were picked at random. They attack simply because they can. Some of them feed on humans like cattle. Some play with us, torment us," he said. "That's why we hunt them down and kill them without mercy."

Declan faced him once more, his attention fully engaged. *To be able to hunt them . . .*

"They call themselves Loreans," Webb continued. "We just like to call them dead sons-of-bitches." He dug into his jacket pocket, then held up Declan's charm. "We found this. Is it yours?"

"Aye, it's mine." Hanging from a cord of leather was a thin medallion imprinted with two birds. His da had gotten it for him at a fair.

My father's dead.

Declan's hand shot out to snatch the medallion, the stitches up and down his body straining. Clutching it in his fist, he grated, "I want in."

"I thought you might say that. But it's not so simple. You're not even eighteen. Maybe if you were older, with some military training under your belt—"

"*Now.*" Declan bit out the word. "Now, goddamn it!"

"And what about the drugs? I read your tox screen."

Declan flushed again. "I'll get clean."

"Even if we made exceptions for you, not everyone gets inducted into the Order. You'd have to be combat-trained, and it's grueling. Rangers and marines have told us that their training was a cakewalk compared to ours."

"I don't give a shite."

Webb's eyes bored into his own. "You'd be dealt pain on a daily basis to harden you, so that you could fight these fiends. And at every second, you would have to demonstrate a single-minded purpose, the obsession to eradicate immortals."

"This is mine by right, Webb. More than anyone's. Ye ken it is."

"You think about this. Long and hard. Because to fight these monsters, son, you'll have to become one. . . ."

Declan shot upright, waking drenched in sweat. Drops of it trailed down his chest, past his dog tags, over his raised scars.

With a shudder, he stared down at the wounds that had been carved into his body from neck to waist. More covered his back and down both his arms to his fingers.

He dropped his head in his hands. The Neoptera had taken his flesh and made him drink the blood of the ones he'd killed. Why? And how much of that blood had tainted his own that night?

Maybe that was how Declan had gotten his strength and speed, his heightened senses. Maybe the drugs kept his change at bay all this time. What else could explain it?

God, to become a thing like that . . .

Nothing that a Glock to the mouth can't cure, Dekko.

He forced himself to lie back, to control the mad drumming of his heart. It was too soon for another injection.

Twenty years later, and I'm still shooting up.

But the dream had been so realistic, gripping him harder than it had in memory. He stared at the ceiling, recalling those ensuing years, focusing his mind on all the work he'd done to get where he was now. . . .

After his detox—a bleak period of unrelenting nausea and bone-jarring tremors—and four months of physical rehab for his injuries, the Order had taken him to their compound.

The training had been as punishing as Webb had promised. Pain came daily, but it did harden Declan. The commanders who hurt him the most were the ones he respected above all others.

When he'd heard other recruits complaining about "brainwashing techniques," Declan had been astounded that anyone might disagree with—or resist—what the commanders were instilling in them.

How could Declan be brainwashed into hating the detrus more than he already did?

Physically, Declan had every advantage over the other recruits. Even at seventeen, he was bigger, swifter, more powerful. Webb attributed it to kicking heroin, the training, the vitamins, and diet.

For once in his life, Declan had excelled, even thrived.

And while he'd learned weapons, hunting tactics, and military strategy, he'd begun educating himself and disguising his accent; he hadn't wanted his enemies to determine *anything* about him.

He buried all traces of his past so that no one could ever connect him to the ignorant seventeen-year-old junkie who'd begged for death while his tormentors laughed around mouthfuls of his blood and skin.

After his initiation into the Order, Declan had hunted

down the offspring and forebears of the creatures who'd butchered his own family. Yet that hadn't been enough to satisfy him. He'd become obsessed with tracking more and erasing them from the face of the earth.

And no matter how much the detrus begged—he *always* made them beg—he'd slaughtered them. Nothing pleased him more.

But then two things had changed.

His abilities had become too noticeable; enter Dixon with her shots.

Webb had given him control of this installation, charging him with capturing and imprisoning the creatures Declan wanted only to kill.

Of course, Declan had obeyed the command, ignoring his own deep-seated needs. After all, the man had saved his life, then given him purpose.

Reminded of all Webb had done for him, Declan vowed to try harder to control himself, his . . . impulses.

I know of no man more disciplined than me. He peered over at the monitor, saw the glowing Valkyrie on one of the bunks with her long blond hair spread out around her head. Like a halo.

I will crush this interest.

Eyes narrowed with hate, he rose and turned off the screen.

EIGHT

"*Magister Chase is making rounds today!*" the shifter next door whispered urgently.

Regin rolled her eyes. "Oh, quick, lemme check my hair." Directly beside their cell's glass panel, she lay on her back with her legs stretched up against the metal wall, her arms folded behind her head. Whatever was the opposite of checking her hair, that was what she'd be doing.

From the bottom bunk, Natalya yawned, waking from a nap. In the back of the cell, Roomie Number Three banged his head against the wall. Or at least, against the wadded up jacket Natalya had jammed there.

Wham . . . wham . . . wham . . .

And so goes week one in the House of Horrors. From her spot on the floor, Regin watched the procession of evil researchers and guards going about their daily evil business.

Warden Fegley, the bane of their existence, had only made the first of his thrice daily rounds. The self-important troll loved to taunt immortals, egging them on to violence, then laughing when security gassed their cells.

And now Chase was making an appearance. Goody.

"Still working out your escape plan?" Natalya asked. "There *is* a time element here, Valkyrie. I'm up for an examination soon. And you'll likely go before me since you were a high-priority capture."

Examination was a euphemism for *vivisection*. Where the subject was dissected while conscious. So far, they'd seen two victims brought by, their eyes glazed over, their chests carved open and held together with staples, like a flesh zipper.

Natalya had told her, "I heard that you experience pain like you've never known. They slice nerves or pluck at them just to see how you tick. You're awake when they crack open your chest to get at your heart. Afterward, they wire your ribs back together."

Unfortunately, Regin didn't have an escape plan yet. The only thing she knew for certain? The more she learned about Declan Chase, the more she wanted to take him out.

He truly was in charge of this entire hateful facility. All operations—from the experimentations to the torturous interrogations—were under his iron-fisted control. He himself was supposed to be a master at torture.

She studied her claws. Just thinking about the Blademan made them straighten and sharpen with aggression. For Aidan, they'd curled, aching to clutch his body close to hers.

"Care to crowd-source your plan?" Natalya asked. "Garner feedback? I actually have some experience with escapes."

"I'll let you know." Regin *did* have that one ace in the hole. Chase would soon be dead if he remembered her. But, hell, she could be vivisected or executed before he ever did.

Regin had begun to see why some of the prisoners were going crazy in here. Their third roomie wasn't the only prisoner who banged his head against the wall. Time passed at an agonizingly slow pace. With no shower available, she'd been eyeing the sink for a whore's bath. Her side had fully healed, but her clothes were stiff with dried blood.

Each second, Regin's anger toward Chase escalated, her temper redlining toward *DEFCON REGIN*.

In the old language, Natalya said, "I recalled something I'd heard about you. Aren't you supposed to have a kiss that drugs men?"

"So everyone says." Regin didn't actually . . . know. Aidan had sworn her lips were like a drug. And with each reincarnation, her kiss had triggered his memories. As soon as their lips touched, his past assailed him.

But the "drugging kiss" rep sounded cool, so Regin had run with it.

Natalya said, "You could kiss Fegley or Chase, then command him to free us!"

What was so bad? They were equally unappealing.

Regin's ears twitched. "Speak of one of the devils." Fegley's cheap orthopedic lifts were squeaking closer.

When the warden appeared outside their cell, he ogled Regin's bared midriff. Gross. Whenever men leered at her, Regin tended to leer back. She canted her head on the floor, turning it one way, then the other. "I finally understand what a dickie-do is. Your gut *does* stick out more than your dickie do."

Natalya guffawed, slapping a hand over her mouth.

His beady eyes slitted, and he walloped his nightstick against the glass directly beside Regin's head. Which made Roomie Number Three's tempo speed up. She clenched her teeth, wrestling with her temper.

"Your time's running out, Valkyrie." Fegley gave another wallop before he squeaked off.

Regin narrowed her eyes, watching him till he was out of sight. "One day I'm going to make that little piggy cry all the way home." With a sigh, she rose and crossed to the boy.

The only thing that broke up this prison monotony was studying their curious fellow inmate, trying to pinpoint what species he belonged to. So far, she'd determined only three things about him.

Since he didn't fit a single species' traits definitively, he must be a hybrid or halfling of some sort.

His gray athletic T-shirt indicated that he played football for the Harley High Tigers.

And he sure was cute.

He was over six feet tall, his build corded with muscle. His eyes were hazel with blue flecks, his brown hair thick and tousled.

The first time Regin had awkwardly patted his banging head to calm him, the fey had raised her brows. To which Regin had eloquently replied, "Oh, eat me."

That night Natalya had wiped the blood from his hair, then covered him with her jacket when he'd slept. After that, the two of them had started to view him as kind of a pet rock, almost like they were the de facto guardians of their very own sea monkey.

Kneeling before him, Regin murmured, “Don’t let that Fegley worm get to you.” Still staring ahead, the kid slowed his banging. “There’s a good . . . male of indeterminate species.” Over her shoulder, Regin said, “We’ve got to come up with a name for him.”

“Why don’t we call him Tiger?” Natalya suggested.

“For his football team? Good idea.”

“Not quite.” At Regin’s quirked brow, Natalya admitted, “He has a trouser tiger. A waistband topper. He might have no other bodily functions, but last night when he slept, he must’ve been dreaming *really hard* about cheerleaders.”

“Nuh-uh.”

Natalya raised her right hand. “Hand to goddess.”

“Speaking of big cats. Cougar, he’s a *zygote*.”

“Can I help if I notice him? I haven’t been around available males in eons.”

“How’s that?”

“I was taken hostage at the Battle of Seven Hills.”

Regin snapped her fingers. “I remember now.” She’d been pissed to miss that epic conflict between the fey and the centaurs. Nothing hurt Regin’s feelings like not being invited to war. “We’d heard you died there.”

Natalya shook her head. “Good old King Volós planned to ransom me, but failed to realize that I was ignoble and no one would pay. It took me a decade to escape.”

“How’d you do it?”

“His nephew—and royal heir—took me out of my

cell to make me his concubine. I acted receptive, right up until I ganked him with my poisonous claws, then decapitated him." Natalya said this dispassionately, but her eyes flickered. Normally her irises were the color of plums, but with emotion, veins of black forked out. "At last I'd escaped. Then less than a week later, I was captured by these wanks. Your takeaway from this story: I need to get laid." She cast a keen glance at the kid.

"He's like six hundred years younger than you are." Regin pointed a finger at the ceiling and declared, "I refuse to be the moral compass of our cell! Most weekends I have an intoxispell bong attached to my mouth like a respirator. I love scatological humor, and I list 'pranks involving nuclear waste' and 'making demons eat things' as my hobbies." Hubcaps, fire extinguishers, pizza boxes. Though she was friends with many of the demon species, she made the rest of them suffer.

"Valkyrie, if there was ever a cradle to be robbed . . . Gods, just *look* at him."

Admittedly sigh-worthy. But Regin merely shrugged. "What are you going to do with him if he wakes? Make porn for the security cameras while I plug my ears and drone *la-la-la*? Besides, he's not fully immortal yet. You claw him and he's dead."

Natalya glared at her claws.

"Face it, Nat, this is one tiger who will never be jumping through your flaming hoop—"

Regin caught the sound of Chase's nearing footsteps. She recognized his long-legged stride, the echo of his heavy combat boots. "Here comes the Blademan. . . ."

NINE

"Is anything wrong, Magister?" Dixon asked, fawning expression in place as they moved down the corridor, assessing new prisoners.

"No." His tone was brusque, his answer a lie.

Declan was having a shite day, and it wasn't even noon.

Tests on the vampire's ring had revealed nothing—which made Lothaire's interrogation this afternoon even more critical.

Declan still hadn't crushed his unnerving fascination with the Valkyrie; her cell was coming up fast.

And he'd found out that yet another magister's prisoners were on the way to his facility, though Declan hadn't even surveyed the ones brought in while he'd been away hunting.

Dixon had offered to bring him up to date on the recent arrivals. He'd accepted because she'd brought him the additional doses and because he'd assumed—rightly—that she wouldn't dare broach the subject of *them* anytime soon.

Now as they passed cells newly filled with more creatures from "myth," she relayed details of their capture and backgrounds.

One cell contained Cerunnos, sentient creatures possessing the head of a ram and the body of a serpent. Another held a number of revenants—zombies controlled by some unseen Sorceri master.

Even a winged Vrekener—a horned demonic version of an angel—had been captured.

Declan grudgingly admitted that this wasn't a bad haul, though not nearly the caliber of his last one. *Nor in the same league as my next will be.* He'd been laying a trap for the most powerful immortal ever to live. A vampiric demon . . .

When they passed the cell of Uilleam MacRieve, the Lykae said, "You're the magister?" His Scottish brogue was thick, his eyes blue with rage.

Declan merely stared at him. In less than half an hour, Dixon was scheduled to examine the werewolf. She and her team would be doing the regular workup, but they'd also be testing a sonic weapon devised to immobilize a creature with his acute sense of hearing.

Turning strengths into weaknesses.

MacRieve bared his fangs. "When I get free from this place—"

Without a word, Declan continued on, ignoring him. If he had a quid for every time one of them said, "When I get free . . ."

I'd be even wealthier than I currently am.

All these immortals smugly thought they'd escape soon, assuming that humans could never contain them. Yet in the centuries of the Order's history, none had escaped.

And no one would be breaking that perfect record under Declan's watch. He'd installed so many security fail-safes that commanders and other magisters mocked him. They called this Installation Overkill.

What they considered costly excess, he deemed standard precautions.

The metal walls of the cells were solid steel, three feet thick. The forward glass wall was made of the same material used for space shuttle windshields. If reentry into the earth's atmosphere couldn't crack that glass, then an immortal with a torque sure as hell couldn't.

But if one *did* breach the glass, then hydraulic bulkheads—barriers of six-foot-thick steel—would drop into place, sealing each of the three corridors. And once those bulkheads dropped, a self-destruct sequence would engage, overridden only by an officer.

Every contingency planned for, he mused, even as concerns about overcrowding weighed on him.

"You seem distracted," Dixon said. "Is it because of your upcoming interrogation?"

"Lothaire will be just one among many vampires," he replied coolly, belying his interest in this one. Though the Order knew more about their kind—their origins, weaknesses, any anomalous powers—than about any other species, aspects of Lothaire proved a mystery.

Certain vampires could harvest memories if they drank blood straight from the flesh. And if one killed as he fed, he could usurp a victim's physical and mystical strengths. Over time, the older ones grew maddened from so many memories, their irises reddening.

Lothaire had that harvesting ability and was one of the oldest vampires alive, yet his eyes hadn't turned fully red. Somehow he'd refrained from drinking as much as his brethren, shrewdly clinging to what little sanity he still possessed.

The Enemy of Old was an anomaly. Anomalies fascinated Declan.

Still the vampire had stolen enough memories to suffer bouts of instability and hallucinations. Declan had observed him slicing his black claws across his wrists to dine on his own blood as he conversed with himself. While at other times, his red eyes had seemed to burn with intelligence and cunning.

Declan wondered which side of Lothaire he'd encounter this afternoon.

In any event, he expected a worthy opponent. Natural born vampires like Lothaire were physically incapable of telling a lie, so they resorted to trickery and verbal misdirection; by all accounts, Lothaire was a master of deception.

No matter. *I will best him. Just as I will best the Valkyrie in her interrogation tomorrow.*

As they approached her cell, his skin pricked with awareness. For the most part Declan had ignored her—until earlier this morning when his curiosity had prevailed, and he'd pulled up her cell on the monitor.

She'd been braiding her hair into haphazard plaits that he somehow found pleasing to the eye—though one would think she'd grow more proficient at braiding after a thousand years. When a fight had broken out in a cell down the ward, she'd bitten her knuckle, then cried out dramatically, *"Can't we all just get along?"*

Did she consider this some kind of game? Once Declan had finished with her tomorrow, she'd understand how dangerous her position was. . . .

For now, seeing the Valkyrie in her cage, imprisoned right along with the other unnatural beings would remind him that she might be fair of face, but beneath the surface she was still one of them. A detrus.

Her beauty just made her more dangerous.

He'd been taught by the Order that they were abominations walking among humans, filled with untold malice toward mankind . . . a perversion of the natural order, spreading their deathless numbers uncontrollably . . . a plague upon man that must be eradicated. . . .

Experience had taught him no differently.

TEN

When she heard Chase's low voice in a clipped conversation as he approached, Regin resumed her customary spot on the floor.

Footsteps closer . . . closer . . .

And then he appeared—pale, angry, with his gaze fixed directly ahead. His pupils were dilated—everyone here knew he was on something. And he still sported those same black leather gloves. Rumor held that Chase hated to be touched, wore the gloves to avoid it. *Freak.*

At his side was Dr. Dixon, the head researcher/dissector. Though Dixon wasn't a pound-candidate per se—she had an athletic figure and even features—she was no looker either. She had lifeless brown hair, and her oversize glasses were the type that only a supremely confident woman could pull off.

Chase seemed to be half-listening to the woman, answering in monosyllables—while Dixon was visibly lusting over him. *The sick mortal two-bit.*

When they paused at a cell diagonal to Regin's, she tried to determine what the woman saw in him.

Regin supposed his thick coal-black hair was nice, and his features were attractive enough. He had a strong chin, defined jawline, and prominent cheekbones with shadowed hollows beneath them. His nose was thin and straight.

He held his broad shoulders erect in a proud military posture, and his soldier garb was pleasingly butch—shined combat boots, a black crewneck pullover with shoulder patches, and camo pants that were fitted around his narrow hips and muscular legs.

All in all, she might turn and check him out if he passed her on the street, but he was nothing like the other magnificent embodiments of Aidan. Not to mention his mental state.

A drugged-up freak of a torture expert? *Have at him, Dixon.*

In the old language, Natalya murmured, "He's noticeably gazing away from you. Why do you think that is?"

Regin had expected him to stare at her in confusion, to demonstrate that he'd begun to feel some pull toward her. Instead, he acted as if she didn't exist.

Which made her bristle. She was always the center of attention. Silent, lethal Lucia had once told her that she loved how Regin always stole the show—because that meant Lucia could go unnoticed in the shadows.

It felt bizarre to be ignored in general, much less by an embodiment of Aidan—who used to stare at her so hard that he'd run into trees.

Answering in the same, Regin said, "How should I know why Chase acts the way he does?"

"Uh-huh." Natalya clearly sensed that there was more to this than Regin was letting on. "You wouldn't have noticed, of course, since you're busy checking out all of him, right down to his tightly muscled backside."

"You take that back, fairy."

"Ah, look at the magister's hand. He just clenched and unclenched a fist. I wonder why."

"As if I care." Finally a reaction!

Christ, I can feel *her gaze boring into my back.*

Awareness of the Valkyrie made him . . . restless. He had difficulty concentrating on anything Dixon was saying.

Just to add to his frustration, the fey and the Valkyrie had begun speaking that language, the one he'd failed to get translated. Yet he knew they were talking about him.

When he and the doctor moved on, the Valkyrie called out in English, "Yo, Dekko, who do I gotta blow around here to get a shower?"

His shoulders stiffened, and he almost answered, "Fegley," but somehow he stifled the retort and continued on—another victory for his iron will.

But once clear of the Valkyrie's cell, Declan found himself still preoccupied. With a feigned glance at his watch, he told the doctor, "We'll review the rest of the prisoners later. Your appointment begins soon."

"They still need to transfer and prep the patient. Besides, we haven't even gotten to the berserker yet."

"Berserker?" She'd piqued his curiosity. The Valkyrie and her sister had spoken of one that first night. The

Order had little intel on the berserkers, because they were exceedingly rare and most were mortal.

"Apparently, he was captured in the presence of other miscreats. He's as strong as any of the prime males in the Lore, and he tests out as deathless."

"An immortal? Then he's an anomaly. Let's see him."

As they approached another crowded cell, one inmate caught his attention, a big bastard who stood apart from the others.

When he met Declan's gaze, his jaw slackened and his green irises flickered, as though a flashlight shone behind them.

Why does he look at me like he knows me? The second prisoner to do so.

And more, this male seemed familiar *to him*.

No, no, Declan would never forget one of these beings. His heart began to pound—that wasn't entirely true. Had this one been there the night Declan had been tortured? Come into his parents' living room when he'd been unconscious?

Dixon frowned at the tension between them. "This is the berserker, Brandr."

"You don't recognize me, do you?" the male asked. "Good. That means we still have time." His phrasings were modern, but his accent had an odd resonance.

"What are you talking about?"

"If you've captured a Valkyrie named Regin, you must stay away from her." His eyes flickered even more. This was obviously very important to him.

So Brandr and the Valkyrie knew each other? Since

berserkers were so rare, he might be the very one that Regin and Nïx had spoken of.

The berserker Regin had longed for. Declan clenched his fists. "You think to order *me*?"

"Heed my warning, Aidan."

Declan tensed at that name. "What did you call me?"

"Your name, brother."

Declan turned to the wide-eyed doctor. "Put him in the schedule, Dixon. He's a level-four candidate."

She gave him a surprised look. That meant a round of their harshest experiments, including vivisection.

Brandr noticed the look. "What the hell are you doing, Aidan?"

"Schedule it *now*." When she scurried away, Declan approached the glass. "I've encountered many of your kind, and one thing remains the same, no matter what species or faction or breed. Deceit. You live and breathe trickery. I don't know your aim—"

"My aim is to escape this place with you and that glowing Valkyrie in tow."

"You think to take me as your hostage?"

Shoulders back, the male said, "I think to take you as my kinsman."

"What the hell are you talking about—"

"*Fight!*" someone down the ward yelled. Other inmates joined in, "*Fight, fight!*"

ELEVEN

One minute, Regin had been bathing at the sink; the next, she'd been abetting an escape attempt.

She'd glanced up to see two guards dragging Uilleam MacRieve past their cell. The werewolf was supposed to be drugged, but he didn't seem completely subdued. His head lolled, but not with each step. Her ears had twitched, and she'd known something was up.

Straightaway, she'd called to the guards, "Oh, boys?" She'd sauntered to the glass in only her black lace bra and panties. "I need some assistance." When they slowed, agog, she'd purred, "Can one of you help me find my orgasm?" Then she'd pivoted, presenting her admittedly mind-blowing ass. "Oh, look, clumsy me, I dropped something." She bent over from the waist.

With the guards distracted, MacRieve had shoved them away, hopping his cuffs to bring his bound hands in front of his body. Claws and fangs bared, he'd attacked.

"Fight! Fight!" the inmates began yelling.

Prisoners all along the ward banged on the glass walls, their shouts echoing down the corridor.

"Zing! Kick their mortal asses, Scot!" Regin cried along with the rest of them. "Fuck 'em up!"

Behind her, the kid banged his head faster, faster. Natalya leapt up to hold him still.

With a howl, MacRieve slashed one guard's jugular, then bit at the throat of the second one, blood dripping from his fangs.

Suddenly, Chase stormed into the fray, bellowing as he tackled MacRieve. They wrestled over the floor, trading vicious blows.

Normally the werewolf would thrash him—the Lykae were among the most powerful of all the sentient creatures—but MacRieve had been weakened by his torque.

Still, Chase shouldn't be winning *that* handily. He wasn't merely subduing the wolf, he was beating the living hell out of him.

Fighting like a *berserker.* A lean bear in winter.

The way he moved . . .

Right before her eyes, his muscles began to tighten and expand, his body growing larger, stretching his layers of black clothing taut. His massive gloved fists cracked bone each time they connected.

When more guards arrived, they had to peel a bludgeoned MacRieve away from the magister's assault.

Once they'd taken the Lykae away, Chase rose, his big chest heaving. His normally pale face was flushed, making his gray irises more vivid. His hair was finally shoved out of his eyes to better reveal those chiseled features.

At that moment, he was handsome, powerful, and so much like Aidan that she gasped. Just as with Aidan, she was uncontrollably attracted to him.

An invisible force. Like two magnets.

He swung his head around at her. Instead of looking surprised by her lack of clothing, his gaze raked over her heatedly, taking in every part of her.

A look both scorching and possessive.

A look that made her pulse race.

His irises flickered. The color of storm clouds lit by lightning. As if unaware of what he was doing, he took two steps closer to her.

She mirrored his action, then raised her hands to the glass. Her claws curled against the barrier between them, her breaths gone shallow.

All else was forgotten. Declan Chase was forgotten. All she could see was Aidan.

Want to be near him.

But when she realized he would soon leave her behind, an old habit rose to the fore. In ancient Norse, the words tumbled out: *"Take me with you, warrior."*

Take her with him?

At that instant, Declan was tempted to do just that.

Christ almighty, her *body.*

He exhaled a shaky breath at the sight of her dressed only in tight black lingerie. Her bra and panties were mere scraps of lace, displaying taut legs, a narrow waist, and curvy hips. High, plump breasts spilled out from the cups.

Her glowing skin was damp and smooth.

When she shivered and her nipples stiffened, he was rapt.

Then he remembered what she was. *Abomination. Enemy.*

Casting her a look of scorn, he abruptly turned away. He strode to his quarters with his fists balled and his mind in turmoil.

Because he was hard.

God preserve me. For her.

Not possible. The medicine prevented him from getting aroused. Hadn't he done two doses last night? And the night before that?

Yet there was no denying the effect she'd had on him.

Inside his room, he paced, fighting the urge to watch her on the screen. *Abomination, enemy,* his mind repeated over and over.

He inhaled deeply—only to release a hoarse breath as the fabric of his pants rubbed his aching shaft.

With a bitter curse he sat at his console and pulled up her cell. She was still staring at the glass, giving him a view of her from the back.

Tight black lace against damp golden skin. Her pert arse was too generous to be covered by her small panties.

He heard a groan, was shocked to realize the sound had come from him. His cock was now *throbbing.*

It'd been so long since he'd been hard, longer still since he'd come. *Enjoy it this once.*

While he might not miss sex, he damn sure missed the feel of spending hot seed from his body.

Stroke himself off to a detrus?

Declan was at risk of beguilement. Knew it. There'd been operatives who'd fallen for immortals—he'd always thought them stupid beyond measure. No miscreat was worth the consequences.

Cast out.

Never.

He shot to his feet, pacing once more. *Get control of yourself.* He could beat this. *No man possesses a stronger will than you, Dekko.*

He had work to do. His duty. There'd just been an escape attempt—with casualties—and he was due to interrogate Lothaire shortly.

Once he'd broken the vampire, Declan would go for an extended run over the sizable island. He knew every part of it—the forests, the mountain caves, the rocky shores, knew where each incendiary bomb was located.

Because I planted them all myself. Declan secretly considered it his own territory. Now he envisioned the miles he'd cover, the way he'd push his body to exhaustion. . . .

Minutes ticked by. In time, he exhaled, confident that he'd regained control. The Valkyrie had sent him reeling, but he'd found his footing once more.

Go break the vampire.

But first Declan needed to erase the security feed of his unexpected reaction to the Valkyrie. He never knew who was monitoring those videos. He pulled it up, scrutinizing their interaction, struggling to understand what power she had over him.

He was about to delete the scene when he realized something that couldn't be right.

At the end, she hadn't spoken to him in English—nor in that unknown language she spoke with the fey.

This was something new. Yet he'd *understood* her.

"I'm not going to lay off until you tell me," Natalya said to Regin in the old language.

For the last two hours she'd demanded to know why Chase's eyes had changed, why *he'd* changed, in reaction to Regin. Unfortunately, the fey had witnessed the entire exchange as she'd tended the kid.

Regin answered in the same tongue, "Just don't tell anyone in the grapevine what you saw."

"Only if you let me in on what happened. Otherwise . . ."

Regin glared. "Fine. After you vow to the Lore never to repeat what I'm about to tell you."

Once Natalya did, Regin outlined her and Aidan's history, his past embodiments, his deaths. She finished with, "And now he's reincarnated once more. This time . . . as Declan Chase."

Natalya gasped. "Then all you have to do is make Chase remember his past? Just get him alone so he can kiss you?"

"Yeah. That's all it ever takes." For some reason, her kiss did a rewind on each reincarnation's mind, sending him back to that one particular moment in Aidan's life, just before he'd claimed her the first time.

"No one keeps me from you," he'd growl.

And then *nothing* could.

He would claim her in a berserkrage and die shortly after from some freak accident or assassination. Over these thousand years, that pattern had repeated itself again and again.

Now, if she was with him when it happened, Regin could use his print to remove her torque and escape, leading others back here to free their allies.

Natalya rose, pacing. "What is your hesitation?"

"I told you what he meant to me!" And earlier, all of her old feelings for him had resurfaced.

"Chase will interrogate you soon. And then you'll be vivisected. More important, then *I* will soon be vivisected!"

"I know this!" Regin was murderously pissed at Chase. But actively plotting to kill Aidan? She recalled the way his eyes would crinkle when he grinned, could hear his laughter as if it were yesterday. *Remember when I vowed I would love you. . . .*

"These mortals plan to exterminate us all," Natalya said. "And they actually seem to be making strides. Still, the fey will live on. But how many of you Valkyrie are left?"

Not enough.

Regin thought of Lucia, out there about to face her worse nightmare alone. *I've got to get to her.*

By hastening the death of a male I've mourned for centuries?

Behind them, the kid spoke for the first time, muttering, "You . . . glow."

TWELVE

Lothaire the Enemy of Old woke strapped to a table in a blindingly white room, the bright artificial light paining his sensitive eyes.

He strained against his bindings, thoughts roiling. *Get to my ring. To get to her.* His master—the Endgame—commanded him. But Lothaire couldn't break free.

For millennia, no enemy had held him. Now a mortal had somehow captured him, had been faster than any human he'd ever encountered.

When Chase strode into the room, Lothaire's fangs went sharp with aggression. Then his eyes narrowed. Something was amiss with this male. Seething anger rolled off him in waves.

"I have questions for you, vampire," he said in a low, raspy voice. "Answer them and you will be spared any unnecessary pain—"

"Who is your commander?" Lothaire interrupted.

"What does that matter?" The man's face was ashen and scarred.

Despise scars. "I am a king. I don't negotiate with mortals at your pay grade."

"A king, is it? That's not what my intel says. In any case, I run this facility. Everything goes through me."

"Then you can bring me my ring. I want to see it."

"We'll get to that. But first, you'll tell me what you know about the Valkyrie."

I know it feels like rapture *to snap a Valkyrie's neck.* He twisted against his bonds with remembered pleasure, sighing, "The Archer. The Archer in the Green Hell." He'd broken her neck like a twig. *I know that Valkyrie are abhorrent.* "Sanctimonious, nosy, prideful."

Chase peered at Lothaire as if he'd spoken nonsense.

"My ring, mortal!"

"This one?" the magister pulled the band from a case in his pocket.

Lothaire's eyes widened. At the sight of his ring, he punctured his bottom lip with a fang for a shot of blood, sucking with need.

"What does it do, vampire?"

Damn it, he wore gloves? "Take off a glove and touch it." *Be the last one to touch it.* "You'll better understand its power."

Chase gave him a shrewd look. "No, I don't believe I will."

"If you keep it here, you will bring evil down upon this place." *She* was coming for him. But he had to get back to *her.* He still had crumbs of her mummy flesh in his pocket. Still had gold flakes from her body.

"What kind of evil?"

"Hers!" Once the waters receded, she and her foul guards would come.

"As no evil can get *out* of this facility," Chase said, "I'm confident the reverse is true as well."

She could reach Lothaire across time if she needed to. A mere mortal jail couldn't keep her out.

"You play with a god's power. She wants the ring."

"What does it do? Why do *you* want it so badly?"

Lothaire just stared at the ceiling, counting down each second to the time when the Gilded One arrived.

"Tell me what it does. Now!" Chase launched his fist against Lothaire's face, the blow like an anvil hit.

Lothaire shook his head hard, then grinned up with bloody fangs. "*Blyad'!* You're no normal mortal."

Another hit, this time with more rage. *No wonder this male was able to take me!* Though Lothaire sensed Chase wasn't an immortal per se, he was somehow enhanced.

Probably taking some chemical to increase his strength. The male's pupils were enlarged, and a sweet scent emanated from his skin. "I wonder what you'd taste like."

"You filthy leech, answer me."

Lothaire sighed. "*Chto ty nesësh'?*"

"Why am I bothering you with this? Is that what you said?"

"You speak my tongue?" Lothaire asked.

"Enough of it. Now, answer me!"

"Or what? What can you do to me that hasn't already been done?" With a laugh, he related, "I've been hung from a tree with the length of my intestines. I've been unmanned with a whip made of razor wire. Naturally, that took *many* lashes. I've watched a Lykae lord eat my eyes after scooping them out of my skull with a rusty spoon. Of course, I could only watch the first; for the second, I listened to him chewing it wetly, until there was a *pop* that he seemed to particularly enjoy."

And when Dorada got hold of him? Now, *that* would be torturous.

"You see, that's the thing with you detrus," Chase began in a contemplative tone. "Your bodies are abominations. If I severed your arms—"

Lothaire yawned loudly.

"—you'd merely regenerate from the injury. You might experience pain, but you wouldn't suffer the horror of permanent *loss,* not like a human."

Lothaire grew increasingly bored by this. "When I get free, I believe I'll show you your spine. I'll hand it to you so casually, politely even, as if expecting you to remark upon it."

Ignoring that, Chase continued, "Of course, mortals also don't suffer from . . . *the sun.*" He flipped a switch, and overhead, the lights changed.

Lothaire's skin began to burn. *UV bulbs.*

Chase ripped open Lothaire's shirt, exposing his chest. Though Lothaire was older and not as sensitive to the sun as other vampires, this was intense. "Chase, my master thanks you for this." With a laugh, he grated, "You prepare me . . . for trials to come."

As charred flesh began to fall from his body, he writhed in agony. His hair turned to soot, the tip of his nose and the ends of his fingers disintegrating.

And he couldn't stop laughing.

"You're glowing," the kid told Regin. He stood to his full towering height and pointed at Natalya. "And your lips are black." He gave a strained chuckle, looking like he was about to start banging his head again. "Snakes have arms and can talk, and men have horns, and—"

"Take a deep breath, my poor lad," Natalya said. "Here, have a seat next to me." She guided him over to one of the bunks and sat close beside him.

"You both have pointed ears."

"I'm a dark fey called Natalya. That's Regin. She's a Valkyrie."

Regin said, "So, you got a name?"

He absently replied, "Thaddeus Brayden, ma'am. Everybody calls me Thad."

Ma'am? "How did you get here? What do you remember?"

"I, uh, I drove to my date's house to pick her up," he said warily.

"Go on." Natalya patted his knee.

"While I was waiting, her dad kept looking at me funny, questioning me about stuff. But then he seemed to calm down, even gave me a shot of whiskey. When I woke up, I was here, seeing *things*. Things that can't be right."

Regin asked, "What are you?"

"A senior, ma'am."

Natalya murmured, "I could just eat—him—*up*." She scooted closer to him until their thighs touched.

Regin glared at her, then asked, "I meant, are you human?"

"Of course, I'm human! Wh-why ask me something like that?"

"Because you're in a Lore supermax," Natalya said. "A prison for immortal creatures."

"I don't understand."

After Natalya relayed the basics about the Order and the Lore, he said, "These people made a mistake. I play ball, go to church on Sunday. I'm an Eagle Scout! I never heard of any of this stuff." He raked his fingers through his tousled hair. "I just want to go home."

Regin snorted. "Don't we all?" Actually, she only wanted to get to Lucia. Would her sister still be in South America?

Natalya patted his knee again. "What'd the dad say before he micked you?"

"That I play ball better than anyone he's ever seen. But I get that all the time, you know," he said without conceit. "I've set all these records and everything. So I thought he was going to accuse me of juicing, but I don't touch that stuff."

"Records, huh?" Regin said. "Sounds like superhuman strength and speed to me."

He exhaled. "I guess. But if I'm not human, then what am I?"

"We don't know," Regin admitted. "You don't have horns or pointed ears, no glyphs or scales."

Natalya added, "I thought you might be a vampire, but you have a tan line."

In a measured tone, he asked, "How do you *know* that I have a tan line?"

"I checked to make sure you weren't a vampire," Natalya said. "You see, we're enemies with the vampire Horde."

Regin narrowed her eyes at the kid. "Hey, you didn't use tan in a can, did you?"

"Of course not. I was out in the sun over the weekend, playing touch football. I was on the skins team."

Natalya was all but purring. "Did you hear that, Regin? The lads played *touch* football. And Thad was *shirtless*."

Regin rolled her eyes. Luckily, Thad was too preoccupied to notice the cougar going into heat right beside him.

"So does this mean I'm like invincible to bullets or something?"

"No, you're still totally vincible," Regin said. "At least until you stop growing and reach your full immortality."

Menacing growls sounded down the corridor as another fight broke out. Thad's eyes started to go buggy again, so Regin snapped her fingers. "Hey, Thad! Stay with us, kid. Tell us about yourself. What are your parents like?" *Really strong? Probably don't look much older than you do?* "Anything unusual?"

"My mom's a widow. My dad died on the work site when I was four. They'd adopted me not long before that."

An orphan. No wonder Thad had no idea what he was.

"I live with Mom and my grandmother now. Nothing unusual. Mom likes to cook. Gram sews."

"So you eat your mom's cooking?"

He glowered. "She's a *great* cook."

Talk about ruffled feathers. "I meant, *do you eat*?" Clearly, *nobody* better talk bad about Thaddeus Brayden's mama.

"Of course I eat."

"When was the last time?" Regin said.

"I had a burger yesterday."

Natalya said, "Not quite so, my boy. You've been here for over a week."

"A week!" He shot to his feet, towering over them. "I'm not even hungry. How's that possible?"

"Some species don't have to eat a lot. Regin's doesn't have to eat at all. There are phantoms, ghosts, succubae, incubi. Maybe half a dozen more." To Regin, she muttered, "My money—and my hopes—are on incubus."

"I can't believe I've been here that long! Oh, man, I missed a game Friday. Coach is gonna kill me."

If the mortals don't kill you first. . . .

"Mom and Gram are gonna be worried sick. I've never even broken curfew." Then his voice went low. "Is my family gonna be safe?"

"We don't know," Regin said. "But since you were adopted, they're probably mortal, which means they'll likely be left alone."

"If anybody touches them . . ." His eyes flickered. *Black.*

She and Natalya shared a look. Black indicated vampire, or possibly demon.

Then Natalya's gaze flittered toward the corridor. "Ah, gods, Valkyrie. Look."

Guards were dragging by Uilleam MacRieve. The werewolf's blue eyes were glazed, his body shuddering, his skin bloodless. Dixon had vivisected him, leaving a line of staples down his broad chest. His ears were bleeding.

"Wh-who is he?" Thad croaked.

"One of my allies," Regin said. The Lykae were now united with the Valkyrie, part of the Vertas army. In fact, Regin was distantly related to Uilleam by marriage. Her halfling niece Emma had wed his cousin, the werewolf king—a king who gazed at Emma with utter adoration and wolven protectiveness.

And the Lykae's prince? He was the werewolf in love with Lucia. The one who had better be protecting Luce since Regin couldn't.

Before all this had happened, Regin had briefly wondered if maybe she oughtn't call them *dogs* or crack Cesar Millan jokes in front of them. Then she'd shrugged and said, "Neh."

At present, she felt fiercely loyal to Uilleam. She leapt to the glass. "We're going to get out of here soon. MacRieve, just hang tough!" She watched until he disappeared from view.

"Allies? We need allies?" Thad's gaze darted to the wall, as if he yearned to start banging his head again. "Have they done that to you? Are th-they going to do that to me?"

Regin looked at Natalya. "Not if I can help it."

I couldn't break the vampire.

As Declan stormed down the winding corridor, guards gave him a wide berth and researchers skittered out of his way. He heard their whispers. . . .

"It was grisly, even by the Blademan's standards."

"I almost felt sorry for a leech."

By the time Declan left him, Lothaire's skin had been

seared away to the bone, his body more ash than flesh. Those UV lights burned vampires the way frostbite attacked a mortal—first the extremities, then spreading up the limbs like gangrene.

Declan had been merciless.

Yet nothing he'd done could make Lothaire talk. Toward the end, all the creature would say was, "She comes, she comes. She's going to want it back. . . ."

Was the "she" even real, or a hallucination?

More soldiers cleared a path, their expressions wary. Declan knew they feared him, often overheard them talking about him. Recently, he'd heard a new recruit mutter, "Chase gives me the ever-living creeps. Like he'd slit your throat just for shits and giggles."

But Declan didn't give a damn how they felt as long as they followed his orders.

As he strode down the ward, he stared down any prisoners who didn't avert their eyes. Did they sense something about him, as the vampire had? "You're no normal mortal," Lothaire had told him.

Paranoia had Declan running a gloved hand over the back of his neck.

His shite day only continued to worsen. He'd been off his game with Lothaire because of his encounter with the Valkyrie. And MacRieve's escape attempt just highlighted the security risks inherent in overcrowding.

Yet Webb continued to accept prisoners, disregarding Declan's repeated recommendations for culling. The two would discuss this soon. *Either I run this place my way, or Webb should come take over.*

Then Declan had a flash thought. What if Webb

agreed with him—and wanted to terminate the Valkyrie?

So be it, he assured himself. Yet the idea sent a chill through him. And he didn't know why! His job, his purpose on this earth, was to destroy her kind, one at a time.

If he couldn't do it, then why was he here? Damn her, what hold did she have over him?

Tomorrow I plan to torture her. Yet I'm drawn to her, attracted to her as I've never been to another.

And he hated her for it.

THIRTEEN

"*Hey, fresh meat!*" a Ferine demon called from his cell as a burly guard led Regin down the ward. "Not so high and mighty when you can't get to us, huh?"

Regin was cuffed, shaking off the effects of poisonous gas, and on her way to be either interrogated or vivisected.

Now demons were going to taunt her? She half-lunged, half-stumbled toward the cell.

"Easy, Valkyrie," the guard said, drawing her back in line. She believed some inmates had called him Vincente.

The demons shrank back from the glass. As she passed, she heard one say, "That Valkyrie made me eat a crab trap last summer."

Regin smirked. She'd thought she recognized him. Her smirk faded when she spied the occupant of the next cell over.

Carrow the Incarcerated, one of Regin's good friends and a party-hearty pal. The black-haired witch stood at the glass, forcing a smile. "It's like a bad hangover that won't stop, huh?"

Behind her was a sorceress Regin recognized, the Queen of Persuasion. Sorceri were tricksy, some good, some evil. "You all right in there?" Regin asked, as if she were still a badass Valkyrie bosswoman who'd fix the sitch otherwise.

Carrow nodded. "The sorceress is cool. So, you heading for an interrogation? Or an . . . exam?"

Regin made with the stiff upper lip when she casually said, "Dunno. Chase or Dixon. One of them will have my foot up their ass directly." She shrugged. "Catch you on the flip side, witch."

About ten cells down from Carrow was *Brandr*—Aidan's kinsman. Who'd taken his vow to his leader and friend *very* seriously.

"Regin!" He leapt up from a bunk.

"Well, well, the gang's all here." Nïx must've given him Regin's whereabouts. Again.

"I'm going to get you out of here," he said, his green eyes aglow.

She snorted. "Let me know how that works out for you, Job MacBangup." Seeing Brandr here just brought her situation into stark relief. "It's curious though—you don't usually show until it's time to bury him."

Brandr flinched, and immediately Regin felt guilty. Both of them had a role to play in this curse. Regin forever triggered Aidan's death. Brandr was forever too late to save him. No matter how hard that man tried.

Many in the Lore had begun to call him Brandr the True.

In a milder tone, she said, "You know who brought me here?"

"Yes, it's *him,* though I barely believe it. Regin, just hold on. I'll figure something out. . . ."

Vincente forced her along the corridor.

When they passed the centaur king's cell, Volós pointed at Regin and slid his forefinger across his throat.

She replied, "Hey, didn't I see you in a donkey show down in Tijuana? No? You've got a twin then—"

"Move on," Vincente said warningly.

She gazed up at the guard. He looked like an ex-prizefighter—heavyweight—with a pronounced brow, a brick-end chin, and a five-o'clock shadow that she'd bet no razor could KO. He was dark-haired, his features a compelling blend of Native American meets mafioso.

He was the first human here not to gaze at her with animosity.

"So, where are you taking me, big guy?" No answer.

Yesterday, guards had hauled Lothaire by after Chase had finished "interrogating" him. The vampire's shirt was ripped open, revealing skin seared to ash. His hooded red eyes had flashed to Regin, and he'd hissed something in Russian.

Lothaire was an enemy—one who'd hurt the Valkyrie in unimaginable ways—so it'd been impossible to muster up sympathy for him. She'd hissed back, "*Do svidaniya*, bitch."

Now it was Regin's turn for an appointment with either Declan or the mad scientist.

In a lower tone, she asked the man, "So am I going to get a zipper in my chest?"

Had there been a barely perceptible shake of his head?

"Am I about to be interrogated?"

Nothing. *Shit, interrogation it is.*

Soon after, he led her into an austere room with a camera in the ceiling, an obvious two-way mirror on one of the white walls, and a table with two chairs in the center.

Vincente pointed to one of the chairs, the one bolted to the floor. "Sit."

"S'all the same, I think I'll stand—"

He shoved her down, hooking her cuffs to a bar in the back of the chair, immobilizing her.

Once she was all battened down, a tech in a white lab coat entered to sink an IV into Regin's arm. The clear line snaked up to a bag, most likely filled with some kind of pharmaceutical torture juice.

Regin got the gist. The interrogator would be able to push a button and serve a dose.

After Vincente and the tech had left, Chase entered, his expression drawn, his ink-black hair still wet from a recent shower. He'd shoved it back off his smooth-shaven face, revealing more of those chiseled features, as well as the thin scars that climbed up his cheek. Dark circles marred his chilling gray eyes.

For all his faults, Declan Chase had a kind of sinister, wretched attractiveness. She took comfort in knowing that, for some reason, the man was as miserable as she currently was.

Without a word, he sat across from her. He wore his usual military threads, but today his wool pullover stretched tighter over his deep chest and broad shoulders. He was more muscled than she'd initially thought.

"Well, don't you look all butch today?" When he shot her a killing look, she stomped one foot. "*What?* What'd I say?" It'd been a compliment.

Up close like this, there was no mistaking his unsettling hatred. Though she'd resisted any escape plan that involved Chase remembering his past, now she realized she might have to declare him a misfire regardless.

She gazed around with a bored air. "This feels just like *Law and Order.* But shouldn't you lawyer up before I throw the book at you? No? So what's in the IV bag?"

"Pain poison. Taken from the Sorceri Queen of Agonies and replicated for our purposes."

A queen was a sorceress more powerful at manipulating a certain element than any other Sorceri.

Bottom line: this is gonna smart.

"Another tool cribbed from the Lore? Like with these torques. And rumor has it that this facility is mystically hidden. You use mysticism when it suits you, even though that's *our* realm."

As if she'd never spoken, he said, "You'll tell me what I need to know, or I'll administer a dose." He held up a control pad with a red button in the middle.

"Torture doesn't work on my kind, just pisses us off. It starts to collect over the years."

"Valkyrie, I will get answers from you one way or another. Either through this painful exercise in futility, as you believe, or through a civilized conversation."

"You call this civilized?" She strained against her

cuffs, leaning in to whisper, "Psst, Chase. The sexual tension between us is grueling."

His face grew even colder, as if she'd just spoken blasphemy.

"So you're the bossman around here, huh? I saw you took down Lothaire. You've got some low-hanging goolies to mess with him."

"Do you have information about that vampire? It might affect your own treatment."

"Turn informant? Sing like a canary? The more I talk, the better I'll get treated?"

He just continued to stare at her with an undisguised loathing.

"Then get ready for an earful! So everybody thinks Lothaire is hotter than the sun he'll never see, but I don't get it." Some of her Valkyrie sisters had deemed him as mesmerizing as a shiny-shiny. "I mean, yes, his body is magnificent—when not extra crispy—but he's a leech, a parasite. His irises are nearly red. Females are always tittering about how you never know whether he's going to kiss you or kill you. And that's just something I'd want to establish up front, you know?"

Chase narrowed his eyes.

"For the record, I like 'em young, dumb, and hung. And clever Lothaire only fits one of my criteria. Plus he's a vampire. I despise vampires. We probably have that in common—"

"You refuse to reveal pertinent information about your enemy?"

"I'll bet Lothaire won't dish about me either. Matter

of fact, I'll bet you don't know much about the Valkyrie at all."

"If that's true, you're soon to remedy my lack of knowledge."

"You've never captured a Valkyrie, have you?" Had her tone been gloating?

"But I have one now."

When his thumb hovered over the red button, she stared at him aghast. "You're truly going to . . . torture me?"

He cast her a puzzled look. "Why *wouldn't* I torture you?"

Because you used to love me, used to cherish me. "I thought we had a moment yesterday? Didn't you like seeing me in lingerie?"

In a monotone voice, he said, "Why did the charge throwers have no ill effect on you?"

He's truly going to do it? Then fuck him. DEFCON. "Chase, I've tussled with vibrators stronger than your *charge throwers.*"

No reaction. "You consumed energy. And channeled it at will. How?"

All Valkyrie consumed it—they were each connected through a grid of mystical energy—but Regin was the only one she knew of who could radiate it through her body. She'd inherited the talent from her birth mother. "So how does one get started as a magister? College or trade school?"

"I don't have the time or patience for games. Now, tell me, why do you . . . glow?"

"I touched a radioactive alien cock once."

He pressed the button.

As her eyes followed a bead of poison traveling down the tube, she muttered, "You're not giving me much of a choice here, Chase."

She remembered all those centuries ago when Aidan had taught her war strategies. If this were a battlefield, then she had only one move open to her—a charge. Could she be his doom once more?

To sit and wait in this facility would mean certain death. Regin hadn't stayed alive for a thousand years by *inaction*.

When the poison reached her arm, she clamped her jaw shut to keep from screaming—it was like liquid fire in her vein. Sweat broke out on her face. Every muscle in her body began to knot.

She gritted out, "When I escape—"

"Valkyrie, no one has *ever* escaped this island."

"Nothing but a roll call . . . of dead immortals?"

"Precisely. Now, tell me what language you speak to your cell mate."

"Immortalian. No? Immoratlivan. Immortinian!"

"Do you *want* me to hurt you?" Another bead inched down the line.

"I want you to go fuck yourself!" she bit out just before it hit.

Her back bowed, her sharpened claws slicing into her palms as she fought the urge to shriek. Lights flared and thunder rocked the building.

Blood trickled from her nose. She tasted more in her mouth.

If he does it again, then my decision's settled.

"I'm told the effect is cumulative—it will continue to worsen." Though outwardly calm as he explained this, his face had paled even more. "But if you tell me about the Valkyrie's weaknesses, I'll administer the antidote."

"Weaknesses? So many. Foremost, we're . . . ticklish."

A third bead dripped down.

"You'll pay!" The pain was blistering, like acid eating away at her from the inside. She threw back her head and shrieked as her body seized. Her arms wrenched violently against her restraints.

Pop. Her shoulder dislocated. Light bulbs shattered above them.

Going to kill him. Going to do the deed myself! When she'd finally endured that wave and faced him once more, her vision was blurred by a film of blood. Dots of crimson had begun to seep from her pores.

He narrowed his eyes. "Your glowing has lessened. Is it emotion-based?"

She spat, giving him a slow, bloody grin. "This will hurt you . . . more than it ever hurts me." *Must make him remember.*

"And again, you act as if we've met."

"I did know you," she said. "Long before all this. Don't you remember me?"

Like a shot, he was on his feet and around the table, his hand gripping her throat. He squeezed her windpipe as he demanded, "Were you there that night?"

She gasped, "Wh-where?"

"Were—you—there?"

"Aidan or not . . . I am going to serve it to you!" Her leg shot up to punt his groin, but he deflected her kick with his other hand.

"What did you call me?" His grip tightened.

She wheezed in a breath. "Prick!" What night was Chase talking about? She couldn't think!

Squeezing harder, harder. "Why did you call me Aidan?"

Losing consciousness. Heart pounding wildly. "Want to know? Bring me . . . to your office tomorrow. Just you and me. I'll tell you . . . *everything*."

When her head slumped forward and her glowing dimmed even more, Declan left her in the room, barreling to his quarters.

He just reached the toilet before vomiting the contents of his stomach. After heaving over and over, he eventually lurched to his feet. Hands gripping the edge of the bathroom counter, he waited for his balance to return. For his control to return. *What is happening to me?*

Administering that poison had affected him nearly as much as her. Though he'd done the same to hundreds of other prisoners.

When he'd tortured Lothaire yesterday, he'd regretted ending the session, wishing there'd been more flesh left to torment.

After Regin, Declan felt like *he'd* been tortured.

And she'd called him Aidan. As had the berserker. If they'd intended to make him paranoid . . .

It's bloody working.

Staring into the mirror, he muttered, "I fuckin' hate her." Yet he still felt that pull toward her.

Even as I was ready to squeeze the life out of her.

A mortal hunter and his immortal prey. *But then, perhaps I'm not quite mortal.* He shuddered.

She wanted to meet with him in his office? What was she planning? They were *always* planning something, living and breathing deceit.

He removed his gloves, then scrubbed his face with two handfuls of water.

To do as she asked was madness, but he needed the answers he'd promised Webb. And Declan knew he wouldn't be able to torture her again.

Why not try meeting her? Having a female prisoner alone in his office would raise some eyebrows, but Declan couldn't care less about that. No one would dare naysay him in his own installation.

I need to know why she called me that name.

After rinsing his mouth, he staggered into his room, sinking into his chair at the console. He pulled up the Valkyrie's cell on the screen.

Vincente and another guard were just returning her, wearing thick gloves because the poison seeping from her skin was lethal to mortals. Vincente laid her on the floor with more care than the other guard would have.

The Valkyrie's body convulsed with each wave of pain, her glow nearly extinguished.

Declan should be observing her impassively. Instead, bile rose in his throat.

As soon as Vincente closed the cell, the male halfling yanked off his shirt to wipe the blood from her. The fey knocked his hand away before he touched Regin's skin and got himself poisoned. Then she punched the Valkyrie's shoulder directly below the joint, forcing the ball back into the socket.

Before Regin passed out, she whispered something to Natalya in that unknown tongue, the maddening language he couldn't even identify.

Whatever Regin said made the fey appear *relieved*. Declan had just put his head in his hands and started to squeeze when he received a screen message from Webb:

> Let me know how your session with the Valkyrie went. Productive, I'm sure. Update: information about their weaknesses takes precedence over all other inquiries, i.e., her source of energy or the vampire's ring. . . .

Then Declan's path was fixed.

FOURTEEN

"*A*gain, Valkyrie?" Carrow the witch said as Vincente escorted Regin once more.

When the guard had shown up to cuff and retrieve her and she hadn't been gassed first, she'd known.

Chase had taken the bait.

"What can I say, Carrow? The magister loves my company."

In an urgent murmur, the witch said, "I saw how you fared his *company* yesterday. Maybe attempt *not* to enrage him tonight?"

On it. "I go with a peace offering. Check it"—Regin leered down at her own chest—"I'm braless."

Carrow shook her head. "Crazy ass Valkyries."

When they passed Brandr's cell, Regin told him in Old Norse, "My time here grows nigh." Though her attitude was confident, she knew several factors would work against her.

First, she wasn't a golden-tongued and persuasive Valkyrie; in fact, she was considered just the opposite—abrasive and smart-assed.

Second, she didn't do subterfuge, preferring to be brutally honest at all times.

Third, she had earned a reputation for flying off

the handle with little provocation. *Justly* earned. Her emotions were notoriously volatile.

Yet now she would have to pretend to be attracted to a man who'd mercilessly tormented her? Instead of giving in to her need to play-dress him in his own intestines?

One move open to her. "*His* time grows nigh as well."

Brandr was at the glass in a heartbeat. His light green eyes were bloodshot, his handsome face wan. Chase must've worked him over too. Still Brandr said, "Regin, don't do it! I'll warn him."

For all that she and Brandr had never gotten along, she couldn't fault his loyalty. "Stay out of my way, or you break your vow. . . ." She trailed off. Were those *staples* peeking out just above his shirt collar?

Dear gods, Chase had ordered Brandr's vivisection? If he'd do it to his one-time best friend, he'd do it to her.

When she and Vincente reached the hub connecting two other wards, the guard squired her into one filled with offices and labs, all empty this late. They followed it to the end, then entered a dark-paneled office.

Chase was already there, seated behind a large desk. He wore his uniform as usual, his dress immaculate. She could even scent boot polish. His hair was off his face again, and he wasn't as pale as usual. *Nice lips,* she realized with a start.

"Lemme guess," Regin said. "You had your introductory spiel all planned, but rational thought deserted you when you saw me stroll in braless."

Chase's angry gaze raked over her breasts. They were pressing against her tight T-shirt even more than usual since her arms were bound behind her back.

"Leave us, Vincente," he commanded.

Without any expression, the man did.

"For the record," she continued, "it's not my fault I came in here looking like Chesty LaRue. You caught me on laundry day, so I have no undergarments on. Though I will cop to a little extra spring in my step for your benefit."

He subtly adjusted his legs behind his desk. Hard-on. Zing! *Regin one; Chase zero.*

Yet his resentment only seemed to increase.

She didn't know when Chase might summon her again—if ever—so she had to make this one chance count. To rekindle his memories, she needed either to coax him to kiss her or to provoke the berserker inside him.

Sex or protracted violence should do it.

"Yeah, weirdly, our cell doesn't have laundry facilities. So I figure I'll wash undies at one time and outerwear at another, always keeping some cover for the cameras. I'm not shy, but frankly, I've had my limit of men chubbing themselves to videos of me. It's moved from simple idolatry to something more sinister." She sauntered over to his desk, hopping atop it, sitting on his papers. "A little too *Caged Heat,* you know?" Those angry eyes were rapt on her bouncing breasts.

Between gritted teeth, he ordered her, "Remove yourself from my desk, Valkyrie."

"Fine, huffy." She hopped down and began exploring

his office. He said nothing, merely restacked his papers as he observed her.

The décor was modern and posh. Aside from the large mahogany desk and matching floor-to-ceiling bookshelves, he had a luxe leather couch and chairs. Office cabinets had been built into the walls. Two enormous windows revealed a temperate forest shadowed by night. Only so many places in the world where trees like that grew. . . .

Yet there were no pictures or decorations. The bookshelves were empty.

She turned to him. "I'm just relieved *you* weren't one of the men going fap-fap-fap to my vid. Or *were* you?" she asked with a stage wink, but his demeanor remained frosty. "So, what's with the gloves? The rumors say you don't like to touch others, or be touched. Care to comment?" She settled on the couch, drawing one knee up to her chest. "I wonder how you have sex. Or maybe you don't."

He'd turned off his anger, his interest, everything. A light extinguished. "You know nothing about me."

"The Blademan's blade is sheathed, huh?" She gave him a slow grin. "I vow to you that I know you better than you know yourself."

"So you keep saying."

Survival time, Regin. She took a steadying breath. *Aidan would want me to live.*

Besides, she didn't have any choice. Lucia needed her help; Regin needed to survive. Yet still she had difficulty with this plan. Centuries of secret hopes and waiting warred with the need to save Lucia—and herself.

Valkyrie won. "Yeah. A long time ago you were called Aidan the Fierce. I've known you for over a thousand years."

The tension in him eased somewhat. "And yet I'm not even forty."

"You reincarnate. A lot."

"Reincarnate. And often, too? Now, this sounds interesting," he said with a sneer. "How many times would this make it?"

"This is the fourth time that I know of."

"Do I look the same?" He was clearly toying with her.

"Your eyes are the same, but the rest of you is always different. I can recognize you, and you always sense I'm familiar. Even now on some level you do, don't you? Our little torture session probably hurt you just as much as me."

"You're insane," he said easily, *confidently*.

"I vow to the Lore that I'm telling the truth. You know I'm bound by that vow."

"Only when it's made to another of the Lore."

His darkening expression warned her she was on thin ice. Of course, when had that ever stopped her? "I know you don't want to believe you have *anything* in common with me. But you *are* of the Lore." She heard his leather gloves clenching beneath the table, knew he was probably envisioning strangling her. "Look, let's make a deal. I'll tell you more info about the Lore than you've ever gotten out of any prisoner, and you'll grant me some concessions."

"Such as?"

"As long as I'm giving you information, you don't torture me or Carrow. Or Brandr and Uilleam MacRieve any more than you have," she said. "Or Natalya and Thad. Just lay off me and those friends, and I'll divvy."

She could see the wheels turning. He fully believed she was nuts. But he also was weighing the odds that she'd reveal something he could use.

Again Chase took the bait. "Agreed. So tell me, Valkyrie. How did you and I meet?"

FIFTEEN

"You were a warlord in the Northlands," the Valkyrie said.

Declan waved her on. But, as she'd done before, she seemed to be wrestling with a decision. *Likely deciding the best way to deceive the mortal.*

Or perhaps this wasn't a game. Many of the older immortals grew maddened. She might believe what she said.

Yet her eyes looked lucid. "A *berserker* warlord."

He froze. Of all the factions she could choose . . . Brandr had looked familiar to him. As had Regin.

No, this was some sort of scam, a plan to undermine him. He stifled his anger, knowing he would have to tolerate this bullshite in order to garner information from her. "Tell me what you consider a berserker to be." To even pretend this was a possibility rankled, but he didn't see an alternative.

"A berserker is a mortal born with uncommon speed and strength," she said. "He worships the bear and can channel its ferocity into a berserkrage, making him as strong as the most powerful beings on earth. At least temporarily. Afterward, he's debilitated." She cast him a measuring glance.

He evinced no reaction, even as a suspicion began to arise. *This might all go back to . . . Nïx.*

"The berserkers swore allegiance to Wóden and fought battles in his name."

Though myths rarely corresponded with reality, Declan had researched the Valkyrie's. "Wóden is allegedly the father of the Valkyrie."

She nodded. "I'm the daughter of gods. Well, two of my three parents are."

"How is there a third parent?"

"When a maiden warrior calls out for courage as she dies, Wóden and Freya strike her with lightning and rescue her to Valhalla. I was in the lightning." She glanced at his expression. "You don't believe me, do you?"

"Immortals are notorious for aggrandizing their own origins. But I've learned never to discount anything completely."

"Fair enough."

"Though I do wonder, if your parents are *deities*, why would they let you be captured by me?"

"Wóden and Freya sleep to conserve power. They take sustenance from worship, and the last few centuries have been lean on the Norse god devotion."

If any of this was true . . . *Information here for the taking.* "Who is the third parent?"

"She belonged to a people called the Radiant Ones, an ancient race of mortals who glowed. Does it soften you toward me to know that a mortal woman birthed me?"

It . . . surprised him. "Where is she? Where are the Radiant Ones located?"

"She's long dead. They all are. I'm the last one of my kind."

"How did they die?"

"Like I said, hers was an ancient race, and they were mortal. Time gives and time takes," she said with a shrug, but her eyes flickered, belying her casual air.

"Berserkers, Valhalla, and Norse gods. I suppose you met Aidan over a horn full of mead."

She stood, sauntering to one of the windows with that hip-swinging swagger that riveted his gaze and ratcheted up his pulse. Knowing she could hear his heartbeat, he tried to control it.

"Actually, I'd just left Valhalla when we met. And I didn't drink mead. I was only twelve."

"Where is Valhalla?"

Over her shoulder, she answered, "It's a different dimension. A godplane."

"So why would you leave? Wouldn't that be like leaving heaven?"

"Yeah, but my sister Lucia was in trouble. So out I went into this strange and harsh world thinking to save her. I was attacked by vampires directly. Barely escaped them."

"Is that why you hate them so much?"

"Partly. The Horde has been hard on the Valkyrie. All of the Pravus army has been. Do you know who they are?"

"I'm aware of your subjective delineations." Their

leagues. The Valkyrie, Wiccae, fey, and Lykae belonged to an alliance called the Vertas. The Horde vampires, some demons, and most of the more beastlike beings aligned with the Pravus.

"Just remember that the Vertas are the ones you want to pull for in the Accession." She cocked her head. "You do know what the Accession is, don't you?"

"Of course. It's a war between all the factions in the Lore, occurring every five hundred years. We just don't know when exactly or where it will play out." When she chuckled, he grated, "What?"

"It's not a single battle. It's a *force* that pits factions against one another. The Accession drags us into conflict, keeping our numbers in check."

Yet more intel. One of the things he'd hated most about detrus was how they spread uncontrollably, unchecked by disease, injury, or old age. Now she was telling him there existed an inherent mechanism to make them kill off one another? "Then why not resist that force?"

"Because it also seeds alliances and brings mates together. Plus, fighting is fun."

"And now humankind will be dragged into your *fun*."

At that, she burst out laughing. "Mortals in the Accession? I think you kids should ride the pine in this one."

Christ, she got him riled. "Both the Vertas and Pravus have taken out specific human targets recently and aggressed against the Order itself. As in the past, we've had no choice but to defend ourselves against the threat both sides pose."

She headed back to the couch. "I hate to correct you, but we just don't *know* about you. I'd never heard of your little dot-org until *you* told me about it. No one I know has."

"A war between immortals and humans is on the horizon."

"Humans aren't going to war against us—they have no clue we exist. The idea's laughable."

"One thing you all have in common? Arrogance. What's laughable is for your kind to believe we aren't aware of you. Part of our mission is to conceal your existence—an impossible task when you flaunt yourselves? You yourself brazenly go out in public with your skin glowing!"

She slapped her palms to her cheeks and cried, "My skin glows?" Then she grinned. "Should I be banished from public simply because I touched a radioactive alien cock once? Now you're just being silly, Chase."

Fuckin' hate her! She was a foulmouthed, conscienceless killer, unfeeling at best and vicious at worst. And now she was assessing him with those uncanny eyes, her ears twitching.

His own eyes narrowed with realization. She was saying these things to provoke a rise out of him, to gauge his reactions. Before, he'd thought her flighty and heedless. Now he recognized that she'd been systematically uncovering chinks in his armor.

"Lookit, I didn't come here to fight. I was telling you all about your being a berserker. Though you don't believe a word of it."

"My parents were normal mortals."

"You must have inherited a recessive gene of something," she said. "It's not unheard of."

"No, but it's convenient."

"I thought I saw recognition on your face when I spoke Old Norse to you."

"Then you were mistaken," he lied. *Going mad*. He'd looked up the language in the Order's databases, but he'd comprehended none of it.

Though he'd understood her perfectly.

"Tell me, Chase, how'd you feel after capturing me in New Orleans? All petered out after your burst of strength?"

"Does anyone *not* feel fatigue after exertion, Valkyrie?"

"I'll bet your senses are really acute. You can see and hear better than anyone you know, can't you?"

He merely shrugged.

"I figured you'd deny your abilities."

"I don't deny them. I deny that I'm a berserker."

"How can you admit to one but not the other?"

"I suspect your oracle Nïx set this up. She made sure you were caught by me, and that you'd been informed of any unusual skills I possess. A mortal berserker would match me most closely. This is all a scam."

"Funny. You weren't stupid in your other reincarnations."

Can't throttle her again. . . .

"I saw you've got another berserker here. Didn't he feel familiar to you?"

"He's in on this too. You two obviously know each other and crafted this plan. I checked on his capture—

he all but lay down to be taken. As if he'd known you would be captured as well."

The Valkyrie nodded. "He wanted in here so he could be near me. He's my . . . protector."

Protector. So they *were* lovers. Why did the idea make him want to beat the berserker into the ground?

Brandr's hands on her glowing skin. Declan couldn't remember the last time he'd wanted to kill this badly. His thoughts grew dim, primitive.

—Mine by right! Meant only for me.—

"Chase, your eyes are ablaze right now. Just go look in the mirror."

He abruptly stood, crossing to the other window. "And give credence to your lies?"

She moved behind him. In a soothing voice, she murmured, "Be at ease."

At once, he felt his lids growing heavy, his muscles relaxing. *What hold does she have over me?*

"What's got you like this?"

His response to her only angered him more. "Your bullshite tales."

"This is all true."

He turned to her. "Then how do you explain what Nïx said to me? I was at Val Hall earlier on the night I captured you. When you drove by, she stared me directly in the face and mouthed, *You're late.*"

"I'm going to kill her!" Lightning flashed just outside the window. "You're right about one thing—Nïx did set this up. But I vow that I'm as much of a pawn as you are."

"To what end?"

"She knew how much I missed Aidan. This would strike her as a perfect solution, forced intimacy and all that. She's probably cackling with her creepy little bat right now."

"Missed *Aidan*? Valkyrie, get your story straight. You just said you were with Brandr."

She gave a laugh. "With Brandr? Please." Another snicker. "No, I said he's my protector. As in, he tries to look out for me."

Declan's relief disgusted him, making his ire escalate again. He moved away from her, back to his desk.

"Why would he sacrifice himself?"

"He was your best friend," she said. "You made him vow that he'd earn ohalla and watch over me."

"Ohalla?"

"If you won two hundred battles while bearing Wóden's mark, he'd grant you immortal life and strength."

True or not, this was fascinating. "What was his mark?"

"Two ravens."

Declan just stifled the urge to touch the charm at his neck. The one imprinted with two birds in flight.

He cast his mind back to the day he'd gotten it. He'd been six, and the nightmares had just started. His da had been worried about him, and though their family could ill afford it, he'd taken Declan and Colm to a fair. A fortune-teller had given Declan the charm, telling him to keep it close to his heart for luck. . . .

"Chase?"

He quickly said, "That's why Brandr is deathless?"

"Yeah, against all odds, he earned ohalla. Now he's as strong as most vamps and demons. Fast, too. When he hits a rage, he could take on even a Lykae."

"He kept his vow this long?" So Aidan had enjoyed Regin as his woman and a loyal friend as well.

"For the first two hundred years, he followed me and Lucia everywhere, ready to step in with the rescuing. We ditched him at every opportunity. Finally Nïx felt sorry for him and told him she'd let him know if I was in danger—or if you were returning."

"Why didn't Aidan earn ohalla?"

"You were working on it, intending to marry me once you became immortal." She sat on the floor with her knees to her chest, her head resting against the window. "You asked me to stay with you while you fought your battles. To me, you should have been merely an interesting mortal, but something about you drew me. I decided to give you a chance." She smiled to herself, murmuring. "As well as my virginity."

He tensed, appalled to catch himself wondering what it would've been like to be her first lover.

He knew what she was doing, knew she was planting the seed so he'd imagine it. And he did, envisioning laying her down and inching his way into her untried sex. Catching her gasp of surprise with his lips . . .

He grew hard yet again. Earlier, one look at her braless breasts in that T-shirt had made him stiff as wood. Before encountering her, he'd gone ten years without so much as a twitch. And now this. Where was his control?

"Even after a millennium, I just have to think about

us together and my claws curl." She twisted around so he could see them.

They *had* curled. His voice rougher, he asked, "What do your claws have to do with it?"

She gave a laugh. "You'll find out soon enough." Before he could demand an answer, she continued, "Life in your camp was satisfying. Life with you was"—she sighed wistfully—"thrilling."

"Who was Aidan warring against?"

"Leeches. Always the Vampire Horde. You'd positioned your army in a strategic pass, and every day you battled them back, to protect the *mortal* villages in the valley below. You, a berserker *from the Lore,* saved thousands of human lives."

He impatiently waved her on.

"You kept your army honed and well trained, and your men loved you, would have followed you into hell."

Declan's men feared and despised him. *And I don't give a shite as long as they follow orders.*

In a distant tone, she began to describe camp life—the dress, the weapons, the mead hall with snarling bears' heads on the walls—until he could almost smell the smoke of fire pits and roasting game, could nearly hear the incessant clang of swords in the training yard.

It was a man's world she described, one that appealed to Declan.

He found himself relaxing, getting caught up in her tale. And all the while she searched his face for glimmers of recognition. "Any of this ringing a bell?"

"Not as of yet. Continue."

"You trained me yourself. I carry two swords to this day because of you. I'd always wanted to wield this great sword, but it was longer than I was tall." Then she frowned. "At least, I *used* to carry those swords."

"I have them stored here." Mere feet from her was the concealed entry into the storage bay. Her weapons were within.

"Do you?" she said nonchalantly, but her eyes had flickered silver. Those swords were *very* important to her. "I still remember the day you gave them to me." Her face grew soft as she said, "It was a day of firsts." A secretive smile played about her lips.

That smile and her sensual tone got his back up. A day of firsts? He could only imagine what kind of firsts. Jealousy toward this Aidan seared him inside, made Declan want to hurt her for loving him. "Yet your Aidan died."

Her smile faded. "Yes. A vampire traced into our home and slew him."

"You care a great deal about those swords—a gift from your first lover. After a thousand years of acquiring possessions, are these your most cherished?"

More flickering.

"They are," he said. "I think I'll destroy them if you don't provide information about your kind."

"Do it. I don't give a damn."

"Immortals can't bluff, Regin. Your changeable eyes always give you away. And from your reaction, I'd wager you'd do just about anything to preserve them. Answer my questions, or I'll melt them down myself."

"You expect me to jeopardize my sisters?"

"Can all Valkyrie channel energy? Start talking, or I'll give your precious weapons to Warden Fegley, let him fuck about with them. Maybe I'll dispatch them to the Horde with your compliments? Vampires should possess the swords that have felled so many of their kind."

Instead of arguing, she rose and sauntered over to him, swinging those hips. A lesser man could grow enthralled with the movement.

"Chase?" she murmured.

He stood as well. "What?" The air around her was electric, pricking his skin, but it felt good—it felt *familiar.* As she drew near, it intensified until he was almost shuddering. He stared down at her silver eyes. Mesmerizing.

Thunder rumbled the walls. "Hold on tight, Magister."

SIXTEEN

Regin's legendary temper? *Redlined.*

Chase stared down at her in confusion. "Hold on tight? What does that mean?"

"It means that you don't *touch* my things!" Her leg shot up between his own, her boot connecting with his ballocks.

"Ah! You fuckin' bitch!" he yelled, fighting to stay upright. "You're goin' to pay for that!" He lumbered forward. "You have no idea what you're rousing."

"Sure I do! A *berserker.*" As she jogged back, she gave a single jerk on her arm, dislocating the same shoulder as yesterday. Before he could reach her, she'd hopped over her bound wrists like a jump rope. "Because that's what you are!"

He swung a wild punch.

She leapt back, dodging his fist by millimeters. While he reeled from the swing-and-miss, she readied for another attack, ramming her shoulder into the side of a bookcase. Her shoulder joint rocked into place with an audible pop.

Again he charged. She feinted and spun around behind him, swinging her joined fists at his kidney. But the collar made her slower, weaker. He was able to seize her arm and spin her around with one hand, his other drawn back in a fist.

She lifted her chin, and Chase hesitated—

She took advantage, snapping her head forward, knocking him in the Adam's apple. Then she swooped down, swinging her leg against his ankles, dropping him to his back.

He shot to his feet, faced off against her. "No more mercy for ye, Valkyrie." Holding nothing back, he launched a haymaker at her head.

She ducked and laughed. "That accent you work so hard to hide is coming out! Are ye feckin' Oirish this time? Eh, boyo?" She leapt atop his desk, punting the side of his head. "Those swords are *mine*! Touch them, and I'll use 'em to slice off your nutsack! For a coin purse!"

When she reared back for another kick, he caught her ankle, yanked. She crashed to the floor.

With a yell, Chase lunged over her, pinning her bound wrists over her head, his hips forcing her thighs apart.

She felt him harden in a rush, even after she'd battered his balls. "Oh, boy! Little Declan's excited to see me! Only little Declan's not little at all. The more things change . . ."

When she wriggled beneath him, his jaw slackened, his lids growing heavy. She'd merely meant to tease him, but this heated contact began to affect her as well.

The enticing ridges of his body, his clean scent, the delicious pressure of his thick shaft against her . . .

She gazed up at his steely-gray eyes and found them so familiar.

Then he shook his head. "Enough! Where do you think you would go if you could best me?"

"I wasn't escaping yet."

He levered himself up on his elbows. "If not an escape attempt, then what was this?"

"A warning not to hurt my swag. Or an icebreaker, considering you're on top of me and we're both hot and bothered. Now, let's kiss and make up."

The Valkyrie was panting, her breasts pressing against his chest. Her lips were parted, full and beckoning.

"Kiss *you*?" As he waited for revulsion to seize him, he found himself wondering how she would react. Would she moan into his mouth?

"It will help you remember me. Kiss me. Come on, you know you want to so bad. You want *me* so bad."

"Never." *Bloody get off her, get away from her.* But he *needed* to be above her like this, to master her, overpower her.

"Never? That boner of yours just called you a liar."

"You little bitch." He ground it between her legs, wanting to hurt her.

Lightning struck just outside. Her silvery eyes went wide. "Again."

Temptress, his mind screamed. She was beguiling him—

She twisted her hips beneath him, rubbing her sex along his length.

He hissed in a breath, rocking against her in answer. *Christ, it feels so good.* "You'd let me fuck you right here, wouldn't you? Take you on the floor like a common whore."

"Another couple of thrusts like that, Chase, and I'll have to demand it." She arched her back.

Her shirt was riding up, revealing the beginning swell of her breasts. Her nipples were still covered, but they'd puckered against the material. *Want to see them.*

An involuntary thrust of his hips made her breasts bounce, uncovering more glowing skin. *Almost to her nipples.*

His cock was throbbing. When he rocked it between her thighs, the pressure made him grit his teeth with both pleasure and pain. With another couple of thrusts, he'd come atop her; at that moment, he wanted to.

It'd been ages since he'd looked down at a woman like this. He cast his mind back, trying to remember the last time. . . .

The night of his torture.

At once, fury drowned out his lust. He shoved himself off her. "Do not touch me again, detrus. *Never* touch me." He ran his hand over his face, then returned to his desk to call for Vincente. "Come remove her."

Apparently unaffected, she rose. "Yeah, you're probably right. I should be going." She feigned a yawn. "You've gotta head back to work and I've gotta head to jail. Big night for me. I'm planning to shiv someone for a bar of soap. I think we might have enough time for a quickie, though."

He cast her a withering look.

"Nothing can stop us from sleeping together. We're like magnets pulled to each other."

That was the thing about magnets—they didn't get to choose what they were attracted to. "Valkyrie, you're never going to have sex again. Not before you're executed."

"Way to kill the mood there, Paddy." She sidled closer, gazing up at him. "Now, Chase, I hope you won't let this spat color your judgment about me. I'm usually good times. In fact, if you keep the terms of our deal, maybe I'll tell you the dirty details of how you claimed my virginity in a berserkrage. How you tore off my dress and tossed me on a bed of furs to do things to me that I couldn't even have imagined."

"You'll tell me a story and I'll spare you? You think I don't see what you're doing? I've read *Arabian Nights*."

"Call me Scheherazade, baby! Actually, she's one tricksy bitch. Who, by the way, still owes me twenty gold pieces and a pound of sesame." The Valkyrie had inched even closer until he could perceive the heat from her body, that addictive electricity. "You know I'm giving you good information. We could continue later, and I'd promise to behave for you. Or be your common whore. Gentleman's choice."

Declan recalled Webb's missive. *If I can't torture her, then I have no choice but to see her again.* "I thought it was forbidden among your kind to talk to outsiders?"

"You *are* one of us."

"Can you possibly comprehend how much that insults me?"

"The truth cuts like a knife, boyo."

Vincente arrived, showing no reaction to the fact that the Valkyrie's cuffs were now in front of her—or that she was blowing Declan a kiss good-bye.

"Take her from here."

Without a word, the man escorted her out. But then, it wasn't Vincente's place to react, to do anything more than follow commands. And the man owed him.

Months ago, Declan had caught him making repeated contact with a particular succubus. Since the Order provided no nourishment for her kind, she'd been withering away from sexual hunger—using everything in her power to lure him to free her. So she could rape the man and feed.

Instead of erasing Vincente's memory, Declan had held the lapse over the man's head, ensuring his loyalty. At the time, he'd marveled that Vincente would risk his career over a female—much less a detrus.

Now I was just rutting over a Valkyrie, desperate to see her breasts.

When the door closed behind Vincente and his prisoner, Declan strode into his bathroom to stare at the mirror. Christ, were his eyes lighter?

No, she's got me imagining things. She's a detrus—everything about her is foul, wrong.

Yet still he was hard for her. He waited for the strain to hit him full-force, would relish the misery as an earned punishment.

Waiting . . .

Just thinking about taking her would be enough to

send that old anxiety skyrocketing. So he envisioned ripping her jeans down to her knees and shoving his cock into her tight little quim.

Waiting . . .

Nothing? He was tense because he needed to fuck, but there was no more anxiety than usual.

In fact . . . it'd *lessened.*

He choked back a crazed laugh. For whatever reason, be it entrancement or not, the strain had all but disappeared.

Right time, right place, right . . . girl? Except for the fact that she wasn't *human*! No, she was a murderer and a blood foe who would run screaming the minute she saw his unclothed body.

Not to mention that he was duty-bound to imprison and eventually execute her.

His shaft didn't seem to care about all that. He scowled down at it. If he did stroke off now, then she would win. He refused. She was one of them. An abomination.

They lure mortal men from their purpose. From my *purpose.* To help him remember it, he tore off his sweater, baring his ruined chest.

Those creatures had peeled away strips of his flesh not at random, but in deliberate circles and lines. The resulting wounds had been too narrow for grafts. Instead, the surgeon had stitched the skin directly together. In time, the scar tissue had grown raised.

Yet even this sickening sight couldn't quell his hard-on. He knew of only one thing that could.

He hastened to his bed, to his case, readying a syringe.

When he'd started injecting this medicine a decade ago, he'd made an effort to be dignified, treating it like an insulin shot. He would ease the needle in, pressing the plunger leisurely.

To somehow differentiate it from what he'd done in Belfast's back alleys.

Now he shot up like a junkie desperate for a fix.

His lids grew heavy with pleasure. His mind was just wasted enough for him to ignore the continued ache in his ballocks, and soon he slept, quickly slipping into dreams. . . .

SEVENTEEN

"*Aidan hastens through battles just to get back to his woman.*"

His men's words rang out behind him, but Aidan paid them no mind. They would hurry back too if they had what he enjoyed.

A golden goddess born from the heat of lightning.

A few of his men teased him that he'd put Reginleit up on a pedestal. As if she belonged anywhere else?

Back at the camp, he dunked himself in the bathhouse springs, scrubbing the vampire blood and gore from his skin. Then he carelessly knotted a filched blanket around his waist as he stormed toward their longhouse.

He found Reginleit sitting by the fire pit inside, lost in thought and staring into the flames. *Contemplating her new life with me?*

But as soon as she spotted him, she stood, her face glowing brighter. "Aidan, you're back!"

As he crossed to her, he was struck anew at how beautiful she'd grown, her body a heaven of curves and softness he longed to lose himself inside. 'Twas as if she'd been created for him—a warrioress with a fierce heart, a sharp mind, and a fiery passion to match his own.

But he had to grin at her silken hair. The crazed braids she'd worn as a girl remained, yet now they were oddly provocative, looking as if he'd just tumbled her.

She leaned up to press her mouth to his, parting her lush lips for him.

With just one taste of her, he groaned, "Your lips, female . . . sweetness itself."

Like a drug . . .

Before he got lost in the mind-numbing pleasure of her kiss, he forced himself to break away. "I've a gift for you, brightling." He swooped her up in his arms, carrying her to their bed.

In a breathy voice, she said, "And 'tis one I've been awaiting all day."

Gods, her mere voice set his blood afire. And when she boldly cupped him . . .

He had to force her hand from him, flattered by her disappointed pout. "Nay, 'tis a true gift." He stood to retrieve his offering from a leather pack.

"I like surprises!"

"You like *presents*. And the mere owning of things." He handed her a bundle swathed in cloth. "I am well aware that I've got an acquisitive Valkyrie for my mate."

Yes, Valkyrie were acquisitive, and he wanted to spoil her, but he had an ulterior motive. He feared for her. Until she turned fully immortal, she was nearly as vulnerable as a human. Vampires were overrunning the earth and would seek to hurt her in retaliation for his decades-long war with them.

She unwrapped the cloth, revealing a pair of short

swords sheathed in leather. He perceived her excitement as she withdrew one of them, holding it up to the firelight. "'Tis so beautiful, Aidan!"

He'd commissioned the pair to be forged from the strongest metals known in the Lore. The blades were perfectly balanced, engraved with glyphs of lightning, and polished to a sheen that reflected her glow.

She stood, swirling both the swords with her Valkyrie's grace, her wrists fluid, the movements so natural that she looked like she'd been born with them in hand. His heart swelled to see her like this. She would become a legendary swordswoman.

"Aidan, I've never been given anything so fine." Her irises shimmered with emotion. Just as they did whenever he brought her release.

After only two weeks with her, the sight of her silver eyes like this had his shaft rising for her.

"I will become skilled with these." She gazed up at him as if he were a hero of the ages.

Looks like that could go to a man's head. Already he stood taller when his woman was near. "I will see to it." *Just as I will see to it that you come to love me.* But he knew it would take time. She was still hesitant about remaining with him for longer than their agreed-upon three months.

Ah, but Reginleit had begun to light up—literally—every time he came into view. And with each battle, he moved closer to the time he would claim her completely. He couldn't fight them fast enough, at times wondering how much longer he could resist the fated pull to her.

When her gaze dipped to his erection tenting the blanket, she murmured, "Perhaps our training can begin in the morn?" She was already trembling, her claws curling for her man. She clearly *had* been awaiting his return.

He took the swords from her and sheathed them in a rush. "In the morn, then. For now, I am going to kiss you as I've craved all day." He swept her up in his arms, carrying her to the furs and laying her atop them. After ridding himself of the blanket, he followed her down.

He made short work of her kirtle, baring her body to his greedy gaze. Where to kiss her first? Her taut nipples strained for attention. He'd see to them.

When his lips closed over one, her back bowed and lightning struck outside.

As he suckled her, she clutched him close, kneading the muscles in his back with growing fervor. He released the damp tip once it was nice and stiff, blowing on it.

"Aidan!"

As she arched for more, he turned to her other one, twirling his tongue around it. She was so damned responsive to him. Her breasts were exquisitely sensitive, her ears as well. And her sex . . . He savored that secret part of her, could lick her for hours. With that aim in mind, he relinquished her breasts and eased downward, settling her thighs over his shoulders.

With his first lick of her flesh, pleasure overwhelmed him. Little wonder that he grew ravenous to taste her, grew irritable in battle when denied his hours of kissing her sweet sex. Yes, he did kill quicker just to get back to this honey sooner.

His tongue snaked over that sensitive bud, but she was already about to peak. He grinned against her flesh. His little goddess was lusty.

"Your fingers, Aidan," she moaned. She loved to be penetrated, even when he licked her. She would come hard around his fingers when he sank them deep inside her.

His Reginleit was so ready to be claimed completely. Merely awaiting him. "You'll come too quick, love."

She made a sound of frustration, but he wanted to keep her on edge. So he drew back, lying down and lifting her to straddle his head. Like this, he could watch her writhe above him, her skin glowing hotly.

He clamped his arms over the tops of her thighs, fixing her tight to his mouth. As he lapped at her core again and again, his shaft stood rigid as a pole.

She moaned low. "Please, Aidan, now . . . *now*."

Unable to deny her, he plunged his stiffened tongue, once, twice, his hips thrusting in time—

She threw her head back as she came atop him. "Ah, gods, yes!" She undulated over his mouth, rocking on his tongue. Lightning streaked outside, and thunder rumbled across the land as he licked her orgasm, groaning in bliss. . . .

Once he'd wrung every last moan from her, they both collapsed on the furs, catching their breath.

Yet then she began to kiss down his neck, continuing a sensuous path to his chest and lower.

Gods, if she could be just as hungry for him as he was for her. He hadn't pushed for this pleasure from her. She was still young, and he wanted to ease her into it. He knew his actions in the beginning could help determine whether she loved the act or hated it—for eternity.

"Reginleit, what are you doing?"

"I want to kiss you. As you keep kissing me."

He coughed into his fist, striving for an offhand tone. "Oh, then, and what do you know of suckling a man?"

She gazed up at him, her ears twitching. "I know from the timbre of your voice 'tis *very* important to you."

"Perceptive, Valkyrie," he said with pride. *And every day I love her more than the last.*

"Teach me how."

With an audible swallow, he guided her head down, loving the feel of her hair gliding over his chest, his nipples. "Press your lips here, Reginleit"—he pointed to the swollen crown—"and give it a lick."

She darted her tongue along the slit, and he uncontrollably gave up a bead of semen. "You do not have to . . ." He trailed off when she eagerly lapped at him, as if she sought more.

"I like this taste. *Your* taste."

She was a prize to be treasured! He cradled her face with shaking hands. "I've much more to give you. Will you take it from me?"

"Is that what your other women have done?" Of her own accord, she nuzzled his testicles, her wicked tongue flicking them as well.

"Ah!" He fought to keep his hips still. "I do not

recall others before you," he said honestly. "You've bewitched me."

"I will take from you."

"Then suck the head hard while pumping your fist beneath your mouth. And you will have a willing slave." His clever Reginleit stroked him so perfectly as she suckled. And all the while, her heavy-lidded gaze remained on his, her eyes silvery with desire.

He palmed the back of her head, his legs falling open. "Touch yourself, love," he rasped. "I want you to come . . . with my shaft deep in your mouth."

She moaned around his flesh as she began masturbating her sex, rubbing it with nimble fingers. Outside, her lightning lit up the night once more.

"Valkyrie, you *madden* me." The pressure built as her mouth and hand effortlessly worked his length, the base swelling as his semen rose for her. Desperate to release it, he just stopped himself from bucking. "Reginleit, my seed! I'm about to spill on your tongue if you do not draw away—"

She robbed him of words as she sucked even harder, demanding his manhood's offering.

He was helpless not to give it. . . .

A wild ocean storm pounded the island, mirroring Declan's turbulent thoughts as he ran headlong into the gale.

Earlier in the night, he'd had the most realistic dream he'd ever experienced—one about the Valkyrie and her berserker. One that had made Declan awaken in a rush, on the very verge of coming, with his hips rocking and his cockhead wetting the sheet.

He'd sworn he could still feel her tongue against him, could still hear her moans.

Declan swiped a hand over his face. *God help me, I was* still *licking my lips for more of her taste.*

Mingled with that aching need had been . . . a lingering *tenderness* for her. And maybe even a thread of guilt for threatening her swords.

Which disgusted him. Had the dream been an entrancement, or something new?

He pushed himself over precarious forest trails, ripping off his shirt, leaving only his fatigue pants and boots.

He ignored the tree limbs that raked his bared chest, ignored his burning lungs as he covered mile after mile. Lightning struck all around and the winds howled, but he savored the wildness of the night, the bite of rain driving against his scarred skin.

Anything but succumb to that dream of the Valkyrie.

Somehow she'd made him experience that scene. *A day of firsts,* she'd told him. Her first time to suck off a man. And he'd imagined it, as if on cue, his mind supplying details to build on her story. Just as she'd intended.

Declan had even dreamed of pleasuring her—a detrus—with his mouth. Which just made him even more suspicious. Because his own predilections didn't match his dream.

Unlike Aidan, Declan had never gone down on a

woman, had never had that kind of time to spare during sex. Not before he would grow sick.

In truth, he'd never much seen to a woman's pleasure at all. And though he was certain he'd *received* oral sex in the hazy days before his body had been maimed, he couldn't quite recall it.

This isn't me. I don't want her for these things. . . .

Perhaps the Valkyrie had some power he wasn't aware of. Maybe a dreamcasting ability, like the dream demons possessed. Which meant an element of mind control.

He was a man who needed constant control over every aspect of his life, a man who worshipped strength and will. *The last time I had them taken from me . . .*

The Valkyrie would pay for toying with him.

He pushed himself until his lungs were heaving and his muscles quaked. Mud splashed up, all over his shuddering body, and still he ran.

Running as if something pursued him.

EIGHTEEN

Chase is having the dreams.

As soon as Vincente escorted her into the magister's office the next night, Regin knew. Chase had begun reliving Aiden's time with her, remembering them sexually.

His eyes were on her like a hawk's, his gaze possessive and *familiar.* He was looking at her like a man who'd seen her naked—and liked the view.

The dreams marked the beginning of the end for each of Aidan's reincarnations. Normally this stage would send her into hysterics.

But now it meant progress. Right? *Press on, Regin.*

"Leave us," Chase told the guard, never glancing away from her.

Vincente turned without a word, his face expressionless as usual.

When they were alone, Regin said, "Vincente doesn't think it's weird for me to be coming here?"

"It's not his job to think. He's only supposed to follow my orders."

Chase's voice was naturally raspy, but tonight it was even huskier, making her ears twitch in reaction.

"So, I was about to lodge a formal complaint

about Fegley," she said. "But this doesn't seem to be a customer-service-oriented establishment." Again, she hopped up on his desk, onto his perfectly stacked papers. His brows drew together, but he didn't bother ordering her away.

"Any minute now, I expect that little tool to say, 'It rubs the lotion on its skin.' He's gonna meet a bad end."

"You're psychic now? Or making futile plans?"

"I'm just old." She sighed. "You see guys like him over and over, and you get to be a crack at predicting it. And speaking of ridiculously ineffectual workers . . . Dixon keeps staring at me with those buggy Where's Waldo? glasses. It's almost as if she's fantasizing about playing with my insides. Oh, wait. She *is*." Regin tilted her head. "I'll bet she fantasizes about you even more."

"Jealous?"

She rolled her eyes at him. "Of *course* I'm jealous."

"I'm surprised you'd admit it."

"You were *mine* first. My dibs are ten centuries old."

"What Dixon and I do is none of your concern."

"Well, if she's your type, then whatever. I just thought a man like you would crave a real woman. Someone who's strong enough to handle your power and sensual enough to slake you." Regin moved to the center of his desk, sitting atop another stack of papers. This time he didn't seem to notice at all.

"At least she *is* a woman. And not a Valkyrie."

"Baby, I'm *all* woman." She spread her legs suggestively, so he was sitting between them. "Uncuff me and let me show you what you've been missing all your life."

* * *

Declan believed she'd do it. He could lay her back on that desk, strip off her clothes, and enter her right now.

The most beautiful woman he'd ever encountered.

And for a moment, everything within him was in perfect accord with the idea.

All day his thoughts had returned to that dream of her and the berserker. He'd grown hard at intervals, wondering how much longer he could go without relieving the pressure that continued to build.

His concentration had been wrecked, his workload escalating. Running an installation of this size was a job for five men—and he delegated little—but he'd never minded, preferring to stay slammed with work.

Now it felt like the reins were slipping from his grasp. Professionally, personally. *Sexually?*

"Come on, Chase," she murmured, "I can *feel* your tension—you're like a powder keg about to blow."

They will separate you from your purpose . . . "I'd never lower myself to bed one of your kind."

She shrugged, but he thought he caught a flash of hurt in her eyes. "Might not be me. But it's not Dixon, either."

"So certain?"

"I *know* you, remember?"

"Prove it, then."

"I know you're in constant turmoil. Your past lives competing with your present." She lowered her voice. "You once told me that it feels like a beast is inside you, frenzied to get out. From the look on your face, you still feel that way."

How the hell could she know that?

Years ago, when Declan had finally confessed to Webb about that constant sense of urgency clawing at him, Webb had nodded knowingly. "It's a *calling*, son. That's what you feel, have always felt." Declan was to channel that into his vocation—destroying the deathless ones.

So why did the strain fade whenever he was with Regin?

"You dreamed about me last night, didn't you?" she asked. "You always used to in the past, told me you did right up to the point when you remembered all."

Immediately on edge, he demanded, "How did you make me experience that dream? Was it dreamcasting?"

"I don't have that ability."

"Bullshite!" His accent slipped yet again.

"Chase, even if I could dreamcast, how could I do it . . . when I'm wearing a torque?"

He swallowed. *No, no, anything's possible in the Lore.* Another being could have affected him, or Regin could even have done this to him before he'd captured her.

"Face it. You are a berserker, and you are a reincarnate."

If I'm one of them, the Order will kill me. His eyes darted. *No, she's got me spooked. This isn't real.*

When he gave a hard shake of his head, she said, "Then how do *you* explain your strength and speed?

Unless you take top-secret military speed or hyper-steroids to hulk out?"

"I do nothing to make myself stronger." Just the opposite.

"Then what?"

Blood that wasn't my own. "Maybe I was nicked in a battle with one of your kind and was exposed to tainted immortal blood. Perhaps I've picked up traits of the creatures I hunt."

"That's not how it works. You can't just *pick up traits.* At least, not permanently. Not unless you die with one's blood in your veins and get transformed into an immortal."

Maybe he *wasn't* turning into a Neoptera?

She grinned at him as she asked, "You haven't died yet, have you?"

I . . . don't know. Those beings could have done any manner of things to him over those days and nights.

His heart sped up as he tried to pierce that haze. *Damn them all to hell, a man should know if he's died or not.*

As if she'd read his mind, she said, "If you hate us this badly, then you or someone you love was hurt by immortals. Considering your scars . . ." She pointed to the ones on his face, the ones that were relatively invisible compared to the rest covering his body.

"So you have me all figured out."

"You're not denying it, then. I'm guessing your parents were killed?"

Killed was too mild a word for what the Neoptera had

done to them. Those creatures had voracious mouths that opened vertically, their lips razor-sharp for cutting flesh. Their tongues were prehensile, stretching inches long.

Declan had felt them probe beneath his skin. Now he barely stifled a shudder.

"Chase?"

"You didn't guess a wife and children," he said absently. "Though most would, considering my age."

"No, you've never been married."

"And how could you know that?"

"In all your lifetimes, you've never even had a relationship with another. I'll bet you've never slept with the same woman twice."

Dead on. "Why would you say that?"

"You hate it with others. You feel sick afterward." In a softer tone, she said, "Because you're missing what we had and want to stay true."

He clenched his jaw, recalling all the times he'd barely kept from vomiting, remembering with humiliation the times he hadn't. . . .

"Aidan—"

His gloved hand shot up. In an instant he had her hair wrapped around his fist, yanking her head down. "Do not call me by that name again, Valkyrie. This will be your last warning."

"Okay, fine," she said mildly, but her eyes had flashed.

Silvery eyes gazing up at me, with her hair coiled around my fist as I guide her down . . .

He released her with disgust.

She was undaunted. "Let's talk in your room. Take me there."

"Why would I possibly do that?"

"Because that's where your bed is, and that's where I belong."

He imagined her in his bed as she'd been in that dream, spread out like an offering, her bared skin alight. Her thighs would be parted with blatant need, those golden curls slick with it. . . .

Duty, purpose, he repeated urgently.

"Come on, Chase."

"Tell me, if I take you to my room and put you in my bed, what do you think would happen?"

"I can draw you a diagram. Hint: I'm slot B, and you're tab A."

"I meant the ultimate outcome. Do you think I'll free you if you please me enough? You're not the first detrus who's tried to whore for her freedom."

"Whore for my freedom?" She laughed again. "What if I just wanted to whore for whoring's sake? Maybe I miss sex with you. Maybe I crave it."

"Wouldn't be surprising. Most immortal females behave like they're in heat."

Her brows rose. "*You* are the one who taught me about pleasure."

Memories from that dream continued to arise unbidden. *—Press your lips here, Reginleit.—*

"And now in another lifetime, you ridicule me for missing it? Come on, Chase. Take me to where you live. Scared I'll find some footy pajamas? A Fleshlight? I want a bath almost as much as you need to watch me take one. I get so much more talkative when I'm clean. Loreans are really fastidious, you know."

"I do know that. The sole aspect of your kind that's positive." He leaned back in his chair. "This subject ends now."

She sighed. "Stubborn. Just like a man I knew whose name starts with A."

"I'm not this Aidan you revere. I'm nothing like him."

"You're so similar it's uncanny. You're both warriors, the strongest and best at what you do. That's been the same with each of the reincarnations."

Curiosity got the best of him, and he asked, "What were the others?"

"You've been a knight, a privateer, and a cavalry officer. Warriors all. Yet each embodiment emphasizes specific facets of Aidan's personality. The first was Treves, a medieval French knight, notorious across Europe. He represented Aidan's ruthlessness and power."

"How did you meet him?"

"Fate. We were both in France one winter for a castle siege."

"Shouldn't you have been in Valhalla?"

Sadness flashed in her expression. "I never get to go back to Valhalla. Once you leave, you're forbidden to return." Before he could ask her about that, she continued, "Lucia—she's my favorite sister—and I were defending the old Earl of Lanbert's castle."

"Why?"

"Lanbert's forefathers hailed from the North, and his

line still worshipped the Valkyrie. Lucia and I decided to reward their prayers and offerings—by pledging swords and bow to the defense of their home. Plus, we were bored out of our gourds."

"Was Treves another ally?"

"Not at all. You see, we were defending the castle against *you*."

NINETEEN

"Against me?" Chase raised his brows.

"Uh-huh. Castle-taking was your thing. You 'commandeered' key strongholds for King Philip all over Europe, and you'd set your sights on Lanbert's keep." Regin drew her calves under her to sit cross-legged on his desk, daring him to say something. Getting comfy when cuffed was damned near impossible.

He glowered but said nothing.

"Every day your army trenched in closer to the castle, almost in trebuchet range. But we'd known it was only a matter of time. Your men were fanatically loyal, and you were a master strategist. Lucia was running out of arrows. My blades were dulled from cleaving bone. We hadn't slept in days. . . ."

When she began describing the setting—the smell of smoke and tar, the lingering rock dust from the battered castle walls, the smithy's constant hammering—he leaned back in his chair, the marked tension in his shoulders lessening.

As she recounted the weeks of battle, the foot-soldier offensives and arrow exchanges, he relaxed even more, resting his hands behind his head. Chase liked these tales.

"Then came the day of reckoning. The trebuchets were loaded, and so close that we could hear the ropes straining. Before you fired them, you rode up to the portcullis, astride a wild-eyed stallion. Skirmishes slowed, quieting until only a stray sword clanged here or there. You were tall, not as tall as you are now, but massive in armor. I would have known you were Treves even if you hadn't been carrying your standard, a red banner with two ravens in flight."

"Ravens?" Had tension crept back into his shoulders?

"The symbol of Wóden, remember? At the time, we just thought it was a coincidence that Treves had it." She slanted him a glance. "You know this mark?"

Chase shook his head. "Go on."

After a hesitation, she said, "For some reason, you raised your gaze to the rampart I defended, doing a double take at me."

In an irritable tone, Chase said, "Perhaps because you *glow*."

"I was cloaked from head to toe," she said with a saccharine smile. "To Lanbert, you bellowed, 'Surrender your castle, or I'll raze it to the ground.' Your ultimatum didn't sit well with me, so naturally, I voiced my opinion."

"Which was?"

"That you should go copulate with a pig. It sounded way cooler in medieval French."

Chase raised his brows.

"But at my words, you jolted in your saddle, your horse growing even more wild-eyed. You called to me, 'You defend that rampart, female?' I answered, 'To the death, prick.' Again, way cooler in medieval French."

"You antagonized the leader of a superior force?"

"What were you going to do? Trebuchet us even harder?"

"So how did *he* respond?" Chase asked.

"*You* called out, 'Lanbert, send down the black-cloaked woman as my war prize, and I will end my siege. We close this eve with peace between us.' Everyone was floored. For Treves to quit a siege without a victory? You'd won dozens of castles—you *never* lost. Even more shocking was that you wanted a woman."

"Why was that so shocking?"

"Because Treves belonged to a *monastic* order of knights. No damsels allowed. Lucia and I didn't know what to make of this. You couldn't know that I was a Valkyrie. But why else would you want me? Of course, Luce made the obligatory war booty cracks, and we yucked it up."

Lucia had finally begun to shake off the worst of Cruach's torture. After centuries, she'd relearned how to laugh.

"You weren't afraid?"

Regin rolled her eyes. "I fear nothing. Besides, we thought it great fun that you were telling Lanbert to send me down. The old earl could no more command me than I could ask Wóden to wake from his godsleep. But by this time, I was fraught with curiosity. I simply had to face you. When I strolled out of the castle, you rode up to meet me."

Regin would never forget how he'd looked. Up close, she'd gotten a better sense of his size, but she hadn't been able to see his face. His visor had shaded his eyes, and the winter sun had been at his back, paining her preternatural sight. "Treves and I . . . bantered." She could still hear his voice:

"You've come to sacrifice yourself to me?"

"Have you not seen me in battle, knight? I sacrifice nothing with this move."

"Woman, you became my prize as soon as you crossed from that keep."

She lifted her chin. "Or you became mine."

"You ordered me to take off my cloak. Though I didn't take orders, I did enjoy shocking people with my wicked-cool glowing. So I pulled my hood back. You hissed in a breath, but you had a surprise of your own. Just as your waving pennant blocked the direct sun, you lifted your visor. I caught my first glimpse of your gray eyes and nearly fainted. They'd begun to glow."

At first Treves had appeared confounded, muttering, *I've never seen you, but you haunt my dreams.* Then his gaze had narrowed with intent, and he'd stabbed his standard into the ground.

"Before I could blink, you'd swooped me up into the saddle in front of you. To your men, you called, 'We war no longer!'"

Now Regin studied Chase's reaction. He hardly seemed to be listening. "And we lived happily ever after," she said, which was not remotely true.

"Stopping there?"

"You seem really preoccupied. You don't like my knight's tale?" She certainly didn't like the end of it. Treves had died in agony before the next sunrise, convulsing in her arms as she'd helplessly watched. After fighting across half of Europe, Brandr had reached them just as Treves took his last breaths.

"Am I *boring* you?" Never in a thousand years had Regin asked that question.

Chase shrugged noncommittally, his dark brows drawn.

What is going on in that complicated mind of his? With Aidan, she'd always known what he was thinking. But this Irishman was continually throwing her. She scooted to the edge of the desk again. "You probably just want to can the chitchat and get to the kissing, huh? It's understandable."

At his quelling look, she shook her head slowly. "No? Well, then I'll give you some advice. Free of charge. You're probably up to your ass with work, and you're hating it," she said. "Chase, you weren't meant to run this place. You're a hunter, a *warrior,* who was born to be in the thick of the fray."

"Do you think that I desire or need your advice?"

"I *am* way older than you are."

"Yet still more immature."

"Easily. You want to tell me what you're thinking about?"

At length, he said, "If each reincarnation personified aspects of Aidan, what were the others?"

"Gabriel the Spaniard was humor and sex. Edward, my young English cavalryman, was . . ." She trailed off, affected as ever by her heartrending memories of him. "Edward was pure love."

"You believe I'm one of these reincarnations. What do you imagine I represent?"

"I think you could be all of them," she said. "But right now, you're Aidan's dark obsession. You're drowning, Chase, and deep down, you know I'm your lifeline."

He steepled his fingers. "I find it interesting that you tell of a man who turned his back on everything he'd worked for. A knight who ended a siege for a woman. Then on the heels of that you *advise* me not to run this installation?"

"I just recounted what happened with Treves. Besides, he was by no means the king's lapdog—he'd questioned his ruler's actions from the beginning and had stood up to him before. There was talk that Treves could seize the throne whenever he felt like it."

Which was why Philip had already had an assassin waiting in the wings. When Treves had disobeyed Philip's command to take the castle, the king had ordered him poisoned.

For choosing me over a victory, Treves had paid with his life. . . .

The Valkyrie's gaze grew distant, her eyes flickering color. When she faced him once more, she said, "Lemme ask you, Magister—have *you* ever stood up to your boss before?"

Earlier he'd suspected that this tale was all part of a setup, serving her agenda. Now she'd just confirmed his suspicion.

While Declan had been relaxing his guard with her, she'd been working him over, every word she'd spoken carefully chosen. "If I don't act like your knight, then I'm a lapdog?" In a disgusted tone, he said, "Perhaps I should betray everything I've ever known for you?"

"I could make you happier than the Order does." So sure of herself.

"I'm not in this for *happiness,* Valkyrie. And I don't question commands, because I believe in the objective—protecting humankind. *My* kind."

"I think you want to leave all this behind to be with me. Chase, I'm only waiting on you."

"Abandon my mission? *Never,* Valkyrie! Who would do this work if not for me?" His gloved hands fisted. No one had ever infuriated him like she did! He was supposed to be emotionless by nature. He injected those numbing concoctions every night. So why were these rages still taking him over?

Without thought, he stormed to his filing cabinet, yanking out a worn file of pictures—photos of the casualties in this war. If he ever doubted his purpose or resented the pain in his battle-worn body, he brought out this folder. Nothing could solidify his resolve more effectively.

He wanted to show her what he fought against, and to observe her reaction. *To see for myself that she won't even blink.*

"If it wasn't for me, then the pack of viper shifters that hit this orphanage"—he tossed a set of four photos onto the desk—"would still be targeting easy prey." The graphic pictures depicted the bodies of children and nuns, swollen and fed upon. "They'd been dragged from their beds in the middle of the night, then envenomed until paralyzed. They couldn't even scream."

She peered down at them, her lips thinned.

"Or how about this?" He flung another picture in front of her. This one showed mauled Wendigo victims with their limbs ripped apart, their bones cracked open. "The Wendigos had sucked out the marrow while their prey was still alive. I destroyed every single one in that pack. Even the humans who'd been transformed into their kind."

As if she sensed she'd do well not to say anything, the Valkyrie remained silent.

The next set of pictures made him rock on his feet; his mother and father tied up on the floor, their flesh consumed to the bone. Their expressions frozen in terror forever. "What about the Neoptera?" he demanded, his voice ragged. "I've eradicated dozens of them during my twenty years with the Order."

For some reason, he shoved the picture of his parents in front of her.

And, damn her, her eyes flickered with sympathy. He slammed his fist down on the desk, bellowing, "Don't you fuckin' dare feel sympathy for them! They were mere mortals, beneath your notice!"

"Of course I feel sympathy!" She shot to her feet, bristling. "That's why I've killed as many of those creatures as I've come across! You're locking up immortals who would be your allies—"

"Ally with you? You're *indolent*. Your own sister said that all you do is fight needlessly and get high." They were toe-to-toe.

"Oh, you're one to talk about getting high, Major Tom! You're flying out of this atmosphere most days."

He ignored that. "You serve no purpose, have *no* reason to exist."

Again that flash of hurt shone in her eyes. "I have a purpose, you asshole! Ever heard of Cruach, the god of human sacrifice and cannibalism? Every five hundred years, he rises, bent on turning all of humanity into maddened cannibal killers. Alongside my sister, *I* fight him. *Me!* I've faced him twice before. Only this time, he's going viral. We're talking apocalypse."

Declan had heard of Cruach before, but they had limited intel on the being. *Yet another immortal threat. Yet more information for the taking . . .*

"I'm supposed to be facing him right now, but you have me locked up here!" She drew her lips back from her small fangs, reminding him of what she was. "Because of you, Chase, the world is teetering on the brink of apocalypse, immortals *and* mortals in jeopardy."

He'd speak with Webb about this, determine a plan of action—

"So I might not have documented my work with handy trophy pics, but it doesn't change the fact that I've put a *god* on ice two times before, and I'm keen to do it a third!"

A red film covered his eyes, and he roared, "*Trophy?*" He buzzed Vincente to come get her—before he throttled her. "Get out of my sight."

TWENTY

Late that night, once Declan finally slept, his body was restless, twisting in the sheets, his mind assailed by dreams. . . .

"What manner of creature are you?" Treves asked the woman before him.

He'd hoped they'd be enemies no more, and even now she was sidling closer to him.

"You do not remember me?" In his tent, her face proved even more radiant, her eyes and hair shining like sun-struck amber.

"I have not met you, had never seen you before this morning." Except in dreams. Yet as soon as he'd heard her voice, he'd felt a stirring in his chest. "Are you a witch?" *One who's bespelled me?*

"No. Not a witch." She removed her swords and cloak, revealing her strange garments—an armored vest of stiffened leather over a fine linen blouse and a kirtle so short that her thighs were visible above her high boots. He swallowed. She had taut, smooth thighs made to cradle a man's hips. Not that he would know from experience.

"I am a Valkyrie, an immortal. One of Wóden's

cherished daughters." She said these words as if they should have some meaning to him. "Have you heard of us?"

"Only myths carried from the lands of the North." He recalled that the Valkyrie were a type of warrior goddess.

This female expected him to believe she was one among them. And why shouldn't he? What else could explain her glowing skin and small fangs, or the pink claws that tipped her delicate fingers?

He removed one gauntlet to run the backs of his fingers over her high cheekbones, his lids growing heavy. Her skin was impossibly soft. With each touch he marveled that such a female was in his keeping. *My prize, and an earned one.*

His forfeiture of that castle would enrage his king, who had steadily been losing patience with him. *I might have a price on my head already.* No matter. As Treves gazed down at her, he knew she would be worth any consequence.

And answering to another was a yoke that had never sat easily upon his shoulders anyway. He and his king would come to terms over this. *Or I'll pluck that crown from his head.*

"You know that I am Treves. What is your name?"

"They call me Regin the Radiant."

"A fitting name, *belle.*" When he tucked a wild braid behind her ear, his eyes widened. The tip was *pointed.* "A Valkyrie's ear?" He was captivated by this creature, now taking her hand and smoothing the backs of her little claws over his face. "Why do you seem so familiar?" And how could he feel half in love with her already? As if he'd fall on his sword should they be parted?

"We met, ages ago." She seemed alternately sad and excited, brows drawn one instant, a breathless smile blooming the next. "But if I tell you, you will think me crazed."

"No more than I, to have dreamed of a woman I'd never seen." Ever since he'd come to this castle, he'd been beset with dreams of her.

"In a past life, you were a berserker, a warrior in Wóden's guard. You served my father." She paused, then added, "And you'd planned to wed me."

Wed her? He drew even closer. "I do not know who you believe I am, but I will gladly be this man."

Her eyes searched his expression as she said, "You were called Aidan the Fierce."

Clearly her affections had already been claimed by this Aidan. "Why do you think me him?" She had mistaken Treves for someone else. *I cannot surrender her.*

I will *not.*

"Your eyes glowed like a berserker's. And I *sense* it's you. The fact that you've dreamed of me convinces me beyond doubt." When he cast her a dubious look, she said, "You've been re-embodied, your soul housed in another form."

Could this be true? Could his soul have lived on from another time?

From his earliest memories, nightmares of angels and devils and biting snow had plagued him till he'd thought he'd lose his mind. Always his chest had given him pain. His parents had feared that his aching heart was weak, that he would die young. As a man, he'd warred to escape the turmoil within him—placating his inward black thoughts with outward black deeds.

Now the ache had disappeared. Perhaps his heart had always been strong, yet it would beat for this female alone. "How could I have returned?"

"When you died in my arms centuries ago, you vowed that you would come for me. I do not know how you've done this. Sometimes we're not meant to know all the things that are possible in the Lore."

"The Lore?"

"It's our world. A world of immortals, where myths and legends live."

She is an immortal; I am not. "You will *not* return to this land, Valkyrie," he commanded, his voice rough from the thought of losing her. "Your place is with me."

Her face brightened even more. "Then remind me why I chose you above all other men."

"I know not how to remind . . ." He trailed off when she began unraveling the ties to his armor, her desires clear. He couldn't rip off his chain mail and tunic quickly enough.

Yet even as his manhood swelled in his trews, he had to admit, "*Cher*, I've never lain with a woman before."

"You have." She smiled, beginning to divest herself of her own clothing. "You just don't remember yet."

His gaze was riveted to her deft fingers unlacing that leather vest. She shrugged from it, then stepped from her kirtle, leaving her garbed in only her blouse. It was so short he could nearly glimpse the juncture of her thighs—and so transparent he could clearly see her breasts.

He gaped at the ravishing sight before him, then swallowed audibly. "I've never wanted anything more than you in my entire life." *You are my life. Somehow I know this. . . .*

She stood on her toes to press tender kisses to his neck, his chest. When she murmured, "Take off your boots," they were as good as gone.

"And your trews."

He tore them off his body.

She backed toward his bed, curling her finger, beckoning him to follow.

After drawing off the blouse, she lay back like a radiant offering. So stunningly beautiful, she took his breath away.

The first woman to grace his bed. *And the last.*

Once he'd lowered himself beside her, she reached for his rampant shaft, cupping her fingers around it. His hips bucked uncontrollably to her silken touch, and a groan was wrenched from his lips.

She began fondling him with languid strokes that made him lightheaded. The pressure within his manhood mounted as she rubbed her thumb over the crown, seeming to revel in the moisture there. "Ah, *cher,* I grow near—"

Without relinquishing her hold, she guided him to lie back. When she straddled his hips, he was transfixed, scarcely comprehending that he was about to know her fully.

She positioned his length beneath her, then began

to lower her body upon it. With each of her panting inhalations, her breasts rose and fell so temptingly. His hands covered that supple flesh, kneading with delight.

Her tight sheath nearly robbed him of his seed. Gritting his teeth, he struggled not to shame himself.

She lowered herself as far as she could, her curling Valkyrie claws digging into his chest.

—As they should.—

Was he going mad? The thought faded when she rose up and inched back down, her core damp and quivering. Rising up. Slipping down.

—She needs me to master her, to overpower her strength.—

How could Treves know these things? Sensing them to be true, he seized her waist, forcing her to her back. When he spread her thighs and seated himself deep between them, she moaned with pleasure, her breasts bouncing as he began to thrust.

He dipped down to kiss her. As his mouth slanted over hers, her lips parted, her little tongue seeking. With his first taste, dizziness swept over him.

"So sweet," he groaned against her lips. *Like drugging poppies.*

At once, memories overwhelmed him. Crimson spatter in snow. Being kept from her when he would slaughter anything that separated them. His savage need to claim her.

He drew his head back, his gaze narrowed. "No one keeps me from you, Reginleit." When he realized his very accent had changed, his jaw slackened with shock.

I am this man she spoke of.

Which meant that she *belonged* to him. "Mine. Woman, you are *mine.*"

"A-Aidan?"

Blood surged within him as a frenzy took hold. "I have come for you." Love for her pounded in his chest, matching the fever of his need.

Her eyes went wide, the irises pure silver. "You've remembered me!"

"From the moment I took your lips."

"H-how?" She arched beneath him. "How could you return?"

He didn't know; as he drove into her body, it didn't matter. "Nothing keeps me from you. *Nothing!*" He cupped her face, pulling her up to him. "Tell me that you belong to me."

"I belong to you." Her claws sunk into his back as she gasped and writhed. "Ah, gods, I've missed you so much!"

He felt her sex tightening around his shaft, knew she was about to climax. *I will take her over the edge, will make her scream with abandon.*

"Follow me!" she cried.

"*Wherever you lead.*" Plunging into her madly, he did. . . .

Declan woke with his back bowed, his hand on his cock, precisely two quick pumps away from spending.

"*Regin!*" he bellowed when his seed erupted. He fucked his fist, imagining it was her tight little quim as lash after lash of scorching semen struck his torso.

He yelled until his voice went hoarse, until the pressure finally ebbed. . . .

He was left gasping for breath, sprawled on his bed—with no pain, no anxiety, no strain. Only after-shudders from the most powerful ejaculation he'd ever experienced.

He'd masturbated to a dream about a detrus and had come so hard, his spend had nearly reached his chin.

I hadn't known *I could come so hard.*

How had he lived without this for so long?

He groaned, wallowing in a kind of sick satisfaction. The guilt would arise soon enough, but for right now, he lay stunned, his limbs boneless.

Sick.

What was happening to him? Just like the Treves she spoke of, Declan felt like he was going mad. And, as in the dream, he'd begun having those stray thoughts, as if someone else was inside him.

In the end, Treves had been *taken over* by Aidan, the berserker's memories overriding the knight's, sublimating them.

The fuck that will be happenin' to me. No, this was an entrancement. Regin was a born killer, an unnatural, deathless female. Damn it, he didn't feel this way about her.

Go run, go train. Go kill *something.* But relaxation made his muscles lethargic, not with sleepiness, just . . . ease.

Yet soon enough humiliation begun to burn within him. Here he was, nearly comatose with pleasure after stroking off to one of them.

Where's your iron will now, Dekko? With a bitter curse, he forced himself to rise and wipe off his chest. *Stay away from her. Ignore her. Fight this—*

His private line rang. Webb.

Just in time to make the humiliation and guilt complete. Declan crossed to his console, answered the call.

"You sound like hell, son. You losing your voice?"

There was something in Webb's tone that immediately set him on edge. Paranoia gripped him yet again. "No, sir." *Just my mind.*

Webb wasted no time. "I've received some disturbing reports about you and the Valkyrie."

"No doubt from Fegley." Though Vincente was privy to Declan's dealings, he didn't suspect the man for even a moment.

"Perhaps it was. The fact remains that I've heard disconcerting things."

"She delivers information to me," Declan said. "Information *you* ordered me to get."

"Then why haven't any transcripts been uploaded?"

Because Declan needed to edit them first—so her pleas for him to kiss her never went on record. "They will be," he bit out, the harshest tone he'd taken with the man since that first night in the hospital.

A long pause followed. "Look, son, guarding the monstrous ones is relatively easy. It's far more difficult to guard the innocent-faced ones, the beautiful ones. The ones that sound like us, dress like us, mimic our species in every way. They call to our sympathy. You're there because you have no sympathy. You're devoid of emotions like that."

Declan's mind flashed back to his training—the intermittent sleep and food deprivation, the combat simulation with live rounds and no pulled strikes. He remembered the butt of a rifle slamming into his temple as his commander yelled, *"You're more of a monster than the creatures out there. . . ."*

At seventeen, he'd been shown photos of what detrus did to mortals. Hour after hour of grisly images for days. No sleep. In the end, his bloodshot eyes had rolled back in his head, and he'd collapsed.

To this day, I punish myself with photos. . . .

"They'll fill you with doubt," Webb continued, "make you question your mission. Is it already happening?"

Making his voice like steel, he said, "Absolutely not, sir." He refused to elaborate, refused to try to convince Webb to see that he was still solid.

He remained staunch, his hatred stoked as hot as ever.

"Good." Webb exhaled a relieved breath. "In any case, I'm arriving next week."

Next bloody week? No! Not that soon. But knowing it was inevitable, Declan said, "Very good, sir." *Have to beat this obsession with the Valkyrie.* Webb would see through Declan's indifferent guise in a heartbeat.

"I look forward to viewing the new addition to your collection. Is everything on schedule for Malkom Slaine's capture?"

My next acquisition. Slaine was a vampiric demon,

a *made* immortal creature. Through some unknown ritual, a demon could be poisoned with a vampire's blood, gifting it with the strengths of both species. Colloquially known as vemons, they were rumored to be the most powerful of the beings in the Lore, stronger even than a Lykae in his prime.

There were only four known vemons alive. Declan wanted to destroy them and forever bury the knowledge of their genesis.

"We've set the plan in motion." Declan had dispatched Carrow the witch to Slaine's home—a hell plane called Oblivion—in order to lure him into a trap. In return, he'd promised to free her and her young cousin.

An easy lie. After his hellish entrancement, Declan held a singular hatred for witches. And the young one had already killed twenty soldiers with her unearthly powers.

Carrow was due back in less than a week. He gave her a six-in-ten chance of succeeding. "Everything's on schedule, sir."

"Excellent. And while I'm there, you and I are going to take some time off. We'll have a proper visit outside of work and all this madness."

To talk about sports and women? Declan had no life outside of work. None. Still he said, "I look forward to it."

Once they hung up, Declan glanced around his chamber. This room represented his entire life outside of his job. The facility itself was his life's work. Now he was in jeopardy of losing it all.

Truly, how much is there to lose, Dekko? No family, no friends. No woman of his own.

No peace. For as long as Declan could remember, he'd craved some kind of ease inside himself. Though he'd never experienced it, he could somehow *imagine* what it would feel like not to know constant misery.

Declan had seen men with an expression that said *All is right in the world,* had envied them their contentment. His own da had had that confident, satisfied mien. At least, before Declan had started having nightmares as a boy. Once he'd begun running with that gang at fourteen, his da never had it again.

Listening to the Valkyrie's tales, simply being near her, was the closest Declan had ever come to it. And tonight's dream . . .

His mind whispered, *Why not enjoy her?*

No! She was undermining his resolve. And with that fall would go any pride he'd managed to salvage over the last twenty years. Whatever power she wielded, he would resist it.

Another of those creatures controlling him again? *Never.*

She would not break him. His will was stronger than hers. Than anyone's.

I'll break her.

And *that* was the reason—the only one—that he still burned to see her.

TWENTY-ONE

"You've, uh, used all your dares, ma'am," Thad murmured.

"And you've used all your truths, Tiger," Natalya countered throatily. "So ask me a truth."

It's too early in the morning for this, Regin thought, bemoaning her second week in this hell hole. She lay on the top bunk, trying to ignore the latest episode of *Good Boy Gone Bad,* guest-starring Natalya, whose voice had turned porn-queenesque.

And Thad truly was a good boy. Over these unending days, he'd proved to be both affable and kind. At least when not faced with mind-bending sights like the Cerunnos or bewinged and behorned demons.

He'd also proved curious. A typical conversation between him and Regin:

"Is there a drinking age in the Lore?"

"Nope. Your high-school self can get slizzard on Zimas every night."

"Is there marriage?"

"Well, sometimes. It's species-dependent, I guess."

"Church?"

"Define *church.*"

But he was starting to flag, with shadows under his

eyes, and he'd lost weight. He ate none of the slop the Order served him and Natalya. His jeans hung on his lanky frame, his build morphing from football player to marathon runner.

Ultimately, Regin had concluded that he was part leech, a halfling vamp, because while Natalya had been busy monitoring Thad's sleep woodies—"*Two words, Valkyrie: nocturnal emission. Just kidding, but I got you to look!*"—Regin had been noticing another part of him giving a salute.

His fangs had lengthened and retracted at intervals. The sweet kid who'd barely been broken of calling them Ms. Natalya and Ms. Regin was a leech, or part one?

Regin's beloved niece Emma was half vamp, half Valk, but Emma could never go out in the sun as Thad obviously could. So what was the kid's other half?

And why do I still like him?

First Emma. Now Thad. Regin was sick and tired of non-evil vampiric creatures messing with her millennium's worth of scathing animosity for their species. . . .

"A truth, then?" Thad asked Nat. "So how many guys, uh, you know—"

"Have I bedded? I'm centuries old, you remember, so if I 'went steady' with one guy every six months, well . . . you get the picture. I wouldn't say an army's worth, but definitely several battalions. Care to enlist?" Over Thad's embarrassed stammering, she said, "And how many girls have you enjoyed, Tiger?"

Regin could *hear* him blushing.

"I've had tons of girlfriends," he said. "I *am* a quarterback, you know. I chase tail all the time."

"You didn't answer the question."

In a low tone, he admitted, "Between football and Eagle Scouts, I haven't had time to find, you know, the *right* girl."

Natalya sighed. "How utterly irresistible of you. Now that you've found her, I dare you to lose the jeans."

He choked out, "Ma'am?"

Thaddeus Brayden, worshipped as a football god in his small Texas town of Harley, had obviously never encountered a female like Natalya. "Of course we should share a bunk," the fey had purred this morning. "I'm nothing more than a fairy godmother. If we share a bed, I can make *all* your wishes come true."

Regin turned a blind eye—because everyone in this cell might be executed at any time. And because she'd forgotten she wasn't a moral person who wouldn't give a shit if the virginal Thad got it on with Natalya.

Just wait till I'm asleep. In the meantime, she stared at the ceiling, mulling over her own situation with Chase.

After their fight last week, Chase had ignored her, letting her languish in her cell. She had no idea where she stood with him or how close he was to remembering her, to kissing her.

This mulling sucked. Regin didn't introspect; she acted. Sometimes she got it right, oftentimes she didn't, and she'd never really figured out how to differentiate between the two.

Because she didn't fucking introspect.

Now apparently she was going to contend with some kind of *internal struggle.* Some kind of on-the-one-hand type crisis. Like the ones her sisters routinely went through.

The ones Regin mocked.

She simply didn't *have* them. She did whatever she wanted to do, and she slept well at night.

Regin muttered, "*Balls.*" Then she finally surrendered to it:

On the one hand, her big berserker had returned to her, and her memories of their times together were burning hot. *Each day I'll love you more than the one before....*

On the other hand, how could she let this misery go on? Her friends, old and new, were suffering. *Like Carrow.*

The grapevine had been abuzz with gossip about her, rumors that Regin prayed were untrue. Word held that Chase had forced the witch to travel to the demon plane of Oblivion—a.k.a., hell—to use her wiles and trap a brutal vampire demon. Or else Chase would kill another prisoner.

Carrow's seven-year-old cousin, a little girl named Ruby.

The Order had captured Ruby—after murdering the child's mother. At that news, Regin had heaved, nearly vomiting energy—

She tensed when she heard Dixon's heels clacking down the corridor. *Evil Order employees going about their evil daily business.*

Regin hadn't thought anything could be worse than

Fegley's belligerent visits, but Dixon had edged him out for prize asshole.

Watching the woman pine for Chase made Regin ill. As if those two would ever have a shot.

Even worse was when Dixon gazed *at Regin*. Like the woman hungered to examine her.

It gave Regin the creeps. She wasn't a puss by any means, but the threat of vivisection was really starting to get to her. Prisoners went off to those labs one way, and they came out another. *Altered*. . . .

She'd just heard Thad's audible swallow and a whispered, "My jeans *completely* off?" when two guards arrived at the cell.

Regin leapt from the bunk. Had Chase sent for her? *Or am I about to be vivisected?*

One guard said, "Here for Brayden. We're moving him."

Thad shot to his feet, his eyes panicked. He subtly reached for Natalya's hand.

"There, lad. It'll be okay."

Regin couldn't say she was surprised by this transfer. Not many of the other cells were coed, from what she'd seen.

The second guard said, "Are you looking for this to be a gas extraction, or are we all going to play nice?"

She and Natalya shared a look. They both knew resisting the guards would be useless. Plus, it'd probably freak Thad out even more.

Regin shook her head. "Just be cool, kid. Remember, I'm not leaving this place without you."

Natalya added, "Same here. You have my word." Then she reluctantly pulled free her hand.

As the guards led him away toward the entrance of the corridor, Thad craned his head over his shoulder, keeping them in his sights for as long as possible.

Regin swallowed. His eyes had been glinting at the end.

She turned to Natalya, who looked bereft. "Come on, Nat, we both knew he'd get sent back to the minors. I've been expecting them to separate him from us ever since he woke from his stupor."

"Doesn't mean I like it. . . ."

Hours later, they heard gasps from inmates up-corridor from them. She and Natalya ran to the glass in time to see the same two guards dragging by Thad's limp body, on their way to the opposite end of the ward.

He was soaking wet and shaking, his pupils the size of saucers. "They told me I'm a vampire," he mumbled to Regin and Natalya. "Now you'll w-want to kill me. . . ." His head lolled as he fell unconscious.

Screaming obscenities at the guards, Natalya slammed her hands on the glass, spitting and kicking, her irises gone black with fury. Regin shrieked right beside the fey, her hands balled into fists so tight that blood dripped to the floor. She was murderously enraged that Thad had been hurt—and that Chase had broken his word to her.

Vincente strode by then. In a low tone, the man said, "He's only going to a new cell now. Worry for yourselves."

Regin sagged against the glass. *Gods, just give me one more chance to take Chase down. Just one more . . .*

As Declan strode through the facility, finalizing preparations for Webb's arrival this week, he decided it was time to bring the Valkyrie round once more.

His trap had been sprung for Malkom Slaine; now all he could do was wait. He'd compiled and edited the information Regin had given him about the Valkyrie, bersekers, and any impending apocalypses.

And by now, enough time had passed that he likely wouldn't throttle her on sight.

Their last meeting had infuriated him; his subsequent dream—wet as it'd been—had only compounded his resentment. *Spend up to my chin. . . .*

Once again, the Valkyrie had sent him reeling. And again, he'd found his footing. If she meant to convince him he was a berserker, she'd have to do better than her tales, her induced dreams.

He would require irrefutable proof. Until then, he'd fight it every step of the way. *Going down swinging—*

"Magister Chase," Vincente called from behind him.

Declan slowed his steps.

"You've, uh . . . you received a message, sir."

"I'll check it when I get back to my office."

"The message didn't come through the usual channels." He handed Declan a sealed transcript folder.

"Then where'd it come from?"

"It was recorded. From the listening device you planted in Louisiana. I matched it to an Aston Martin, red, current year, Orleans Parish tag."

"So? Someone must have driven that car, and we picked up a conversation. Those bugs are voice-activated."

"The car wasn't started. And only one person was inside it. Just read the transcript, sir. I suggest in private."

"I have another task at hand. Tell me who it's from, and I'll decide."

Vincente lowered his voice. "It's from a Valkyrie named Nïx. She left the message specifically for you, using your own bug."

How the hell had Nïx found the hidden device? He could only imagine what she would have to say to him.

Without a word, Declan turned back toward his office, ripping open the folder as soon as the door closed behind him.

He started to read. . . .

—Begin transcript—

Testing. Hello, hellooo, anybody out there? Check, check, one, two. Soft pee. Puh, puh. Resonance! Soooooft pee. Alpha bravo disco tango duck.

This is Nïx! I'm the Ever-Knowing One, a goddess incandescent, incomparable, and irresistible. But enough about what you think of me. It's a beautiful day in New Orleans. The wind is out of the east at a steady five knots and clouds look like rabbits. . . . But enough about what you think of me!

Now, down to business—

Squirrel!

Where was I? [Long pause] Why am I in Regin's car? Bertil, you crawl right back out of that bong this minute!

Oh, I remember! I am hereby laying down this track for Magister Declan Chase. If you are a mortal of the recorder peon class, know that Dekko and I go waaaaay back, and he'll go berserk (snicker snicker) if he doesn't receive this transmittal. . . .

Chase, riddle me this: what's beautiful but monstrous, long of tooth but sharp of tooth and soft of mind, and can never ever tell a lie?

That's right. The Enemy of Old can be very useful to you. So use him already.

P.S. Your middle name's about to be spelled r-e-g-r-e-t.

And with that, I must bid you adieu. Don't worry, we'll catch up *very* soon. . . .

[Muffled] *Who's mummy's wittle echolocator? That's right—you are!*

—End transcript—

Declan sank back in his chair, muttering, *"Jaysus."* Why in the hell would she communicate with him?

And she'd alluded to him being a berserker.

Fighting it all the way down . . . Why would she say she'd be seeing him soon? Perhaps she planned some kind of incursion to free Regin?

Regret about what?

He called Vincente to his office. "Did anyone else see this?"

"Only the one who transcribed the message."

"Bury it." Declan scowled at the transcript. "And bring me Lothaire."

TWENTY-TWO

"Gods, Magister," Lothaire said as soon as a cadre of guards left him in Chase's office, "try to contain that."

From behind his desk, the magister demanded, "Contain what?"

Lothaire's cuffed hands fisted behind his back. "That frenzied energy rolling off you in waves." It distracted him from his seething need to disembowel the man.

Chase had a look in his eyes, an almost *demented* light. The man was losing it. "I don't know what you're talking about, vampire." His visage was pale, his scars seeming more prominent.

Hate scars. I'm physically flawless—why can't everyone be? Everywhere Lothaire went, people stopped and stared. Of course, then they usually ran. "You don't? Ah, if only I could lie so easily."

The magister didn't address that, merely observed, "You appear . . . saner today."

"Alas, you are remarkably less so." *Demented and not quite mortal.* What was he? Lothaire had contemplated this for days. "It seems we are to meet in the middle." *I don't have* time *to be maddened—because of you.*

"But you're not healing as I would have expected," Chase observed.

The torture had left Lothaire wasted. "That's because Magister Chase's hospitality leaves much to be desired." The Order provided no blood for vampires—Lothaire hadn't fed in weeks. And without blood, he was barely regenerating.

Beneath his shirt, ash remained where his flesh should be. There were gaps in the skin that should be covering his ribs.

So hungry I can count my ribs. He almost laughed. *Not so flawless at present.* But Chase would carry his marks to the grave. *I will heal once I feed.*

If only Lothaire could take down Chase and drink him. His fangs throbbed at the thought, his gaze rapt on the man's neck.

Chase noticed. "You sick son of a bitch. You think to take my blood?"

"When I truly want it, you'll know. Because my fangs will be shoved deep in your neck." Lothaire shrugged, turning to survey Chase's office.

The only discernible hint of his personality was that there was no hint of his personality. Lothaire strode to one of the windows, gazing out over the rainy landscape. *She* was out there in the world. Both his doom and his salvation. He wondered how strong this glass was. *Drink Chase, break the window. . . .*

But he couldn't leave this place without his ring. "What do you want, Magister?"

"You're the oldest immortal here, and it's said you know more secrets about the Lore than almost anyone."

"True and true." For eons, Lothaire had crept through the night to drink his enemies down. And with each drop of blood taken from the flesh, he'd harvested knowledge.

His victims were legion.

"Most important, you're a natural-born vampire, so you can't lie. And I need information."

"Why should I assist you?"

"I'll torture you otherwise," Chase said so easily, still thinking himself the master of his domain and all within it. But not for long.

"Perhaps I'll make you go through the motions," Lothaire said. "I did relish your frustration when you couldn't get me to talk last time." Even when those lights had melted his flesh from his bones. . . .

"Then so be it."

Foolish! the Endgame admonished. *If you don't survive the Gilded One, then your female will be in jeopardy.* And to survive, Lothaire needed supplies from this magister. "I do wonder why you've not tried to bargain with me? Immortals enjoy a good bargain." *I know this well.*

Lothaire's nemesis Nïx might be the Ever-Knowing, but he was the Ever-Doing—forever collecting debts. Over the millennia, he had amassed an army's worth of debtors.

And every move I make serves my Endgame, the ultimate prize.

"What do you want?" Chase asked.

"My ring."

"Out of the question."

"Keeping it here invites the wrath of an unimaginable power." La Dorada, the Gilded One, a sorceress of pure evil. *The waters recede more each day....*

Just before his capture, Lothaire had spent weeks traveling into the deepest part of the Amazon, following the Valkyrie archer Lucia and her werewolf lover as they sought Dorada's hidden tomb. At the last instant, Lothaire had swooped in to steal that ring directly off Dorada's mummified body, knowingly triggering the tomb's floodgates and waking her from her slumber.

He smirked now. He'd left the Valkyrie and the wolf in the lurch to deal with the cataclysmic aftermath.

"An unimaginable power?" Chase exhaled impatiently. "I suppose I'll just have to chance it. Unless you're ready to tell me what the ring does."

"No. I am not." Lothaire's smirk faded. *Now* I *am left in the lurch, imprisoned here for Dorada to find, trapped without the ring.*

She would bring her vicious guards here with her. "I will answer one of your questions—unrelated to me or my ring—if you have twenty pounds of sodium chloride placed in my cell."

That earned a double take from the unbalanced magister. "You want... table salt? Why?"

"Why? I believe that is a question related *to me*."

Chase glowered. "I can't authorize your request."

"You can authorize anything you want. Remember, everything goes through you. This is *your* realm. Call your hulking minion, and order him to stow salt in my cell. It's that simple."

"I give you my word it'll be done."

"But you don't *keep* your word, Magister Chase. You promised the witch that she and her ward would be released if she brings you the demon Malkom Slaine. But we both know they won't be freed, even if she succeeds. You would be stupid to do so."

Chase didn't even have the grace to flush. At length, he radioed Vincente. "I want twenty pounds of salt placed in Lothaire's cell. You heard me. See it done."

Lothaire inclined his head. "Ask your question."

"Are there reincarnations? I need to know if reincarnates exist." Chase very much wanted an answer to his question. And he very much wanted it to be *no*.

Curious. "Of course there are reincarnations."

Chase sank back in his chair, his face paling even more.

"I even know a few. They owe me debts of honor." But then, most of the key players in the Lore did. *When their accounts come due, the world will quake. . . .*

Lothaire studied Chase's expression: consternated and alarmed, with a touch of belligerence. From the whispers in the ward, Lothaire had learned that Chase was particularly interested in Regin. Now a query about reincarnates?

"And with your question, Magister Chase, all becomes clear to me. The final piece of the puzzle. *You* are the legendary berserker who returns for Regin the Radiant." He grinned, baring fangs. "How ironic to say this, but *ne za chto*—welcome. Welcome to the Lore. . . ."

TWENTY-THREE

I could be a part of their world. One of Lorekind—a term Declan had always derided.

As he strode toward Regin's cell—with nothing but a pair of cuffs and burning intent—paranoia rode him hard. He felt as if every inmate's eyes were on him, but then they could likely perceive his turmoil. Just as Lothaire had.

Time to face the facts, Dekko. Regin might be telling the truth.

Lothaire had confirmed that reincarnates existed. Hell, Lothaire had specifically said Declan was the berserker Aidan.

If Declan could accept that he was a reincarnate, then what would stop him from accepting he was a berserker? And vice versa?

Which would mean that some long-dead warlord was fighting to take over his already damaged mind.

And I'm ceding territory to him.

This would be the first time Declan had felt such a loss of power—and an impotent loss of will—since the night those things tied him down and fed from his flesh. . . .

Am I more a part of their *world than I've ever feared?*

He narrowed his eyes as he passed prisoners. *Are they all bloody lookin' at me?*

Going mad. Long time coming.

When he turned to stare one creature down, Declan caught a reflection of his eyes in the glass. Dear God, were they glowing?

He knew how to fool psych evaluations, but how could he disguise a physical reaction like that?

And lying to Webb would prove much more difficult. He could almost see the disappointment and disgust on the man's aging face.

No, Declan couldn't accept this, couldn't simply surrender his entire existence. *Fight it all the way down.*

Which was why his footsteps were taking him to Regin. She was the key. Hadn't she said he'd remember all with their first kiss?

He was ready to test it out. *Fuck it.* To prove either him or her a liar at last.

Chase stood outside Regin's cell with his eyes blazing, looking . . . shell-shocked.

For some reason, his soulless, cold façade seemed to be cracking right before her eyes.

He opened the cell without the usual b.s. security protocols, then stormed inside. His hand shot out to seize her upper arm, yanking her to her feet.

Though Regin didn't resist as he cuffed her, Natalya snapped, "What the hell are you doing, Magister?"

She told Natalya in the old tongue, "This could be my last chance. Let it go."

The fey backed away and answered in the same, "Good luck, Valkyrie."

The cell door closed behind them. As Chase dragged her down the corridor, his grip on Regin's arm was like a vise.

"Chase, let up!"

"Silence." With another yank, he forced her along the ward to his quarters.

They passed Carrow's cell. She was indeed absent, but there were three new inmates in addition to the sorceress from before: two more Sorceri—Portia, the Queen of Stone, and Emberine, the Queen of Flames. Both hard-core evil.

And then there was Ruby, the motherless little witch, imprisoned in this house of horrors. Had Chase himself been the one who'd orphaned her?

The girl gazed up at Regin. Her green eyes were puffy from crying, but she put up her pointed chin and defiantly wiped her nose on her sleeve. *Kid's just like Carrow.*

And if Chase got his way, Ruby would likely never leave this place. At the thought, Regin's temper redlined.

When they passed Brandr, he banged on the glass. "What are you doing with her, Aidan? Calm yourself!"

Chase didn't answer, only tightened his grip on her arm and hastened her past.

Brandr's roar of frustration echoed down the ward.

Once they were inside Chase's office, he clasped her around the waist and lifted her onto the back of his couch. Standing before her, he gazed down at her face. "You wanted us to kiss, Valkyrie?"

Now? He wasn't the only one who could feel rage. It would take everything in her not to turn away in disgust. Could she control her temper for once?

"Answer me."

Keep it cool, Regin. Smile and be flirty. Say nothing insulting. But she couldn't come up with anything else!

"Your lightning's going off like mad." His brows drew together. "And your eyes . . . stark silver. Why are you shaking?"

She bit out, "Waiting. For. Your kiss."

He exhaled with annoyance, dropping his hand.

"You're not going to do it?"

"As soon as I'm confident you will no' bite, female."

The Valkyrie folded in her lips, as if to stem her words.

Declan had never seen this furious and terse side of her. He found he didn't like her quiet, had grown accustomed to her informing him of what she was thinking at all times.

The idea that she wouldn't be receptive to his attentions had never occurred to him. And he wasn't quite sure how to go about this. She wasn't even the same species—*God preserve me*—and he hadn't kissed anyone in twenty years. "What the hell is wrong with you?"

At last she spoke, words spilling out in a rush. "What's wrong with me, Chase? Really? What could possibly be *right* with me? We had a deal. As long as I told you my tales, my friends weren't to be tortured. Friends like Carrow."

So that's what this concerned?

"You knew I'd find out. You know the inmates talk!"

He didn't bother denying it. "I have a daily transcript of everything uttered in the facility."

"So you knew, but you just didn't care. You don't have to keep your word to a lowly creature like me?"

"She wasn't tortured, Valkyrie. Not by me."

"You forced her into a hell dimension—you don't consider that torture?"

"Not in the strictest sense of the word."

"Did you kill the little witch's mother?"

He frowned. "Another got to the job before I could. I was on base when it happened."

"My gods, you sound disappointed."

"As you pointed out, my work here keeps me from my hunting."

"I didn't mean hunting witches!" she cried.

"They are treacherous and malicious beings."

"With their enemies, maybe." She was clearly grappling to check her anger, but her lightning continued to fire. "And what about Thad? Just another broken promise?"

"He was scarcely touched."

"He's just a *kid*." Her lips drew back from her small fangs. "And how long will it be before you poison me again? How long before you let Dixon cut me open like she's been dying to do?"

Though he'd been keeping Regin's exam off the log, he couldn't stall it indefinitely.

The Valkyrie's pique didn't bode well for his aims—but she'd seemed to relax when she'd talked of the past.

"I've kept you from being examined so far because of your tales. I believe I'm due for one."

When she merely gaped at him, Declan decided to bargain with her. Trading concessions with the vampire had proved simple enough. "You said you wanted two things from me. Tonight, I'm prepared to offer you one, and possibly both. For a tale, I'll let you bathe."

He thought he spied a calculating glimmer in her eyes. But then she smiled, and it vanished so completely he thought he'd imagined it. "I *do* want a bath. And you *do* want to watch me take one."

The most beautiful female he'd ever seen wanted to bathe in front of him. And he was just craven enough to stride to the concealed panel of his room and say, "Then follow me."

TWENTY-FOUR

"So this is Declan Chase's lair," Regin murmured as she gazed around. *I got inside!* Somehow she'd conquered the worst of her temper, and now she'd been rewarded.

His quarters were similar to his office—devoid of personality, shadowy, and freakishly neat. The interior had three levels, one with a king-size bed and a massive computer console, a second with a kitchen and what looked like a weapons armory, and a third with a workout area. There were no windows.

Dark and creepy. With a forced smile, she said, "It suits you."

He sat at the console, still thrumming with tension. Something had happened today that had rattled the hell out of him. But she didn't give a damn what. She was here only to deliver one heaping order of downfall. The man before her had proved himself irredeemable.

She sauntered over to join him—and found some of the most technologically advanced surveillance and computing systems she'd ever imagined.

Budget? Unlimited. Like congressional-spending unlimited.

"Wow, look at this setup. NASA called. They want Houston back."

What a reality check. Mortals actually had power—they were organized, well-funded, determined—and they were going to use it to destroy Lorekind.

Chase was leaving her no choice but to strike against him.

She scooted over, about to hop up on the desk. Without taking his eyes off her face, he moved a neat stack of papers, absently clearing the space for her.

She took it. "Do you watch me a lot on those high-def feeds?"

"On occasion."

"Uh-huh. So now you can watch me in person. Live nude girls in your bath. Be a good magister and unlock the cuffs, won't you?" She gave him a heated look as she added, "Unless you think I can take you?"

When he hesitated, she said, "You can either remove them or strip and bathe me yourself. Gentleman's choice."

His Adam's apple bobbed as if he was picturing the latter option. But then he flicked two fingers at her. "Turn around. And eyes forward."

Eyes forward? She didn't give him a chance to change his mind, quickly twisting to give him her back.

She heard him pull off a glove, so tempted to peek. What didn't he want her to see?

Declan's scarred hand looked monstrous next to her perfect, glowing skin. A timely reminder.

I will never let her see these scars.

Once he'd unlocked the cuffs and hastily dragged

his glove back on, she hopped off the desk and began exploring his quarters, just as she had his office. He merely observed as she investigated the refrigerator, opened drawers and closets.

She tried to open the weapons locker and couldn't. "What's in here? Your personal arsenal?"

Precisely. But he said nothing. She grew bored with it soon enough and continued her exploration, heading toward the bathroom.

From inside, she called, "Taking you up on your bath offer! Tale to follow. I'll just yoink some shampoo and soap." Then she began running the water.

He strode inside in time to see her traipsing naked to the bath, that exquisite ass swishing, the ends of her blond hair swaying just above the small of her back.

He took a stutter step, hardening at once. Running a hand over his mouth, he turned and began to pace outside the door. *Go watch her bathe. She's naked but for her collar. In my keeping.* He experienced a sharp masculine thrill to have a female like that under his power.

"I don't suppose you'll reconsider washing me?" she called. "Maybe my back? Or my front?"

Though she was a forbidden immortal, he almost wished he could do both. He scowled down at his gloved hands.

Steam began to waft from the bathroom. When sweat beaded his upper lip, he hated anew the layers of clothes he was forced to wear. With a muffled curse, he entered the hazy room to find her reclining in the tub, blanketed by a mound of bubbles. She raised one glowing leg in the air and smoothed her hands down it.

He imagined following her hands with his mouth. . . .

Most immortals weren't shy about nudity, but she behaved as if they'd done this a hundred times. *A man watching his woman in the bath.* Of course, in her mind, they *had* done this a hundred times.

With as much nonchalance as he could manage—considering he was hard as wood—he sat on a bench by the wall. Enough distance between them.

She smiled at him. "Come join me."

"No' likely." To have her slippery skin rubbing against his? Half of him shuddered with want, the other half recoiling. He could only imagine her reaction to the sight of his scars.

Though Declan might not deserve to be, he was a proud man; he would never risk that humiliation.

"Your loss." As she began leisurely washing her hair, the tips of her ears peeked out. Pointed ears. Another example of how alien she was.

Yet now he was so far gone that he could admit he found them intensely attractive.

When she briefly ducked under the water to rinse her hair, the bubbles began dissipating, almost revealing her breasts. Would they match what he'd seen of her in his dreams?

He distrusted this female, had the urge to throttle her at times, might even hate her. *And still I've got to see her breasts—*

"Ahem. Should we get to the tale?" She'd caught him peering hard at her chest.

"Go on, then."

"Tonight, I'll tell you the story of when you were Gabriel, a lusty pirate. You found me five hundred years ago during the last Accession."

Wasn't this the reincarnation representing humor and sex? Declan could recognize that Regin was humorous, the things she said outrageous, but he was missing the humor gene. Nor was he a good lover. And he didn't see those traits changing anytime soon.

If Declan had been jealous of Aidan and even of Treves, this pirate should send him through the roof.

Regin relaxed back in the bath, or at least, she *appeared* to relax. She was on a mission.

She might not be a golden-tongued Valkyrie, but she was resolved to take down Chase, intended to go full guns and turn up the heat.

All I need is one kiss.

She would detail Gabriel's relentless seduction, their sensual battle of wills waged nightly in his sultry cabin. She had struggled to deny the Spaniard to save him from the curse; he'd used everything he knew to seduce her. . . .

"Gabriel was a privateer who answered only to his queen," Regin said. "His flag—a crimson pennant with two ravens in flight—struck fear in anyone who had the misfortune of seeing it."

Had Chase just flinched at that?

"He overtook the ship I was on, taking me captive."

"How did you recognize him?"

"His eyes glowed. Just as yours did after you gutted me in the street." *Filter, Regin!*

When Chase's jaw tightened, Regin quickly continued, "He knew we had some kind of connection. But he didn't question it, just accepted it. He turned his back on queen and country, wanting only to start a life with me."

Regin fell silent, remembering how nothing could dissuade Gabriel. No matter what she said, no matter how she tried to warn him: *"You must believe me! If you do not free me, you will die in some ghastly way. I'm cursed. You understand about curses—you're a Spaniard, for the gods' sakes!"*

"A curse would be living without you by my side," he said so smoothly.

"At least get me to land." So she could consult a witch about how to save Gabriel before he died, to find a way to beat this.

"Land? We do not make the Indies for months."

"The Indies?" she shrieked.

"Sí. By that time, you will have surrendered to me."

In the end, Regin hadn't had much choice. . . .

Suddenly Chase said, "I don't want to hear of the Spaniard."

She blinked at him. *And there goes that plan.* "I thought that's why I'm here."

"I want to hear what you'd tell the next reincarnation of Aidan." He got a shrewd look in his eyes. "What you'd tell him . . . about *me*."

TWENTY-FIVE

"About you?" The Valkyrie raised her blond brows.

"That's right."

"I'd tell him . . ." She dug one fang into her bottom lip. "I'd tell him how Declan Chase freed all my friends and allies, then let me pimp-slap Fegley till he pissed himself."

Declan merely glowered.

"Then I'd tell him that I hadn't really known much about Chase, not until the magister and I ran away together. On this very night, he flew me to his hometown of . . ." She trailed off, as if waiting for him to answer.

Why not play? She'd already determined his accent. In fact, he'd stopped bothering to disguise it around her. "His hometown of Belfast."

Clearly surprised he'd answered, she canted her head at him, and her wet hair streamed over one glowing shoulder. "Exactly. Belfast. He showed me around the city while telling me all about himself. For instance, he outlined his likes and dislikes . . ."

Likes and dislikes? Declan had no ready answer. He knew what he hated—his enemies—and he knew what he loved—destroying them.

As if sensing he was stuck, she said, "He liked, um . . ."

weaponry." She cast him an appraising glance. "And working out."

As close as any. He inclined his head.

"He disliked the bubbles concealing a certain glowing Valkyrie's breasts."

No' goin' to deny that.

"After our tour of the city, we stayed at this posh Irish resort—"

"Cabin," he interrupted. "He'd have taken you to a cabin in the mountains or near the sea." He crossed his arms over his chest. "Chase didn't stay at resorts."

A shadow of a grin surfaced, then she seemed startled by her reaction. "Well, this cabin was in the Mourne Mountains, just south of his hometown."

"You know the area?" His da had taken him hiking there when he was a lad.

"I've been there once or twice or a hundred times over the last millennium. So we went to the cabin, and explored the moorlands. Chase hadn't realized what good times I was. We laughed and got up to mayhem of the practical joke variety—until anyone within a ten-mile radius of us had evacuated. But don't worry," she assured him, "no mortals were harmed in the making of the mass evacuation."

"Good to know." Those damned bubbles dissipated too slowly. He still couldn't see her breasts.

"And all the while, both of us knew how the night would end. But we were purposely prolonging the anticipation. By the fire, I fed him Guinness *and* . . ."

"And Galway Bay oysters."

Again she seemed to curb a grin. She liked this

game. Or more, she liked that *he* was playing it. But then, wasn't she the fun-loving Valkyrie, the prankster?

"Once his hunger was sated, I couldn't take it anymore—I was dying to show him how much I appreciated my freedom. And I was aching to demonstrate how much I missed him. We decided to share a bath in front of the fire—"

He opened his mouth to tell her that wouldn't be happening, but she quickly said, "He didn't feel comfortable at first, because . . ." She trailed off again.

He smirked. *You're on your own, lass. And the water's gettin' deep.* "Nice try."

With a challenging lift of her chin, she said, "He wasn't comfortable because of myriad reasons that we soon worked through. Completely. I reminded him that it was just me. Just his Regin. And that I'd seen him in so many guises and had known him in so many lives."

Her eyes got a faraway look when she said, "We'd been through too much together to ever hold back from each other." She faced him again. "Declan realized that I'd never judge him and that he could always trust me. Once he relaxed, we started kissing and petting each other, exploring each other with slow, grazing touches." Her voice was growing throaty.

Declan was literally on the edge of his seat. Though his body felt strung tight as a bow, his mind's turmoil continued to ebb. He dimly thought, *This is what it's like to feel normal.* Somehow this Valkyrie made him feel . . . right.

"Soon neither of us could stand it any longer. He saw how my claws were curling for him—"

"I ken what that means now," Declan said, cutting her off. Then his eyes narrowed. "Let me see them."

She raised her hands from the water to display her little shell-pink claws.

—Curling for her man.— He swallowed. "You're gettin' aroused right now."

"I don't deny it."

"Then by all means, woman, *keep talkin'*."

Another reluctant grin. "He lifted me from the bath and laid me down on the rug." She pointed to the one beside the tub. "Which, coincidentally, looked a lot like this one."

"And what'd you do on it, then?"

"We were both dripping water and breathing heavily as he knelt between my legs. His hand trailed down my body, caressing with the back of his fingers. Descending inch by inch. On the way down, he circled my navel with the pad of his forefinger, round and round—"

"And then?"

She grinned at his impatient tone. "And then his fingers dipped to my sex. Is that what you want to hear about?"

"Aye, I'll hear of that."

"With his first touch, he gave a groan. In his husky voice, he told me he loved how slick I'd gotten for him."

Would I find her so right now? God help him, he knew he would.

"He began leisurely stroking me, making me roll my hips up to his teasing touches."

A sudden thought occurred. *I could tease her.* Since he suffered no strain with her, he wouldn't have to speed through the act, gritting his teeth as he tried to come. *I could play with her.* He swallowed. *Play with her all night long.*

Except he wore gloves. How would she react if she saw his scarred hands? His body?

"By the time he finally delved his fingers inside me, I was whimpering with need."

—She needs them deep.— Inward shake.

"But Chase was merciless, slowly thrusting them, readying me." She'd begun panting, the tops of her breasts almost visible.

"Readying you," he repeated. *Would I have thought to do that?*

"He knew it'd been two hundred years since I'd had sex last."

"Two *hundred.*" And Declan had thought *he*'d been celibate for an age.

"I stay faithful to him, always have. But Chase would prepare me anyway, since he was quite large." Her gaze fell on his erection, bulging against his pants.

When her eyes went silvery, he found himself easing his knees open for her to better see it. Lips parted, she glided through the water closer to him; he yanked the bench closer to her.

"We're like magnets," she breathed.

"Kneel up." If he was going to hell . . . "Let me see you."

With no hesitation, she did. Giving him a clear view of her breasts.

He ran a shaking hand over his mouth, muttering, *"Jaysus."* They were flawless, fuller at the bottom, with tawny nipples proudly upturned.

Déjà vu rocked him. Losing his mind . . .

She placed her hands on the end of the tub, leaning toward him on straightened arms. Her body was trembling so much that her breasts quivered, suds dripping from them. Her nipples were so tight they had to ache.

Not as much as my cock is achin' from this sight. The urge to run the heel of his palm down his shaft grew nearly irresistible. "Keep goin'."

"H-he covered my body with his own, removing his fingers to replace them with his shaft. Inch by inch, he sank into me while I writhed in delight—"

"Wait." Eyes narrowed, he leaned forward as well until he could feel the electricity sparking off her. *Addictive.* When their faces were only a few inches apart, he rasped, "He didn't kiss your pretty little ears or tongue those stiff nipples?" *I would have. Wouldn't have been able to stop myself.*

She sounded like she'd stifled a moan. "For that first time, he was trying to keep me from coming before he could claim me. He knows I love to climax when I'm being filled, but sometimes I orgasm too quickly."

Almighty. He had to cough into his fist before he could grate, "Do you, then?"

She nodded. "And he knew he had plenty of time for that. He planned to have sex with me at least . . ." She trailed off once more.

Gaze locked on hers, Declan told her, "He'd fuck you till you lost count."

* * *

Thunder rumbled outside from Regin's lightning. She was on fire for . . . *Declan Chase?*

The customary coldness in his eyes had been replaced with a wicked glint. His face was flushed with color, highlighting his handsome features—that chiseled jawline and those broad cheekbones. His firm kissable lips . . .

Somehow he'd turned everything around, tantalizing her with glimpses of what Aidan used to be like when he was aroused—carnal, a touch playful, yet definitely in charge.

And still Chase was so different from Aidan. He was complicated; she never seemed to have any idea what he was thinking. His thick accent made shivers dance over her skin.

And the way he gazed at her . . .

Those heated looks tinged with that unmistakable *yearning* were doing funny things to her. This wicked, sexy Irishman made her feel punch-drunk.

Gods, his mouth was so close. She wanted it on her own.

"Go on, Regin."

"Our tongues were twining, our lips locked so tight that we were breathing for each other. My claws sank deep into the rigid muscles of his ass to drag him closer, but by this time I was just hanging on for dear life—because he was pounding between my thighs with all his might."

Chase groaned, rubbing his palm along his length, making her gasp. But when he realized what he'd done, his cheeks flooded with color, and he fisted his gloved hands beside his hips. "And then . . . ?"

Drawing from memory, she told him, "Just when I thought I'd pass out from pleasure, he clasped me against his big body with his arms like bands around me, while he shuddered and plunged. I tried to last, but I couldn't stop from coming. He groaned in my ear that he could feel me squeezing him, that he'd give me what I needed. That he was going to come so hard, it'd feel like a thrust inside me. He had to throw back his head and yell—"

"Could you feel his spend?" Chase demanded, his breaths quickening.

Now she moaned, as much from the memory as from his question. "It flooded me, so hot that I orgasmed again."

They must have reached Chase's limit; without a word, he lunged forward, lifting her from the bath.

Declan set her on the bathroom counter, wedging his hips between her thighs.

"Chase?" Whatever she saw in his expression made her fall silent, simply letting him feast his eyes on her.

He was spellbound as streams of water descended from her slender neck past the delicate line of her collarbone. From there, droplets slipped between the swells of her breasts to her flat belly and lower, drawing his eyes to the small patch of blond curls between her legs. Just like in his dreams.

Now he nearly went to his knees at the sight. "You're so beautiful, Valkyrie." *And I have no idea what I'm goin' to do with you.* He'd meant only to kiss her, but now he wanted . . . *more.* "I need to touch you." He quaked with the need. *Explore every golden inch of you.*

When was the last time he'd felt anticipation—or experienced anything that he couldn't get enough of?

"I'm yours, Chase. You can do whatever you like to me. Just take off your gloves."

Frustration whipped him. "You think I don't want to?" He knew the whispers in the ward, knew everyone believed he didn't like to touch or be touched.

Right now, he wanted to feel her more than anything. But to reveal the backs of his hands to her . . . ?

An idea arose. "Do no' move from this spot, Regin. Do you understand me?"

She gave him a sarcastic salute that made her breasts bob. He bit back a groan as he turned toward his room.

He ransacked his meticulously stowed belongings until he found what he sought, then returned to her, holding it up like a prize.

She raised her brows. "I think I'm underdressed."

With that sinful gleam in his eyes, Chase had returned with a civilian necktie. He didn't ask, just wrapped it tight around her head, blindfolding her.

Then she heard him tearing off his gloves, his excitement palpable.

Earlier he'd told her, "Eyes forward," as he'd removed her cuffs. And now this. So why didn't he want her to see his hands?

For long moments, she waited for him to make a move, her anticipation building. She could feel his gaze on her naked body and suspected he was deciding *where* to touch her first.

Finally he grazed the pads of his fingers over her cheekbone. She shivered as he rasped, "Soft as silk."

Gods, it'd been so long since a man had caressed her.

Another long hesitation. Then he ran a finger over the pointed tip of her ear.

She began to squirm.

"You like that?"

"Uh-huh." Wondering where he'd touch her next grew maddening.

When he traced the tip of her other ear and her nipples tightened into aching points, he hissed in a breath.

Touch them, she inwardly begged.

Instead, he brushed his big knuckles along her jawline. "You look so delicate, Regin. Deceptively so."

Though she couldn't see, the scene was vivid enough to her. With each hesitation, she knew he was deliberating over which part he wanted to feel next. As if he was sampling her.

And she wanted to sample back. When she raised her hands, he said, "Ah-ah, Valkyrie. Just me touchin' you." He drew a finger from her inner ankle up to her knee.

She bit back a cry, dropping her hands. *Wicked, complicated man—*

He swept his thumb over her bottom lip, and she softly moaned, just stopping herself from darting her tongue to his finger.

She'd begun swaying from the sensual onslaught. "Chase, do you . . . do you like the way I feel?"

Moments passed in silence. Then his finger circled her nipple.

When she cried out, arching her back for more, he groaned, "*I like it.*"

TWENTY-SIX

Declan had never seen anything like the sight before him. The Valkyrie was trembling, panting, her nipples rock-hard. Her responses had him in a lather to come—the little sounds she made, her expressive mouth, her soft, sensitive skin.

He could stroke himself off right here, but this teasing her excited him like nothing ever had. In this, his will was her will. If he decided he'd keep her on the edge, then that was where she'd stay. The idea was erotic as hell.

How had he missed out on this for so long? To go without stroking a woman's giving flesh?

But even as the thought arose, he knew his reaction was due to her. The Valkyrie was special to him in some way, her pleasure important.

For twenty bleak years, he'd convinced himself that he was cold and unfeeling, that he wasn't burdened by a man's needs.

No longer. *I need* her. "Where do you want me to touch you, Regin?"

She jutted those breathtaking breasts.

"There?" Just to keep her guessing, he would *not* be touching her there. Not yet.

"Uh-huh."

Instead, he leaned in, grazing his lips over the tip of her ear. *Sexy little ears.*

She shivered wildly. "Chase!"

Thrilling. After a pause, he reached around her and dragged his nails across her arse.

Her plaintive moans came quicker and quicker.

I could make her orgasm. Just from this game. He'd never felt a rush like this, as if a mystery he'd long pondered was being revealed—

She pressed her hand against her flat belly and began sliding it down.

She would touch herself? In front of him? He groaned, wanting to see her rubbing her sex, but that was for another night. "No, Regin."

"Then let me touch you." She reached for his chest.

"Put your damned hands down," he snapped, knowing she'd be horrified by the feel of his skin. "Sit on them."

"Chase—"

"Do it."

After a hesitation, she did. He rewarded her by tracing her ear with his lips again. Directly beside it, he murmured, "Are you wet?"

She could only moan in answer.

"Show me, then." He skimmed his finger along one taut inner thigh, and she dutifully spread her legs, revealing her glistening sex. At the sight, his cock pulsed so hard, he thought he might spill at once.

His control was in shreds. *Have to feel her there,*

explore her flesh. He skimmed the backs of his fingers down her belly to her navel, just as she'd detailed earlier. When he circled it, her lips parted around a whispered, "Oh!"

"You know what comes next. You described it to me." His fingers trailed from her navel down, lower . . . lower . . .

"Chase!" Her skin glowed even brighter. "What are you doing to me? I-I'm *close.*"

He'd bring her over the edge. With his other hand, he finally rubbed his thumb back and forth over one nipple.

"Oh, my gods," she breathed, licking her lips. His gaze was rapt on her darting tongue.

Declan had imagined her kiss, had dreamed of it. No longer could he deny himself the taste of her sweet lips. *To catch her cries as she goes over the edge?* With his fingers still teasing, he leaned in, dipping his head, his lips hovering just above hers.

"Chase?" It was as if a spell had been broken. Before she'd been arching to his touch, her body begging for more. Now she drew back from him. "Wait, I . . . just hold on a minute, just let me think."

"Woman, you've been pushin' me for just this."

She lowered her head, whispering, "I can't do it."

"You can." He pinched her chin, holding her face up. "You *will.*"

"Shh." Her ears twitched. "Someone's here."

"You're just saying that—" Then he heard it too. Footsteps within his chambers, heading for the bathroom. He was about to kill whoever was stupid enough to interrupt this.

After I've waited so goddamn long?

She reached for the tie, and he yanked on his gloves—

"Son, get away from her."

"Webb." Here. Three days early.

When Declan threw a towel over her, he saw her silvery eyes were wide. He moved in front of her, hissing under his breath, "I will protect you." Then he turned to his commander, battling the urge to bare his fucking teeth that the man had seen her unclothed.

"Declan, what the hell are you doing with this prisoner?"

Risking everything . . .

Regin couldn't decide whether she was irate or grateful about this Webb's interruption.

How had things with Chase burned so totally out of control? She was supposed to put him under her spell. Instead, just the opposite had happened. . . .

Webb swept his gaze over her with a look of revulsion. Her eyes slitted. *Right back at you.*

He was big, not tall like Chase, but burlier. He wore a military uniform and sported a salt-and-pepper buzz cut.

By Chase's reaction, Webb was a superior officer. Yet Chase faced him with his shoulders back and said, "I want her."

"You *what*?" Webb's gray brows shot up, his forehead creasing.

Dude's about as shocked as I am. She knotted the towel around her chest, then hopped down to watch the exchange.

Chase stretched his arm in front of her protectively. "I'll continue to do whatever you ask, but she belongs to me."

"Listen to what you're saying!"

"You're going to let me take her from here, to an older facility. Someplace where I alone will see her."

Chase was *telling* a superior what's what? Gods, his arrogance was magnificent—and so familiar. Aidan had expected Wóden to bestow ohalla on him; now Chase was *demanding* Regin as his due.

"No, you don't want her, son. She's just made you think that you do. Ask the Valkyrie why she's tried so hard to get you to remember this Aidan."

"What are you talking about?"

"Tell, him, female," Webb said. "Tell him how you've been trying to kill him."

Oh, shit.

Chase turned to her. "What is this?"

From behind him, Webb said, "She believes you're her lover reincarnated."

"Aye. She's told me as much."

"Has she told you that every man she's slept with has died within hours of it? She believes you're cursed to perish in each lifetime as soon as you claim her."

Shit, shit!

"Deny it," Chase commanded her.

She gazed up at him, knowing she should lie. . . . "I can't deny it."

"And her lips have a drugging effect—like a narcotic," Webb continued. "That's why she was coaxing you to kiss her. She planned to seduce you, and then you'd perish like the others, allowing her to escape."

Between gritted teeth, Chase said, "How do you know this?"

"The transcripts from her cell. We had her conversations translated by a new source. She told her cell mate that this was her plan for escape—your death."

What new source? When I find out—

Chase launched a fist into the wall beside her head. "You fuckin' bitch, deny this!"

She sucked in a breath at the lost look in his eyes, the palpable pain. "What did you expect me to do, Chase? Calmly await my torture?"

His fists tightened even more, his muscles growing as rage welled inside him.

She stared up at him. "Hit me, Magister. Make this easy for me."

Again Declan couldn't. *Damn her!* He roared, "Get her away from me!"

Webb grabbed her arm, shoving her out of the room. "Declan, come to my office in an hour. We'll talk once you've had some time to process all this."

And then they were gone. Leaving him alone in his chambers, where he'd likely go mad.

So it's over. The excitement he'd felt. The pleasure. *The highest high to the lowest low.*

Feeling dead inside, he sat at his console, watching the feed of her cell for the last time.

Such a fuckin' fool, Dekko. You knew they weren't to be trusted.

He saw Webb shove her into the cell. She was still in that towel, her clothes bundled in her arms. She swung her head up to face the camera, eyes silvery.

Declan ran his gloved fingers down the monitor over her image. Then he punched the screen.

TWENTY-SEVEN

"I never expected this from you," Webb told him. His military bearing was even more pronounced tonight, though he used to relax around Declan. "Never from you, son."

Webb's censure was killing him. Declan respected him more than any other man. It was bad enough that Declan had fucked up so completely, but for Webb to know about his transgression was too much.

"Your clearance will be downgraded. Your print won't work on prisoners' bindings."

Not mind-wiped? Not cast out?

"And Fegley will take over your captures."

"You're putting him in charge of Malkom Slaine?"

"Fegley's loyal to this cause. Loyal to the bone."

"He gets off on the power here."

"As opposed to getting off on the inmates here?" Webb rubbed his hand over his face. "You know I look upon you as a son. And your work here isn't finished. I will try to smooth this over as best as I can."

Fixing things for me yet again.

"But, Declan, I have to know you can beat this obsession with the Valkyrie."

"Consider it beaten." There was no gut-wrenching

pain in his body, no urgency or crippling tension. Inside he felt cold as ash.

It didn't matter whether Declan believed she had the power to destroy him. *She* had, which meant she'd been actively endeavoring to murder him. All the seduction, all the charm to win him over . . . all bullshite.

He'd been an easy mark, yearning for what she'd seemed to offer.

And until he'd discovered the truth, he'd at last had the briefest taste of . . . peace.

Now he knew exactly what he was missing. *Fuckin' hate her!*

"How can I trust that?" Webb demanded. "When you broke every regulation to see her repeatedly in your quarters? You of all people should know what they're capable of. Have you forgotten about your parents? How do you think they'd feel about your involvement with a female *who's not human*?"

Declan stared straight ahead, berating himself for this fall far worse than Webb ever could.

"It's us against them. There's no middle ground. You're either on our side or you align with the detrus that *fed* on your family. Fed on *you*. What's it to be, Declan?"

"I'm loyal to the Order."

"Good. Then you'll accompany Fegley in Slaine's capture, shadow the warden for once. Just as a precaution."

The idea grated. "Why?"

"Because you're the only one who could stop that

demon if he got loose on our plane. After that, you'll take some time off base."

"*Now,* sir?" Who would interrogate Slaine? Who would make sure his blood got destroyed so no one was ever tempted to miscreate another like him?

Webb steepled his fingers, a gesture Declan now realized he'd emulated. He'd emulated much about the man. "I'd been coming to see you tonight to tell you some exciting news, the kind you crave most. But now I don't know if you deserve the mission. . . ."

Declan's body shot through with tension. "You found Neoptera." Their nests were rare; it'd been years since Declan had encountered any of their kind.

"Yes. In southern Australia."

Only a few hours away by chopper. This could be an opportunity to prove himself—and the chance to do what he loved above all things.

Slaughtering Neoptera. *Hatred so vicious it burns cold.*

"I need this, sir."

"Yes." The man gazed at him shrewdly. "I think it's exactly what you need."

The stench of rotting flesh engulfed Declan and his men as they closed in on an abandoned warehouse. The smell of old victims.

Which meant that they'd found the Neo nest. At last.

He and his team had dusted off directly after Slaine's successful capture, and for the better part of a week they'd hunted along the murky quays of southern Australia.

He waved half his men toward the back of the building to block off the only other exit. They wore night-vision goggles and had their sidearms drawn. No TEP-Cs tonight—this was going to be a close-quarter bug hunt.

Declan had unsheathed his sword and was ready to get his hands dirty. Ready to prove himself.

He'd gotten through Slaine's capture without throttling Fegley—a feat in itself. Acting as a mere fail-safe in the background, Declan had done nothing, just watched another heading *his* mission.

He'd even held his tongue as Fegley had taunted him. Apparently the warden had put two and two together: Declan's interest in the Valkyrie, followed by his downgraded clearance.

"Golden boy Chase," he'd said. "Not so perfect after all. Got caught with his hand in the cookie jar."

Declan shook away those thoughts, needing to stay focused. Already he was in strung-out shape. For days, he'd been unable—or unwilling—to sleep. *To dream.*

When they reached the entrance, he motioned for his team to activate their goggles, then feigned doing so as well, though he'd never needed them.

Inside the dark warehouse, the stench was pervasive. Four bodies lay tied, gagged, mutilated. An adult male and female and two children. *A family.*

Memories threatened to swamp Declan—scenes from a time when *he* had been bound and tormented, knowing death was coming.

Pleading for it.

Seeing the victims' wounds made his own skin crawl. His raised scars grew hypersensitive, as if he could still feel the injuries that had wrought them—

A male Neo swooped down on him, delivering a blow that hurtled him across the space. Four other creatures attacked as one.

Declan tasted blood, ripped off his goggles. His heart began thundering in his ears, his muscles burgeoning.

He spat a mouthful of blood, then charged into the fray.

Gore splattered thickly over the walls as Declan stabbed the last Neo, pinning its powerful body to the ground.

This one was the fourth he'd felled. His team had taken down the other.

Looming over the creature, Declan pierced its thorax to immobilize it, then unhurriedly twisted his sword as it thrashed. Its compound eyes stared up at him with sentience. When it lashed out its prehensile tongue, Declan eagerly punished it with another onerous twist of the blade, unable to disguise his satisfaction.

His men regarded him uneasily. They were hardened black-ops soldiers—mercenaries, assassins—and *he* was raising brows?

Never had he experienced camaraderie with them. For them, the Order was a job. It was Declan's life.

And they could never appreciate retribution like this—because they hadn't earned the right to it. . . .

In time, he slammed his boot down against the

Neo's head, wrenching free his sword to strike the killing blow.

But as he raised his weapon, Declan hesitated.

For years, he'd dreaded the effects of Neo blood, had wondered endlessly why they'd forced him to drink of their dead.

Now he realized they'd probably done it just to keep him conscious and alive for longer, nourishing him as they fed from fresh prey.

There was a more likely explanation for Declan's abilities. *Going down swinging . . .*

Had he accepted that he was a berserker? No. But the mere possibility made Declan shake loose his old dread, made him accept that these beings would have no hold over his future.

They would never take more from him than what he'd already yielded—days of his life, pieces of his flesh . . .

My family.

With a savage yell, he swung, decapitating the creature. *Done. It's done.*

Inhaling for calm, he ordered the team to do a cleanup, then trudged out into the humid night air to wipe down his sword.

With no more leads in this city, they'd be returning to the facility days early. Probably just as well; once this adrenaline rush waned, he'd be completely exhausted.

As he gazed down the dimly-lit quay, he acknowledged that the Valkyrie had been right about one thing. He was never meant to run a facility, to torture day in and day out. He was a hunter through and through. He *should* be in the thick of the fray.

And again, his thoughts returned to Regin.

As far as she was concerned, he was dead inside. He didn't give a damn about the Valkyrie, didn't hate her, just felt numb when he thought of her.

Aye, cold as ash.

So why did I order Vincente to watch over her while I was gone?

TWENTY-EIGHT

Declan arrived back at the base at six in the morning, limping, bleary-eyed with exhaustion, his fatigues blood-splattered.

Returning "home" from battle, like in that dream of Aidan's.

When the berserker had washed off the blood and gore, he'd found the Valkyrie waiting for him, *needing* him. Gazing up at him like he was a hero.

—Her face lights up when I come into view.—

Now, God help him, Declan's feet wanted to take him to her cell. *Oh, aye, Dekko. So maybe she can try to finish you.*

Instead, he forced himself to stagger to his solitary, grim quarters. He just needed some sleep. Then he'd think more clearly.

He gazed around his room—why had he never realized this was his own cell? A soulless hollow space. Just like his life.

Here he had no sweet kiss and soft woman waiting for him. No family. Just emptiness.

These goddamned detrus had more of a life than he did.

He sank down in front of the console, fighting the

overriding urge to see Regin. It'd been a week. Just a glimpse . . .

He pulled up the feed of her cell. She was asleep, curled on her side. She wore only her T-shirt and panties, with her hair spread over her shoulder.

Achingly beautiful.

He was expected to hate this female as much as the creatures he'd just hunted? To equate her kind with theirs? Impossible.

He exhaled. Numbing drugs or not, his emotionless existence was clearly over. He did feel, and all too strongly.

I want her so much. Even while she wants me dead.

Why wouldn't she? How many times had he told her he would execute her, or that he took pleasure in hurting her?

He couldn't begrudge her actions—she'd taken him at his word and attempted to protect herself, doing whatever it took not to be on the "roll call of dead immortals."

All's fair in war. Best not take things personally. He was a big boy; if he could dish out the pain, he'd better be prepared to take it.

No, if he was honest, he'd admit he'd been infuriated by his reaction: disappointment so deep it'd been like a physical blow.

Declan wanted whatever he'd believed he could find with her. Craved it more than a full needle.

A knock sounded on his door. Probably Dixon this early. Speaking of needles. *Better have what I need, Doctor.*

He flipped off the screen, buzzed her in. She carried a case. *Very good.*

When she saw him, her eyes widened behind her glasses. "Those hunts really take it out of you. No sleep?"

"None." He'd been too busy searching—and too desperate not to dream of Regin.

"I see. I'm sure you've had a lot on your mind as well."

Maybe he was paranoid, but Dixon seemed to be acting strangely around him, more reserved. Probably figured out what had happened with Declan and the Valkyrie. If Fegley had, then Dixon sure as hell would.

"I'll catch up on some sleep now," Declan told her, his eyes riveted to the case.

"You'll need to. Webb scheduled you for Slaine's interrogation."

"It hasn't been done?" Perhaps his commander's confidence wasn't totally gone.

"Slaine was too injured from Fegley's ham-handed capture. The subject's been recovering for days."

Declan had been at the capture, had seen the terrible power that demon had wielded. Though he'd never admit it to another, Declan couldn't have brought in Slaine uninjured either. "When is it scheduled?"

"Eighteen hundred. Gives you twelve hours to rest up." She held up the case. "Your new, improved formulation should help. As you ordered, it's much stronger—you can go every other day at least."

As soon as he had the case in hand, he parted his lips

to dismiss her, but she merely said, "Get some rest," and left.

Alone, he turned the monitor back on, staring at the Valkyrie. What wouldn't he give to sink down behind her, draw her close, and sleep like the dead?

A dangerous thought. A nearly undeniable pull. *I'll be taking my dose now, before I do something even more stupid.*

He opened the case, filled a syringe. His chest ached for something intangible; his vein swelled greedily. He gave in to at least that need, plunging his syringe.

Ah, fuck me, that's strong. Like the old days.

He collapsed back on the bed, the needle still in his arm. Chemicals rushed through his brain, his thoughts clouding. But his wasted mind remembered something he'd been too enraged to recall before.

Right before Declan had tried to kiss Regin, she'd told him she couldn't do it. . . .

Blackness swallowed him.

When Regin awoke that morning, the grapevine had news. Chase had just come back from some mission after disappearing for days.

And she didn't know how she felt about his return.

All week she'd been consumed by guilt, conflicted over her loyalties, pacing that cursed cell. Every time she railed at herself for not kissing Chase, she would remember the excitement of being with him, the pure sexual charge of his game. That night, for such a brief window, Regin had *liked* him.

Until Webb had crashed the party.

The man was obviously close to Chase, had called him *son*. In turn, Chase had gazed at the man with clear respect.

But after Webb's interruption, Chase had been disgusted with Regin and so ashamed of what he'd done with her. She couldn't stop recalling the pain in his voice, the hurt in his blazing eyes.

Now she awaited her "examination," knowing her time drew near. Chase had been enraged—he would never stall for her.

Altered . . .

Every hour that passed was grueling. Natalya was regaling her with tales of old battles to keep her distracted, but time pressed heavily on Regin. She was continually lost in her own thoughts.

One spot of good news in this ordeal? Carrow had somehow survived Oblivion and lured her target, Malkom Slaine, into the Order's trap. On the day of his arrival, Regin had seen the vampiric demon—arguably the biggest, meanest looking brute she'd ever beheld—dragged half-dead down the ward.

Yet after all the witch had risked to meet her end of the bargain and save Ruby, Chase had broken his word; he hadn't freed them.

And he'd called the witches treacherous? *Bastard.*

But as far as Regin knew, Thad and MacRieve hadn't been singled out again—

Gas hissed from above, clouds of it beginning to diffuse from the ceiling. Though she'd expected exactly this at any second, Regin stared up in disbelief.

Natalya murmured, "I'm so sorry, Valkyrie."

Regin shrieked with frustration, pounding the glass of her cell. She held her breath as long as she could. *Fight it!*

Vision growing hazy, lids so heavy . . . Both she and Natalya collapsed to the floor.

When Regin woke, she was strapped to a table with bindings she couldn't break. Her claws were like razors, but she couldn't wield them.

An IV snaked from Regin's arm; electrodes covered her skin. She craned her head around, saw Dixon and other scientists in white lab coats. In the corner, Fegley stood smirking.

Chase wasn't here? Regin spied the camera above. Probably watching it from the comfort of his room. She refused to give him the show he expected, wouldn't scream or cry.

He'd once told her that she would beg for mercy, but she'd be damned before she did. She was Reginleit the Radiant, an ageless daughter of gods.

"Shall we get started?" Dixon asked the others, her eyes glittering above her mask as if with fascination. "We have *a lot* to cover in a short amount of time."

Bone saws and scalpels were lined up on a table. When Regin saw the shining metal of a chest cracker, her bravado faltered. She turned to the camera. "Chase, you have to remember me! You'll regret the living hell out of this if you let it happen!"

One of the scientists casually remarked, "Commander Webb has expressed a particular interest in this one."

Regin shrieked, "I'm going to eat Commander

Webb's heart!" Her stress made the lights flare. All the technicians hunched down, their eyes darting.

"Dr. Dixon, her pulse is two fifty and climbing."

When Dixon raised a scalpel, Regin gazed at the camera. "I can withstand this, Chase. But can you?"

TWENTY-NINE

Declan woke to a pounding on his inner chamber door.

Vincente, no doubt. He turned bleary eyes to the clock. *It cannot say half past five.* He'd slept almost twelve hours?

Dreamless hours in a deep black void.

He flushed with a queasy kind of shame to see the needle still in his arm. Plucking it out, he eased to his feet. Dizziness washed over him as he lurched toward the bathroom.

A single dose had rocked him. *Every other day at least.*

More pounding on the door.

Declan yelled, "I'll be there in a goddamned minute."

In the bathroom, he stopped and stared at the countertop where he'd touched the Valkyrie. With narrowed eyes, he recalled her telling him, "I can't do this."

Hadn't she pulled back from him?

Yet even if she'd decided not to go through with her plan, how much of that night was real? He wondered if she'd desired *him* or merely reacted to a man's touch. She'd said she hadn't been with a man in two centuries, but surely that had been one of her many lies. . . .

He faced the mirror, barely recognizing his reflection. Pupils dilated, skin clammy. He turned away in disgust, then stepped into the shower stall.

Under scalding water, he scrubbed his body, washing away all the traces of his hunt, of his twelve-hour stupor. He rolled his shoulders back, but couldn't work out the tension knotting there.

When he hung his head under the spray, pressing his palms against the tile, his gaze fell on his track marks. *As bad as I was in Belfast.* Declan hadn't thought of himself as an addict since then, but now there was no denying it. He could shoot up for the rest of his life, chasing what he'd felt with the Valkyrie.

He'd tasted peace with her. Somehow, she was the key. To be denied her . . . ?

Christ, what did he even want from her? Having never been satisfied in this area of his life, he had no idea what he needed. No target to aim for.

All he knew was that he wanted *more* of Regin. More time with her, more contact . . .

More.

He'd waited his entire life for this, comprehended with perfect clarity that he'd waited for her. *I can't go back to an existence like before.* Grim. Soulless. Strain. *I won't.* He'd eat a bullet first.

Which meant he had to make a choice. He either accepted Regin as his, while accepting her nature and what she was.

Or he ended himself.

He exhaled a long breath as he admitted the truth to himself—he *didn't* see her as he did the rest. No longer. The Neo hunt had only crystallized what he'd already wrestled with.

When Declan looked at her, he didn't think of her as some vile detrus; he thought of her as . . . his.

He *could* accept her. He gazed down at the scars covering his body. Regin would never accept *him*.

You've come full circle now, Dekko. How ironic.

Hating those marks so bitterly, he threw back his head and bellowed with misery, slamming his fist into the tile. *Want her so fuckin' much.*

The pain in his hand felt welcome. So he did it again and again till the tile cracked and shards piled around his feet.

He raised his face to the spray. *Take her, escape this place.* He could *make* her love him. Somehow. He'd had better odds. But then he'd come back from worse ones, too.

Turn his back on his duty? On Webb, the only friend he had in the world?

Slow down . . . just think this over. Tonight, after he completed the interrogation, he would go running, giving himself a chance to contemplate everything. He'd cover the entire island if he had to, but he would make a decision.

He dried himself, then dressed in his fatigues, boots, and pullover. Last came the hated gloves. They were too tight today, especially over his bloodied right hand.

Everything felt confining, as if his skin itched. He

loosened the strap on his watch. Ten minutes till six.

He stormed from the room, nearly leveling Vincente on his way out. As Declan strode down the corridor, the man followed.

"Magister Chase, I've been knocking and calling for hours."

"Not now." He spied Webb waiting at the door of the interrogation room.

"This is urgent—"

"Right on time, as usual, son," Webb said, before immediately dismissing Vincente. "That will be all."

The guard left with a cryptic glance at Declan.

"We've heard good things about your hunt," Webb continued. "A pristine job, and back early, too."

Declan had always soaked up the man's praise. Now guilt surfaced. *I'm thinking of betraying him?* The man who'd given him a home, a job, purpose. "Thank you, sir."

"We have high hopes for Slaine's questioning. Don't let me down."

"No, sir."

Webb slapped him on the back.

As Declan entered the interrogation room, he was struck anew by the massive size of the creature, by its vampire fangs and demon horns. No, Regin didn't look like a monster or a murderer, but this large male did.

"Why have you taken me?" the demon demanded in thickly accented English, renewing his efforts to get free.

"All in good time, Slaine." Declan felt sweat beading his upper lip. Christ, that hit was still roiling in him, and he hadn't eaten all day. His hands shook. Would Slaine notice?

Dixon entered then, ready to collect samples from the demon.

"His blood's been drawn," Declan told her. "The second your lab's done, you'll destroy it." If a mortal drank that blood . . .

"But his orders—"

"Destroy it!"

She nodded, but she wouldn't look him in the eyes. Paranoia flared again.

Once Dixon collected the vials and left, Slaine said, "What do you want with me?"

"There's much interest in you. In your *genesis*. Today, you're going to tell me all about it. And tomorrow, my physicians will examine you, to see what makes you faster, stronger."

"So you can make more like me?"

"So we can make sure your kind is never miscreated again."

"Maybe you should just . . . cry?" Natalya said as she sat on the edge of Regin's bunk.

Regin lay on her side, curled up as much as the ghastly wound allow. Under her shirt, pasty skin had swelled up around an angry line of seeping staples. Her skin was dim all over. "Leave me alone," she said in a deadened tone. With effort, she turned to her other side away from the fey.

Ignore the metal wire holding your ribs together, ignore the staples in your skin.

Natalya was undeterred, actually beginning to stroke her hair. "Crying can be therapeutic. Or so I'm told. Never have done it myself. But I do know the pain will fade soon."

Regin wasn't afflicted only with physical pain—though that had been worse than any she'd ever known; humiliation seethed inside her as well. For her entire adult life, she'd been a creature with which one didn't fuck. Now she was defeated, and at the hands of a man who should've defended her.

How the demons and vampires in the ward had gloated!

"Did they put every part back under the hood, Valkyrie?"

"Nice piercings."

"Surgical steel's your color."

Both allies and enemies had witnessed her at her lowest. Even the ones who hadn't seen her still knew how intensely she'd reacted. As Natalya had told her, "You were like a nuclear reactor. Your lightning and thunder shook the building."

Regin had yearned to be strong, had been resolved. Which was why her reactions had stunned her. After a thousand years of knowing herself, suddenly she'd been *altered*.

In that operating room, she'd behaved in ways she'd never anticipated. Like a stranger might. Not like a stalwart Valkyrie would.

"Chase promised me I would beg," Regin muttered. "He was . . . right." A Valkyrie, begging *mortals* for mercy. Shame scalded her.

"The magister was there?"

"He ordered it but didn't have the stones to show. Fegley was there smirking. Dixon, of course." Regin would never forget the doctor's eyes behind those freakish glasses—studious and calm as she'd probed and sawed. There was no hate, no patent sense of righteousness.

Because Dixon truly believed Regin was no more than an animal to be utilized in the pursuit of science.

In the background, her fellow surgeons had carried on a casual conversation as Regin had screamed in agony. . . .

When she shuddered, Natalya laid her hand on Regin's shoulder. "There's one thing that'll make you feel better—and strike fear in the hearts of your enemies once more."

This demeaning ordeal wasn't merely an ego check. Anytime a Lorean was perceived as weak, others called open season. If Regin ever did escape this place, she'd be endangered from this defeat. "And what would that be?"

"A trophy. Taken from Chase's body and carried on your person. Like a fashion accessory. I'm going to own a memento from Volós before I die."

Despite her pain, Regin grew curious. "What did he do to you?"

"He tortured me for a couple of years, mainly as court entertainment. Then I was largely forgotten in his vile dungeon for about six years. Until his nephew visited."

"The one you killed."

"Correct." In a faraway voice, Natalya said, "Every night in that cell, I sat plotting revenge. With every rat

I caught and ate raw for sustenance, with every lash of a barbed whip, I only grew harder, losing myself in fantasies of killing Volós." Black veins forked out across her irises. "And before I destroy him, I'm going to tell him to send his nephew my regards. I can see it playing out so clearly in my mind."

"We've got to escape this place first. And I'm not feeling particularly bullish about our odds right now."

"You're feeling downtrodden because you've been dwelling on what Chase has done to you. Instead you should think about what he'll soon *surrender* to you. Come, Regin, tell me. How would you kill him?"

Regin gritted her teeth and sat up. "A sword stroke from his gullet down to his balls. It'd be just deep enough to kill him, but not outright. There'd be enough time for realization and horror to set in. Naturally."

"Naturally. And Fegley?"

"Cut off the tool's tool. Then nick his femoral artery."

"For Dixon?"

Regin was liking this game. "I'd force her to swallow razor blades. Let them slice *her* body open from the inside."

"Now you're talking! That notorious Valkyrie pride is surfacing—I can see it. Think of it, Regin. Retribution is within reach for both of us. Let's make a pact to help each other get our revenge."

"I'm *in*." Regin swiped her sleeve over her eyes. "Hey, Natalya?"

"Yes?"

"I'm really glad we had this talk."

THIRTY

Hours later, Declan conceded defeat with Slaine. But only temporarily. Though the demon despised Carrow the witch for luring him into the Order's clutches, Slaine still wanted her, even believed she was his mate.

I'll use that. Threaten the life of a male's woman, and he would do anything, say anything.

Pitiable, he told himself, even as he feared what he'd do if someone had a blade at Regin's throat.

Out in the corridor, he again noticed that Dixon wouldn't meet his eyes, even turned to avoid him. Farther along, he came upon a smirking Fegley, rapping his nightstick against his palm.

Vincente was nowhere to be found, though he'd obviously needed to talk to him. Disquiet settled over Declan as he strode to his quarters.

Back at his console, he pulled up Regin's cell. She was curled up on the bottom bunk, her back to the camera. Her fey cell mate was pacing.

A knock sounded at his door. After a short pause, Webb entered. "Better luck next time with Slaine, son." His tone was odd, his expression almost . . . guilty.

Now Webb was acting strange? *Gotta cut back on the medicine.* Paranoia had him by the throat.

"I need to take the vampire's ring off-island for more study," Webb said. "And transfer a prisoner as well. Unfortunately, I must leave tonight before the storm hits."

Declan was only half-listening, keeping the monitor in the corner of his vision. Was Regin's skin dim? "The ring's in my safe."

"I've collected it already."

"Which prisoner are you transferring?"

Just as Webb said, "The one you're no doubt watching," Regin turned on the bed—revealing a line of staples below the hem of her shirt.

Vivisection.

The room spun. "What . . . the Valkyrie was . . ."

"Examined? Yes, while you were resting today. I'd hoped to have her shipped out before you finished with the demon." Then he exhaled. "You and those monitors. Never could hide anything from you. Well, not much, anyway."

Declan shot to his feet. "No. She wasn't scheduled," he said slowly. "Some other creature was."

"I decided to have her examined before her transfer."

Sagging against the console, Declan rewound the feed of the O/R to this morning. Regin had just awakened strapped to the operating table.

He could do nothing but watch in horror, his heartbeat roaring in his ears, his mind threatening to break once and for all.

This had been done by Declan's order hundreds of times before, but he'd never truly understood. . . .

As they'd begun slicing her skin open—without anesthesia—she'd shrieked, her body twisting in the restraints. Tears had leaked from her stunned eyes. Again and again, thunder had boomed, shaking the camera.

She'd felt *everything.*

When they'd cracked open her rib cage, Declan clutched the edge of the console, crushing the wood to splinters. Never had he felt so sickened. Not even the night his entire family had been murdered.

Once Regin had grown insensible, just before speech became impossible, she'd begged Chase to stop it.

And Fegley had told her, "Who do you think ordered this done to you? You didn't think that he'd retaliate against you?"

That lying son of a bitch! I will bash his skull!

With a roar of fury, Declan turned to Webb. "Why the fuck would you do this? *Why?*" he bellowed, not recognizing his own voice. *She cried for me to save her. . . .*

In a faltering tone, Webb answered, "Now, just calm yourself."

He fears me. He should.

"This is one of thousands of examinations. Why would you care about a detrus who sought to kill you?"

No, she stopped me before I could kiss her.

"She's got you bewitched. Tonight I'm moving her from the island, so you can throw off this spell. I'll fix it, just like I fixed the last one." Webb ran his hand over his face, looking much older than his years. "Then you can return to life as you knew it. To a life of purpose and service."

Declan felt a murderous rage, and confusion following on the heels of it. Because he wanted to kill the man he'd looked upon as a father.

"You want to harm me right now, don't you, son? After all I've done for you? Can't you see that this is an enchantment?"

It wasn't. *Unless Regin got to me when I was just a boy.* He'd been waiting all his life. . . . "Answer me! Why would you do this to her?"

"We have to uncover their weaknesses. The Valkyrie could prove more dangerous to the Order than any other faction. Hell, that glowing one wants you dead even now. Play the feed where she talks to her witch friend."

Though he could imagine what she'd said, Declan did. As the guards dragged her past the witch's cell, Regin's skin had been ashen, her legs trailing limply. He could see the grisly staples climbing above the collar of her shirt and down her flat belly.

Bile rose in his throat.

"Carrow . . . is that y-you?" She'd coughed blood. "Can't s-see."

Carrow leapt to the glass. "I'm here!"

"Kill him, witch! Curse Chase. He ordered this. He is Aidan the Fierce. T-tell my sisters."

Declan shoved his fist against his mouth.

Regin had been right to trick him, had been smart

to do everything in her power to escape. *What should I have done? Calmly awaited my torture?* She'd known this was in store for her.

And I didn't protect her.

"Son?" Webb began backing away—because, Declan dimly realized, *he* was stalking closer.

"I understand what you must be feeling." Webb stumbled up to the next level of Declan's room. "But this is manageable. Maybe it's time for you to know what you're battling, so you can comprehend why you feel this unnatural pull to her."

"What are you talking about?"

"Son, you're . . . you're a berserker."

"You bloody *knew*. For how long?"

"We knew you were different from the beginning. You killed two Neoptera with a bat when you were just seventeen years old. Dixon only recently put it all together after she studied the immortal berserker. Though you're still mortal, you share key markers with him."

Might have been swinging, but I've still gone down. Declan was of their world. "But if you knew I was different . . ." He trailed off, his eyes narrowing. "It was *you* who sent Dixon to help me camouflage my symptoms."

When Webb didn't deny it, Declan said, "Did you tell her to keep me high, so you could control me, so I'd continue to be a good little soldier?"

"It's not like that, son. She suggested an . . . enhanced medical regimen, and I agreed. You seemed more satisfied."

"Even though you saw what I went through to get

clean the first time! Why not tell me, and let *me* figure out how to deal with it?"

"I was protecting you. You already had more obstacles to overcome than any other man I've ever known. I thought this knowledge would break you."

It might have, before Regin. Declan's brows drew together. Their kind— He stopped himself. *No,* my *kind have one mate.*

All his life, he'd wondered what he yearned for, obsessing over it every minute of the day, sickened with the need to find it. He'd nearly lost his mind. Declan flexed the hand he'd used to punch the tile in his shower earlier.

At last, he could stop wondering. Regin was . . . his. To possess, to protect. He swung a lowering glance at Webb. The man before him had hurt Declan's woman. Had removed her from his reach, possibly forever. "You had to suspect that the Valkyrie is mine. Still you did this to her?"

"Now, wait just a minute! You told me that you'd beaten your obsession. I believe you called her a detrus whore. How was I to read your mind?"

"Bullshite! Then why hide this from me? Why send me off the island? I wasn't supposed to be back for days!"

"The Valkyrie are a real threat. That subject is the key to developing a weapon to fight them—a device that disrupts a Valkyrie's energy supply. There's potential, but we need to test it on her again."

"That subject?" Declan lunged forward, his hand shooting out to wrap around Webb's throat. "That subject is *my woman*!" *How Regin cried for me . . .*

Webb's eyes went wide with fear. He tried to talk, but Declan tightened his grip.

I loved this man like a father?

Suddenly the power surged, the lights wavering. *My bloody installation doesn't have power surges.*

Webb's radio sounded: "Commander, our security nets are picking up some strange interference. We thought it was more of the Valkyrie's lightning, but this is different. . . ."

More of her lightning. The bolts that Regin had given off with each mutilation. *And I slept through it all, high in my room while Dixon cut on her.*

By this man's order. *Punish him.* He squeezed harder.

The radio blared again: "Commander Webb? Something is approaching."

Declan felt that ominous pressure strengthening, as if the air had grown leaden. But his mind was bent on slaughtering this man. "She's mine. You don't touch what's mine. You will not take her from here. I'll protect her with my life."

Regin hadn't been separating Declan from his purpose. *She* is *my purpose.*

"Commander, we need an authorization from you or Magister Chase to go to code red—"

"RIIIIINNNNNNGGGGG!" some being shrieked, a sound as he'd never heard.

Lothaire's words about the gold band flashed in Declan's mind: "She's coming. She's going to want it back." He'd described an unimaginable evil descending upon them. . . .

This new threat diverted some of Declan's rage. *Webb might just make it out of this office alive.*

With the last of his control, Declan eased his grip. The man staggered back, wheezing in breath and rubbing his neck.

Declan called in the code, then said to Webb, "Get out of my sight. Take the helicopter and leave here. *Now.* Before I finish what I started."

Just as an alarm began to wail, the lights wavered again, then failed altogether. No backup electricity fired, no emergency lights. The alarm faded to silence.

Darkness. The only sounds came from the gale intensifying outside.

Impossible. Some force had taken out all his many redundant systems.

Still rubbing his throat, Webb hastened to the emergency exit. "I'll go. But remember—you have a target on your back. Every creature in here wants you dead."

That's why I'll keep them in their fuckin' cages. Declan met his gaze. From the man's expression, he figured his eyes were flickering. "If I see your face again, I'll end you."

"After I saved your life? I was a father to you for twenty years."

"Which is why you're still alive—"

Three crashing booms sounded in succession; the corridor bulkheads had descended, sealing the wards. Both he and Webb knew what that meant. There'd been a breach in at least one of the cells.

The deployment of those bulkheads triggered an hour-long self-destruct sequence, one that could only be overridden by an officer—*after* the facility had been secured.

Without the override, incendiary bombs would detonate all over the island, wiping this place off the map.

Webb asked, "Can you secure the facility?"

He had to try. With any cell breach, the installation was considered hot, a quarantine situation. There was no evacuation of personnel. If he failed, everyone would die in the bomb blasts.

Declan set his watch as he rushed to his armory. He donned a plated tactical vest, then shrugged into his dual holster with its pair of Glocks. After strapping on his sword belt, he grabbed two MK 17 assault rifles, packing armor-piercing rounds.

He turned toward the door, ready for battle.

Just before Declan left, Webb said, "If you radio me before the sequence ends, I'll override remotely. Good luck, son."

Declan's shoulders stiffened, and he didn't look back. "I'm no' your son."

THIRTY-ONE

"*RIIIIINNNNNNGGGGG!*"

With a grimace, Regin limped to the glass—*ignore the metal, ignore the staples*—to peer out into the darkened corridor. "What the hell's going on, Nat?"

Just moments before the power had abruptly failed, she'd heard a male's outraged bellow, thought it was Chase's. *Yeah, that's right, boyo, I survived your little science experiment this morning.* Hour by hour, she'd been healing. At least physically.

After that bellow, she and Natalya had felt a weighty malevolence descending over them, some shrieking creature.

Natalya joined her at the glass. "I don't know what's out there, but maybe we'll get a chance to break out."

Regin glanced down at her chest. How far could she get like this? Outwardly, the wound was in the reddened, itchy stage of regeneration. Inwardly, who knew? As she'd begun to move around, she'd determined that she still had her full range of motion—but it hurt like hell.

She'd be damned before she slowed Natalya or anyone else down.

As the storm outside grew even more violent, the

grapevine went abuzz. Yet the inmates repeated only one phrase: "*La Dorada.*"

Regin rolled her eyes. "Who or what is La Dorada? Sounds like a snack chip—"

"*RIIIIINNNNNNGGGGG!*"

"A really pissed-off snack chip."

The shifter next door whispered, "She's the Sorceri Queen of Golds and of Evil. They say she's come for Lothaire, the Enemy of Old."

"*RIIIIINNNNNNGGGGG!*"

"You want your ring?" Lothaire yelled from down the corridor. "*Then come and get it, you bitch!*"

"Lothaire, the S.O.L., sounds like." *Serves him right.*

Then the shifter said something that really got Regin's attention. "Farther up the ward, Dorada's removed torques from other Sorceri and some members of the Pravus."

Natalya said, "Then there will be an escape. As soon as one of them is strong enough to break the glass."

Regin exhaled a deep breath, wincing from the movement. "Like Portia and Ember." Two of the Sorceri in Carrow's cell, rumored to be lovers for centuries.

Portia, the Queen of Stone, could move Mount Everest into her backyard if she felt like a climb. Emberine, the Queen of Flames, could shoot fire from her hands or turn herself into flame. A single blast from her could grievously wound an immortal. A human—or a young immortal—would stand no chance.

Carrow and her little cousin Ruby were trapped with those Sorceri. *Gods help them.*

"Volós could shatter it," Natalya said distantly. "With one kick." The creature was huge, eight feet tall and packed with muscle. "I could face him here. Finally."

The floor began vibrating beneath them. Small fissures cracked in the cement, sending up clouds of grit.

"Is that what I think it is?" Natalya asked.

"Feels like Portia's getting frisky. Hold on to your ass," Regin said. "Thad must be wigging. If we get free, we snag him then go straight for my witch friend."

"Agreed."

The shifter relayed, "Portia's bringing up a mountain of stone."

When the rumbling strengthened, Natalya said, "If a mountain keeps rising, doesn't that mean the surrounding land will start falling away?"

Regin nodded. "Yep. And we're on the surrounding land." Smoke began oozing down the corridor. "Looks like Emberine got loose." Could Carrow escape those two with a little girl in tow?

Again and again, glass shattered as more creatures were freed.

"La Dorada's coming," the shifter whispered. "Ah, gods, she's coming."

Seconds passed, then . . . La Dorada skulked into view. She was half-mummified, but sodden. Gooey.

Regin let out a low whistle. "*The Mummy Returns* meets *Dingoes Ate My Face*."

Strips of rotting gauze clung to the sorceress's body.

Her face was slimy with pus and appeared to be missing a couple of chunks, as well as an eye.

Surrounding her like a pack of guard dogs was a dozen Wendigos. They were as contagious as ghouls, but much faster and smarter. Of course, the average loogie was smarter than a ghoul.

"Look at the gold," Natalya breathed in awe.

Dorada wore cool gold pieces—a golden crown on her lumpy head and an elaborate breastplate over a surprisingly intact rack. With each of the sorceress's steps, gold flakes drifted down.

"She's altogether ooky. But I'm not picky." Regin banged the bottom of her fist against the glass, ignoring the pain radiating out from her chest. "Yo, beautiful. Come pop this collar off me."

Natalya hissed, "Are you mad?"

"What's she gonna do? Vivisect me? Imprison me? We've got a pact to fulfill, remember?" To Dorada, she cried, "Seriously, sweetheart, shake that mummified ass over here." Regin kicked the glass. "Lemme the fuck out—"

La Dorada swung her head around, peering at Regin with her one eye.

"Okay. That's freaky. Lookit, Gollum, if you spring me, I'll help you find your Precious."

Regin could have sworn the sorceress's mouth gaped with a toothless smile. Then she slinked away.

"No, no, no!" Regin cried. "I'm about to *do* evil! Help a bitch out!"

But she was gone, leaving Regin and Natalya trapped

like sitting ducks, still wearing their torques, while Pravus soldiers began prowling the ward. Once they'd eliminated the humans, they'd be coming for their true adversaries.

They'll come prowling for us.

As Declan marched out of his sanctum into the sealed-off research ward, he swept an assessing glance over the area.

Down the corridor in front of the multi-ton bulkhead, three dozen soldiers had set up a secondary barricade, just as he'd instructed them in repeated exercises.

They'd improvised with lighting, illuminating the ward with randomly placed outdoor spotlights and chemical glow sticks.

At this end, farthest from the bulkhead, dozens of terrified scientists and other support staff huddled. They'd evacuated here as per the contingency plan he'd made them drill again and again. He dimly noted that they looked relieved to have spotted him.

Dixon wasn't among the evacuees. Had she been, he would've tossed her to the fucking wolves.

Vincente was absent, the loyal guard who'd apparently been trying to tell Declan about Regin.

But Fegley was here. *And I don't have time to kill him right now.*

The need to defend his base burned within Declan. *My land.* My *territory.* He ruthlessly drove thoughts of Regin—and of Webb's revelation—from his mind. If he didn't secure the facility, all would be lost. Including her.

Declan pointed at Fegley and said simply, "You're as good as dead." The man cringed.

At the barricade, Declan called for the senior officer. "Where are the breaches?"

"In ward two, Magister. Soldiers trapped behind the bulkhead radioed that there are at least twenty confirmed cell breaches. There's some kind of foreign miscreat in there, a being from the outside. Nothing can stop her. None of our weapons. She's somehow removing the torques from specific prisoners."

Impossible. But then, how the hell had she even gotten in here? "Which prisoners?"

"The most violent ones, sir."

Regin was in that ward. "Why haven't the soldiers gassed the place?" Each guard carried canisters of nerve gas and a breathing apparatus as part of his standard gear.

When the radio crackled with hoarse yells, Declan snatched it up, ordering, "Deploy your canisters. Now!" No response. "Confirm the order and carry it out!"

"Sir, the Sorceri . . . raising a . . . and fire . . ." In the background, screams of terror rang out. Glass cell walls continued to shatter.

"Goddamn it, gas them!" Gurgling sounds followed. Then utter chaos.

The guards flanking Declan went bug-eyed. The floor began vibrating. Then came a sound Declan couldn't believe.

The steel cell walls in ward two were groaning as they . . . crumpled.

Just then some force battered their bulkhead, denting the six-foot-thick metal.

The civilians screamed; Declan clenched his slackened jaw, then ordered, "If it goes, fire at will." The guards clutched their weapons—MK 17s, TEP-Cs, grenade launchers. "Steady . . ." He cocked and aimed his own rifle.

These were hardened soldiers, handpicked by the Order, but they knew what awaited them if they fell into the hands of these enemies.

A fate worse than death.

Another pounding of unimaginable power. Then another. "Steady . . ."

The bulkhead flew open in a rush of sparks, like a door kicked in. A shock wave of air and sound clouded his vision, deafening him. Dust and smoke everywhere.

Through the murky gap left behind, winged demons soared above. Cerunnos slithered in.

"Hold them back!" Declan yelled, firing at the demons, burning through a clip in seconds. He grounded four of them, then stormed to the opening to meet the threat head-on. A volley of bullets whizzed past his head as his men covered him.

Declan fought his way past the onslaught, but as soon as he caught his first look at the facility, his breath left him. Dozens of prisoners ran free. The bulkhead to ward two had also been breached, and a . . . a *mountain* was rising within.

Two Sorceri females stood nearby; Declan recognized Portia and Emberine—the Queen of Stone and the

Queen of Flames. Neither wore a torque, which meant both possessed their full ungodly powers.

With a wave of her hand, Portia continued to draw up that colossal pediment of rock.

Emberine was beside her, incinerating any soldiers who'd had been caught outside the research ward. One shot to the chest rendered their bodies to ash.

If that stone rose any higher, the entire facility would be demolished. Declan wouldn't be able to save anyone on this island from the self-destruct. He wouldn't be able to save Regin.

Regin. Declan finally understood what his victims had felt when he'd tortured their mates.

A madness to protect.

Have to eliminate the Sorceri. He yelled once more to the guards, "Hold the line!" then charged straight into hell.

As he tore through the riot, he dimly realized that the creatures without their torques were uniformly those from the Pravus alliance.

That "being" had come from the outside to free only one army.

Now the Pravus preyed on their weakened Vertas enemies.

Regin was injured and likely still wore her torque. If the glass of her cell shattered, she'd be left unprotected. As a Vertas, she'd be targeted. . . .

Finally he garnered enough room to raise his rifle and take a bead on Portia. He squeezed the trigger and held it, but before the spray of bullets could hit the female, Emberine melted them in midair.

Then the Queen of Flames turned on him, eyes filled with malice. A fireball blazed in her raised palm. He leveled his aim at her, emptying a clip, but she'd already hurled the ball at him with the speed of a rocket.

A kill shot.

It took him right in the chest, exploding him across the facility.

THIRTY-TWO

Dorada is in the building. Lothaire mused. Here, just as he'd predicted.

His nemesis Nïx might have her foresight, but Lothaire had *insight*. He could calculate what Loreans would do with exceptional accuracy.

The bitch had come for her ring—able to track whoever had touched it last over the entire earth. But she was also here for retribution. And she wouldn't give a damn that he'd been working for her side in the war between good and evil for millennia.

"I told you we'd escape soon," Lothaire grated to the demon male across the corridor. Since Malkom Slaine's arrival, Lothaire had tried coaxing him into an allegiance, patiently explaining the value of allies in the Lore.

He himself had made pacts with all kinds—whatever the Endgame required. In ages past, he'd fought side by side with a Valkyrie when all he'd wanted to do was torment her. He'd aligned with various demonarchies that thought he was the devil incarnate.

He'd even quelled his abundant pride and sworn fealty to a vampire king—one who sat upon Lothaire's own throne. . . .

Yet though Slaine was part vampire, he hated all "leeches." He just sat there obsessing about his witch, plotting his revenge, refusing to ally with a red-eyed vampire.

Though I know everything about this world, and Slaine knows so little.

Though he was a slave in Oblivion, and I'm soon to reclaim my kingdom.

The ground quaked beneath him. So Portia was raising a mountain? Then the whispers were true—Dorada *was* removing the prisoners' torques.

At least from the evil ones. He knew he'd receive no such boon from her.

Twisting metal clanged, echoing down the hall. The walls began to warp. The glass of his cell couldn't take much more of this pressure.

Perhaps escape could be had before Dorada reached him?

No. She neared even now.

He'd brought her down upon himself recklessly, had known better. But he would have done anything for that ring—the Endgame demanded it—and he'd never imagined he'd have to contend with her in this state.

"One way or another, this ends tonight." Lothaire paced, as ready for battle as he could be, considering he still wore a torque—and was starving.

For weeks, he'd been denied blood, and Chase's torture had left him compromised, his skin still missing in places.

But at least that bastard had given him salt. Lothaire filled his pockets with it.

Everyone in the Lore knew that a Wendigo's contagious bite or scratch would transform even an immortal into one of its kind. But they didn't know much else because few survived an encounter with them intact.

Yet centuries ago, one wizard had discovered what salt did to those creatures—a wizard who'd died under Lothaire's fangs, unwillingly yielding his memories and knowledge. . . .

"I am ready to have done, Dorada!" Lothaire yelled. "Face me, crone!"

Seconds later, he spotted her just outside Slaine's cell, a walking corpse, surrounded by a frothing pack of Wendigos.

She was even more hideous than the last time he'd seen her mere weeks ago. His eyes narrowed. Though she should be invincible, scorch marks branded her decomposed skin. The mortals had shot—and wounded—her.

Why hadn't she regenerated to her full power before she'd attacked? *Too anxious to get to me?*

Wait, Dorada was removing Slaine's collar? Lothaire hadn't thought Slaine was particularly evil. And he was usually right about these things.

Who am I kidding? I'm always *right.*

Then Emberine appeared and shattered the demon's cell wall with her fire. Slaine the slave, freed of his torque and his jail? The injustice of it all.

Dorada swished to a stop in front of Lothaire's cell and shrieked, *"RIIIIINNNNNNGGGGG!"*

"You know I don't *have* your ring, *suka*."

La Dorada raised her withered arm. In a wave, the Wendigos rushed the glass of his cell. As they repeatedly barreled against it, blood and contagious saliva smeared the fractured glass, their claws clattering down it. . . .

The barrier shattered. The stench of them—of her—nearly felled him.

But as the creatures charged, Lothaire dug into his pockets, tossing salt. The granules burned their gaunt skin, shriveling it like a leech's.

He aimed for their faces to blind them. Putrid flesh gave up smoke, yet they kept advancing through that haze.

He dodged their knifelike claws, swinging his fists to send them flying. But they recouped in turns, continuing their attack.

Out of the corner of his eye, he spied Slaine climbing from the wreckage of his cell. As Lothaire clashed with the Wendigos, he bit out, "Slaine? A hand here."

Dorada swung her head at the demon to shriek, *"RIIIIINNNNNNGGGGG?"*

Slaine strode away, calling over his shoulder, "Where's your allegiance now, vampire?"

If you're not with me, you're against me, Lothaire thought as he repelled another charge. *You've erred for ill. . . .*

Again and again, he cast the rabid creatures out. But the quaking beneath his feet intensified, keeping him off balance. The roof began to sag above him as the facility threatened to collapse. He waged a losing battle.

Suddenly, the cement beneath the Wendigos fractured, the jagged line widening—

In a deafening rush, the ground opened up, creating a yawning ravine; five Wendigos plunged into that blackness. The others hung on to the edge, scrabbling for the steel rebar that jutted from broken concrete.

Under the immense pressure, the two rock faces of that new crevasse jerked forward and back as if the earth breathed.

Lothaire rammed the heel of his boot atop the Wendigos' elongated fingers, dropping them one by one.

Across the divide, La Dorada shrieked at him, her expression promising pain.

"Come and finish me, then!" he bellowed, but his muscles were shuddering, his body too weakened from the Wendigos. . . . So this was how it would end?

Dorada would keep him from what he desired so violently? The centuries of toil, the sacrifice.

At the thought, fury spiked within him, coursing through his ancient royal blood. *Think of* her. *So young, beautiful. Think of those innocent eyes gazing up at me with delightful fear.*

A red haze covered his vision. The ground quaked once more. The crone teetered at the precipice.

With the last of his strength, he sprinted to the edge and vaulted to a ledge of rock just beneath her. His hand snaked out to seize her ankle. He gave a vicious yell and yanked.

La Dorada screamed as she crashed to her back.

Holding on by the fingertips of one hand, he pulled against her mighty strength . . . dragging her . . .

She dropped over the edge. But as she fell, she caught his right leg with her claws, dangling below him.

"Join your dogs, bitch!" He slammed his left boot into her hideous face, crushing one side. Another kick took her sole eye. A last kick—

Dorada plummeted, her fading scream carried up for long moments. . . . Then silence from below, what had to be hundreds of feet down.

His relief was short-lived. The rock face began to grind forward, closing the distance between the sides. A stone mouth with rebar teeth.

Sweat broke out on his body, dripping into his eyes. He reached for the steel rods above him . . . stretching . . . higher still . . .

Missed.

Again, he tried to climb. His muscles were too deadened, starved for blood. The urge to release his grip grew undeniable.

One finger slipped. Then another. . . .

THIRTY-THREE

Battles. Everywhere. Directly in front of Regin and Natalya. But just out of reach.

As the mountain continued to rise, the entire building wobbled. The glass of other cells succumbed to the pressure, but theirs held strong.

All she and the fey could do was watch the havoc outside their cell. Though all the creatures in the Vertas had their torques, none of the Pravus did.

Regin laid her palms against the glass. "Put me in, Coach . . ."

"I'm bloody ready to play," Natalya finished.

Packs of shifters wrangled, the Vertas mammal shifters versus the Pravus amphibious ones.

Winged demons skulked through the ward, dragging humans into dark corners to share for sex. Horde vampires fed from the mortals at the same time. Volós thundered up and down the corridor, his long mane of hair tied back in a queue, his hooves matted with gristle.

Mere feet away, five starving succubae waylaid Uilleam MacRieve. The females were torqueless, which meant they were probably a hundred times stronger than the Lykae would be right now. They attacked as one, launching him directly into the glass wall of Regin's cell.

She cried, "Break the glass, MacRieve!"

His fists were flying, but the females were dusting off his blows. "Wee bit busy, Valkyrie!" He fought as if his life depended on it, roaring and flailing.

Regin murmured to Natalya, "Most guys aren't usually too keen on getting away." The succubae had ways to make males crazed with lust. "If he falls under their spell, I'm gonna look away. Really. I am."

"I bet he's fighting it because he's found his mate."

Regin frowned. Then it would destroy him to be with another female, even under these circumstances.

Eventually the ravenous succubae took MacRieve—a Lykae male in his prime—down, pinning him to the ground. The shock he must be feeling . . .

When one of them ripped off his shirt, he spat in her face. "You bluidy whores! Rot in hell!"

Beneath her hands, Regin felt the glass cell wall bulging out. More splinters fractured across it. "Natalya, on the count of three, we charge the glass. Hard. You harder than me. Because of my recent fileting and all."

Natalya nodded, and they crossed to the back of the cell. "One . . . two . . . three." They ran, ramming their shoulders against the glass. *Impact.* The wall shattered, sending them sprawling forward. The pressure shot shards like bullets into the corridor, riddling the succubae, tearing them apart.

Lying flat on the ground, MacRieve was mostly unscathed. He leapt to his feet and attacked the five, his claws slashing through their necks, finishing them off one by one. "My thanks to you, Regin." *Slash.* "And to your friend."

"*De nada,* werewolf," Regin said, scanning the area for a sword, a freaking pipe, anything.

Natalya snatched up larger shards of glass, stabbing them through her jacket sleeves for later use. She collected still more, carrying them between her knuckles, ready to throw.

Regin cocked her brow at a dead guard's machine gun. She hooked her foot under it, hiking it up to catch it.

Natalya said, "Have you ever fired one of those?"

Lorekind scorned them. The weapons were so tackily *human*. "Look, I've seen *Terminator.* How difficult can it be? Now, let's go find Tiger!"

MacRieve said, "Whoa, where are you going, Valkyrie? The exit's the other way. I'll help you get there safely."

"No dice. Got someone back there."

He pointed in the opposite direction. "And I've got someone up there. Gods speed, females." He loped off.

She and Natalya raced away as fast as Regin could manage. While they searched for Thad, Regin also had her eyes peeled for Fegley, Dixon, and most especially Chase.

"Is that Tiger?" Regin pointed far down the corridor. "At the edge of that big gap?" Through the smoke, she couldn't be sure.

Natalya swiped her hair out of her face. "It's him.

Wait . . . what's he doing? Isn't that where Lothaire's been kept?"

"Yeah. Exactly where La Dorada was heading." They tried to get his attention, but there were too many skirmishes. "Nat, go snag him! Quick, I'm right behind you."

"I've got this!" Natalya bolted away, with Regin lagging behind, limping over uneven ground. The floor was still swelling up and collapsing as if it bubbled. Flaming rafters had begun hurtling down all around them.

Yet even over the din, Regin's ears twitched. "We've got company," she called to Natalya. Pravus shifters had picked up their scent and were trailing them.

Within moments, she and the fey were surrounded by the dregs of the Lore—a motley collection of creatures with viper eyes, forked tongues, and scales. Some had crocodile fangs and plated skin.

Regin cocked her weapon, brought it to her hip. "You don't want to mess with us. I'm about to mince meat and make hay with this thing."

The largest one laughed. Until Natalya's glass shard plugged his jugular. Regin aimed and pulled the trigger. The gun kicked as bullets sprayed.

It was shredding their torsos like *cheese,* halving their bodies. "Let's *do* this! Rock out with your cocks out!"

When they'd all been dropped, Regin's injured chest was screaming in pain, her ears ringing. Her gun was hot, and she thought she might be a little infatuated with it.

Natalya said, "Let's go!"

"Right behind you—"

Volós stepped in front of them, blocking their way, his body stretching nearly the width of the corridor.

"You killed that evil woman, Mister."

Lothaire gazed up, spied some young male peering past the edge of the overhang. In no way had Lothaire destroyed La Dorada. He'd only bought himself time.

"I saw you do it—we're going to be all right now!"

He wanted to sneer, "Do I look all right, boy?" But his cause was greater than merely himself. And now victory was possible. He simply needed assistance with this predicament.

His lips curled at the naïve immortal above him. *And then I need to replenish my strength.* "A hand, if you please."

"Sure thing." He lay flat at the edge, extending his arm down. "I'm Thaddeus Brayden. Call me Thad."

Lothaire took his hand, his eyes locked on Thaddeus's neck, on the spot just below the metal torque. His fangs throbbed for that skin.

As always, he had to be very careful whom he fed from—he balanced forever upon a razor's edge—and younger was ever so much better for him.

With a surprising strength, Thaddeus hefted him up to safety. "What's your name?"

What manner of creature was he? Usually Lothaire could tell at once, but this boy's species eluded him. "I'm Lothaire. The *Ally* of Old." Not a lie. A female had once called him that. "On to terra firma, then."

"Terra whatta? Oh, yeah, sure thing." Once they'd moved from the gorge to more stable ground, the boy said, "Good to meet you, Mr. Lothaire."

"Seems I owe you a debt of gratitude, Thaddeus." Lothaire seized him by the neck, yanking the boy's back to his own chest.

"Wh-what the hell are you doing?" he demanded, futilely struggling.

As Lothaire lowered his head, he murmured, "Now I'll owe you a blood debt as well." He sank his aching fangs into the male's hot neck, drawing deep. . . .

THIRTY-FOUR

"You don't want to mix it up with us tonight, Flicka," Regin warned the centaur king. Of course, he did *not* have a torque and had somehow scored not one but two swords. "Just let us pass."

He stalked closer, swinging those swords with supernatural speed. Eyes on Natalya, he said, "Vengeance is *mine.*"

"You have no quarrel with the Valkyrie," Natalya said. "Let her go."

"She's a leader in the Vertas. This is our opportunity to crush all of you."

Regin calmly aimed her rifle. "You're an easy target. Lots of surface area to wound. Big-game hunting's my new fav—"

He charged them; Natalya screamed, "Regin, fire!"

"I'm going to grease him right now!" she yelled, pulling the trigger.

Nothing.

She banged the gun against her upraised knee, then tried again. *Oh, shit.*

Volós bore down on them with his swords swinging, one ton of irate centaur male.

Regin ducked and chucked her rifle at him—he

sliced through it. Natalya flung six shards of glass at him. They plunged deep into his flanks, but he didn't seem to feel them.

With a scream, the fey leapt for Volós's side, swiping her poisonous claws across his body. But the centaur was unaffected.

Regin realized why. The torque had neutralized all her powers—which meant her poison.

While Natalya gaped, Volós kicked out his back legs, his hooves speeding for Regin's chest.

Fire. On me? Wake up. . . .

Declan forced his eyes open, shaking off the blackness.

Fuck! His armored vest was on fire. He jerked upright, shrugging free of the armor, knowing it was the only reason he still lived.

He scanned the area for the Sorceri. But they were gone, no doubt certain they'd killed him.

And while he'd been out, the Queen of Stone's mountain had risen until the facility's entire framework shifted.

Realization sank in. There was no containment, no retaking the installation. This structure was about to crumble to the ground. It was done. There'd be no self-destruct override.

So how long until the sequence timed out? He squinted down at his watch.

Less than half an hour left.

Mere minutes to get Regin to safety, and only one shite option available to him.

As soon as he'd lurched to his feet, nearby creatures

turned their heads in his direction, ears or noses twitching. Eyes zeroed in on him. *"Blademan,"* they whispered. *"It's the magister."*

They attacked in a wave. He reloaded the rifle and opened fire, burning through another clip.

Too many of them. No time to reload. He shouldered the rifle and drew his sword, slashing his way toward Regin's ward.

In midstride he slowed, canting his head. *Regin's scream.*

Over the pandemonium, the roars and explosions, somehow Declan had heard her.

He pushed hard in that direction, evading opponents instead of engaging them. Sounds seemed to dim until all he could hear was his heart thundering.

His body began to change. Blood pumped to his muscles—they drank it in as though starved for it, growing, strengthening.

Finally he knew what to call this.

Berserkrage. A beast stirs within me.

For the first time in his life, he didn't resist, gave himself up to it. Never had he felt the transformation like this. *Because I've never done what I was born to do.*

Protect her.

Lothaire recoiled from the boy, spitting a mouthful of blood.

Blood that was part vampire, yet masked by something else he couldn't place. Lothaire wasn't often surprised, but this had taken him unawares.

Blyad', we don't drink our own! He spun Thaddeus

around, clutching his upper arms. "What are you?" He gave him a shake. "What—are—you?"

The boy turned owl eyes up at him. "Th-they told me I'm a vampire."

Lothaire spat once more. "Then they've only got half the story." He released him with disgust, his fangs aching so badly they'd likely turn blue.

"Are y-you gonna bite me again?" he asked, his gaze darting toward the frenzied combat ahead.

Lothaire scanned for another victim. "Consider me immune to your charms." He started forward, beings diving out of his way.

"Uh, okay. I'm just gonna trail behind you, mister, if you don't mind. Let you run interference."

Without slowing, Lothaire said, "You are as insignificant to me as a fly."

"I'll take that as a yes. So where're we headed?"

Lothaire absently said, "To find the Blademan." *And get my ring. Finally.* He stormed toward Chase's office.

When ghouls mindlessly rushed them, Lothaire dispatched them readily. Any creatures stupid enough to attack him paid with their lives.

The boy had begun gazing up at him worshipfully.

As he should.

"Wait, Mr. Lothaire," Thaddeus yelled from behind him. "Those're my girls up ahead! Or they used to be. Might wanna kill me now that I'm a vampire and all. But they're fighting with that gigantic horse thing. Can you take him out and save them?"

Lothaire cast him a chilling glance over his shoulder. "Aid a Valkyrie and a fey?"

The boy swallowed. "For that debt of gratitude?"

Lothaire eyed the centaur. Volós had pledged no allegiance to him.

If you're not with me . . .

Regin leapt back, narrowly avoiding Volós's hooves, tripping over a headless body. Natalya was still ducking under Volós's swords, but he was too fast. *Just a matter of time.*

Surveying the area, Regin spied another gun—this one attached to a downed guard's hand. She clambered across the floor to it, but the man was still alive, barely. When she yanked on his rifle, he yanked back with one hand, holding in his entrails with the other.

As she played gun tug-of-war, she saw Thad a short distance away. "Tiger! Ah, thank gods."

He turned to her with a wobbly smile, calling out, "You don't wanna kill me?"

"You're such a douche!" she yelled in answer, which made him grin wider. Then she noticed who he was with.

Thad was following *Lothaire* like a puppy; the kid hiked a thumb at the vampire, then gave her an okay signal.

"No, Thad, get away from him!" She snatched the gun free, aiming at Lothaire.

Click. Click. Empty? Balls! *Hate guns.*

But as she watched in disbelief, Lothaire stole behind Volós, casually raking his claws across the centaur's back legs, severing tendons. Volós began teetering, his legs bending at weird angles.

Like a shot, Lothaire was in front of him, calmly

sidestepping Volós's swords as if he could predict exactly where the centaur would swing. The vampire stretched out one long arm and severed Volós's throat in a rush of blood.

When Lothaire cupped a handful of it to his mouth, Thad cried, "Dude! That's disgusting."

"It's mother's milk." The vampire walked on as if he'd merely stopped to tie his shoe.

Still scrambling for purchase, Volós dropped one sword to clamp his gaping throat; Natalya took advantage, catching the weapon. She used it to lop off Volós's forelegs, sending him toppling forward.

"Give your nephew my regards!" With a scream of victory, the fey took his head.

Revenge. One down, one to go. "Grab your trophy, Nat, and let's book."

As Natalya sliced the queue from the back of Volós's head, Regin grabbed Thad's shoulder. "What were you doing with Lothaire?"

Thad pointed. "He's getting away! We've got to stick with him."

"No way, kid. That leech is bad news! Evil as hell."

"Not all vampires are evil—I'm not! And he saved you two, didn't he? He's strong enough to get us out of here. After we find the Blademan."

"Blademan?" Regin gazed at Lothaire fearlessly striding forward through the commotion. He was like a snowplow as beings cowered. *Lothaire can take me straight to Chase.* "I'm following him." She snagged Volós's second sword from his clenched fingers.

"Oh, fine!" Natalya said. "Just be wary, Thad. And

take this." She handed him her sword, preferring to load glass shards between her knuckles again. "Swing first, ask questions later."

When the three of them caught up to Lothaire, he frowned at his new retinue of immortals but didn't deign to annihilate them.

As they passed Carrow's cell, Regin peered inside, but the occupants were long gone. No piles of ash remained either, so Regin was hopeful. Brandr too was missing.

She spotted Chase just as Lothaire tensed in front of her. The magister was fighting his way through the ward, somehow fending off waves of creatures.

Regin and the vampire said in unison, *"He's mine."*

Lothaire turned to her with silky menace, his bloodstained face as hard as a marble statue's. "Chase remains alive for now. Or you *do not*."

Regin was raising her sword and opening her mouth to argue when vampires traced all around them.

Red-eyed Horde vampires. Who looked surprisingly enraged at Lothaire.

"We've been searching for you, Lothaire," the largest one said. "Did you think we wouldn't find out that you betrayed the Pravus?"

Another added, "The Enemy of Old has clearly allied with the Vertas, now working with a Valkyrie, a fey, and a . . ." He gestured toward Thad.

The leader said, "You freed the rage demon king. He guards the well with his queen. There's no retaking it."

"Was that I?" Lothaire shrugged nonchalantly, but his eyes were reddening. "Ah, yes. It was."

Regin had heard about him freeing Rydstrom, a

Vertas demon king, and had mulled the vamp's motives. But then she'd learned that Lothaire had extracted a high price for his cooperation: Rydstrom's vow to give the vampire *anything* he wished in the future.

"Shall we get on with this, then?" Lothaire sighed. "I've pressing business to attend to."

The vampires appeared astonished by his gall. Most of them began to converge on Lothaire, Natalya, and Thad, but a trio closed in on Regin, separating her out.

One told her, "You've slaughtered so many of our brothers, Valkyrie, over your unending lifetime. At last you'll pay."

"We're not going to kill you," said another. "Not at first."

They began tracing all around her, delivering blows, then disappearing before she could strike with her sword. The torque made her so sluggish. . . .

One backhanded her, whipping her head around. Blood flew from her lips, her staples straining.

Another's hit sent her skidding across the glass-strewn floor, leaving a trail of crimson like a mop swipe. The third lifted her limp body by the neck and a thigh and flung her into a swaying stone wall.

Before she could scramble out of the way, the wall collapsed over her, pounding her body into the floor. Pain exploded all over; consciousness wavered.

The vampires weren't finished. One snatched her hair to drag her from the rubble as she shrieked.

As if in a dream, she heard Chase's answering bellow.

Suddenly the glint of a sword flashed at one vampire's throat. His head tumbled to the ground.

The remaining pair turned on their attacker.

Chase. Standing just there. His eyes were blazing, his body larger, his muscles swelling with his berserkrage.

They rushed him. With uncanny speed, he sliced through one's neck, seizing the other by its throat.

Squeezing, squeezing. His brutal power . . . The vampire's eyes bulged just before Chase separated its head from its body.

Then Chase ripped free the masses of concrete that covered her as if they were feathers. "Hold on, Valkyrie." With unexpected gentleness, he scooped her up, clasping her to his chest. "I'm gettin' you out of here."

"Hate you." She was too weak to fight him. *So dizzy.* To black out now, with enemies all around? Her Valkyrie instincts screamed for her to be wary.

"Hate me all you want—after I save your life."

As Chase lifted her, she gazed back at the fight. Lothaire was still surrounded in a battle to the death. Natalya and Thad had escaped? Yes, Natalya had somehow snagged a charge thrower and was threatening to fire it as she backed herself and Thad out of the clash. He was scanning the area, yelling, *"Regin!"*

Regin drew a breath to call for them—

"Ah-ah, Valkyrie." Chase shoved his gloved hand over her mouth as he took off in the opposite direction.

Only when they were clear did he remove it.

"Why . . . save me?" As she struggled, his pitiless face grew blurry.

Gazing down at her, he growled, "Because I'll protect *what's mine.*"

Darkness took her.

THIRTY-FIVE

Declan cradled Regin's limp body in one arm; with his other, he struck with his sword, clearing a path for them.

Still filled with that incredible power, he effortlessly slashed through the melee. With every back and forth swing of his blade, he cleaved off heads, adding to the carnage.

Mangled bodies lay everywhere. Heinous creatures devoured fallen soldiers, raping others. Some beings had weapons, which meant that the storage area had already been raided.

He glanced down, saw a female's severed arm, still covered in a sleeve from a blood-soaked lab coat. Dixon's oversize glasses lay crushed beside it in the same copious pool of blood. She couldn't have survived that.

So Vincente was missing, Fegley likely fallen, and the doctor was done—

The floor shifted beneath his feet. Rocks still rose, flames soaring. The entire area was unstable, could cave at any second. Time was running out.

If he could get to a truck, he could drive to a small airstrip a few klicks away. There was an old twin-prop plane that *might* start. But the impound lot was too far from here.

With luck, there might be a vehicle in the warehouse loading bay. As he headed there, he spared a glance at Regin's new injuries. Too much blood to determine the extent of damage, but he could tell the staples had held at least. She would heal. She'd glow again.

I will see to it.

When he'd saved her from those vampires, he'd wanted to yell with the rightness of protecting her. The instinct to make her his woman and defend her to his last was primal, ingrained in him.

God help him—because he'd surrendered to it completely. Declan had nothing else to hold on to, no other reason to fight what he was feeling for her.

Now it grew inside of him, flaring to life like an out-of-control fire. *Mine.*

I'd die to protect her. The realization didn't shock him, just confirmed what he'd been grappling with for weeks.

Once he reached the loading bay entrance, he shoved open the double doors. Inside, cracks in the roof allowed rain to pour inside, and the ground buckled. The area was dark, yet he could see clearly. Another mystery explained—berserker senses.

Scanning . . . scanning . . . A truck! He sprinted to it, slowing as he neared. A section of rafter had crushed the engine. "Fuck!" Twenty-one minutes left. He turned back to the entrance.

Brandr blocked his path, his sword raised.

The man took one look at Regin, and his face fell.

Declan thought he muttered, "I've failed him." Then he charged forward. "Put her down, you sick fuck!"

Declan raised his own sword, pointing the tip at the berserker. "I don't want to fight you," he said honestly. Whatever Declan thought of him, the man had protected Regin in the past. "And I've no time for this."

Brandr seemed to grow larger, his eyes wavering, but the torque stopped him from hitting his berserkrage. "Give her to me!"

Standoff. "Not goin' to happen."

"Then we fight—" Brandr went still. "Wendigos near. I smell them."

Red eyes appeared in the shadowed corner of the warehouse, blocking the sole exit. Dozens of the creatures scrabbled closer, their fangs dripping, the claws of their feet skittering over concrete.

Declan clutched Regin tighter. "Fuck me." She stirred, giving him a fitful shove against his chest, but she didn't wake.

Brandr mumbled, "Yeah, feck me, too."

"We put this aside for now," Declan said. "If your aim is to get Regin out of here safely, then we're in accord."

"Take off your glove, Blademan, and free me of this collar. Or we've got no shot."

"I can't unlock it."

"And I should trust that?"

Though the words stuck in his mouth, Declan said, "I vow it to . . . the Lore."

At that, Brandr hissed a curse. "One scratch, Chase. That's all it takes. I will put you down if it happens."

Declan laid Regin against the back wall. "Same here,

Brandr," he said, turning toward the oncoming threat.

The largest Wendigo made a guttural sound, and the pack charged them.

Declan and Brandr fought alongside each other, their swords slashing, drawing arc after arc of the creatures' brown blood.

"When this is over, she goes with me," Brandr said, decapitating one in a spray of brown ooze.

"Over my dead body." Declan took another's head.

"Not a problem. After what you did to me and to her? You want to give her more of that?"

With each of his sword strikes, Declan felt that same déjà vu overwhelming him. Somehow, he knew when Brandr would swing, could sense when to sidestep the man's sword. There was an ebb and flow between them, even as they continued to argue.

"I didn't do that to Regin—didn't order it! I didn't even know about it." *Slash.*

"Bullshit!" *Sword whistling.*

"It's true."

"It doesn't matter, Blademan! It happened under your watch. You captured her. You're responsible. Gods, man, her skin is *dim*!"

The berserker was right. *All of this is my doing.* He had to atone. "I'm tryin' to get her out of here alive. There's a plane. But we're running out of time. . . ."

"That's the least of our worries right now."

For every Wendigo they took down, it seemed another appeared, closing in. He and Brandr began fighting back to back with Regin in the middle. *That's how berserkers fight. Back to back, guarding the prize.*

When the pack tightened the circle even more, and Declan barely deflected the swipe of a knifelike claw, Brandr said over his shoulder, "They're too close. Too many. I'll do Regin. Then you."

Declan swung madly. "We're not bloody there yet!" But in his heart, he knew they were.

Another near miss. No more room to maneuver—

Suddenly glass shards protruded from the fronts of the Wendigos' throats and legs. The creatures reeled, frantically clawing at the glass.

Declan cleaved through one's neck. "Ask questions later!"

He and Brandr took advantage of the Wendigos' injuries, felling one after another. Finally, no more emerged to take their places.

When a host of convulsing, headless bodies fanned out from them, Brandr called, "Who the hell's in here?"

Out of the shadows, Natalya the fey sauntered, with glass shards between the knuckles of each hand and a charge thrower strapped over her shoulder.

Brandr murmured, "Well, hellooo, trouble."

She nodded. "With a capital T, if you please."

That halfling followed her, out of breath, his eyes a touch wild, his sword coated in brown Wendigo blood. He hauled a sizable pack on his back. Containing what?

"Did we hear something about a plane?" Natalya said.

Ignoring her, Declan scraped his sword along the bottom of his boot, cleaning the contagious blood off his own blade. He sheathed the sword, then collected Regin against his chest.

Still unconscious. How injured was she? *Has to*

be internal bleeding from the wall falling. He kept reminding himself that she'd live. How many times had he cursed an immortal's resilience?

"Have you called for boarding yet?" the fey asked. "I'm a medallion member, and I'd prefer a vegetarian dinner."

Declan turned toward the exit with Regin, saying over his shoulder, "Bullshite. We're full up." He'd let Brandr aboard because he owed the man—but no more of these miscreats.

The fey's voice grew menacing. "How shall this play out, Blademan?"

He heard the unmistakable buzz of a cocked charge thrower and turned slowly. "You've only got so many shots with that thing."

"Which is why I didn't utilize it against the Wendigos. In any case, all I need is one to end you."

One shot would, in fact, electrocute him.

"Think, Chase," she continued, "if we meet other creatures—perhaps some of the many who want you dead—we can help you fight."

"She might have a point," Brandr said. "How many more Wendigos do you have here?"

"Dozens."

Brandr swore under his breath. "And that being from the outside, that Dorada, brought even more. What about ghouls?"

"Hundreds."

"Then we need her," Brandr said. "And the boy."

"We need the charge thrower and nothing more." She wasn't budging. They wasted time. Biting out an oath, he said, "We've got minutes to reach the plane before this island *disappears*. If any of you fall on the way, I'll step over your corpses." With that, Declan sprinted out of the warehouse, leading them down a smoke-filled service hall, then out into the blustery night.

Rain pelted them, but Regin remained unconscious as they sped toward the airstrip. The smaller runway there was an older alternate to the current one where transport planes touched down, unloaded, and immediately took off.

Yet something caught his attention far on the other side of the facility grounds. It was Vincente, running hand-in-hand with that succubus. He was shirtless; she was no longer wasting from hunger—

Just feet behind them, a vampire stalked closer, sword raised.

"Vincente!" Declan yelled a warning, but he couldn't be heard over the storm.

The vampire swung; at the last second, the succubus shoved Vincente out of the way and took the hit in her arm. Vincente whirled around and shot the leech in the face with a combat shotgun then scooped up his bleeding female.

Declan's mind could hardly wrap around this. *The succubus took the hit for a mortal.*

"Vincente!" he yelled again.

The guard's head jerked up this time. They met eyes. Declan waved him over, but Vincente shook his head. When Declan pointed to his watch—*place is about to blow, boyo*—the man nodded, then hastened toward the forest.

"God speed, Vincente," Declan said, continuing on. In the distance, he caught sight of the hangar's tattered wind sock flapping in the storm. He muttered to Regin, "Almost there." So far, they'd had no encounters with other creatures—at least, none that wanted a fight.

As they closed in, the fey asked, "Where's the airport?"

"You're lookin' at it."

"Is that a hangar or a barn? I'm confused."

The wide entrance doors were padlocked. Cradling Regin in one arm, he used his free hand to wrench free the chain, surprising even himself with his strength. Then he and Brandr shoved open the doors. Inside was an old aerial reconnaissance craft, a weathered six-seater prop plane.

Brandr raised his brows. "*That* is the plane?"

Declan unlatched the Cessna's door, hurrying up the steps. "It'll get us to where we're going." He laid Regin along the back bench, then climbed into the cockpit.

"Is there no other way off this rock?"

There was one, a ship in a berth on the west side of the island. It was even more of a long shot than this and impossible to reach in time anyway. "You want on the plane or not?"

Brandr followed, taking the copilot's seat. "Beggars can't be choosers, huh?"

The fey and the halfling dashed in behind him. The halfling's pack took up a seat.

Natalya reached for the pull-up door, but hesitated. "Well, well, look who's come calling."

Lothaire stood just inside the hangar. He had two MK 17s strapped over his shoulders and a bloody sword in hand. His clothing was riddled with burn holes. Bites and gashes covered his exposed skin.

Natalya asked, “How’d you escape all the vampires out for your head?”

In a monotone voice, Lothaire stated, “I’m that good.”

She aimed her charge thrower. “Maybe, but you’re not getting on this plane, vampire.”

Thad peered out. “Let him on, Nat!”

Brandr and Declan both twisted back in their seats, bellowing:

“No’ a feckin’ chance.”

“No fucking way.”

Lothaire gave her weapon a withering glance, then canted his head sharply. “I do not care to board this plane, as it happens. We’ll talk when you come back down.” With that, he turned and strode outside.

Come back down? “Crazy Horde vampires,” Declan muttered as he fired up the engines on each side of the cockpit. When both started and the propellers began turning, Declan hid his relief.

Another miracle? The fuel gauge read full. But God only knew how long that fuel had been sitting.

“How many miles is it to the mainland?” Natalya asked. She was sitting on Thad’s lap in the sole remaining seat.

“Eight hundred.”

Brandr gave a laugh. “This thing won’t make it that far!”

“There’s an alternate island site nearby.” Basically a dirt runway and a camp. “We’ll figure out what to do there." He glanced down at his watch. The incendiaries would detonate in two minutes.

"We've got more company!" Thad said, face glued to the port-side window. "Wendigos on the runway."

No time for a systems check. Declan pushed in the throttle, and the plane lumbered forward out of the hangar.

He taxied down the runway, forced to shave off as much length as he dared to avoid the nearing throng of Wendigos.

To take off, he had to reach a minimum of eighty miles per hour. Eighty, with cold engines, a short runway, and gusting winds. At the far end of the track, a stand of fir trees whipped in unison, like a moving wall. *Have to clear them.*

Brakes engaged, he shoved the throttle in, RPMs spiking, engines rumbling. Over his shoulder, he snapped, "The shite in your pack better be really important, kid."

"It totally is!"

With a curse, Declan released the brakes, and they surged forward. Gaining speed, gaining . . .

At any moment he expected to feel the plane rocked on its arse from a bomb's blast wave.

Natalya said, "Those trees are coming up awfully fast, Blademan."

Brandr yelled, "Chase, balls to the wall!"

"I'm throttle down," he grated.

Fifty miles per hour. Sixty.

At the last possible second, he heaved back on the yoke. The nose shot up, the tail sandbagging. "*Come on, come on.*" He held his breath. . . .

The wheels scraped the tops of the trees. They flew clear.

When they'd reached a minimum safe altitude, Declan's eyes briefly closed. "We're away."

The three conscious passengers exhaled with relief.

"We made it! This has to be the coolest thing ever," the halfling said. "To outrun those Wendigos?" His expression was animated. "Never been in a plane before!"

Oh, yes, you have, Declan thought, just as Natalya said, "Lad, you must have been." She spoke to Thad but glared at Declan as she said, "You were flown here when the magister's men kidnapped you—an eighteen-year-old boy—away from your mother and gram and wholesome Texas life."

The halfling turned back to the window. "Miss 'em." Then he absently told Natalya, "I just turned seventeen."

Natalya's face screwed up. "*Oh.*"

"Hey, Nat, take a look at the place."

Declan gazed back at the facility. Or what was left of it. "*Jaysus.*"

In the center was a mass of stone, a new mountain towering among the flames. Cement blocks swirled above the ruins. Even in the pouring rain, flames climbed high, like a picture of hell.

My life's work.

The fey murmured, "You reap what you sow, Blademan."

She was right. As of this night, all the work he'd done—all the effort and discipline—had netted him no home, no work, no life. Not a friend in the world after Webb's betrayal.

And it was a betrayal. Declan saw that clearly now. *He knew what Regin is to me. My female.* And yet Webb had hurt her in unthinkable ways.

Declan gazed back at Regin, laid out across the bench. What would he do now? Where to go? All he knew was that he wanted to be near her—and she'd never want to be with him.

"I thought the island was going to disappear," Brandr said.

Declan glanced at his watch. The self-destruct was now nine minutes overdue. "It was supposed to have." He surveyed the landscape below. Not a single detonation. Something must have jammed them.

For better or ill, he suspected there'd be no blasts tonight.

"What's that?" Brandr pointed ahead.

Declan faced forward. Squinting, he wiped the windshield with his sleeve. A cloud of dark shapes hovered in their path. He slowed his speed, descending to avoid them, but they dropped down as well.

The answer hit him just as Brandr said, "Winged demons."

Dozens of them. They attacked in a swarm, their claws shredded down the sides of the fuselage, across the wings.

Declan shoved down the yoke in a sudden dive, trying to shake them free. The stall alarm on engine one blared.

Brandr clamped the dash as the plane plummeted. "What do they want?"

Natalya said, "My guess is the magister's head on a platter!"

Engine one rumbled, smoked, then died. The starboard wing was trashed, the other barely holding on. Engine two roared, straining to keep the plane at altitude.

The yoke vibrated wildly as Declan fought to maneuver back toward the runway. "We're goin' down." Though trees grew at one end of the runway, a sheer rock face capped the other.

Have to slow our speed. There was nothing else to be done, no steering a plane this disabled.

Brandr gazed at him, a hint of sympathy in his eyes. Because a mortal probably wouldn't make it.

And no man could die with more regrets than Declan. He would never have the chance to make things right with Regin. Would never kiss her or claim her. Too ashamed of his scars to ever reveal them. Too cowardly to risk her rejection.

Should've taken the chance, Dekko. He almost wanted to believe he'd come back in another life.

Over the screaming engine, Brandr yelled, "I'm sorry, Blademan. Looks like you're about to check out. Again."

Declan yelled back, "Just get her off this island!" *If* she survived the crash. He glanced back at her. She was battered, appearing so delicate, not the larger-than-life Valkyrie he was used to. How much more could her body take? "Do it within six days!" Before the Order struck the final blow to this island.

"I almost believe you give a shit about her!"

"Protect her, berserker," Declan said. "Vow it!"

"I already have." With that, Brandr climbed out of the cockpit into the very back to sit beside Regin, gathering her body up in his arms, clasping her close. To Natalya, he said, "Come, female, I can buffer you too."

The fey climbed back, then reached for Thad, pulling him close as well.

"Natalya?" The boy's voice broke.

"You'll be fine, my lad," she assured him, but her face was drawn with fear. "If I had a pound for every plane crash I've been in . . ."

As the ground rushed closer, Declan's heart began pumping blood, thundering in his ears.

But he still heard Brandr murmur, "Till we meet again, Aidan."

THIRTY-SIX

Lothaire stood in the pouring rain watching as the plane came screaming back toward the runway.

He pinched the bridge of his nose. He'd ordered the winged Volar demons to bring it to the ground *gently*. This touchdown would prove anything but.

If Chase died, all his knowledge of the ring would expire with him. Lothaire had ransacked his office, but couldn't find it—

The craft landed belly first on the last quarter of the track, the initial impact ripping the fuselage in half, severing the tail from the rest of the plane. The cockpit half didn't slow, barreling toward a wall of rock.

One wing and its engine separated, exploding into a ball of fire that rocked the night. The blast pitched the cockpit and remaining wing end over end until it crashed into the side of the cliff.

Lothaire hurried toward it. If Chase lived, Lothaire could drink him, harvesting all of the magister's memories.

At the thought, his fangs dripped in his mouth. *Such hunger* . . . He'd have to take care not to drain the man down.

When he approached the mangled cockpit, the scent

of aviation fuel swept over him; the remaining engine sparked and flamed in the hissing rain.

Just a matter of time before it too exploded.

He found that Chase lived. Barely. Blood streamed down his face from a gash at his temple, whetting Lothaire's appetite even more. The plane's frame had collapsed around his lower body, metal indentations trapping his legs inside.

As Lothaire impassively watched, Chase gripped his legs behind the knees and yanked, but he was pinned tight—

Those winged demons descended all around the crash site like vultures.

Some of demonkind, such as these from the Volar demonarchy, believed Lothaire was the devil himself, born to lead all demons back to hell. Naturally, he'd fostered this rumor. Now Lothaire bared his fangs. "I said *gently*."

One muttered, "He unexpectedly made the craft dive."

"Be—gone." With fear in their eyes, they took off at once, great black wings swooping, fanning the flames.

Lothaire dropped to his knee beside Chase. "Where's my ring?"

"Fuck off, leech!" He brandished his sword from a sheath at his side.

Before Chase could strike, Lothaire fisted his wrist, wresting the sword free. "I recognize this blade. You stabbed me with it, twisting it inside me." Lothaire pulled the scabbard free, then donned his new sword. "For sentimental value. Something to remember you by."

Next he seized the magister's hand. "And now to be

rid of this collar." Though the man resisted, Lothaire tore off his glove.

More scars? Raised marks covered the back of Chase's hand.

With a shrug, Lothaire flattened the pad of the man's thumb against the torque's lock. "Once I'm free, we're going to find out exactly how much pain you can endure while remaining conscious. I won't stop until you tell me where my ring is." He leaned in to say at his ear, "I'll be sure to make you feel your *loss*."

Chase sneered, "My print won't work."

Lothaire pressed his thumb on the pad again. "You lie." He snatched off Chase's remaining glove to test his other print. Nothing.

"If you want your torque removed, go find Fegley. Tell him I sent you."

"Didn't you hear? The warden is dead. Emberine burned the man alive." After his hand had been removed to use as a key. But the *suka* wouldn't bargain for it, had threatened to incinerate it if Lothaire neared her.

So I'm still trapped. "Then you remain of use to me, Chase. You know of another way off this island."

"Of course I do."

"You *will* share it. But must I dismember you first?" Once Lothaire drank Chase, he'd garner knowledge of any potential escape to be had. But those stolen memories were difficult to access at will, no matter how hard he'd trained to do just that.

Most of the time the memories came in the form of dreams. *How much sleeping will I be doing until I escape? Until I seize* her?

The magister's body twisted as the flames began to lick closer to his legs. As if he could see his female, Chase stretched one arm out, reaching in her direction. His eyes glowed with fear—but clearly not for himself.

He would be particularly keen to bargain. "I *do* hope your female's faring better than you. If she survived the crash, she could be at the mercy of those winged demons. Lusty devils. They won't kill her; they'll keep her as a concubine. For centuries. They'll breed on her as well, of course."

Chase yelled, thrashing against the metal.

"You want to get to her more than anything," Lothaire murmured. "You want it so badly, you're dumbfounded that you can't get free."

Another violent thrash.

"Now you understand what it's like to be kept from your female when she is in danger. To have some enemy gloating, while you are trapped and powerless, unable to defend her. But what if I pulled you free and you were able to go to her?"

"Do it! Free me!"

"You'd have to cede things in return. You stole my property, jailed me for weeks, starved and tortured me. So many debts to pay. The scales between us tip so heavily against you, I probably should just kill you."

"You want to deal? Then do it!"

"My ring. I must have it."

"It was taken off the island tonight. I don't know where."

"*Blyad'!* Then what else do you have? What will clear the slate between us?"

"The Order will strike this installation within six days," Chase grated. "But there's a boat a few days from here. I vow to lead you to it, if you free me now."

A few days? *Cutting it so close.*

Lothaire would require blood in the interim. Normally he fed only every week or so, but he was still regenerating. And he'd need all the power he could steal to compensate for this torque.

"I'll allow this to cancel out my stolen property and to pay for jailing me for weeks. You will be my guide—and my prisoner." He examined his black claws. "Next?"

"*What?*"

"To pay for starving and torturing me. What could possibly be recompense for that?"

Chase's eyes darted. "I don't . . . know. Damn it, pull me free so I can think!"

"I can't stand to see all this good blood going to waste, seared to nothing."

The magister's face paled even more. "The fuck you'll be drinkin' me!"

"When you tortured me, I told you I'd make you pay in ways you couldn't imagine."

As ever, I was right. Lothaire almost sighed. *The world is so tediously predictable.* Speaking over Chase's furious railings, Lothaire said, "Until we escape, I want you to *yield* your blood to me."

Submitting to my bite. Nothing would humiliate a man like Chase more, nothing could bring him so low. Though Lothaire was calculating—choosing to serve the Endgame, rather than his emotions—he *was* a vindictive son of a bitch.

* * *

"Never." The scent of flames and volatile aviation fuel oozed over Declan. "Just free me!" The nearing fire, the *frustration*. He was going to burn to death without reaching Regin. And if he died, who would get her off this island before the Order retaliated?

The vampire said, "Someone will pay for the damage you did. Perhaps your woman? Yes, I should go pierce her bright flesh. If she lives yet."

"Don't you *fuckin' dare.*"

"Poor Regin. She could be bleeding out, or about to burn like you. Ah, she looked so weak, too. She could actually perish." He tsked. "A legendary being like that, her life force extinguished forever. Because you wouldn't surrender mere drops of your blood. And possibly a memory or two."

"No, no!"

Lothaire rose. "Her blood will be sublime."

"Don't touch her!" *Touch what's mine, and I'll punish you.*

Lothaire knelt once more. "I want all the blood I can drink from you, Magister. Whenever and *however* I choose to drink it until we leave this island."

However? Declan didn't understand, couldn't think. The metal frame of the plane was heating all around him, searing his skin. He would give his life to save hers, but surrendering his blood to a detrus . . . ?

To have another one of these creatures feeding from his body?

"Never mind. I'll return with her head, so the two of you can fry together." Lothaire turned once more.

"I vow it." Declan bit back a yell as pain racked him. "Now free me!"

"Very well." After several tries, the vampire hauled him loose in a rush. As Declan labored just to rise up on his battered knees, Lothaire snatched free two seat belts, using them to tie Declan's hands behind his back.

"What the hell is this, vampire?"

Lothaire shoved one hand against the side of his face and clamped the other over his shoulder.

"*No!* What the fuck are you doing?"

"Exacting, no, *accepting* a payment from you. I promised you that you'd know when I wanted to drink you. Because my fangs would be shoved deep in your neck." The vampire dipped down, murmuring, "They're about to be. And with your invitation."

Declan flailed, roaring with fury. *Another detrus feeding on me! Another one touching my skin!*

"It can be quite enjoyable if you relax."

But no matter how hard Declan struggled, he couldn't get free. He felt the vampire's breath against his neck right before the bastard pierced him. There wasn't the pain he'd expected, just a disgusting fullness.

The rage, the unspeakable humiliation . . .

Lothaire drew deep, his tongue working as he lapped and sucked. When the vampire groaned, Declan shuddered with revulsion, dizziness washing over him with each greedy pull from his neck.

Finally the vampire released him with another groan, sitting back on his haunches. "Your blood is *steeped* in power." Running his tongue over a fang, he said, "Among other things. I believe I might be high. But I *like* it."

"You wanted my memories, leech? They're all yours." All the torture, misery, hate. Declan gave a crazed laugh. "You'll fuckin' choke on them!"

THIRTY-SEVEN

The magister's blood was delicious and drugged. Yet what a bitter aftertaste!

No matter. Lothaire couldn't remember the last time he'd tasted blood so powerful. His skin began regenerating in a rush, strength filling him.

Out of his countless victims only a handful had ever fueled him as Chase had.

Berserkers. Those rare creatures. Who knew?

If he could have blood like this *and* lose the torque . . .

"You filthy parasite—I will kill you for this!" Chase's muscles began to swell, his eyes glowing, but he'd probably burned through his berserkrage surviving that plane crash.

"Admit it, Magister, you liked it a little." Lothaire hauled him to his feet.

"One day I'll cut off your fuckin' head."

"Words hurt, Chase."

The man opened his mouth to say more, then gritted his teeth. "This isn't finished." Through the pouring rain, he lumbered in the Valkyrie's direction, following the swath of the plane's landing.

Lothaire trailed him, keeping a keen eye on his new investment and blood supply. When they reached the other half of the plane, the berserker, the fey, and Thaddeus had just crawled from the wreckage.

The fey's cheek was gouged open. Thaddeus appeared unscathed, sounding out some primitive Texan-esque whoop, then yelling to the sky, "We freaking *lived*!"

Brandr had an unconscious Regin cradled in his arms. One of his eyes was swollen shut and blood trickled from his nose. But Regin looked no worse than before the crash.

When Chase sagged in relief, Lothaire yanked him upright.

The man's scarred hands clenched and unclenched behind him as he so clearly longed to have her in his possession.

Lothaire drawled at his ear, "You want her so badly? Perhaps you oughtn't have had your lackeys mutilate her. Just a thought."

Natalya reached for her charge thrower. "What is the leech doing here? Again?" But her weapon had been damaged.

"Chase is my prisoner, and the Valkyrie goes with us."

Brandr nodded slowly. "You *are* as crazy as they say."

To keep his bargain with Chase, Lothaire would have to defeat these three and take the Valkyrie.

Or I can use them. Lothaire assessed them one by one. A ragtag army.

The fey had skills, the berserker would be an extra sword. Thaddeus's hidden strength could come in handy. Currently, the lad was dragging an overstuffed backpack out of the tail of the plane. Seemed he was smart enough to provision himself.

"Chase is leading me off the island," Lothaire said. "He knows of an alternate means of escape. We could include you. For a price."

Natalya rolled her eyes. "What now?"

"Allegiance to me, until we depart this place. You'd vow no malice against me."

Brandr shook his head. "That thing, that La Dorada, will be coming for you. Unless you killed her?"

"She's out of commission for a time." The sorceress had been rash, coming for him before she'd regenerated enough. He'd capitalized.

Natalya pressed her fingers to the wound on her cheek. "Do we have a choice but to side with you?"

"Not unless you want to stay here. And Chase informed me that the Order will be retaliating soon. Unite with us, or die."

"Then let's allegiate or whatever!" Thaddeus said. "I want out of this place! You've got my vow."

Natalya gritted out, "Mine as well."

Brandr scowled. "I vow it."

Lothaire tensed as a new scent wafted in the air. A foul scent. Through the rain, he spied glowing eyes in the woods. "Wendigos. On three sides."

When Declan spotted the creatures skulking closer, his instincts screamed for him to get Regin away. There were three times as many as before.

"Only one place to run." Natalya turned her gaze toward the dark forest just beyond them.

"No, we can't outrun them with these torques." Brandr swiped at his bleeding nose. "And we'd be going directly into their most advantageous terrain. We need to stand and fight."

Natalya scoffed. "All of us barely defeated a fraction of their number."

"If we run, you know what will happen! They'll infect us. I'd rather die—*in a fight*!"

"You could run, and I could stay to fend them off," the vampire offered. "For some reason, I feel amazingly refreshed." He swung an amused look at Declan that made him grind his teeth. "And it seems I'm quite handy against them." He fingered something in his pocket.

Natalya tossed away her busted TEP-C. "So, Lothaire, you're going to fight them out of the blackness of your heart?"

Lothaire said to Declan, "Mortals always have a rabbit hole. There's a secure shelter somewhere on this island, isn't there? Somewhere you'd all be safe this night?"

Beginning to recognize Lothaire's calculating look, Declan gave a tight nod, not bothering to hide the scathing hatred boiling inside him. "And what would it take for you to fight the Wendigos?" What *more* would he want?

"Whenever I ask for something in the future, you will do it for me. Anything. Without hesitation. Vow this."

Another deal with the devil?

"Make no bargains with vampires," the fey murmured. "You always lose in the end."

Too late.

Brandr shook his head. "You can't agree to an open-ended deal like that, especially not with a leech like him."

"Do I have a bloody choice?"

"Chase, they're pure evil. I've fought them all my life," Brandr said. "Hell, I've probably fought *him*!"

Lothaire calmly said, "An unlikelihood, as you still live."

Brandr lunged for the vampire, his free hand balled into a fist, but Natalya stepped between them.

"The Wendigos are closing in," Lothaire said. "I'm going to need your answer."

"Chase," Brandr said warningly.

"This is the only way to save her, and you know it," Lothaire said. "Don't you want to safeguard her?"

At that, Brandr cursed under his breath.

Because he knows I'll make this deal and any other to protect her? "You have my vow." *Put it on my goddamned tab.*

"Very good." Lothaire's red eyes glowed as he so obviously relished the upcoming fight. "Go. I'll stall them."

The halfling began shucking off his heavy pack. "I'll stay with Mr. Lothaire and fight." To Brandr, he said, "You get Natalya and Regin to safety."

With an eerie menace, Lothaire slowly turned to Thad. "No. You won't, young Thaddeus."

"I can help you—"

Lothaire's fist shot out, connecting with the kid's mouth, sending him flying onto his pack. "Run. Along."

Glaring over her shoulder, Natalya helped Thad up. The boy ran his forearm over his bleeding lip, casting Lothaire a stunned look. As he clambered to his feet, his eyes flashed black.

Brandr said, "Let's go. We're running out of time."

Thaddeus adjusted his pack, and Natalya snagged their only weapons, a pair of swords. Brandr still carried Regin—the sole thing Declan wanted.

They set off. But at the edge of the forest, Declan turned back to Lothaire. "How exactly will you know where we go?"

He laughed. "You won't get rid of me that easily, Magister." Fangs glinting, he murmured, "I'll pretend that you're prey and hunt you."

THIRTY-EIGHT

The group plunged into the forest, with Declan in the lead, making for an older abandoned facility. He'd been there a decade ago when he'd taken over the island.

In the background, they could hear the ongoing fighting, with earthshaking explosions and sporadic gun chatter.

Maybe Lothaire would be decapitated in the coming battle. *And rob me of the joy of doing it myself?*

Other creatures moved among the trees from time to time, though not the deadly Wendigos. *Not yet.*

The gale buffeted them, hampering their vision. They leaned into the wind, toiling up an ever-ascending terrain toward one of the many mountains in the island's interior.

Normally he'd be sprinting this trek so easily, but he'd been weakened from the berserkrage that had probably saved him in the crash.

And weakened from blood loss.

Worse, Lothaire seemed to have sucked out any medicine left in him.

Still Declan wanted Regin in *his* arms. "Untie me."

"So you can carry her?" Brandr ducked under a

branch. "Now that I've got her, I'm not giving her over."

"Then free me, in case we meet an enemy."

Natalya said, "You *are* an enemy. You might have some weird reincarnation history with Regin and Brandr, but our history's only four weeks long, and it hasn't exactly endeared you to me." She leapt over a washout. "Let's see. Charge thrower to the face during my capture, imprisonment, threat of torture hanging over my head, enforced abstinence."

Brandr did a double take at that. "We might have a history with Chase, but that didn't stop us from being strapped down to a table and eviscerated without anesthesia." His ire growing with every word, he said, "Our rib cages were cracked open, then wired together—under his orders."

Declan grated, "Not Regin."

"Oh, yeah, that's right. You didn't know about her. Even though you run everything here? Or *ran* everything."

From behind them, the halfling said, "Is there really another way off the island?" He was out of breath, no doubt from lugging that pack—what must be a week's worth of food.

"Aye."

Brandr snapped, "Well, tell us what it is."

Declan shot him a look. "You're still an immortal to me. The fey's right. We *are* enemies. Seems that knowledge might just keep me alive."

"We didn't *have* to be enemies," Brandr said. "You're the one who fucked up, Aidan."

"Don't call me that!"

"Aidan, asshole, whatever." He shoved Declan along. "Just shut up and keep moving."

Taking orders from the male infuriated him, but Declan had no berserker strength left to break his bonds, no choice but to lead them forward.

They continued in silence for at least half an hour before they reached the old research facility, a bunker tunneled into the side of a mountain. It was the first modern one on this island, circa nineteen fifty.

Declan led them through a series of rock cutouts, much like a labyrinth, winding deeper into the mountainside. When the trail appeared to dead-end at a sheer rock face, he edged to the right and kept going.

"An optical illusion," the halfling murmured. "Coo-ell."

They finally arrived at the bunker entrance, a thick metal door covered with lichen and moss.

"All right." Brandr said, "So how do we get in?"

"Untie me, so I can enter a code."

"Just tell me how to do it."

At the man's implacable expression, Declan said, "Tear away the moss. There's a manual code pad. If I can remember the code."

When Brandr uncovered it, Declan rattled off a series of numbers for Brandr to enter.

Clicking gears sounded. With a hiss, the door cracked opened. Declan entered, and the others followed. The air was stale, the inside pitch dark. Regin's glow was so dim it barely made a dent in the pressing black.

Brandr shut and locked the door behind them with an echoing clang, and Declan led them down a flight of narrow stairs into a large room. The exam room. Rows of metal tables—with restraints—stood in the center. Cages lined either side, while desks and cabinets occupied the front and back walls.

Oversize ventilation grates covered the ceiling. Blood drains dotted the tiled floor. Archaic-looking tools hung from wall pegs.

Thad whispered, "This place gives me the creeps."

Brandr rubbed his chest, no doubt reliving his own torture. "The ones in the cages had to watch?"

Natalya added, "Regin's going to lose it when she sees all this."

Declan gazed around, trying to see it from their point of view. Though the Order's research work hadn't changed much in sixty years, the manner of it had. The new facility's atmosphere was sterile, distanced.

This was raw, blatant, leaving nothing to the imagination.

Regin *would* lose it. She *should*. He glanced at her in Brandr's arms. She was shivering and soaking wet. *And still not waking.*

Brandr gently laid her on one of the desks, then began exploring. "There are more rooms?"

"Smaller exam rooms and some lavatories. The water should still work."

"Will there be a key here to remove the torques?"

"No, none." Wanting Regin close, Declan sat on the end of the desk beside her, ignoring Brandr's scowl.

"I guess we're bunking here tonight," Brandr told the others. "It'll give all of us a chance to recover."

"And to eat." The halfling began unpacking his bag

atop another desk, pulling out energy bars and bottles of Coke. He, Brandr, and the fey began splitting the take.

"Where did you get all this?" Brandr asked.

Natalya said, "Thad cleaned out the PX store. He's a natural at looting. I was quite proud."

Thad beamed. "Well, the Scout motto *is* Be Prepared."

Declan realized that he hadn't eaten in eighteen hours and had no more medicine in his system to dull his appetite. Withdrawal already threatened. He was alternately starving then nauseated, hungering for food while missing his nightly shot with a feverish intensity.

But he'd be damned before he asked them for something to eat.

They'd just finished their meal when banging on the door sounded. Everyone tensed.

Natalya said, "Has to be Lothaire. Are we certain we want to let that vampire in?"

Thad felt his busted lip. "He cleaned my clock."

"We all swore allegiance, remember?" Brandr started for the stairs. "Besides, he will help us keep Chase alive for the time being. He stays for now."

Moments later, Brandr returned with the vampire.

So much for my hope that Lothaire would die.

The vampire strolled in, casting his surroundings a bored look. "Breathe a sigh of relief. I've returned." While he'd been out, Lothaire had acquired a hooded camo jacket and a bush hat. More claw marks riddled his shirt and pants, and blood trickled from a wound down his chest.

My blood. Filthy leeches. Declan's hands fisted as he reminded himself that Lothaire had saved them all this night. And might come in handy in the future.

But at what price? *Make no bargains with vampires.*

Lothaire leapt onto a tall cage, sitting atop it with his back against the wall. He began removing his many weapons—one of which was Declan's sword. A vampire wielded *his* weapon. *Just as I'd threatened to do with Regin's.*

"Yes, you returned," Natalya's eyes narrowed, "but you've got Wendigo scratches. You'll transform into one of them."

"Luckily, I have salt." He took a handful from his pocket, rubbing it into the laceration on his torso.

Natalya raised her brows. "Salt halts the transformation?"

"Do you know how many people I had to drain to come by that knowledge? You're welcome, fey."

"Good to know. Now, what's happening out there?"

"More fighting. The facility is one giant kill box."

"What do we do now?"

"We get information from Chase." Lothaire winced as he tended a particularly deep gash. "How long before more mortal troops arrive?"

"They won't. I said the Order would strike. Not how. They'll bomb after one hundred and fifty hours."

Lothaire said, "Why so much time?"

"It's a Hail Mary protocol. The island is seeded with

incendiary bombs for a total self-destruct, but for some reason, they didn't detonate."

Natalya said, "Technopaths could have detected them and disarmed them."

Declan had suspected the same. "The soonest the Order can deploy an aerial attack is six and a half days. They can't strike before Friday at noon." It didn't escape his notice that he'd begun saying *they* instead of *we*.

His life with the Order was over. But Webb had it wrong. That didn't mean Declan had to throw in with these miscreats any more than necessity demanded.

Unfortunately, it looked like they'd be along for the ride—all the way to the escape boat and beyond. "In the meantime, there are other adversaries to contend with."

Lothaire said, "Some of the vampires and demons will simply trace from here now that their torques are gone."

"Some?" Brandr swigged his Coke.

"Others will remain to pick off the Vertas while they're at their weakest. It's what I would do. Actually, I'd trace more of my brethren back to this place and exterminate them all."

Brandr whistled low. "Fish in a barrel."

In a thoughtful tone, Lothaire said, "We will have to chance that they don't."

"Then what?" Thad said. "How do we get out of this place? How do we get home?"

Declan grudgingly said, "There's a boat on the far

west coast of the island. It would take about three days through the forest on foot."

Brandr said, "Which is the Wendigos' natural habitat. The woods will be crawling with them."

"The only other option is to stay above the tree line while crossing the mountains. Which will tack on two days."

Thad belched into his fist, then said, "Never been on a mountain before!"

"So the mountains it is," Natalya said. "Doesn't sound too bad. We only have to stay alive for a spell, then we cruise home."

Declan gazed at Regin. And then she would leave him and never look back. Or maybe she would remember that he'd rescued her from those vampires and feel gratitude. *Aye, gratitude.*

Brandr added, "When we get back, we can get a witch to remove the torques. Regin's good friends with several of them." Then he frowned at Declan. "Wait a second. You said the mainland is eight hundred miles away. What kind of boat are you taking us to?"

"A bloody big one."

"What do I do then?" Thad asked. "Can I go back home?"

Everyone looked at Declan. At length, he said, "No. Your family is mortal, so they're safe, but if you return, that magister will simply recapture you. Take you to another facility."

"There are more of these places?" Natalya cried.

Declan shrugged. *Four others.*

Thad said, "Thanks for letting me know Mom and Gram are okay. I appreciate it."

Gratitude from the kid, after all that had been done to him.

"Hey, is there like a witness relocation program for us?"

Natalya said, "We'll figure something out for you and your family, lad. I promise." Then she turned to Lothaire, "So, vampire, who is La Dorada?"

Thad asked, "What'd she keep screaming about a ring for?"

Declan grated, "And how the hell did she get into my facility?"

His tone dripping condescension, Lothaire crooned, "Ah, children, it's not yet story time." He closed his eyes and turned away, saying over his shoulder, "To anyone who contemplates even nearing me while I sleep: I will garrote you with your own viscera."

Declan was about to demand an answer when he heard a muted whimper. Was Regin waking at last?

Yes, her eyes were darting behind her lids, her brows drawn. He leaned closer, hands clenching behind his back again. He would fix this with her. She'd never known a man with a will like his. *I'll* make *her want me back—*

She opened her eyes. Narrowed them on him.

Then she hissed.

Regin shot upright, locking gazes with Chase. He'd been looming over her while she was defenseless?

She wasn't now.

Launching herself at his throat, she shrieked, "I'll kill you!" She dug her claws in around his Adam's apple, but he wouldn't fight back.

Brandr lunged forward, prying her from Chase's throat. "You can't, Valkyrie!" He looped an arm around her waist, pulling her away.

"Watch me!" She lashed out at Brandr, knocking her head back against his face.

Chase simply stood there, tense as a board, his neck bleeding.

Brandr muttered, "I can't let you do that, Regin."

"Why not?"

"He knows a way off the island, a boat just a few days from here. He's going to lead us to it." At her ear, he said, "You know I can't let you kill him anyway."

"Did you not see what he had done to me?" she cried. "They cut me open by his order!"

Chase's eyes blazed. "I didn't order it, didn't know about it!"

Brandr released her, standing between her and Chase.

"And I'm supposed to believe that? How could you not have known?" Natalya had told her she'd thrown off electricity like a reactor. "Were you gone?"

Even after everything, part of her wished he'd been gone, wished he'd had absolutely no part in it.

"I swear that I didn't know," he answered, his tone evasive. "And that I would've stopped it if I had."

Lying about something. She was too drained to think, too injured. She gazed around with growing disbelief. Saws, scalpels, exam tables, and cages surrounded her.

"Ah, gods, where are we?" She rubbed her chest, reeling on her feet. It was like a warehouse of old torture tools.

Then she spied *Lothaire* atop one of the cages, relaxing with his hands folded behind his head as if he'd just been napping. "*Him?*" She reached to her back—for swords that weren't there. "Do you know what he's done to the Valkyrie? What the hell is wrong with you people?" Her breaths grew shallow, wheezing. "I can't be around them . . . I can't." She coughed, a rattling sound. "And I-I can't stay in this place—"

Regin's legs gave out. Her knees met the hard floor as blood bubbled from her lips.

THIRTY-NINE

Declan shot forward to help her, ignoring the bloody hand she raised to ward him away.

Brandr shoved him back. "She doesn't want you to touch her!" He knelt beside Regin. "Listen to me, Valkyrie. The wire holding your rib cage together doesn't come out on its own. Nor the staples. I'm going to have to cut them out of you." Regin's silvery eyes grew stark.

Oh, bloody hell, no. "She'll heal on her own. She'll regenerate." *They always do.*

Brandr cast him a black look. "You had this done to me too, remember? And I know that I was ripping those staples out of my chest over an entire day. I had to dig for the wire, unknot it, and pull it free—in between the times I blacked out. At least she'll have someone to help her."

Regin was still coughing, blood dripping from her lips, her staples straining.

Declan's gut churned as realization sank in. He knew this had to be done.

"Is there some kind of remover here?" Brandr asked. "For the staples. Maybe some kind of anesthetic?"

"They would have used sutures back then. And any chemicals were removed from the bunker."

"I'll need a blade." Brandr lifted her into his arms.

"Take your pick." Lothaire smirked. "We're surrounded by them."

Natalya found a scalpel, gravely handed it to Brandr.

Brandr jerked his chin toward a pair of clippers. "Fey, can you grab those bolt cutters as well?"

They weren't used to cut bolts. Declan stepped forward. "I'll see to her."

Regin cried, "He's . . . not touching . . . me!"

From his vantage on the cage, Lothaire exhaled loudly. "Whatever you do, be quick about it. If the storm abates, her lightning will be like a beacon to the Pravus. And I for one need rest before I face yet another army of immortals."

"I'm doing this, Chase," Brandr said simply.

On some level he must trust the berserker, Declan realized, because he allowed Brandr to carry her into a back examination room.

As Declan watched from the doorway, the berserker laid her on a metal table, then took off his shirt, balling it under her head. "Regin, when you feel like passing out—just let yourself. This is going to get rough."

"You know I can't . . . with enemies here. Vampire. Chase."

I'm not your enemy. No longer.

"Just turn off those Valkyrie instincts for once. I'm not going to let anyone harm you. I've waited a thousand years to protect you." He brushed his hand over Regin's hair. "Let me do it now." Then he marched to the door.

Before Brandr slammed it in his face, Declan met eyes with her. He parted his lips to say something—*I'd take this pain for you. No one will ever hurt you again.*—but no words came out.

Outside the room, Declan began to pace. He hadn't protected her. He'd gotten her out of the facility, but this had happened when she'd been directly under his watch.

He'd done nothing except hurt her from their first meeting. When he'd gutted her in a dirty street. When he'd poisoned her.

And when she needed me most, I was high in my room, failing her.

Each time Brandr excised a staple, Declan could hear her biting back a cry. The strain was crippling him. But now it was accompanied by the onset of withdrawal symptoms. Teeth-clattering tremors threatened.

At her first real scream, an answering roar was ripped from his chest. Where was his vaunted willpower now? His lack of emotion?

How many times had Webb told him, "You're devoid of emotions like that"?

I'm not. That gnawing anxiety overwhelmed him until he nearly doubled over with it.

Then came another scream, thunder clapping immediately after. Everyone stared at each other, leery.

The storm intensified, seeming to rock the mountain until even Lothaire raised his brows.

Regin cried, "No, no, Brandr, now just *wait*—"

When she shrieked, Declan rammed his head against the tiled wall, gritting his teeth. *This is my doing.*

Have to get to her. He strained against his bindings, his heart beginning to thunder as it pumped blood to his muscles. Coursing, coursing . . . With another yell, he busted the straps, then charged to the door.

Natalya planted herself in front of him.

"Out of my way." —*Nothing keeps me from her.*—

Just as he raised his hands to toss her to the side, Brandr came out. He had streaks of blood up his bare chest. He barely gave Declan's freed hands a glance. To the fey, he said, "She won't pass out, and the next part is going to be bad."

Declan snapped, "That *wasn't*?"

"What can I say? Your bitch Dr. Dixon did a hack job on her."

Because she was in a hurry to finish before I woke from my stupor.

"The wire got mangled into Regin's rib cage, and some of the bones have already grown over it." Brandr looked at Natalya. "I need someone to hold her shoulders down. Either you or the boy."

Natalya nodded. "Of course I'll do it."

"Use the restraints," Declan grated.

She hissed, "How easily you say that."

"I *tried* using them," Brandr said. "Regin has to be perfectly still or the wire's going to pierce her heart. I can't strap down her chest because of the size of the opening."

Declan ran his hand over his face. "Neither of them will be strong enough to hold her still."

"And you will be, Chase?" Brandr demanded. "It's clear you've begun to think of her as yours—"

Lothaire guffawed.

"—so can you watch me slice open your woman?"

Natalya drew Brandr aside. "You're not considering this? The fiend looks like he's about to have a psychotic break."

Declan didn't deny that, just said, "I'm no' askin'."

Brandr studied his expression. "Maybe he *should* see it."

When Natalya reluctantly deferred, Brandr turned back to the room.

Am I ready to see this? Declan inhaled deeply. *You reap what you sow.* He entered, halting in his tracks at the scene before him.

Brandr was squeezing her bloody hand in his, and Regin was gazing up at him, crying, shaking her head miserably. "We c-can do . . . the rest tomorrow."

She was bare from the waist up. A line of pitted skin crawled up the middle of her torso, and blood tracked down her sides. Between her breasts, Brandr had sliced the line wide open until her skin gaped over her rib cage. That hideous wire jutted up in the center.

Declan shoved his fist against his mouth, swallowed back vomit.

"This will be over soon," Brandr promised her. "And you'll never have to go through it again. Close your eyes, Regin. If you trust me, you'll close them."

At length, she did.

Only then did Declan cross to the table. He could see why Brandr needed her perfectly still. The man was going to have to lower those cutters directly beside her beating heart.

How many times had Declan cursed an immortal's resilience?

Now he prayed for hers.

Regin lay in a twilight, her mind refusing to go under, even as Brandr began clipping in her chest.

The gruesome sound of those cutters—*snip, snip*—echoed in the room. She thought she was still begging him to wait till later to do the rest. To give her a chance to recover from the staples.

Reasoning with him like a coward.

Her tone was mewling, like a little girl's. She was appalled at herself.

Oh, gods, had he let Chase inside? She opened her eyes, but a murky film shaded her vision. Was that brute holding her shoulders down? She flailed against him, but he was immovable. "Let me go, let me go!"

"Regin, be *still.*" Chase's voice sounded thick. *"Please."*

She kept struggling. Metal scraped bone.

"Damn it, Chase!" Brandr pulled the clippers out. "You've got to keep her still!"

"Aye," he rasped. His big hands covered her mouth and nose.

Terror flared. Suffocating her? *Can't get air!* She kicked her legs out, digging her claws into his hands.

Instead of helping her escape, Brandr muttered, "You are the coldest son of a bitch I have ever met."

Blackness took her, and it was almost a . . . blessing.

When Declan removed his hands from Regin's face, Brandr gazed at him like he was a monster.

"See to her before she wakes!" *Can't do that a second time.* Her little claws were still embedded into the backs of his scarred hands. "What are you waitin' for?"

Brandr shook his head hard, then returned to the knot. "I've almost got it. It's tangled, though." Clipping, untangling, clipping. "One piece left—"

A spray of blood erupted from her chest.

"What the hell happened?" When Regin's lids slid open, Declan snapped, "Goddamn it, she wakes. . . ." But her head lolled to the side, her eyes sightless, *deadened.* No, not *waking.* "Regin!" he roared. Her heart had stopped, punctured; no breath filled her lungs. He swung his head up. *"What the fuck did you do?"*

"I'm not a surgeon—I'm just trying to clean up what *your* people did to her!" In a rush, he yanked away the last of the wire.

Declan squeezed one of her hands in both of his, willing her regeneration to take hold, that preternatural healing that coaxed her kind back from the brink again and again. *Live, Regin.*

Brandr had just finished when she sucked in a breath, her lids sliding shut. Life returned, though she remained unconscious.

"It'll take more than this to kill her," Brandr said. So why was he so visibly relieved, running his arm over his sweating brow? "She'll heal quickly if we can find something to hold her skin together for a few hours. But there's no tape, no sutures." As he searched for an alternative, his gaze flicked over Declan's uncovered hands but he didn't address them. "Maybe if we knotted some fabric around her torso—"

"I'll hold her. To keep the wound edges pressed together."

Brandr narrowed his eyes. "Am I wrong to trust you?"

"Again, I'm no' bloody askin'."

The man gave a nod, but hastened to add, "Only till it closes or she starts stirring. If she wakes against you, she'll just fight and reopen the wounds."

Declan gingerly lifted her from the table, then sat on the floor against the wall. With her back to his chest, he wrapped one arm over her breasts, and the other around her waist, squeezing her against his body. Her head rolled on his shoulder. She was so small and frail. Her skin was cold. *Dim.*

"I'll return to check on her."

Once the door closed, Declan shuddered out a breath, his sight gone blurry. He lowered his forehead to her shoulder. *"My God, Regin,"* he rasped. How much more could she take? "Stay with me, brave girl. Hold on."

Her body might heal, but would her mind? She'd told him torture collected over the years. . . .

"I wish to Christ I could take this pain from you." Unable to stop himself, he desperately rubbed his cheek against hers over and over, murmuring her name repeatedly. "I'll never let you be hurt again. Never. For the rest of my life." Then he froze. Their faces were wet?

"You're cryin', lass?"

He jerked his head back, brows drawn in confusion. *She* wasn't.

FORTY

Need to sleep, Lothaire thought. *To get information about the ring. Time is running out.*

But he cracked open his eyes when the berserker finally emerged from that back exam room. The male looked shell-shocked. His hooded eyes were bleak but glowing as they searched out the fey. When his gaze fell on her, his body coiled with tension.

At the unmistakable look he was giving her, she stood, her breaths shallowing. "H-how is Regin?"

"She'll be fine," he said, his footsteps unwavering in her direction.

Ah, but Lothaire wasn't the only one watching this transpire. Young Thaddeus's eyes were flickering.

Without stopping, Brandr grabbed her hand, murmuring low, "Need you. And you need me."

She gazed at Thaddeus—who tensed to act, yet didn't—then followed the berserker as if in a daze.

When they disappeared into the night, Thaddeus kicked the leg of a table.

Lothaire exhaled. "You don't want her anyway. Her blood's poisonous to our kind. If you bedded her, you would feel the need to drink her. And at your age, you wouldn't have the control to stop yourself. Is one fuck worth your life?"

"Why are you even talking to me? You busted my lip earlier."

"So I did."

Thaddeus glared. "When you hit me, was that like to . . . to get me out of harm's way? Or something?"

"I did need you out of the way."

"You didn't answer my question," Thaddeus mumbled, sinking back down onto the floor, nursing a bottle of Coke.

"That's not what you need to be drinking, *paren'*. I saw how you reacted to the scent of the Valkyrie's blood." Thaddeus's fangs had shot longer, and he'd grown hard, squirming in his seat. His expression had been alternately lustful and aghast.

If Lothaire hadn't recently gorged on the magister's high-octane blood, even he might have been affected.

"I give you a week, maybe two, before you're driven to bite someone."

"I don't know *how* to . . . to bite or drink! But you could teach me."

"And what could you possibly do in return?" Lothaire waved a negligent hand. "Play football for me? Break in my jeans really well?"

"At least tell me what else I am."

Lothaire didn't actually *know*. So instead, he said, "Our slate is relatively clean." But not quite. "You would do well to keep it that way."

He didn't have time to tutor a fledgling vampire. More important developments were afoot.

Lothaire needed Chase and the Valkyrie together.

My Endgame demands it.

If Nïx had been steering the Vertas, he'd just as easily been steering the Pravus—he could see the chessboard so clearly, hundreds of moves ahead. That soothsayer could foresee people's actions; Lothaire could predict their reactions.

Now a blood debt from a Valkyrie lay within reach. But first he needed to set two pawns on a path together. So how to get Chase into Regin's bed? To rekindle their fabled tale?

Using all my considerable talent, if need be.

Don't move a bloody muscle, Declan commanded himself. The longer Regin slept and healed, the longer he could hold her.

And right now, he *needed* to hold her. Withdrawal gripped him hard.

Normally the drugs would leach little by little out of his system. Now they were just *gone,* sucked out by a goddamned vampire.

Sweat beaded over his skin, and he had to gnash his teeth to keep them from chattering. His legs were restless and tremors racked him, but he fought to keep still, ever careful not to wake her.

Because the contact with her battled the worst of his symptoms.

He'd hurt her; she hated him. And still, having her in

his arms soothed him in ways unknown to him before. He'd been dead-on when he'd realized he was seeking this every time he'd planted a needle in his arm. *Never again.*

An hour passed, then two.

She'd just stirred for the first time when Brandr returned. He was soaked through, appearing in better spirits. He reached for Regin. "She's healing, her skin knitting already."

Her wound was reddened, but it had indeed closed completely. Declan reluctantly released her, his arms cramping as Brandr collected her. "Where are you taking her?"

Again, the man's gaze fell to Declan's uncovered hands, but he didn't remark upon the scars. "Out with us."

"Then put a goddamned shirt on her!"

Brandr raised his brows. "Aidan's definitely in there. Somewhere." He worked Regin's shirt over her, gently threading her arms into the sleeves before he left with her.

Alone, Declan found the door to the lavatories, searching until he located a sink that still pumped well water. He scrubbed his face, then looked into the mirror, hissing in a breath.

His irises were . . . glowing.

Because I'm a berserker. With the spirit of a bear stirring inside him. *My eyes will be changeable with emotion.*

No wonder they were now. Shame and regret roiled within him. *She's lost to me . . .*

Declan had recognized that he had a choice: possess Regin, or end himself. He'd lived too long with the strain.

As he'd predicted all those years ago, it was about to break him.

Lost . . . Which made his decision easy.

When he returned to the main exam room, Brandr was cozying up to the fey while Thad glowered in their direction. Lothaire, still atop that cage, looked like he was actually sleeping. *No doubt keen to get to my memories. Have at them, leech.* Declan didn't see Regin. "She woke?" Alarm spiked in him. "Where is she?"

Thad said, "She's outside, cleaning up."

Declan turned to go after her.

"I wouldn't follow her if I were you," Brandr said. "She's about to blow, and she took a sword. Even injured, she'll kill you."

Natalya added, "Give her some time to lick her wounds in private."

"I can't let her remain out there. No' alone."

Brandr shook his head. "An armed, thousand-year-old Valkyrie filled with an unholy rage? Who would be crazy enough to face her right now?"

Me. Declan was already sprinting up the bunker stairs. He pushed out into the gale and sped heedlessly down the treacherous terrain.

Not far from the bunker, he found her in a small clearing. She knelt in the mud, topless, with lightning exploding directly above her. Her hair was a soaked mane covering her bare back, her pointed ears peeking out.

Her shirt and a sword lay beside her. She was angled so that he could just see her face as she peered down at her chest. With a light touch, she inspected her wounds.

Guilt nearly felled him. If he accepted that some members of the Lore weren't evil—like Regin and Brandr—then his commanders had been right.

I am *more of a monster than the creatures out there.*

First the strain, and now this guilt over the things he'd done? *Too much for one man to shoulder.*

Regin raised her face to the pounding rain, muttering to the sky, her expression one of pure fury.

When he saw that, he knew she could never be brought to forgive him. Never.

So it's over.

She slowly donned her shirt, then reached for the sword. In a flash she was on her feet, weapon raised. Lightning struck mere feet behind her; she didn't flinch. "Time for you to die, Chase."

It's long over. . . .

Chase's eyes were glowing in the night, filled with . . . *shame*? "Do what you need to."

"You think I won't?" He was a madman who'd harmed her friends and imprisoned children. Who'd captured her and let mortals cut on her.

He yelled, "Then do it!"

She gasped at the unbearable pain in his expression, the hopelessness. What in the gods' names had happened to him in this lifetime?

No, it doesn't matter.

He strode toward her across the clearing, growing more incensed with each step—as if he were pissed that she hadn't attacked him. "Swing that fuckin' sword!"

Regin clutched the hilt. "You have a death wish?"

"See—this—done." Getting closer. "Why are you hesitating?"

She didn't know!

"You want to put me down? Aye, you should yearn to. Do it now!" When he was a few feet from her, he lunged forward; she raised the sword point to his chest. Right at his heart.

But she couldn't drive it home.

He shoved his chest against the point until it sank into his skin. "Goddamn it, do it! Don't you want revenge, Valkyrie? All that pain you suffered was my doing! Mine! Directly from the start."

Lightning struck with her frustration, thunder booming instantly. The winds howled around them.

"Do you know what I was thinking before I captured you in New Orleans? That you were just another job to complete before I got to return home. Another detrus added to my personal *collection* of them. That night, I stabbed you with my sword. Remember how I twisted it inside you?"

She remembered all too well, the pain, the betrayal. *One of many to come. . . .*

"And don't forget when I tortured you. The poison was so strong that you dislocated your shoulder from your seizures. Oh, and that vivisection? I must have ordered them on hundreds of your kind. Maybe thousands. And I never once doubted that I had every right to."

"Because you believe immortals are unnatural?" she bit out. "That we're animals?"

"*Less than* animals." As if he was quoting someone, he intoned, "Abominations walking among us, filled with untold malice toward mankind. A perversion of the natural order, spreading their deathless numbers uncontrollably. A plague upon man that must be eradicated."

"Then why save me from those vampires tonight? Why allow the vivisection, then turn around and rescue me? You could've stopped what Dixon and those fucks did to me!"

"You want to know why I didn't stop them? Because I was high in my room, Regin. With a needle jammed in my vein. While you were getting butchered, I was knocked out, oblivious to the world."

Her lips parted wordlessly.

"Think of everything I've done to your friends and allies. That's what I do—I hurt your kind. I take them from their homes, from their families." His eyes were haunted, his lashes spiked with moisture. Voice hoarse, he rasped, *"Put me out of my fuckin' misery, woman. Do it."*

Gods, he was so damaged, so . . . ruined. As she gazed at his eyes, dim impressions arose in her mind. Her face wet with warm tears? Why couldn't she remember?

Suddenly, he gripped her shoulders—to yank her into him.

FORTY-ONE

"*No!*" The Valkyrie raised her leg at the last minute, kicking him back, then threw the sword across the clearing.

She hadn't run that steel through Declan, though he'd all but forced her to.

"Why can't you do it?" he bellowed.

"I don't know!" She sounded dazed. "Do you really want me to? You're that miserable?"

When he'd been staring down that sword, he'd accepted death. But now he realized that if he died, she'd have one less protector. He had to get her off this island first.

"You don't deserve my mercy," she said, her voice breaking. Tears welled in her eyes. The sight of them pained him far worse than that sword ever could have.

"No. I don't." Still, he had the mad urge to explain his actions, to explain why he'd grown so callous to immortals, why he'd believed her kind had to be controlled. Why it'd fallen to him.

The training that made me a monster.

Yet he knew he could never make her understand.

"I've been tortured before, Chase. But never like this. They talked about golf and movies while they . . ."—she bit back a sob—"while they played with my womb."

Warring impulses raged inside him. Declan wanted to yell with wrath, to comfort her, to annihilate any who'd dared touch her.

"You promised me I'd beg. Oh, how I did. And I will always hate myself for that. I begged *you* to make it stop! You can't comprehend what it's like! The *violation . . .*"

"Maybe I comprehend more than you think!" Seeing Colm's throat slit, watching his parents being eaten alive. *Feeling the flesh peeled from my goddamned body.*

His words seemed to enrage her. "If you've witnessed it a thousand times, then you're an expert at it? Is that it?" Her lips were drawn back from her teeth. "You *disgust* me. You know nothing. *Nothing*!"

For her to discount what he'd been through? "I know everything!" he roared as he tore off his shirt.

She gasped, blinking rapidly as if she couldn't believe her eyes.

"Don't tell me what I can or can't comprehend!" He turned to show her his back. When he faced her again, her expression was horrified. "I know what pain is, Regin! I know what it feels like to be powerless."

Lightning struck again. She stumbled back a step, then another.

Slipping away from me forever. He reached for her, but she shook her head slowly.

"You stay away from me, Chase. Whatever you want me for, whatever you think might be between us, forget about it. It's just . . . *dead* between us!" She turned back toward the bunker, covering her mouth as if she was going to be sick.

As he watched her hurrying from him, he had a flash memory from long ago. From the day the Order's physicians had removed his bandages.

His first thought upon seeing what was left of his chest had confused him, had made no sense in the context of his life.

When he'd gazed in horror at his skin, he'd thought . . .

She will never want me like this.

Regin ran blindly back to the bunker, losing energy, vomiting it free of her body.

Scars covered Chase's chest, back, and arms. The wounds were curving, ritualistic. He *had* been tortured. And he was clearly still living with the aftereffects.

Track marks lined his inner arms.

The sight of his scars hadn't sickened her; the *idea* of them did. They'd rocked her because she could imagine the pain behind them.

Who'd done that to him? She remembered speaking to him about his hatred of immortals, remembered guessing that some had hurt him and his family. He'd never denied it.

She could piece together a likely scenario. A number of them had killed his loved ones. He'd survived the ordeal, then joined the Order for revenge.

She slowed, some memory tickling at her consciousness, but she couldn't recall it. . . .

No wonder he hates us.

She flung open the door to the torture warehouse, wincing at the pain in her chest. As soon as she could grab a decent weapon, she was gone from this place. She'd go it alone before she stayed near Chase.

Chase. With his defeated eyes, lost expression, and palpable yearning.

Damn it, I don't have internal struggles! If she hated someone, she hated them. Period. She'd vowed to mete retribution on him.

So why was she feeling that old pull to him? Why did she want to go and erase that haunted look in his eyes? *Shh, warrior, be at ease.*

Aidan had been so beautiful and proud, a king in his world. He'd never known a single defeat until the very end of his life.

Chase was . . . he was *wretched*. He'd clearly been dealt tragedy early. If each reincarnation emphasized a facet of Aidan, then Declan Chase was the worst of him.

Pain and hate personified.

His body had been maimed. Yet his face . . . As she'd backed away from him, her lightning had struck, illuminating his visage.

A face made more beautiful by lightning. He'd looked like some kind of tormented, dark angel.

And that tragic beauty and raw longing called to her as no other embodiment had. . . .

When she entered the exam room, Lothaire gazed at her from his perch, his eerie reddened eyes following her movements.

"What are you looking at?" Soon she'd confront him

about his past crimes against the Valkyrie, but not until she'd healed more. *Not until I have a shot at bringing home his fangs to my sisters.* Then she'd slay him.

"Some of us are trying to sleep, *suka*."

"I've got your number, you son of a bitch."

He casually hissed, muttering in that thick Russian accent, "I'll be getting yours, drop by drop."

Whatever that meant.

At the back of the room, Thad was asleep sitting up against the wall. Natalya was dozing with her head in Brandr's lap.

Regin frowned at this, then continued her search for a weapon. She'd left that sword outside.

Brandr eased Natalya's head to the ground and crossed to Regin's side. "Is Chase still alive?"

"Unfortunately."

"It's definitely Aidan in there. Could scarcely believe it before. But now I'm certain of it." His brows drew together. "What are you looking for?"

"I need a weapon, but I don't want to take the last sword."

"You're leaving? What about our escape?"

"If I stay, I'll kill him," she said. "I vowed to the Lore to get revenge on him."

"Regin, if you'd seen him earlier, the way he reacted to your being hurt . . . Your vow's been more than fulfilled."

She was unconvinced.

"In a few days, the Order's going to bomb the island. There's only one way off—a boat on the far shore over these mountains. If you're not on that boat, you're dead."

"I'll find it and meet you there. If I don't show in time, then leave without me."

"You can't go alone."

I might not have to. When Regin had been out in that clearing, just before Chase showed up, she'd sensed . . . a Valkyrie's presence.

Was one of her half sisters on this island even now?

"The journey's going to be dangerous," Brandr said. "And I hate to say this, but right now, Chase is the strongest of us here."

"A mad dog is strong, but you don't trust it with your life!"

"I'll put him on a leash then, tie his hands. Would you stay then?" When she hesitated, he said, "You won't make it off this island alive without him. And since I'm sworn to protect you, then I won't either."

In a lower tone, she said, "And what about Lothaire?"

"The vampire fought off Wendigos tonight, allowing all of us to escape here. Chase had to make some kind of bargain with him."

"So he cut a deal with an evil leech—"

"To save *you.* Look, I'm not asking you to forgive Chase. But maybe just try to understand him."

"Do you know how many of our friends and allies are on this island? How many died this night? How many lives have been ruined? He's behind all of that! He believes we're all animals—including you!"

"I know this! I just want you to be aware that he made sacrifices tonight. That he's at least trying to make amends."

"What do you want me to do? Get cozy with him—so he can die anyway?"

"Regin, this is the first time I've really been around Aidan since he died. You've known him in the past, for however briefly." He ran his hand over the back of his neck. "But I've always been too late. I saw the knight breathe his last. I was with you when we buried the Spaniard's empty coffin. I was running for the cavalryman, yelling a warning seconds before he was shot. I just . . . I want to see what this is like. To have him back."

Brandr misses him, too.

"But he's not the same," she said in a softer tone. "You'll only be disappointed."

"Then you can leave him behind after we escape. What could it hurt to wait a few days . . . ?"

Even over the storm, Declan heard someone nearing, but he was too bloody weary to bother covering his scars.

Fuck it. Let everyone see what he really looked like. . . .

Brandr approached, his eyes narrowing at the sight. Yet he said nothing, just stalked around the clearing, kicking a rock here, throwing a stick there.

Colm used to do that whenever he had something pressing he'd wanted to discuss. "Say what's on your mind, berserker."

"What the hell are you doing out here?"

Sitting in the rain like a fool, wanting to howl from

losing her. Though he'd never had her to begin with! Just as he'd known, one look at his ruined skin had made her run. Why had he hoped she'd react differently?

When Declan didn't answer, Brandr said, "Did an immortal do that to your chest?"

"Oh, aye, lots of them," he snapped.

"Tell me you killed them." Brandr's eyes gleamed in the night. He sounded almost . . . pissed for Declan.

He gave a curt nod.

"This certainly explains why you hate all of us."

"I hated you because it was my goddamned job to! And because I never bloody knew there was an alternative."

"And what about those, Chase?" Brandr pointed to his track marks. "What are you into?"

Shame filling him, Declan stared at the puddle deepening around his boots.

"You're shaking now. How bad will the withdrawal get?"

"I've gotten through the worst of it." *Regin saw me through it, and she didn't even know. . . .* But he wasn't free from the symptoms yet.

"Are you going to stay clean?"

"That's the plan."

Seeming to make a decision about him, Brandr said, "Regin wants to leave."

Declan shot to his feet. "Not a chance—"

"Unless you are tied up, like a prisoner. I've got some exam restraints back at the bunker."

How bloody fitting. "You and I both know I can hit a rage and break any bindings."

"And she knows there's enough time in that short window to take your head."

"If I do this, then she stays?"

Brandr nodded.

Declan drew on his pullover, then handed Regin's discarded sword over to Brandr. Wanting his penance, he returned to the bunker, allowing himself to be bound.

Inside, Thad and Regin were sitting up against a wall together, her head on the boy's shoulder. *Don't thrash him. He's young.*

When Natalya gestured for Brandr to join her, the berserker dropped down on the floor beside her.

Lothaire was still dozing.

Declan sat off to the side away from everyone, feeling—as usual—like an outcast. He used all his willpower not to stare at Regin. And failed.

The dark circles under her eyes and the pallor of her skin were like physical blows to him, redoubling his guilt.

When their gazes met, he didn't bother hiding what he was feeling. *I want you so much. I'd give anything to redo the last month. To rid myself of these scars for you.*

Expression brimming with hostility, she turned from him. When Thad put his arm around her shoulders, she curled into his side.

Declan's fists clenched behind him as he resisted the urge to break his bonds and snatch her away from the halfling.

When his legs grew restless and his shaking intensified once more, he leaned his head back against the wall to stare at the ceiling. This wasn't nearly as punishing as it'd been earlier, but without her in his arms, it was worse for him.

Need her. He gnashed his teeth, struggling to keep his legs still—

Suddenly Lothaire shot upright, out of breath and patting his chest from neck to waist. His face was drawn and clammy with sweat.

Declan narrowed his eyes. *The vampire just dreamed of my torture, experienced it.*

When Lothaire's red gaze fell on him, Declan murmured, *"Fuckin' choke on them. . . ."*

FORTY-TWO

Regin woke in a rush. She'd been dozing against Thad again, who still snored beside her.

Throughout the night and morning the two of them had slept on and off, recuperating as they waited for some of the battles to die down.

Rubbing her gritty eyes, she glanced around. She saw lots of torture instruments but no torturer. Chase and everyone else were outside the room.

When Thad began nuzzling her neck, pressing his opened lips against her, she smacked him in the back of the head. "Don't go vamp on me now!"

"Whaa!" He shot upright, his fangs sharp. "Where am I?"

She glanced at his fangs, then down. "Oh, my gods, when do you *not* sport wood? There are bathrooms in the back, so go burp the worm or whatever."

Blushing furiously, he muttered, "I-I'm really sorry." He pulled his T-shirt lower. "I don't know what's happening with me."

"You were either about to bite me or kiss me or both. Not a chance, kid! You've got better odds with Natalya—and those are looking up at zero." At his mortified look, Regin exhaled. "Look, I had a rough night, and I'm taking it out on you."

"I get it. It's cool." He scrubbed his hand down his face. "So, uh, Natalya's *totally* out?"

"Yeah, Brandr cockblocked you. Sorry. But one day, you'll find someone nonpoisonous. . . ." She trailed off when Natalya came down the steps from the outer door.

Thad shot to his feet, finger-combing his hair.

"Wakey wakey, eggs and bakey," the fey chirped as she strolled into the room, looking rested and relaxed. "Come on, it's high noon, and we've got a boat to catch!"

And clearly, you got laid, Regin thought with a spike of jealousy. When she got back to New Orleans, she'd take a lover. No more being faithful to Aidan.

She'd take two. Hell, there was that pack of leopard shifters that'd been sniffing around her. *I'll lift tail for every single one of them.*

Regin rose, every muscle in her body protesting. "I'm taking a fiver." She scuffed toward the lavatory she'd found.

Natalya ruffled Thad's hair with her knuckles, discomfiting him even more, then followed her inside.

As Regin rubbed water on her face, Natalya hopped up on the next sink over. "So how about those revelations from last night! I suppose they're hampering your revenge plans. Because of the whole Chase-didn't-order-your-torture development."

"Just means he gets to live."

"Well, the important thing is that I got *my* revenge."

Regin tugged up her shirt to dry her face, then peered at her injury.

"Your skin's completely healed," Natalya said, her tone impressed.

"There was a lot of lightning last night—it helps. I'll be as good as new in a few hours."

"But you're not glowing."

Regin shrugged. "It might not come back." Her mother's had been forever dimmed. After Wóden and Freya had rescued her from the vampires that killed everyone in her village, her skin had never glowed as it once had. And it'd been covered with vampire bite scars.

I learned to count by them, never knowing how much I was hurting her.

"Oh, here"—Natalya stood, reaching into her jacket—"first time I've ever had women's lingerie in my pocket that wasn't my own." She handed Regin her bra. "Though it probably won't be the last."

Regin slipped off her shirt to don it, vowing to burn these clothes when they got back.

Natalya pinched her own cheeks, then vogued in the mirror for a few poses. "So, what are you going to do with Chase now? Not going to soften toward him at all?"

Last night, Regin almost had when he'd revealed his scarred skin to her—and when he'd been suffering through withdrawal.

He'd been off to the side by himself, silently shaking in the dark. *Going through that alone . . .*

Then Regin had remembered all he'd done to her. "After his laundry list of crimes? Historically, whenever someone abducts, poisons, or stabs me, I don't do second chances. Historically. I'm going to get on that boat, then get the hell away from him at the earliest opportunity." She'd find Lucia, and pick her life up where she'd left it.

"No attraction there?"

"Nothing there whatsoever," she said, ignoring Natalya's snort of disbelief. "Speaking of attraction. So, you and Brandr? Thad was crushed."

"The kid's seventeen. Just turned. In any case, Brandr and I scratched an itch. No big deal."

"Uh-huh."

"It wasn't all that wonderful, to be honest. I was afraid of poisoning him, even with my torque, and he was worried about hurting me. Basically, instead of one of us zigging while the other zagged, we both zagged. But you want to hear something crazy?" She leaned in to say, "I can't seem to stop looking at Lothaire. I caught him washing off earlier—shirtless—and was gobsmacked by the sight of his body. His physique and face are flawless, like a sculpture or something. Those hooded eyes of his—"

Without a word, Regin turned toward the door.

"What?" Natalya called, following her. "Name one thing about him that's not perfect!"

Over her shoulder, Regin said, "Maybe his razor-sharp vampire fangs? Maybe the fact that his 'physique' is fueled by a liquid diet? And those hooded eyes you were about to rhapsodize over? They're the color of *blood*."

Natalya grumbled, "Details, details."

They met up with Thad outside the lavatories, then the three emerged from the bunker into pouring rain and whipping winds. Lowering clouds promised more of both. Goody.

As a Valkyrie, Regin could withstand extreme temperatures, but that didn't mean she enjoyed being soaked and chilled.

They navigated the rock cutouts, then crossed to the nearest clearing. The landscape here was rocky with peaks in the distance, each bleaker than the last, like they'd be named Mount Donner Party or Need-A-Mind-Eraser Point.

The rest of the males caught up to them there. Chase's wrists were bound in front of him now. Brandr, that ever-loyal ass, must've retied them.

The magister didn't approach her, didn't try to speak with her, but he cast her a darkly possessive look.

Nope, nothing there whatsoever. At all. Less than nothing.

Declan realized with a jolt of alarm that Regin's skin was as dim as it'd been last night. Surely her wound was healed for the most part by now—she moved without stiffness—but her skin remained ashen.

What if it never returned to normal? *If it's the last thing I do, I'll figure out how to fix this.*

After an initial glance, Regin didn't look at him again. No surprise, considering all he'd done to her. And that'd been *before* he'd revealed his scars.

All night he'd wondered what the hell had possessed him to do that.

She gazed around at the scenery with plain distaste. Though a carpet of firs spread out below them, the mountaintops were bare—not because of snowfall, but because the peaks were too craggy for trees to grow.

He'd always enjoyed the desolate landscape high on the mountains, but she lived in a warm bayou town, resided at the edge of a swamp. If she hated this place now, it'd only get worse the higher they got. The rain would grow nearly constant, the wind gusting.

She pushed a sopping braid from her face. "Another day in paradise."

Could any female hate a man more than she does me?

Regin's attention turned to Lothaire, who still looked affected by his nightmares. If vampires experienced others' memories as if they were reliving them, then how could Lothaire not be tortured by what he'd dreamed?

Declan had once thought he wouldn't wish his past torment on even his worst enemy. Recalling Lothaire's bite, he decided, *No, I'm good with it.*

"How are you going to keep up with us during the day?" Regin demanded of the vampire.

"Overcast skies, superior nutrition, and my purloined army gear for cover." He tipped his wide-brimmed bush hat toward her. "And you?"

"Isn't your girlfriend La Dorada coming for you?"

He stilled, as if *listening* for her. "Not as of yet. Soon though."

"You stay outta my way, leech, or I will go lord-of-the-flies on your ass." Again, she instinctively reached back for her swords. Swords that could never be replaced.

They'd surely been buried in the facility's collapse.

Lothaire sighed. "Regin the Eloquent."

"Eat me." She passed them all without a glance. "Just tell me where we're heading."

Declan said, "If you want to be on point, we're going west—"

She unerringly turned due west and started climbing. Natalya and Thad joined her, and the three began conversing, mainly answering Thad's constant stream of questions.

Brandr hung back with Declan, while Lothaire brought up the rear.

In a low voice, Brandr said, "My gods, man, I've never seen you look so routed."

"You've seen me only a handful . . . ah, you mean as Aidan."

"Hell, even when you were dying, you looked more enthusiastic than this." When Declan said nothing, Brandr bit out a curse. "Listen, it isn't over. She has feelings for you."

"Oh, aye. Very strong ones. Hatred, for instance."

"If that's the case, then why couldn't she kill you?"

"She told me I didn't deserve her mercy—" Declan tensed when Lothaire closed in from behind.

"Are we talking about the Valkyrie, Magister?"

"Don't call me that! I'm no' one any longer." *What am I now?*

He was . . . *nothing.*

"You're on a clock," Lothaire said. "Once she escapes this island, she will leave you behind without a second thought."

And I'll follow. That'll be the way of things now.

Brandr said, "After a thousand years of warring with leeches, I never thought I'd say this sentence, but . . . the vampire's right. You have to win her back before we reach the boat."

"Win her *back*?" Declan snapped under his breath. "I never had her to begin with!" *Dead between us.*

There'd been only one night when he'd felt they had a real connection—when she'd been in his home, in his bath. She'd spun him tales so appealing that for a split second, he'd thought about freeing the miscreats she aligned with and flying her to bloody Belfast.

At the time, it'd seemed like madness; now it looked like a missed chance.

But, he reminded himself, there'd been no connection. It had all been an act—one designed to kill him. She might have pulled back at the last minute, but the intent had still been there. "Just save your breath."

"You *can* win her," Brandr insisted.

Declan actually held a measure of trust for the berserker. Yes, Brandr had proven himself repeatedly, but even Declan would admit there was something more. As if they'd known each other . . .

Now a thread of hope arose at the man's words. Maybe he knew enough about Regin to aid him. *Aye, and maybe you're chasing the wind.* "How can I?" Had he said that out loud? Fuck.

Thad scuffed back to join them, still burdened by his pack. "So, what are we talking about?" He fell in beside Lothaire.

The vampire said, "About how Chase can win back the Valkyrie."

Chase cast him a killing look over his shoulder.

"Well, men," Thad began in a solemn tone, "this sounds like a brewski moment to me."

Declan frowned when he heard a pop-top opening. "You brought *beer* with you? That's what filled your pack?"

"Regin said there's no drinking age in the Lore. And I was thinking I was going to die and all. It's not just beer, anyway. I've got condoms, cologne, toothpaste. Essentials."

So we have no food.

Brandr said, "Sounds like you were planning on getting laid before you die."

"I was, until you—how'd Regin put it?—until you *cockblocked* me."

That's my foulmouthed lass.

"What can I say?" Brandr shrugged. "But by all means, pass the beers around."

Thad handed the berserker one, then offered another to Lothaire, who merely raised his brows. "You want one, DC?" the kid asked.

Declan stiffened. "You didn't just call me that."

With a cheery grin, Thad handed him a warm can.

This situation was surreal. Here he was, hiking a mountain trail at the bottom of the world with a reviled vampire enemy, a vampire lad, and a berserker.

And this was the closest Declan had come to male bonding since he'd run with a gang back in Belfast.

Losing my mind. Fuck it. *Consider it already lost. A*

sunk cost. He raised his bound hands and accepted the beer.

"Sorry it's warm."

"How I like it," Declan said, though he could scarcely remember the last time he'd drunk alcohol of any kind.

Thad swigged from his can. "So how far did you guys get?"

Brandr said, "If you want my advice, Chase, you need to convince her that the old Aidan is in there. Maybe make an attempt to be more like him."

In a disbelieving tone, Declan said, "Be more like Aidan." *I can barely figure myself out . . .* He had no idea what or who he was, but now he was supposed to emulate someone else?

"Start being honest with her. Aidan always let her know what he was thinking. And he fairly much treated her like a queen."

Lothaire sneered, "That's the worst bloody advice I've ever heard!"

Agreed.

Brandr bowed his chest. "And why's that, leech? She cared for Aidan once—she will again."

"Precisely. She cared for *Aidan,*" Lothaire said. "I knew of Aidan the Fierce—no mortal could kill that many of the Horde without my hearing about it. And I know that he was a bold, blond Viking who was like a god among men. Women wanted him and men wanted to be him." He sighed. "Reminded me of myself." Then he jerked his chin at Declan. "Chase here is a coal-haired, scarred, underhanded, emotionally deficient

Irishman. Who, incidentally, is loathed universally by immortals and mortals alike."

Just lay it out there, leech. But Lothaire was right. Who was Declan to compete with Aidan—the man Regin had so clearly loved?

Not for the first time, Declan felt a blistering hatred for the man. A jealousy that ate at him. *Even if I might be Aidan. Sunk cost.*

Lothaire said, "I have a much better plan."

"Why help him?" Thad asked pointedly. "When you don't help anybody else?"

Lothaire exhaled ruefully. "Incurable romantic."

Incurable romantic, my arse. What was Lothaire's game? What would he gain by this?

Brandr said, "A millennia-old source of unadulterated evil dispensing relationship advice? We'll pass."

"If he takes my advice and it doesn't work, then I'll release him from one of his vows to me."

Declan's thoughts had been so filled with Regin, he'd forgotten how in deep he was with Lothaire—a vow for all the blood the vampire could drink and an open ended one, for *anything*.

Which meant . . . *I'll be killin' Lothaire as soon as he stops being useful.*

Brandr shook his head. "If your advice doesn't work, Chase could drive her further away."

"Is that even possible?" Lothaire countered. "Now, the first thing. Brandr tells her nothing, none of that greasing the wheel." Imitating Brandr's voice, Lothaire said, "Aw, Regin, he's been tortured. His life's miserable. He just wants you so badly, and psst, the poor guy's a *drug addict—*"

"You do drugs, DC?" Thad was appalled.

"Did," Declan bit out. "Past tense."

Brandr looked like he wanted to kill Lothaire. "If I tried to grease the wheel, it's because Chase could use some help right about now. All the help he can get."

Lothaire briefly gazed heavenward. "Chase is clearly a reluctant sharer. Which should incite her curiosity about what's going on in his head. She's a disgustingly self-righteous Valkyrie, filled with the need to fix things, to right wrongs. If anything needed fixing . . ." He waved a hand to indicate Declan from head to toe. "As wrong as he can be."

Declan remained silent, even though this reasoning seemed sound. *Jaysus, Dekko, taking advice from a leech who's blackmailing you for blood?*

His jaw clenched so hard that he *almost* kept himself from grating, "Second thing?"

Lothaire said, "Ignore her. Regin is accustomed to being the center of attention wherever she goes. In her circle, she's the showstopper, loud and brash compared to the silent sister she's always around. If you ignore her, Regin will grow even more curious about you."

Ignore Regin? When even now his gaze was scope-locked on the back-and-forth swish of her hips and arse? Need hammered at him. Without those shots, lust was riding him hard.

Brandr snapped his fingers in front of Declan's face. "Oh, yes, this is going to work like a charm."

"No, it'll totally work!" Thad finished his beer, offering a second round. When both Declan and Brandr refused, Thad cracked open another one for himself. "I ignored Sally Ann Carruthers for an entire semester. My mom came home early one afternoon and found her waiting for me. Get this—Sally Ann was waiting *naked* in my *bed*. Mom dragged her out by her ear."

Quirking a brow at that, Brandr asked Lothaire, "And the next part of your plan?"

"Tonight we will all make sure she has a chance to go off by herself. Then Chase will use violence to break the ice with her."

Declan repeated, "Violence."

"Live by the sword, love by the sword," Lothaire said.

Thad belched. "I got nothing on the violence. I was taught to respect women."

"He can respect her in the morning. Or not." Then Lothaire began outlining a plan for this very night.

With each word, Declan realized the strategy made a certain sick sense. He'd have to go out of his comfort zone, but if this plan could work . . .

Thad said, "This is definitely beyond my realm of experience. But I do have a tip, DC. My gram told me there's one thing a man always forgets to do whenever he bungles something—simply say he's sorry. Don't forget to do that." He pulled another beer from his pack. "Going to see if my girls are thirsty." He trudged ahead to join Regin and the fey.

Brandr seemed resigned to Lothaire's plan, but added, "If this works, Chase, you still can't kiss her."

"Because her lips drug men? Is that even true?"

"Aidan once admitted to me that her lips were like a drug, but I don't believe he meant literally. Hell, you two were locked at the mouth most of the time. However, I do think it makes you remember your past life sooner."

The idea of losing himself to Aidan's memories no longer sounded so bad. Especially if Declan's memories of torture, of addiction, of hurting Regin would all fade. Instead, he'd remember what it was like to be respected by his men rather than feared, to be adored by Regin rather than hated. "You truly believe in this curse?" Stranger things had happened in the Lore, but Declan had been cursed before and knew how it felt. Wouldn't he *sense* his impending doom now?

"I've seen it happen too many times," Brandr said. "So no kissing her, and no berserkrage with her. And by no means can you claim her."

Not claim her? If that Valkyrie parted her thighs and actually wanted Declan between them . . . ? "Boyo, understand me"—his gaze pinned Brandr's—"if I get a chance with her, I'm fuckin' takin' it."

FORTY-THREE

Is someone out there in the dark? Regin's ears twitched. *Watching me?*

She stilled in the water of the stream she'd found not far from their camp.

With narrowed eyes, she scanned her surroundings—a marshy plateau cradled high in the mountains. Here the stream widened into a chest-deep pool before spilling over into a waterfall.

Her sword and her recently washed clothes were laid out on a nearby boulder, a mere lunge away.

A second passed. Then another. Could just be the misting rain that continued to fall.

She continued her bath, scrubbing sand over her arms in agitated swipes, fearing she might be on the verge of introspecting again.

The unmerry band of six had traveled all afternoon and most of the night, but had decided to break till dawn. Though Regin was good to go—her chest had healed completely—Brandr, Chase, and Natalya needed to eat, were out hunting right now.

And Thad had begun to flag. Three beers hadn't helped him. He'd grown maudlin, missing his family, friends, and school. Regin had told Natalya, "The kid needs to be drinking blood, not suds."

The fey had replied, "Are you offering, Valkyrie?"

No matter how much Regin liked Thad, she wasn't ready to tap a vein for any vamp. Not hating a vampire was one thing; filling an empty beer can with your blood to feed one was another. . . .

All afternoon, Chase had been ignoring her, just as he had when she'd been in that cell. Unable to stand it, she'd taken Brandr aside, demanding to know what the four males had talked about. He'd shrugged and said, "Ask Declan." She'd smacked Brandr on the back of the head and stormed off.

But she couldn't stop thinking about Chase, about the scars he'd revealed to her. They'd looked old, which meant he must've been young when he'd gotten them—

The memory that had tickled her consciousness the night before finally surfaced, and she recalled the picture he'd shown her of the couple who'd been eaten alive by Neoptera.

Those curling, deliberate wounds the man and woman had suffered matched the distinctive shapes of Chase's scars. She remembered the ragged tone of his voice, the knotting of his shoulders. The way he'd pounded his fist on the desk.

A gasp left her lips. *They were his parents.*

Declan Chase's *mother and father.*

Had he watched the Neos devouring his family as his own flesh was stripped?

The couple had been middle-aged. Which meant

Chase had been young when the creatures had . . . had *fed* on him. She shoved the back of her wrist against her mouth.

He must've barely survived. How terrified he had to have been.

She gazed at the cloudy night sky. Yet just because she could understand his motivations didn't mean she could forgive his crimes. He might have had nothing to do with her vivisection, but he'd still tortured her, he'd still brought her and her friends to this hell-on-earth island as his prisoners.

Had MacRieve and Carrow even made it out of the facility alive? Was that vemon Malkom Slaine out stalking the witch and her ward? Regin had faced a vemon in the past and was lucky to have escaped with her life. They were phenomenally strong and fast. If Slaine wanted revenge, then who could possibly protect Carrow?

And because of Chase, Regin had been kept from Lucia. She had no idea how her sister was faring out in the world. Would Lucia be foolish—or desperate—enough to face Cruach alone?

Regin ducked her head under the water. What would she want with Chase anyway? There was no happily ever after with him. He scorned immortals. As of yesterday, he was a jobless, homeless drug addict, with a target on his back the size of the entire Lore.

And that was *if* he lived. *If* they didn't kiss or have sex. Otherwise he'd kick it before anyone in the Lore got a chance to off him—

She stilled when she sensed Chase nearing. *Couldn't*

ignore me for long, eh, Paddy? She peered over her shoulder, found him standing at the edge of the water.

Without his cuffs. *Damn it, Brandr.*

Then she frowned. Chase's mien was determined, his dark brows drawn together over his blazing gray eyes.

Determined to do what?

His pullover sweater and pants seemed tighter on him. As if he'd grown over the day, which made no sense—

He grasped the bottom of that pullover to remove it. *Does he think he's coming in with me?*

"Pool's taken. Run along, Chase." He didn't, so she opened her mouth to deliver a caustic chew-out. The words died on her lips when he dragged the sweater over his head, revealing his flexing torso.

His scars seemed to be stretched flatter than when she'd seen them last night, as if his chest had grown. As she surveyed his torso, she found herself staring as much at his sculpted slabs of muscle as she was at the scars covering them.

Rock-hard ridges descended to the low waist of his camo pants. Her gaze dipped to his flat navel, then to his goodie trail. And lower . . . She swallowed. He'd begun stiffening in those pants.

She yanked her gaze up, determined to look at anything else. Around his neck he wore dog tags, and a big, butch military watch was strapped to one brawny forearm. With the combat boots, low-slung pants, and tacticool accessories, he looked good. Even scarred, he looked better than good.

Was he gorgeous, like the original Aidan had been? No. But he was intriguing.

And right now, Chase looked like a man who knew what he wanted and who was on the cusp of taking it.

Magister Chase, the man, was . . . *sexy.*

When he sat on a nearby boulder, pulling up one knee to unlace a boot, that eight-pack of his rippled. She watched with a reluctant fascination as he removed both boots.

Then he stood, his hands at the fly of his pants, pinched fingers tugging down his zipper. She was going to tell him to stop. Any second.

Shoulders back, he let the pants drop, stepping from them.

Breathe, Regin. His shaft was semihard and growing, rising from a patch of crisp black hair. Pulsing with aggressive jerks, it distended before her eyes. Behind that taut flesh, his balls hung down, heavy but visibly tightening.

The clever and relatively young Declan Chase met two out of her three criteria.

He'd always been generously endowed, but this . . . Her claws were curling for it.

Stop staring at his dick, slore.

Yet the rest of him affected her almost as much. His legs were powerfully masculine, dusted with black hair that led up to his groin. His hips were lean, the muscles up his sides flexing.

She was transfixed. But when he took a step closer, she snapped out of it. "Thanks for the view of your junkyard." She turned away, continuing to wash her arms. "But you'd do well to stay away from me, Magister."

"No' a magister anymore, no' one of the Order."

She shrugged. "Oh, because you've lost your installation?"

"I'm no' a magister anymore, because you wouldn't be a magister's woman." He strode into the water.

FORTY-FOUR

Declan edged closer.

In a way, this was like a military op. Yet never had an objective meant this much to him. And in no plan of attack before had he ever felt this much conflict within himself.

Stripping in front of her was one of the hardest things he'd ever done. Storm a Cerunno nest? Routine. Attack a demon stronghold? Child's play.

Putting himself under her scrutiny to risk certain rejection? Grueling.

He'd somehow held himself still as she'd leisurely inspected every inch of him. For some reason, he didn't think she was repulsed by the sight of him. God in heaven, maybe even the opposite. When her eyes had flickered, he'd grown hard under her gaze.

Nothing to lose, Dekko. If this didn't work, then at least he'd be freed from one of his vows to the vampire.

Her slim shoulders tensed as he eased up behind her. Heedless, he reached forward and pulled her hair off her nape. About to kiss the smooth skin above her torque, he leaned in—

She threw an elbow back, catching him in the mouth. "Don't you dare!"

As he'd hoped, that one hit wasn't enough, was only the shot that set off an avalanche. She whirled around, fist drawn back to pound his cheek.

He shook it off, swinging around to kiss her neck.

"Stop that!" She punched his mouth again. He pressed his newly bleeding lip to the other side of her neck.

"What is *wrong* with you?" Another hit to his face left his jaw singing.

But he merely rubbed his chin over the tip of her pointed ear. Every time she struck, he responded with a kiss or touch. "Is that supposed to hurt, Valkyrie? You hit like a wee girl."

"A wee girl!" she screamed, punching his kidney over and over, backing him toward the shore.

Never had he been so happy to take a beating. Of course, she wasn't at full Valkyrie strength, and he was lingering on the very cusp of berserkrage.

When he tripped backward onto land, she leapt atop him, straddling his waist as she drilled his face like a punching bag.

Instead of deflecting her hits, he grasped her perfect breasts, groaning from the weight of them in his hands. Soft, damp flesh against his palms. Her nipples were tight points. . . . With a groan, he rocked his hips up beneath her.

She knocked his hands away; he let her.

"You keep ticklin' me like this, Valkyrie, and I'll think you want me to tickle back." Was she even aware they were both naked and she was straddling him? He could feel the heat of her quim against him, slick warmth in the cool air. "I can do this all night, lass."

"You prick!" she yelled between breaths, hammering his sternum. "Maybe I can't land a painful punch because of all the *drugs* in your system!"

His gaze bored into hers. "Never will touch them again," he told her, and he meant it.

"Or maybe you don't feel my hits because of all that ugly scar tissue buffering you!" She dragged her claws over the marks.

Shame filled him. Anger ignited. *She'll never see past them.* Just as he'd known.

Then his eyes narrowed with realization. "I might be ugly, Regin, but something's got your claws curlin'." She'd seen him completely undressed, and she was still getting aroused. Wanting to roar with triumph, he grew more aggressive, leaning up to brush his lips over one stiff nipple.

After a heartbeat's hesitation, she backhanded him away.

"Slower to defend on that one, no, lass?" He pinned her arms to her sides so he could nuzzle her other nipple. Though she resisted, he took it between his lips, tasting that bud, tonguing it . . . With a hoarse groan, he began to suckle, his eyes rolling back in his head.

Had she moaned? His cock pulsed painfully.

In a siren's voice, she said, "Chase, let me go. So I can touch *you*."

Yes! Without releasing his suck on her nipple, he slid his hands down to rest on her hips.

"You want my touch, Blademan?" She reached

back, raking those claws up his thighs, leaving bloody furrows. "That's all you'll get from me—pain!"

He sucked her harder, till her nipple throbbed to the tip of his tongue. Pain? He felt none.

Gods, Chase's mouth was so hot on her breast, his lips closed tight around the peak.

He was thrumming, the muscles of his torso flexing sensuously beneath her. She'd never truly comprehended how big Chase's body was next to hers. *So like Aidan.*

Yet so different. A Celt with a wicked tongue and a gravelly voice.

His kiss tempted her; but for right now, it felt better to smack him around. She shoved him back, slapping him across the face.

"That's it, Regin, do what you need to."

"Oh, I will." The last three weeks had been like a pressure cooker, and now she was about to explode. Every hit made a knot inside her unfurl. He wasn't the only one who could feel rage—and seeing the blood she'd drawn all over his body made it ebb.

One of his eyes was swollen. His lip was busted. The skin over his broad cheek was split. His legs were bleeding.

And still he was hard as rock.

He took her hips and settled her lower on his torso, pressing her to his erection. "I want you so much. It's like a fever in me."

She knocked his hands away. "Why would I ever

want you back? You think I'm just going to forget all you've done to me?"

"No, no' forget. But I can salvage this thing between us. I'm ready to do whatever needs to be done."

"Salvage, huh? See, I've been remembering more from last night. You *suffocated* me." She boxed his other ear. "Was it hard to do?"

His face went cold, evincing that cruelness she'd hoped never to see again. "Just pressed down till you went limp. What's hard about that?"

"Ugh!" She backhanded him again.

"Of course it was bloody hard," he roared, the tendons in his neck straining. "One of the hardest things I've ever done. Brandr was about to puncture your goddamned heart. Happened anyway."

"Your hands were steady enough when you were cutting off my air!" Another resounding slap.

"Because they fuckin' needed to be! Damn you, woman, you *died*! And there was . . . *nothing I could do.*" His voice was thick.

Was Chase feeling an emotion other than hate? Dim memories arose. Her face damp with tears? Chase murmuring in her ear to hold on for him?

She narrowed her gaze. "Did the big bad Blademan lose control of his emotions last night?" *Slap.* "Did seeing me like that compwetely bwake your wittle heart?" *Backhand.* "Did you cry man tears?"

He flipped her to her back, rising above her. "Cried over you like a wee babe." He pinned her hands over her head. "I *can* feel, Regin. And it killed me to see you like that!" His eyes began to glow. "Which really pissed me off, Valkyrie. Because any last hope that I could live without you vanished."

Declan wedged his hips between her legs as the need to make her his burned within him. "It will always be you, Regin." His free hand curled under her thigh to position his shaft.

"No, Chase!" She scrambled back from him, fighting his hold on her wrists. "Never!" She'd begun panting, breasts rising and falling, her nipples swollen. "You can't do this. No sex!"

"Does this mean you're feelin' something for me, Valkyrie? Maybe you want me to live now?" He leaned down to kiss her, but she yanked her head to the side.

"Do *not* kiss me," she hissed, her eyes flashing.

"No kissing of *any* kind, then?" As she tussled against him, he moved her bodily to a nearby bed of grass.

"What are you doing?" she snapped.

He captured her wrists in front of her, then knelt between her legs. "I just want a taste of you, Regin. I've dreamed of doing this to you."

"Forget it!" She tightened her knees.

He maneuvered his shoulders to work her thighs wider, then dipped his head to her blond curls. "One kiss, and I'll stop."

"Chase, damn you—"

He pressed his mouth to her quim and gave a lick, silencing her and shocking him. *"Ah, fuck me!"* She was delicious, her sex quivering and wet. He'd planned to ask her if she wanted him to stop. *Impossible.* He set back in, his tongue delving for more.

She moaned and lightning struck overhead. His permission.

He released her wrists, and her hands flew to his head, not to shove him away, but to thread her fingers through his hair—the first time she'd touched him without anger.

More. He breathed her in.

"That's it, Regin. Let me do this to you." When she undulated to his mouth, his cock pulsed even harder, moisture beading the head.

With each roll of her hips, he rocked his own, spreading his knees wider. He thrust against air, imagining his shaft was buried deep where his tongue plunged.

Heaven was pleasuring her with her lightning overhead to let him know he was doing it right. With each kiss, her skin glowed brighter, and something like . . . like *joy* swept over him. *I can satisfy her.* In time, he *could* fix this between them.

"You're delicious." Between licks, he groaned, "*Hot . . . wet . . . heaven.*"

At his words, she gave a strangled cry, and her legs fell open in total surrender. *In invitation.* He traced her glistening core with the pad of one finger.

"Inside," she moaned. When he eagerly slipped it into her tight sheath, her head thrashed. "Don't stop *that,* just don't stop. . . ."

"You need these fillin' you, don't you, lass?" With a hungry flick of his tongue, he wedged another finger inside. "I'll get them nice and deep."

"Chase, I'm close!"

"Regin, come for me!" He bore down on her with his mouth, his fingers thrusting in time. *"That's it, baby."*

Her back bowed. A bolt of her lightning struck so close he felt the heat of it. "Chase!" she screamed as she began to orgasm.

When she clamped his head to draw him closer, he almost spilled on the ground. As he licked in bliss, his spine tingled, his heavy ballocks tightening. He commanded himself not to come as he wrung every shiver from her, every last cry.

He broke away only when she pushed against his forehead. When he rasped his stubbled cheeks against her thighs, she trembled anew.

For long moments, she stared up at the sky. Then she propped herself up on her elbows, meeting his gaze, her expression utterly inscrutable.

"Regin? Say something. I do no' like it when you're quiet."

Chase had pulled a fast one on her. *Zing!* This had all been a carefully crafted and executed plan. *Get the volatile Valkyrie so pissed, she loses control.*

And according to plan, she was now naked, on a bed of grass, with Declan Chase between her thighs.

The playah got played. She'd been . . . predictable. Everything had burned out of control.

And was threatening to again. When his gaze dropped from her face back between her legs and he tightened his arms around her thighs, she said, "Don't even think about it."

With a darkening expression, he rose up on his knees, looking as if she'd just taken away his new favorite toy. His body was taut as a bowstring, his muscles rippling, his shaft jutting with need.

"What the hell, Chase? What was this?" He'd used her own personality against her, and she'd fallen right into his trap. She should throw *him* a curveball. She should tease him, get him within a heartbeat of coming, then strut off, leaving him with a view of her sweet ass.

I'm going to femme fatale him! Like her sisters would. Oh, yeah, the playah's back in the house—

"Should be obvious what this was, no? If you're still confused, I can draw you a diagram."

Her eyes went wide, her hand fisting in the mud beside her bed of grass.

"Hint: slot B is delicious—"

Splat. Without thought, she'd thrown mud all over his face. *So much for femme fatale.*

He sputtered in disbelief, then roared, "*What the ever-livin' feck—*"

Splat, splat. Muck covered his torso. And gods help her, his reaction almost had her cackling.

"That's how you want to play?" He snagged her ankle, dragging her closer to smear a handful of mud across her thighs. Though she scrambled to get away, he coated her belly with a generous swipe, then tossed a glob over her breasts.

"Dick!" She beaned one of his legs with another salvo, bringing the heat.

He released her to scoop up mounds of ammunition in both hands. In an ominous tone, he said, "Regin, there're two ways we can do this—"

Splat. Tagged his other thigh. Which left only one place that she hadn't hit. A big target.

He followed her gaze down. "Do no' even think of it. You do it, and you'll be cleanin' me up."

Splat.

FORTY-FIVE

Declan gazed down at his mud-coated groin. "Little witch." He dropped his handfuls, then lunged for her, scooping her against his chest to head for the stream.

He swung her up and tossed her in, following right behind her. She gasped, swiping hair out of her eyes as he dunked under and scrubbed the mud off his face.

"I warned you." He snagged her wrist and brought her palm to his chest, wiping away the streaks. "You made this mess, you clean it up."

She narrowed her eyes, no doubt to curse him, but his other hand on her breast silenced her. "I'll be doin' the same." He brushed his thumb over her nipple, and her lids went heavy. When he released her wrist and cupped both breasts, she sucked in a breath.

A heartbeat passed, and another . . . "Damn you," she whispered. Then, of her own accord, she glided her soft hands over his chest. With each stroke she uncovered more skin. Scarred skin. But she didn't shy away. In fact, once she'd cleaned away the mud, she traced some of the marks, her gaze following her fingers.

I'd kill to know what she's thinkin'.

With one hand, he began rubbing her belly, cleaning

her as promised. With his other, he smoothed mud from her thighs.

She reciprocated, reaching down and sweeping her palms up his legs. His knees went weak as her hands climbed higher.

"How was your plan supposed to end?" she murmured, her fingers grazing just below his aching ballocks. Would she touch him there?

"With me makin' love to you." He began kneading her breasts.

Even as she arched to his hands, she said, "That won't happen."

"Then I'd call it a win if I get to pleasure you again." He lightly pinched her sensitive nipples, making her sway. "I want to be a good lover to you." Now that he'd discovered he could pleasure her, he wanted to excel, to be the best she'd ever had.

"And what about you?" She gripped his shaft with her palm, and he jolted upright. "Doesn't this ache?"

Voice breaking low, he said, "Like the devil." A slow stroke had him groaning, "*That feels so good.*"

"Just cleaning up the mess I made."

"You keep doin' that, lass, and I'll add to it."

She peered up at him with silvery eyes. "That's a shame. 'Cause I had plans for this." She gave him a squeeze.

If not to make love, then . . . His jaw slackened. *She wants to go down on me?*

Never had it been so important not to come. Gritting his teeth, he somehow kept his seed as she scrubbed him thoroughly.

Twice he almost spilled it—when she ran her thumb in circles over his cockhead, and when she firmly grasped his ballocks while she stroked. Before this night, he'd had no idea how much he would particularly enjoy the latter.

"There. All done," she said in a throaty voice. "I'll bet it's so clean I could eat off of it."

Brows drawn, he swallowed audibly. "One way to find out."

Still holding him, she turned back toward the shore.

Regin had a mountain of a man naked on a bed of grass, with her kneeling between his legs, her palm cupping his shaft. And she wasn't feeling so much played as powerful.

We won't do more than scratch an itch, she assured herself. Just as Natalya and Brandr had done.

With his accent thicker than she'd ever heard it, Chase said, "Leadin' a man by his cock, lass?"

His husky voice made her shiver, her nipples puckering even harder. She was melting for this wicked Celt. "That a problem?"

He shook his head gravely. "Can no' think *why* that phrase has a negative connotation."

Never taking her eyes from his, she bent down and ran her tongue over the swollen tip.

He exhaled a ragged breath. *"Almighty."* A wet lick around the crown made him shudder.

He leaned up on his elbow to watch her, the muscles of his torso rippling. With his other hand, he brushed her hair back. "Want to see your beautiful face. Been waitin' all my life to be with you like this."

Her heart seemed to flutter. *No, just scratching an itch.*

Chase certainly didn't think that. As she brought her lips over the head, she gazed up at his expression—dark brows knitted, gray eyes ablaze with yearning.

When she grasped the base of his shaft and sucked him deeper, he breathed, "*Ah, fuck me,*" and gods help her, she wanted to at that moment.

He drew his knees up, his hips subtly thrusting as he cradled the back of her head. His thighs were quaking, brawny muscles contracting. Already close.

She broke away to say, "You like this?"

"I *hate* it."

She almost grinned. His reactions were seducing her all over again. The low rumbling sounds he made. The way he was so obviously struggling to hold out.

The hand on her head was shaking as he pressed her down for more.

Nothing had ever turned her on so intensely as this. Her nipples ached, her clitoris throbbing for release. She reached between her legs, stroking wet flesh, her eyes closing with bliss.

When she moaned around him, he rasped, "The only thing that could make this better is you comin' on my tongue again."

She blinked open her eyes in confusion. He'd pulled out of her grip, maneuvering her body to lie beside his until she faced his shaft—and he faced her sex.

With his fingers splayed tight over her ass, he gave a harsh growl, then buried his mouth between her legs.

She could feel his hot breath, the desperate flicks of his strong tongue.

"Chase!" She almost went over the edge right then. When he raised one knee, rocking his hips toward her, she eagerly drew his length to her mouth again, suckling it with greedy pulls.

"*Unh . . .*" He groaned against her flesh and bucked to her lips.

But when she grasped his balls and tugged, he broke away to yell, "Ah, more o' *that*! You're makin' me—"

She sank the claws of her free hand into his muscled ass, clutching him closer. He jerked in surprise, roaring, "God almighty! Comin', Regin!" then returned to licking her madly.

Yes, yes, yes! Sucking harder, she ground against his tongue, beginning to come in a wet rush. She was screaming around his engorged shaft when he erupted, pumping his semen free.

Mindless with waves of pleasure, she drew him deeper, deeper. . . .

FORTY-SIX

"God in heaven, woman." Declan lifted her, laying her against his side. "That'll change a man's outlook on life real quick."

The best way to bring a male back from the brink? Hot oral sex with a Valkyrie. And he finally understood what her little claws were all about!

As a light rain fell over their heated skin, he wrapped his arm around her shoulders, groaning in satisfaction. *Complete peace.* For the first time in his life.

The strain was gone, and in its place was something like elation. Oh, aye, elation and excitement coursed through him. He finally believed he could look forward to *more* with her.

His woman. A future worth fighting for. All the things that had been missing from his life for so long.

More.

"That shouldn't have happened," she muttered.

"I'll argue that point to my dyin' breath. Do you deny you enjoyed that? You're glowin' bright as day, and you came hard enough. Twice."

"Oh, please! I hadn't rubbed one out in more than

three weeks. Diaper play would've gotten me off at this point."

"I'll make a note."

She stiffened beside him. "This doesn't change anything."

"Regin, it changes everything! You're attracted to me." *And I can be what you need in bed.* "Anything else I can fix."

"Like your scathing hatred for my world?"

He pinched her chin, tipping her head back. "Then *show* it to me! Show me why I was wrong to hate it."

"It's too deep-seated in you, too ingrained."

"Maybe it was before, but I must be shakin' it. Hell, I don't know up from down anymore. Nothing about me is fixed."

She murmured, "You're *unfinished.*"

"Aye, precisely."

"I need to go."

When she moved to get up, he shoved her against his side and slapped her arse to keep her there. "You stay with me."

She snapped, "What do you want from me, Chase?"

He drew his head back in confusion. "I want *everything.* You're *mine,* Regin." He'd earned her by right of every miserable second of his life. "Let me tell you how this is goin' to go down. I'll get you and your friends off this island, and then you and I will figure out a place to put down roots." Her lips worked soundlessly. "Speechless? Would've thought that an impossibility." He nipped the tip of her ear. "I might have four or five decades of life left—a blink of an eye in your lifetime.

I will have you till I die, so you're just goin' to have to suck it up."

"What gives you the right to demand all this?"

"If your man Aidan actually hitched a ride with me, then I'm entitled to the use of his woman for a few years. And I want to seal this deal with you tonight."

"No way, Chase. You can't have sex with me."

"You want me to." He studied her expression. "Christ. You *need* me to."

"Doesn't matter."

She hadn't denied either! "Because of the curse."

"Among other things."

"Like what?" Then it dawned on him. "You're worried I'll get you pregnant?" His brows drew together. "Never thought about that before." He remembered looking around the home he'd known for a decade, thinking how grim and silent it was. How soulless his entire existence was.

Now possibilities spread out before him, ones he'd never imagined for himself. *I could be a . . . da?* The corners of his lips curled.

It struck him then that his entire outlook must have shifted. Because the idea of a sprawling lightning-struck house filled with Valkyrie daughters and berserker sons felt *exactly right*. "Regin, I've got money saved up. I can take care of you and our bairns."

"Okay, that wasn't what I was talking about. Valkyrie aren't fertile unless we eat for a few weeks."

He'd had no idea. Fascinating.

"But since you brought it up . . . Dude. You're a jobless, homeless drug addict. Great daddy material."

Straight-talking Regin. "I'll never touch the shite again. I don't need to suppress my strength or get mindless again—I need to be strong and clear to protect what's mine." He squeezed her tighter, pressing his lips against her hair. "As for the job, I've money enough to keep you in Aston Martins, Valkyrie. And to buy a home. Or two." When she raised a brow, he explained, "For twenty years I've had zero expenses. I haven't spent a dime of my substantial salary. And many of my captures carried bounties. Now, what *was* your point?"

"What if you had a 'freak' child? It seems like that'd be your worst fear, to get a *detrus* pregnant."

"Don't ever use that word to describe yourself again. That was my mistake—not seeing that there are differences among the immortals. Good and evil, just like with humans."

"Yeah, well, your realization came too late for me." She shoved away from him, rising to her feet.

With a sigh, he let her go. His skin felt bare and cold without her. All these years avoiding touch, and now he wanted nothing more than to have her warm little body against him.

When she strode over to her clothes, the sight of that naked arse had him hard all over again. Voice rough, he said, "Stay with me." Had that sounded like a command?

Her back stiffened, then she pulled on her knickers. "Forget it."

Here goes nothing. He exhaled and said, "I am . . . sorry."

* * *

Regin froze. Without turning, she asked, "What did you say?"

He grated, "I'm sorry that I've hurt you repeatedly. And that I hurt . . . people you care about."

"An apology?" She faced him. "That must've been difficult."

"I thought I was doing my duty with you. With all immortals. I followed my commander's orders blindly." He scrubbed his hand down his face. "We . . . went too far."

That haunted look in his eyes. She was drawn to his pain, wanting to soothe it. Aidan had never *needed* her. This man before her needed Regin like a lifeline.

"Webb was your commander?" At his nod, she said, "You seemed close to him."

"He was like my father and best friend rolled into one. He saved my life from a pack of Neoptera. That's what did this to me."

Those creatures were terror personified. She'd suspected, but to hear it confirmed . . . "How old were you?"

Instead of answering her, he held out his hand. "I'll only talk about this if you sleep the rest of the night by my side."

"You sound like Lothaire, making everything a transaction."

"Maybe he's right to."

With a roll of her eyes, she sat down a couple feet from him, pulling her knees up to her bare chest. At once, he yanked her back to his side.

She exhaled, defeated. "How old?"

"I was seventeen."

"That picture you showed me, it was of your parents."

He tensed against her. "Aye."

"I've never heard of anyone surviving a Neo attack."

"Webb saved my life before they finished me."

Finished him. Everything began to make sense. His family had been massacred, he'd been maimed. And the man who'd saved his life warred against immortals.

"He gave me a reason to keep going. Taught me everything I know."

Meaning he'd been brainwashed, and at such a young age. Declan Chase had never had a chance. "What will happen with Webb now?"

"If he finds out that I lived and went AWOL, he'll put a bounty on my head." There was a thread of something like grief in Chase's voice.

"That's harsh."

"I . . . I almost killed him."

"What? Why?"

"He's the one who ordered you vivisected. Hid it from me. He'd learned I was a berserker by then, so he would've known that you were mine." Chase's eyes glowed with menace. "Yet he still hurt you. When La Dorada arrived, I was squeezing the life out of him." His hands fisted even now.

He'd harmed the man he looked upon as a father? Over her? She'd heard his outraged bellow that night. . . .

"I am done with the Order, done with Webb. Face it, Regin. You're the only friend I have in the world."

He thinks we're friends? "When did you start to feel differently about me?"

"That night in my bathroom marked the beginning of the end for me. I actually considered runnin' with you to bloody Belfast. Would you have gone with me then?"

So fast it would've made his head swim. But she didn't need to encourage him. Instead of answering, she brushed his track marks. "What happened here?"

"I used to inject a drug to keep my rage and strength in check. It had an opiate in it as well."

"How long have you been doing it? Some of the marks look old."

"Over a decade." He hesitated, then said, "Before that . . . I shot heroin. When I was younger in Belfast."

Oh, gods. "Because you always felt sick inside?" His past lives competing with his present, the nightmares and memories. . . .

He shrugged, but he didn't deny it.

Then she should have found him as a boy before he got so twisted. Instead of running from Aidan's latest incarnation, she should have protected him. Guilt was like a lead weight over her chest.

How loyal am I? I abandoned Aidan to fate. Left a young Declan Chase at the mercy of the world.

As if sensing her turmoil, he said, "Come now, lass." Whenever Aidan had wanted to look into her eyes, he'd gently cupped her face in his hands. Not so with Declan. He gathered her neck in the crook of his arm and held her steady as he gazed down. "Let's no' talk about that. You're with me now."

Even after everything that had happened, Regin found herself nodding against him, her arm gliding across his deep chest.

"But I want you to understand that I'm not tryin' to replace Aidan. Know I can't. You loved him too bloody much."

I didn't. Not irrevocably. The Valkyrie believed that one of their kind could recognize her eternal mate when he opened his arms and she realized she would forever run to get within them. Regin had been so *close* to running to Aidan, but she'd fought those feelings. "I . . . didn't love him." *Hadn't allowed myself to.*

"What? Why didn't you fall for him?"

"I needed him body and soul, but my heart was still my own."

Chase stared up at the sky, and the corners of his lips curled. A thousand years ago, Aidan had evinced that same expression. *Anticipation.* "Then, Valkyrie, it's still mine to win."

In time, his breaths deepened, and he passed into sleep. As Regin watched, his eyes began to dart behind his lids, his arm tightening around her.

He's dreaming. Her own eyes welled with tears as she whispered, "*Shh, be at ease. . . .*"

FORTY-SEVEN

She can't remain on the battlefront with me, Edward thought, his gaze following Regin as she paced his tent. Wending around his myriad weapons, she trailed her fingers over the waist jacket and crested helmet of his cavalry uniform.

Her lovely visage was drawn, her ethereal glow lighting the interior. Already his soldiers thought she was a witch who'd entranced him.

She couldn't remain with him—and he couldn't part from her. Which meant he'd be going into her world, he hoped as her husband. Yet the Valkyrie was proving . . . recalcitrant.

"You're too young, Edward!"

"I'm twenty-five. Men my age marry."

"Men your age usually don't turn their backs on everything they know. Finish your tour on the peninsula, then go home to your London mansion. Marry a mortal girl who wears dresses and doesn't have pointed ears. I will bring you nothing but tragedy."

When she picked up his saddle blanket and saw his embroidered personal crest, her face grew stricken. "Two ravens in flight?" She gave a bitter laugh. "Edward, you must let me go. You have to forget about me."

He cast her a rueful smile. "What makes you believe I could possibly do either?" She didn't understand the depths of his feelings, could never be made to. He stood, crossing to her—even moments without touching her proved too long to endure. He rested his hands on her slim shoulders, wanting so badly to kiss her, but she forbade it.

For how much longer can I deny myself a taste?

"Regin, it will always be you. This curse can't be stronger than what I feel for you."

"That's exactly what Gabriel said. On the day he died."

"It's just coincidence, love. All of it. Aidan fought vampires his entire life. Is it a surprise that, in the end, he was murdered by one? Treves had repeatedly angered his king—a coward who had him poisoned. And Gabriel? My God, Regin, how many pirates died in shipwrecks?"

"You're forgetting one thing—the timing. All of these deaths happened within hours of them bedding me. I'm your curse! Why can't you accept that . . . ?"

Declan shot awake, eyes darting as he took in the murky morning. *Not in a tent?* For a moment, he couldn't place where he was.

Then he spied Regin. She was up, getting dressed, glowing like the sun in the persistent rain.

She tilted her head at him. Under her gaze, he resisted the nearly overwhelming urge to throw on his clothes. *Still new to me.*

But she gave his scars little attention, and he relaxed, musing about how she'd slept curled against him. Just as protecting her had fulfilled him, so had merely holding her.

Fulfilled. Such an alien feeling, he'd scarcely known how to label it.

The rightness of her in his arms alleviated his lingering withdrawals, gave him something infinitely more pleasurable than the shots had ever provided. . . .

Just as he contemplated dragging her back down with him, she said, "We need to get back."

"Aye, I know, then," he muttered, rising to don his pants. Regin watched him unabashed, and again he thought she *might* just be liking what she saw.

But when he dragged on his pullover, they both frowned. His clothes were tight.

"Aren't you supposed to . . . go back down? Muscle-wise?"

"But I didn't hit a berserkrage. Maybe it's because I'm clean of drugs?"

"Um, you shot up the day before yesterday."

But a vampire sucked me dry. He shrugged.

"Were you dreaming just before you woke?" she asked, shivering with cold.

"Here, lass." He crossed the distance to her, yanking off his sweater. "The material stays dry, it'll keep you warm. Arms up, then."

With a roll of her eyes, she lifted her arms so he could tug it down over her. It nearly reached her knees. He took the opportunity to clasp her against his chest, resting his chin on her head. "You will no' put your arms around me?"

"I don't want to encourage you. Now, answer my question."

"I dreamed of you and Edward in his tent, discussing the curse. He felt the same way about it as I do now—that it's bullshite."

She pushed against him until he released her. "Edward died the next day."

"How?"

"A sniper fired on his troops. He pushed me out of the path of a bullet. The back of his head was just . . . gone. A mortal sacrificed his life over an injury that would've taken me a day to recover from. I've been as good as widowed four times. And with this lifetime, you've been doomed for five."

"If last night was my *doom,* Regin, then you can sign me up for a hundred more go-rounds."

She narrowed her gaze. "Don't you dare ridicule me or this . . . this situation! I nearly lost my mind with each death. Aidan bled out in our bed. I held Treves as he yelled in anguish from poison. My pirate? My beautiful Gabriel? A violent storm bashed his ship apart. A falling mast crushed him, killing him instantly. His body was swept overboard, and I-I couldn't find him . . . c-couldn't bring him back."

"Damn it, lass, this curse will no' affect you and me."

"With everything you've seen in the Lore, how can you doubt this?"

"I don't doubt that curses exist—I've *been* cursed by a witch, and I remember how it felt. I'd *sense* something if a curse was hanging over me." He brushed his knuckles down her silky cheek. Would he ever grow used to the luxury of simply touching her skin? "I do no' know how to convince you of it, but I feel this in my gut. We're beyond it."

"Even if there were no curse, and even if I could forgive you for all you've done to me, I can't get past what you've done to my friends. You've got a lot of fates on your head."

"What if I get everyone in our crew off the island? Would you forgive me then?"

She shook her head. "That would still leave Carrow, Ruby, and MacRieve. And Lucia must be alive and well. Every single one of them has been jeopardized by your actions."

"How Lucia?"

"I'm supposed to be with her when she faces Cruach."

"You know I've no control over her fate."

"The stakes are steep for me, Chase. I could never forgive you if Lucia was forced to fight an enemy as vile as that by herself, because I was *otherwise engaged*. She's everything to me."

"Then you've laid out my tasks. I'll take care of them one by one."

Regin folded up the pullover's lengthy sleeves. "How's that?"

"I won't be gettin' on the boat with you."

"What are you talking about?"

"Regin, I'll scour this island for all of your friends first."

"You'll get yourself killed, before the curse ever gets a chance to do it."

"If the alternative is not having you, then so bloody

well." He shrugged. "But you forget, this is what I do. I hunt immortals. And this is *my* island. I'll find them."

"And Lucia?"

"She's stayed alive this long. So I'm counting on her to live one thousand years *and four weeks*. If I can get everyone to safety, will you give us a shot?"

"What about the cur—"

"Don't answer now," he interrupted, his tone curt. That curse talk maddened him. He felt with a certainty deep down in his bones that he had a future with her. He'd be damned if they'd argue over something that he *knew* didn't apply to them. "Just think about it."

As Regin and Chase made their way back to meet the others, she studied him under her lashes.

Before, he'd been intriguing to her, attractive, even sexy. This morning, he was *devastating*.

His wet hair whipped over those lean cheeks. His camo pants clung to his sculpted legs and ass, until her claws curled painfully. Had his steely-eyed gaze always been so breathtaking?

Their activities last night had certainly agreed with the man. Chase seemed to have grown overnight—and shed a couple of decades' worth of tension. The stiffness in his back and neck was absent. Now that his lips weren't pressed into a grim line, she could see his even, white teeth, making her fantasize about what his smile would look like.

She doubted even Chase knew. The man didn't have a single laugh line anywhere on his face, not even a hint of one.

As they neared the others, she asked, "Don't you want your sweater?"

His expression darkened. "Do *you* want me to wear it?"

She frowned. "I don't care either way."

He smoothed a braid from her face. "Then I'd rather it keep you warm."

When they rejoined the group, almost as one, their gazes locked on his bare, scarred chest.

Brandr looked troubled but sympathetic. Thad gaped, while Natalya winced. Lothaire didn't bother hiding his derision.

Chase jammed his shoulders back, chin raised, and her heart gave a pang. Beautiful Aidan had never had to back down before anyone, had never been embarrassed a day in his life.

But maybe Chase deserved this scrutiny and more from the people he'd hurt. *Walk away from him. Let him feel this alone.*

Yet her hand decided to reach for Chase's, and her stupid fingers felt the need to lace with his.

The look he gave her as he tightened his grasp was one she'd never seen from him before.

Tenderness.

Brandr broke the silence. "Come on, then, let's get moving. We need to cover a lot of ground today."

As the others set off, she tried to make light of the situation. Because Chase was clutching her hand—like a lifeline. "Did the big bad Blademan just have a funny feeling in his chest?"

His gaze pinned hers, and he rasped one word. *"Aye."*

FORTY-EIGHT

What a difference a day can make, Declan thought as the six of them climbed a mountain trail.

In that short time, he'd gone from the lowest low to the highest high.

Yes, they were on the run for their lives, beleaguered by a squall, but he felt a hundred pounds lighter. For the last several hours, he'd led Regin through gusting winds and biting rain, blocking both for her. And each time he'd glanced over his shoulder to check on her, her eyes had flickered—with definite interest.

Chest swelled with pride, he realized he might have a shot at *more.*

When the group took a break before a particularly steep ascent, he squired her back the way they'd come. Out of sight of the others, he leaned down to kiss her damp neck. The lass let him. "Been needin' to do that since we left the stream." He nuzzled her ear. "Have you thought about my offer?"

She pulled back. "Offer? It sounded more like a decree. So, in this imaginary world, where we're a couple and all my allies are safe and sound—and there is no curse that's about to kill you—what do we do with our time?"

"You wanted to ally before. We could be partners, split bounties. I'd still get to hunt Neos and Cerunnos. Slay some Horde vampires, right?"

"You'd let me go into battle with you? Not afraid I'd get hurt?"

"I've seen you fight. I pity anything that crosses you. You're the most capable female I've ever known. Besides, I'd never let you be hurt."

"Uh-huh. And didn't you tell me that we'd find a place to put down roots? Be informed that I've already got one. Lucia and I have always planned to live in adjacent houses on some seashore. How would you like a Valkyrie for a neighbor?"

"You will no' scare me away so easily as that. For more of what you gave me at the stream, I'll reside in Val Hall's attic." He leaned in to murmur, "I now ken the appeal of your little claws. I've got your marks across my arse."

"That a problem?"

"I'll be ireful if I go a day without them," he said gravely. "Besides, a seaside home sounds about right. I told you I like the mountains—and the shore. I grew up on the Irish coast, you know."

"And how would you be with my family?"

"Scarce." At her raised chin, he said, "I can manage with them. And I already have an in with your sister Nïx. She sent me a message a week ago."

"What? How?"

"I'd bugged your car. She sent me a message through the damn bug."

"What'd she say?"

"That I should question Lothaire, and that she'd see me soon."

Regin had been sensing a Valkyrie presence for two days now. Was it *Nïx* on the island? "And?"

"And a bunch of other gibberish."

"Nïx doesn't speak gibberish. Everything she says is for a reason."

"She told me my middle name would be regret." Chase held her gaze. "Your sister was right. I'm goin' to spend the rest of my life makin' everything up to you."

"Whoa, Chase, you're acting like I'm a done deal. And I'm the furthest thing from it."

"You've given me your terms, and I'm goin' to prevail."

"Let me know when you puzzle out how to get around a thousand-year-old curse. I'll be curious to see."

He opened his mouth to reply, but Brandr called out, "Hey, Chase, we need to decide on the best way up. Preferably taking the path less mined with unexploded incendiaries."

"Aye, then." To her, Chase said, "We'll continue this discussion later." He took her hand, leading her back. After chucking her under the chin, he jogged off to confer with Brandr.

Natalya joined her directly. "I've been waiting to talk for hours. But I didn't want to interrupt Chase—as he seized on any opportunity to touch you. Assisting a Valkyrie over a downed sapling? How romantic."

"What'd you want to talk about?"

"Just to commend you on your revenge last night. It must have been fiendish. Of course, I can only imagine since there wasn't a mark on Chase this morning, only residual bliss."

"He heals fast! I whaled on his face. Must've been thirty hits."

Natalya's lips quirked. "You're glowing like a Lite-Brite."

"Shut it, fairy."

"I don't know what kind of upskirt mojo you've got going on, but that man is different."

Regin gazed over at him as he pointed out something to Brandr. Chase's demeanor was still gruff, but the strain around his eyes was diminished.

He'd grudgingly accepted his sweater back—it was far too big for her to climb in—but he'd rolled up his sleeves, displaying his brawny arms. The flat scars over his skin looked almost like tribal tattoos.

And damn, if he didn't look bigger every hour. Maybe the drugs he'd taken *had* kept the berserker in him in check?

Natalya gave a little wave at Thad. The kid sat under a rock overhang, trying to talk to Lothaire, but the vampire didn't look lucid. "So now that you've sampled Chase," she said in a low tone, "are you going to keep him?"

"I can't forget about the curse," Regin said firmly. Because she was tempted to do just that. To take that wicked Irishman behind a rock and have her way with him.

"Over my dead body," Regin said. "Two-bit hookers, every one of them."

Thad scratched his head. "Mr. Lothaire said every male needed a purring nymph or two chained to the foot of his bed. As pets."

Natalya gasped. "All right, lad, no more talking to Lothaire."

Though Regin was strong enough to confront that vampire over his crimes against the Valkyrie, unfortunately, Lothaire had come in handy.

If their crew of six passed groups of evil demons, he always appeared in time to defuse the situation. The demons fawned over him like he was Elvis or something, saving them a fight—and saving them time.

They were already cutting it close to get to the boat. For the last five days, they'd pushed hard through the mountains, but the never-ending storms and wind made for slow going. And on the second day out, they'd spotted throngs of Wendigos teeming in the forests below, so their crew had clung as high as possible to the rocky peaks, taking extra time.

All the while, Regin had continued to sense another Valkyrie, yet couldn't pinpoint it enough to go searching. She'd asked Chase about it, but he'd sworn no other Valkyrie had been in the facility.

"Nat, are my fangs looking *any* bigger?" Thad murmured, his tone dire. "Be *honest*."

As Natalya oohed and aahed over his "manly" fangs, Regin only half-listened, glancing over her shoulder at Chase. Earlier, he'd tried to draw her into conversation, but she'd been too out of sorts. Now she was lost in her own thoughts, about to introspect like a son of a bitch.

She feared she might be a jot more than infatuated with this reincarnation. Like on her way toward falling-off-a-skyscraper-onto-your-face in love with him.

Which she could never allow.

But gods, that man appealed to her in so many ways. Regin liked that he was complicated, and that he was *trying.* She admired that he'd overcome so much and was striving to be a better man.

Other males might feel sorry for themselves or rail against fate. Not Chase. He just picked himself up again and again.

For each of the last four nights, the two of them had gone off by themselves. He'd never tried to kiss her mouth or make love to her—as if he knew she'd pull the plug on their arrangement. After they'd slaked the worst of their need, they talked into the morning, with her curled against his chest. He'd pet her hair while she traced his scars, wishing she could take away the pain that had rendered them.

Last night, he'd finally told her of the days and nights he'd been a captive of the Neoptera. Though his tone had been brusque—as if he were relating a military report—he'd physically reacted to the memory. Sweat had dotted his upper lip and brow, his eyes lit with misery.

Afterward, when he'd eventually passed into a fitful sleep, she'd lain awake, dazed, wondering how he could possibly have endured that pain.

And to what end? Why would he survive so much just to have his life ended now?

Though he slept little, when he did he continued to dream about his past lives. One night, he'd experienced the battle when Gabriel had captured Regin's ship. Another night, he'd relived the Spaniard's wicked bed play with her. She'd woken to Chase's fingers plunging deep inside her as he stroked himself in time.

His intense gaze had swept from his busy fingers to her mouth. When he'd wet his own lips, she'd quickly said, "No kissing."

"I can wait you out, Valkyrie," he'd rasped. "Now that my prize is in sight. . . ."

Each dream sent her panic escalating. Soon he would remember all, and then Aidan would rise to the fore, taking over.

Declan Chase, the man, would be no more, his life just a memory, his body soon to perish.

The cycle continued, the curse grinding on.

"I need your help," Declan muttered to Brandr as Regin climbed ahead with Thad and Natalya.

Brandr raised his brows. "You know that's what I'm here for."

Declan did know that. The man was proving to be a staunch ally. Still Declan had difficulty asking others for assistance. "How do I talk Regin past that curse?"

Brandr said, "You don't, if you want to stay alive."

He ground his teeth in frustration. In his mind, the rescue from the island was as good as done. All her conditions could still be met. The only thing that stood in their way was this curse.

Declan intended to eliminate *anything* in their way, to do whatever it took to claim her as his own. The last few days with her had been amazing. Life had never been so bloody easy for him. He didn't have to disguise his accent with her, didn't have to hide his body. He felt no strain.

He'd never imagined that a woman could fit him so well. He liked the way she thought, liked that she said outrageous things and threw mud in his face. Regin had *flavor.*

His lass was the opposite of soulless.

They'd talked deep into the night, getting to know each other better. She'd confided her secret fear—ghosts—and her addiction to video games. And she was droll. Though he was out of practice laughing, his lips had curled when she'd itemized the things she'd made demons eat.

The one subject she refused to talk about? The distant past. She feared him remembering more, feared triggering that damned curse. "What do you suggest then, Brandr? Because I'm no' givin' her up."

"As if you could."

"No, I'm done for. Would be happily so if I could get her to feel the same way."

"Have you considered trying to become immortal?"

Three weeks ago, Declan would've been insulted by this question. Now it made him regret that he couldn't be. "You think I'd immortalize this battered body?" He waved his hand to indicate his chest. "Besides, I know the risks inherent in turnin'. I just want a few decades with the lass."

"You won't get it. If you sleep with Regin, you'll die. Period. The only chance you have is to become an immortal *before* you claim her."

"And how would I do that? You know the transformation is no' foolproof." The catalyst to become another species was death—and it didn't always work.

Demons turned only a fraction. The Lykae had better odds, but it often took a newly transformed werewolf decades to control his inner beast—if it could be tamed at all. "Can you transform another into an immortal berserker?"

"I have no idea, but if I had to say, I'd go with no. I've never heard of it happening. The ones with most success at this are the vampires. Which would never work."

"Aye, I despise them, could never become one."

Brandr lowered his voice. "And we know how Regin feels about them."

"She hates them for killing her man."

"Regin hated them long before that. Her mother's entire race was exterminated by vampires."

Declan ran his hand over his face. "I did no' know that."

"And if you did become a vampire, her Valkyrie blood would be irresistible to you. There's no way she could spend eternity as a host to one of them, not even for you. Face it, Chase, your only hope is to abstain with her."

Declan caught Regin glancing over her shoulder at him with silvery eyes. "Then I've no chance in hell," he said dryly. "But I'm no' convinced of this, Brandr. I'm strong—stronger than I've ever been. I'll no' go out so easily, now that I've something to live for."

"I wish it were that simple. Listen, Regin has alliances with the witches. They might be able to help you—if you don't claim Regin before we reach New Orleans."

"The witches will do no favors for me."

"We can figure something out. But only if you can wait . . ." Brandr trailed off as Lothaire approached them. "What do you want, leech?"

He rubbed his tongue on his fang. "Chase's end of the bargain."

FIFTY

"Come, don't be shy, Magister," the vampire murmured, his eyes riveted to Declan's neck. "I grow peckish."

"Don't bloody call me that!" He gazed out past a craggy rock face, back down the trail where the others awaited them. Brandr was supposed to tell Regin that they'd gone to scout ahead, but Declan was uneasy.

And it sat ill with him to sneak around like this, to cede his blood so shamefully. "You aren't even supposed to drink this often," Declan said. "Older vampires can go for weeks. Do you *want* more of my memories?"

"Surely the rest can't be worse?"

When Declan only raised his brows, Lothaire said, "In any case, I lost blood fighting the Wendigos and need to refill my coffers."

Declan gritted his teeth, rolling up a sleeve. *How far I've fallen*. Allowing himself to be drunk.

But he had no choice. If he'd had any lingering doubts that he was a member of the Lore, they'd been extinguished; Declan felt *compelled* by the vow he'd made.

"It'll go faster through the neck," Lothaire said. "And

I know you want to be quick. Don't want your female to catch you *in flagrante dentate,* do you?"

"Forget it."

"I seem to recall that your vow stipulated whenever and *however* I chose to drink you."

Declan's hands tightened into fists as Lothaire moved behind him. "You're a fuckin' parasite." *I could* never *become a vampire.* Filthy leeches.

"Words still hurt, Chase. Besides, you should be thanking me. My advice about the Valkyrie clearly worked. And speaking of females, if I call you by one's name while my fangs are plunged deep in your neck, just run with it." The vampire leaned in.

Only one more day of this vow. Just one more day.

Declan's jaw clenched when Lothaire punctured his skin with a groan. The vampire's hands clamped his shoulders, those sucking sounds nauseating. Again and again, Lothaire drew greedily—

Over the blustery winds, Declan heard a horrified cry, swung his gaze up. "Ah, God, Regin!"

"What kind of sick kicks are you into?" Regin screamed as she bolted away.

Lothaire had been drinking Chase—and the man had been *letting* him.

No wonder Brandr had stood at that pass like a guard, telling her to stay put. Her ears had twitched, alerting her that something was up. But she'd figured Chase had taken Lothaire out to kill him—not to *feed* him!

She'd sneaked off after them because she wanted to interrogate Lothaire before he died.

Worse, it'd taken her several seconds to react to the sight of them together. She'd been almost hypnotized by the scene as Lothaire drank. Chase's masculine face had been tense, his gray eyes focused on the ground. Lothaire's face had been starkly beautiful, his pale blond hair brushing Chase's shoulder.

Light and dark. One terrible, one tragic.

And Lothaire had been . . . hard. "Oh, gods!" she cried as she ran back along the trail. *Hot poker for my eyes! Hot poker!*

Why couldn't she have stumbled upon Chase and Brandr necking? That would've been crazy hot.

"Regin, wait!" Chase ran after her, his bite mark torn and bleeding. He must've jerked away from Lothaire. "I didn't have a choice!" He grabbed her arm. "I had to make that vow to him. Without his aid, we wouldn't have made it past the first night."

She flung herself from his grip. "He can learn things about me through your blood. Can learn about my sisters!" She briefly covered her mouth. "He can see everything we've done! I don't want that leech to know what we do in private."

Lothaire strolled up, making a scoffing sound. "As if I don't watch you two live from a distance." He licked his crimson lips. "His staying power is increasing. As is yours. Bravo."

They both scowled at him.

"I made a vow," Chase told her. "I'm compelled by it. You understand this."

"Fine. Then you should've kept your distance from me until you were released from it."

He pinched his forehead. "I knew I had only days to win you."

Brandr, Natalya, and Thad caught up to them.

"What's going on here?" Brandr demanded. "Damn it, Regin, do you never do as you're told?"

She blinked at him. "It's taken you a millennium to get that?"

Lothaire said to her, "Valkyrie, I've seen little about your sisters that I don't already know. Mostly I've been treated to Declan's torture at the hands of my former allies, the Neoptera."

Regin swung her head around at Lothaire. "You're *talking* to me? You really wanna do this, leech? Clear the air?" Again she reached back for her swords and came up empty. With a glare, she dropped her hand to the sword at her hip. "Then let's go! The Valkyrie know what you did to our queen. You hid Furie somewhere, torturing her for decades. Rumor has it you buried her under the sea to drown a million deaths."

But Lothaire frowned disdainfully. "I assure you I do not know where Queen Furie is."

"We have it from a very reliable source that you do. Your old king said so."

"Who was crazed till the day he died."

Regin narrowed her gaze. Lothaire was physically incapable of lying. "Then . . . then where is she?"

"Again, I do not know—"

Chase raised his hand, hissing, "Listen!" He flicked his fingers for her sword. Without thought, she tossed it to him. In one fluid motion, he caught it, then flung it end over end down through the treetops below.

A Cerunno uncoiled with serpentine agility, narrowly dodging the blade.

When it slithered away with a bullet's speed, Regin cried, "We've got to catch it!"

"It'll be long gone, Valkyrie," Lothaire said. "You can't match pace with one of that kind, not when you have a torque. Besides, you need to be running in the opposite direction. The night of our escape, I saw the Cerunnos amassing with all the Pravus allies. Among others, there were vampires, shifters, and some Sorceri—Portia and Emberine, specifically."

"Then those bitches will be coming for us! We've got to attack them first."

Lothaire gave a harsh laugh. "They're too powerful. You're not much stronger than a mortal right now. What hope do you have against a being who can move mountains?"

Natalya said, "As soon as Portia knows we're on *this* mountain, she'll level it."

Lothaire turned to Chase. "You and I are faster than the others. We need to lead the Pravus away from this group. Make a lot of noise while descending as swiftly as possible, and hope they follow us. Or this mountain will fall."

Chase gave a curt nod, then faced Brandr. "You take the others to the boat. Due west from here there's a covered berth in a leeward cove. We'll meet you there before sunset."

"Oh, no, no. This is a shit plan." Regin crossed to stand before him. "For one thing, Valkyrie don't *flee*. We *fight*."

"We're running out of time," Lothaire intoned.

Chase pulled her close to say at her ear, "Then do this to protect Thad and Natalya." The bastard was playing on her sense of loyalty. And it was working!

When he drew back, she said, "This is still a shit plan. I can fight—I can help you!"

"I ken you can fight. Which is the only reason I'd let you out of my sight." His confidence in her abilities continued to surprise her. "But right now, we *are* faster than you and the others. You know this is the most logical move."

She did, but was pissed that they were in this position.

When she pursed her lips, he said, "If for some reason we don't show by sunrise, take the ship." Then Chase shared a look with Brandr. "You watch her back."

Brandr gave a curt nod.

In Old Norse, Regin murmured, "Take me with you."

Chase's brows drew together. "This is the best choice, lass." Trying to make light, he chucked her under the chin. "Is the big bad Valkyrie worried about me?"

Peering up at him, she said one word. "Yeah."

Chase dragged her close with the crook of his arm. "Mind yourself, Regin." Against her hair, he vowed, "I will no' be long apart from you."

The Endgame commanded action, Lothaire thought as he and Chase sprinted through the brush. *And I'm about to obey.*

"Come, Magister, you're flagging. Did I drink too much?"

Chase was utterly exhausted, more than from merely ceding blood. He was depleted—as if from a berserkrage. Between breaths, he snapped, "Do no' bloody call me that!" He cast another glance back in the Valkyrie's direction.

"You look worried. I'm sure Regin will be fine. We should be concerned more for ourselves down in this forest."

"If something happens to me, what would it take to get you to watch over her?" Chase wiped sweat from his brow. "To make sure she gets off the island alive?"

"More than you can give. Such as a firstborn to go with my others. Matching set and all."

"Then just move your arse. There's a clearing up ahead."

They broke from the trees onto a bare plateau. Chase stopped, stared. "What the hell is this, Lothaire?"

Pravus beings—fire demons, Horde vampires, shifters—had all congregated here around Portia's makeshift stone temple. The structure looked like a roofed Stonehenge, with Emberine's flames crawling over its stones like living things. Portia and Ember strolled out, gazing on with interest.

Lothaire tilted his head at Chase impassively. "This is a day trade. You for my freedom."

"You son of a bitch!" He lunged for Lothaire, but a cadre of vampire guards traced to intercept him.

"I delivered you unto them for the late Fegley's severed hand, or, more importantly, his thumb,"

Lothaire explained as the guards whaled blows on Chase. "As for your fate—the Pravus are planning to gather here at sunset and make a proper sacrifice out of you."

Chase thrashed as the vampires forced him to an upright slab of stone, binding his limbs to it. "How long have you been plottin' this, you fuck?"

"Emberine came to me this morning. As soon as she'd realized she hadn't killed you in the facility." Apparently she and Portia would've attacked the group earlier, but they were wary of young Thaddeus. At last Lothaire had discovered what the boy was.

They were right to be wary.

As the guards took turns beating Chase, Ember tossed Lothaire the rotting, discolored hand. "Your payment, Lothaire."

"*Spasibo.* With my deepest thanks." He took the bloated thumb and pressed it against the lock on his torque. Nothing. He turned the hand upside down, trying it the other way. Still nothing. "My dear Emberine, I hate to be a bother, but the warden's print doesn't work."

She laughed, and wisps of fire flew from her lips. "I never said it would work. I merely vowed that it was Fegley's."

Portia snickered. "Come, Lothaire, days have passed since the hand was . . . harvested. Out in the rain, it's decomposed."

Blyad'! That they would dare pull this stunt with him?

He hadn't seen this coming, hadn't predicted it—

because now there was a new variable. His weakness. His inability to remove this collar.

So I'm no closer to escaping this place. To rescuing her. His fangs sharpened with rage. But his master dictated coolness.

Lothaire gave them his most charming smile, the one he usually reserved for imminent victims. "Shall we negotiate for a ride from this island? One of these demons or a brother vampire could trace me from here in a heartbeat."

Portia said, "What do you have?"

Lothaire answered, "I can get you the Valkyrie."

FIFTY-ONE

Where is he? Regin thought as she paced along the water's edge. *I'm going mad without him here.*

Hours ago, they'd arrived at the shore. Just as he'd promised, there'd been an enormous boathouse in a protected cove. The boat was actually more of a ship, like one of those coast guard cutters.

Thad and Natalya were aboard, making coffee and surveying charts, while Brandr waited on the beach with her.

Dusk would come soon. "I don't like this, Brandr. Chase should've been here by now."

"I've never seen you this worried." He sank down on the sand, resting his elbows on his knees. "But that can't be right. Just days ago, you wanted the man dead."

"A lot's happened since then." She wasn't merely worried, she was *sick* with worry for Chase—like claw-biting, hair-pulling, pacing-for-hours worried. Because she might be . . . she might be falling for Declan Chase.

At the thought, guilt racked her. She'd refused to allow herself to love Aidan because he was mortal, and yet she seemed to have no control over her emotions where Chase was concerned.

Which made no sense. The stakes were even higher.

Before she'd held her heart back because she'd feared Aidan dying of old age. Now she knew Chase's death loomed, and she still couldn't stem her feelings for him.

Because, gods help her, she wanted her scarred, surly, fucked-up Irishman more than she'd wanted her perfect Viking.

Brandr skipped a stone into the cove's calm blue water. "And this morning, you were flying off the handle because Lothaire drank from him."

"After I realized my eyes would eventually stop burning, I calmed down. I understand why he did what he did. I don't like it, but I understand."

"Can you imagine how hard that must've been for a man like Chase? To allow a vampire to take blood from him?"

Yes. Yes, she could. Her Celt was *trying*, struggling to make the best hand out of what fate dealt him. "Damn it, where is he? We never should have split up—"

"Valkyrie," Lothaire said. He stood at the edge of the tree line. Alone.

Panic surged through her. "Where's Chase?" *I can't lose him. Not again.* Her lips drew back from her fangs. "I'm going to kill you, leech!"

Must get back to Regin. Every minute since his capture, Declan had waited for his heart to start pounding, for his strength to return. Now the sun was setting.

He'd begun to suspect that Lothaire's feedings somehow forestalled his berserkrage. Which the leech had likely put together—and used to weaken Declan today. How long would the effects last?

Have to get free. Surely, Regin would know better than to trust Lothaire. She would never be tricked as Declan had been. She hated that vampire.

But what if Lothaire tells her I've been injured? She'd admitted she would worry for Declan; the vampire could prey on that.

Declan had to escape before Lothaire lured her to this place—a vile, tomblike camp filled with blood foes.

These creatures had beaten him repeatedly, mocking his pain and ridiculing his scars.

Between those beatings, he'd listened to their conversations. They either thought he couldn't hear them or didn't care because he'd soon be dead.

He'd learned that Carrow and her ward had made it off the island, along with Malkom Slaine—who'd acted as protector to the two. And he'd heard that MacRieve had organized Vertas shifters, holing up in the mountains and rigging traps for the Pravus.

Apparently, three of the beings Regin worried for still lived—

The two Sorceri females swept into the temple. Myriad beings, probably three dozen of them, followed the pair inside, eagerly gathering for the show.

"Night comes, Magister," Portia said. "Make your peace."

Declan had no reason to think he'd suffer a less painful fate than Fegley's burning. Yet all Declan cared about was protecting Regin from them.

Raised voices sounded from outside the temple. Declan swung his head up. *Regin's voice.*

Lothaire was forcing her into the clearing. He'd tied her wrists behind her back.

"You sold me out, leech?" she cried. "I'll kill you!"

Declan thrashed against his bonds.

In a bored tone, Emberine said, "So you fetched us the Valkyrie?"

"They're so trusting, it's like leading lambs to slaughter," Lothaire said. "However, this prisoner should be of particular interest to you—she's the magister's woman. That's why she's here. All I had to do was tell her she could save Chase."

"No!" Declan bellowed. "Lothaire, don't do this!"

Emberine studied his reaction. "Intriguing." She asked Lothaire, "What do you plan for her?"

"I intend to snap her neck, a particular fondness of mine. Eventually, I'd like to drink her to the quick, but of course, the killing blow is reserved for my gracious hostess."

"I'll rip your fuckin' head off, vampire!" Finally Declan's heart began pounding, his blood coursing to his muscles. But he still couldn't hit his berserkrage.

Emberine waved Lothaire on, leaving sparks in the air. "By all means."

As Regin flailed, the vampire snaked an arm around her head, palming her chin with one hand. He reached the other across her neck to seize her shoulder.

"No! Nooo!"

Regin met eyes with him, as if she were trying to tell him something—

The vampire snatched both of his arms in opposite

directions. Declan watched in horror as Regin's head twisted. Face lax, body limp, she collapsed to the ground.

He roared with fury. *She's not dead. Not dead.* She would live through this. If he could get free. *Save her.*

These fucks *cheered.* He stifled another yell as rage flooded his body, the strength of a berserker growing rampant inside him. *One hand free.*

"Come, Emberine," Lothaire said. "The honor is yours."

The sorceress created a fire sword in her palm. Playing to the crowd, she raised it above her head teasingly. All attention was on her.

Another arm free.

The crowd began to chant Ember's name. *Punish them.* A red haze covered his vision. Thoughts came at random.

With one final violent thrash, Declan escaped his bonds. As he stalked toward Regin's body, he seized the vampires closest to him, yanking them into each other, bashing their skulls.

Never taking his eyes from her, he ripped anyone between them limb from limb. *Closer.* Blood sprayed over him.

Nothing keeps me from her.

FIFTY-TWO

Three . . . two . . . one.

Regin's legs surged forward, kicking the sorceress's ankles and sending her crashing to the ground. With another kick, she slammed her boot heel down onto Ember's throat. At that moment, Thad, Natalya, and Brandr burst into the temple with weapons raised. Lothaire drew his sword, slaying two nearby demons with one swipe of his blade.

The leech's plan was working. *Might let him live.*

When Regin popped up unharmed, free from the fake knot at her wrists, she met Chase's wild gaze. She couldn't imagine his bewilderment; his mind should be a chaotic frenzy by now. She'd never seen him so big, so fully berserk. Across the melee, he ravaged through demons and vamps to get to her.

Lothaire tossed her another sword. "I told you this would work." His tone was casual, even as he laid waste to his former allies.

"Maybe if you hadn't screwed over Chase in the first place, huh?"

Ember gaped from the ground, her lips working silently before she hissed, *"Die, Valkyrie."* She shot to her feet, raising her fire sword.

But Regin had already swung. "Gotta dis*arm* you. Bitch," Regin said as Ember's arms fell to the ground in a cloud of wafting ash.

Ember screamed, her butchered limbs spurting streams of fire like blood. But Portia was ever watchful of Ember; a massive boulder hurtled toward Regin, leveling anyone in its path.

At the last minute, Regin ducked. The stone crushed Ember's head.

Portia shrieked, speeding toward them. A swarm of something that looked like locusts followed her. Not locusts.

Sand.

"Lothaire!" Regin yelled. "Take out Portia!"

At that, other demons and vampires turned to him. "Lothaire betrayed us! *Again.*" A dozen or so demons and vampires traced away at once, dragging their wounded.

Turning to Portia, Lothaire eerily chided, "If you're not with me . . ."

Deciding to fight another day, the sorceress snatched Ember's hair around her fist, then latched on to a vampire about to trace. The three disappeared.

Regin's gaze found Chase once more. His eyes were focused on her, unwavering, even as he reached to his side and snagged another foe, wrenching its head from its neck.

Behind him lay a trail of carnage, one headless, twitching body after another. His speed was mind-boggling. All those years ago, he'd told her that he'd done incomprehensible feats in order to get back to her.

Now she was seeing them. *A lean bear in winter . . .*

Not far from him, Thad, Natalya, and Brandr fought back to back, dispatching the rest of the fallen Cerunnos and other creatures that had no means of tracing away. Soon the temple was filled with gore, but cleared of live adversaries.

Only the original six of them remained.

And Chase was storming toward her. Regin sheathed her sword and ran for him as well. "Chase!"

When he caught her up against his chest, she clutched him with all the strength in her body. *I ran into his arms.*

Her eternal mate. *I* couldn't *hold my heart back.* "I was so worried!"

Voice ragged, he said, "Nothing keeps me from you." His gaze was fixed on her lips. "*Nothing.*"

"No, Chase!" His words filled her with fear. Words from the past. *Is it too late?* She beat against his chest, clawing to get free. Declan could *never* remember.

Because I want him.

But he slanted his mouth over hers, plunging his tongue between her lips before she could yank her head away.

"Nooo!" She kicked him until he finally drew back.

"Sweet as honey," he rasped. "The others had it wrong. You're no' like a drug." Setting back in for more, he groaned, "*Better than . . .*"

She head-butted his throat with a vicious snap. "Chase, stop this!" To the others, she said, "He's remembering. Help me!"

When Brandr, Natalya, and Thad stepped forward,

Chase set Regin on her feet, still gripping her arm with one viselike fist. Pure menace emanated from him as he leveled his gaze on the three. Blood had spattered his torso, lines of crimson crisscrossing his scars. "Nothing keeps me from her."

He was a berserker in full rage, with his chest heaving beneath those chilling scars—a terrifying sight for most, yet Regin's heart clenched for him. *He's magnificent.*

Brandr advanced on him. "I can't let you have her, friend—"

Chase launched a punch; his fist connected with Brandr's face like a cannonball. Brandr's head whipped around, his body lifted off the ground before it dropped. Limp.

When Chase narrowed his gaze at the others, Natalya and Thad both held up their hands.

"We'll let you two work this out between yourselves," Natalya muttered. "See you back at the boat." They each grabbed one of Brandr's arms and started dragging the man away.

Lothaire said, "No hard feelings, then, Blademan? Everyone makes a bad day trade now and again. . . ." He trailed off at Chase's look. "Very well, I'll be at the boat. We'll talk then."

It's left to me. Have to escape Chase. "Ah, gods, I don't want to do this." When he turned to her, she brought her sword hilt crashing into his temple.

FIFTY-THREE

"*Regin!*" Declan roared, his mind mired in confusion as he pursued her through a rain-swept forest.

With each step, his body quickened for her, while memories of a far-distant past bombarded him.

Kissing Regin's sweet lips by the light of a fire while a blizzard howled outside. Laughing with her upon a bed of furs. Teaching her about pleasure.

But those memories were dim compared to the last five days.

Kissing Regin's body under the blaze of her lightning while the wind gusted over them. Lying side by side, talking in murmurs. Learning how to pleasure her. . . .

She was his. She owned his heart and commanded his soul and would forever.

Why would she flee him now? When he needed her more than he ever had?

He swiftly caught up to her as she tore along a streambed, farther and farther into a narrowing canyon. Until it dead-ended with high walls all around. "Nowhere to run, Valkyrie."

She dashed across the stream and back, searching for a way out. "Damn it!" She raised her sword. "I'll use this."

He stalked closer. "Nothing comes between us."

Not time, not death. He lunged forward, snatching the sword from her grip, tossing it away. "Why would you deny me?"

"I have to—you can't do this!"

"I can and I will." His hand shot out to loop around her waist, dragging her close. "I need you so badly, Regin."

Her eyes went silver. Yet then her expression hardened. "If you take me tonight, it won't be without a fight."

"So long as I take you."

When Chase dipped down to kiss her again, Regin punched him with all her strength.

He drew back with his brows drawn, not in pain, but in confusion. The hit hadn't even fazed him. He was stronger than he'd ever been, faster too. And she wore the torque.

Utterly impossible to best him.

It was her nature to fight, to rail—but she'd fought Aidan in the past. *And look where that got me.*

No more.

Maybe if she stayed calm, she could bring him back from the brink? Steeling her resolve, she raised her hand to cup his cheek. "I need your help."

He frowned down at her.

"I have to talk to you. And I need you to be calm." She brushed his wet hair from his forehead. "That's it. Be at ease."

When the mad light in his eyes ebbed somewhat, she continued, "I want to be with you for longer than one night. And to do that, we've got to stop this. We've got to pull back."

"Nothing will stop me from claiming you this night. *Nothing.*"

"Then you're going to widow me again? Don't you care about me?"

He gripped her nape. "I fuckin' love you, Regin!" Rain spiked his lashes as he gazed down at her, commanding her, "Love me back!"

Can't lose him. "J-just wait, Aidan!"

His eyes went wild again; he threw back his head and roared, his neck straining.

"Please, Aidan, be calm!"

When he faced her again, he bellowed, "I am *no*' goddamned Aidan! You're talkin' to *Declan*. Do you no' see *me*, woman?"

"N-not Aidan?" She blinked against the rain. "What? How?"

He gave his head a harsh shake, clearly struggling to gain control of his emotions. "I've got his memories. No' the other way around. He's a part of me. That's all."

"You're still . . . Declan?" This had never happened before! Maybe the outcome could be changed as well? *Or maybe you're grasping at straws.*

Voice hoarse, he said, "Aye, it's me. I will never be your perfect Viking, Regin! I've made unforgivable mistakes. I've no family or friends, and my men hold no love for me. I'm scarred inside and out. And I'm bloody askin' for you anyway!"

You're the one that I want. Yet then she shivered with fear. "But the curse—"

"Has no reign over me, no' over us. The past has no hold!" He brushed his battered knuckles along her cheek again and again. "Can you see *me,* see the man that I am? Accept me, Regin, because I'm holdin' on to nothin' but you."

A thousand years ago, Aidan had taken her hands in his own and asked her to accept him. Tragedy had followed for all his days. "Declan, I'm . . . afraid. I'm scared to."

"You *know* this is different. You have to feel it too."

Do I? Or do I just want him so much?

He dipped down, his lips slanting over hers. He gave a sharp groan at the contact, but he was gentle, tempering his brutal strength for her. And she loved him for it.

Gods, how she loved him.

In the past, whenever the frenzy had seized him, she'd been swept up, answering his beast. Now some long-dormant part of her was waking, clamoring for his kiss, for his claiming.

Resisting it went against her every instinct. She couldn't deny that primal pull—not when her heart craved him just as feverishly.

Want him so badly, love him so much. . . .

The conflict within her grew stronger. She feared, but she *hungered*—soon *she* was deepening the contact. Even as she lamented her weakness, she savored his firm lips and lapped at his tongue.

When he returned her forays with wicked flicks, shivers raced over her. He kissed her until they were breathing for each other, until she got lost in the bliss, scarcely aware as he began stripping her, then himself. She only realized she was naked when she felt the rain on her sensitive skin.

By the time she lay back on their discarded clothes, she was panting with need; he looked on the verge of losing control as he moved between her legs.

His body was taut with readiness, his brawny arms and pecs bulging. His shaft was a heavy rod, straining toward her.

Lightning flashed, shadowing his scars in relief, like brands over his skin. But each raised lash called to mind his strength, his will to survive.

Magnificent male.

As her gaze was lovingly tracing over every inch of his body, he'd been regarding hers just as intently. "Look at you, my beautiful Regin. You think I'd surrender you to another? You are *mine.*" He fisted his hand in her hair, yanking her up to him. "Say *my* name, Regin."

She breathed, *"Declan."*

He leaned forward to suck her earlobe. "I'm goin' to fuck you till you scream it. Fuck you till we lose count."

She gasped, his words making her tremble.

"But I need to get you ready." He drew back, his smoldering gaze riveted to her sex. "Spread your thighs for me."

When she eagerly obeyed, he bent down. She could feel his hot breath against her flesh as he nuzzled her curls, making her nipples pucker into aching points.

"Never get enough of this." He pressed his opened mouth to her, his tongue snaking over her clitoris.

"Ah, yes, yes!" she cried over the thunder booming through the canyon.

His low growls, his hungry mouth. Already she grew close.

When he delved his finger inside her, he groaned, *"Gettin' so wet, baby."* He wedged another one in, thrusting them just enough to ready her—while keeping her on the brink.

The pleasure soon bordered on pain. Gazing up at the sky in agony, she begged, "Declan, *please*."

"What do you want, Regin? Tell me and it's yours."

She couldn't fight this. *Inevitable.* But it was different this time—because Declan remained himself. "I n-need you inside me."

"You're wantin' my shaft, then," he murmured against her. "I'll make you come so hard with it."

She gave a strangled cry. Gods, she did want it—she ached for it, shamelessly rolling her hips.

He rose, pressing wet kisses up her body, his dog tags trailing up her torso. A hard suck on each of her nipples made her head thrash.

"Ah, please!"

The corded ridges down his torso rippled when he knelt between her legs, his biceps flexing as he clamped her hips and jerked her closer.

He fisted his length. When the broad head found her wetness, she cried out; his eyes went heavy-lidded, his jaw slack.

He began running that swollen tip up and down, groaning in anguish each time it briefly breached her core. "You're goin' to be so tight and wet for me."

Keening his name, she mindlessly undulated, rocking on the crown.

"That's it, lass, move on me!" In that husky voice, he told her, "Get your honey all over it."

His gravelly words sent her to the very edge. When he fitted the broad head inside her, she demanded, "Deeper."

He bit out, "Need to . . . go easy—"

"Deeper." Her claws sank into the tight muscles of his ass.

"Ah, Regin!" He surged home, filling her with thick, pulsating flesh. *"Mine!"* he roared in triumph.

His shaft was unyielding inside her, stretching her, forcing her body to accept his. When he seated himself as deep as he could go, she surrendered with a scream, her sheath contracting around him. *"Declan!"*

As her orgasm burned through her, his steely gray eyes held her gaze. "I can . . . can *feel* you comin'."

When the waves of pleasure finally crested, they didn't recede. She was still as frantic for him, her lightning forking out over them.

He raised himself on straightened arms. Head hanging down, his tags rattling around his neck, he gave one forceful shove over her. Gnashing his teeth, he dug his knees into the ground to heave his big body over her again.

The third time, his back arched, and he raised his gorgeous face. His expression was agonized.

On the fourth shove, he bellowed, "Regin!" That agonized expression transformed to one of ecstasy just as she felt him ejaculate inside her.

Jet after jet of his scorching seed.

He bucked his hips in a frenzy, flooding her . . . until she helplessly came from it.

FIFTY-FOUR

"*Need—more,*" Declan grated between breaths, mere moments after she'd wrung from him the most mind-shattering pleasure he'd ever imagined.

He lay atop her, heart thundering overs hers, his swollen shaft still buried deep inside her. The haze began to lift, yet Declan was by no means sated. "I . . . I can no' *stop,*" he bit out.

Though he might have vague recollections of taking her in the past, this was still new to him. Those memories were distant, didn't feel real to him.

She was real to him. *I'm not givin' her up to anyone. Never.*

"Who says you have to stop?" she murmured, her body so warm and giving beneath his. Her silvery eyes were brilliant in the night, her blond brows drawn with passion. Her silken skin was bright with it.

"My woman's wantin' more?" he rasped, beginning to rock over her, reveling in their mingled wetness.

Her lids grew heavy. "Always." Her voice was throaty from her screams.

He raised himself up on straightened arms. "Tell me what you need, Regin." He wanted to pleasure her more than she'd ever been, to be the male she remembered above all others. He craved learning her body so well he knew it like his own.

"Try me."

Gauging her reaction, he began to languidly stir his hips between her thighs. "Do you like that?"

Arms falling back over her head, she purred, "I *hate* it."

But when he gave her quick pumps deep in her core, her head thrashed, and the addictive spark between them flared hotter.

He clasped her hip, his thumb sifting through her blond curls, seeking her swollen little clit. When he rubbed it, she went wild, digging her heels down to buck beneath him.

He groaned, "You like to move on me, lass?" Rising up on his knees, he positioned her over his lap.

At once, she wrapped her arms around his neck, parting her lips for more of his kiss. He covered them with his own, licking her tongue. Her mouth was indescribably sweet. . . .

Clutching her luscious arse, he wrenched her down his length while he thrust his hips up. She moaned into their kiss.

Knees spread, he plunged into her with more force. When she tightened her hold around his neck, her straining nipples raked across his chest, whipping him into a lather. He ignored the tingling in his spine, the heavy ache in his ballocks. *Won't come before she does.*

Another harsh thrust . . . and another. Her moan grew continuous, her thighs locked around his waist, her arse writhing against his palms. *On the edge.*

He used all his strength to take her, pounding up into her until his skin slapped hers, until her head fell back and she could do nothing but hold on as he pistoned beneath her. Mouth against her damp neck, he rasped, "You're goin' to come for me again?"

"Yes! I'm so close . . ."

He tugged her hair down. "Do you want more of my spend inside you?"

She sobbed, "Yes, yes, yes!"

"Then wring it from me," he commanded at her ear. "Take it from me with your tight little quim."

"Declan!" she screamed, as she began to come wetly around his shaft.

A guttural sound broke from his chest when he felt her sheathe tugging him deeper, its slick clench undeniable.

In a daze, she moaned, "I want to feel it. Ah, gods, I want *you*. Want you."

At her words, pleasure racked him. His eyes rolled back in his head as he growled, "Yours, everything I am . . . yours." With one last brutal thrust, the throbbing pressure in his cock gave way, erupting in a searing rush of seed.

Chase clutched her as if he'd never let her go, one of his big hands palming the back of her head, the other gripping her ass. His hoarse exhalations fanned against her neck.

Still quivering with pleasure, Regin squeezed her own arms around him.

They clung to each other, as if they both feared something was about to pull them apart.

For how long they stayed like this, she didn't know. But when she managed to lift her eyelids, she saw that dawn had broken, the sun rising above a cloudless forest. She could hear gulls and waves. They must be close to the shore.

"Never lettin' you go, woman." He ran his cheek against hers. *"Love you."*

And still Declan remained, his memories foremost. Which was good. Because she was in love with Declan Chase. *I want my Irishman.*

Had the sand in the hourglass started to flow?

He drew back his head, wrapping the crook of his arm around her neck. Gazing down at her with fierce gray eyes, he said, "You belong to me, lass. It will always be you."

It will always be me—but will it ever be you? The stark light of day filled her with dread. *What have I done?* She'd talked herself into believing this time would be different. She should have fought him harder. But she'd been so desperate to love him.

Some things might have changed with this reincarnation, but the end result would be the same. Four times before, the man she'd made love to had been dead within hours. Those four times, her body had still borne the marks of his abandoned lovemaking—when his body had gone to the grave.

She shuddered. *Ah, gods, how could I have?* Chase would die; the hourglass would empty. And this time, she wouldn't survive losing him.

When her tears welled, his eyes went wide. "No, what's this? Shh, baby, please do no' cry."

As tears tracked down her face, she stared beyond him, awash in dread. The brief show of sunlight surrendered to gray. Rain misted once more.

"Lass, talk to me. You ken that I don't like it when you're quiet. This is because of the curse?" He petted her hair, rocking her. "I'm not goin' anywhere. Nothing will separate us again. Wouldn't I sense it if the end was near? I've never been more at peace in my entire life. It's . . . pure peace, Regin."

With an angry shove, she clambered off him, disentangling herself from his body. "What about me? What about *my* peace?" She swayed on her feet as realization hit her. Aidan had never been the one cursed.

She was.

Regin was the one left to suffer, to mourn. *To forever know what I'm missing.*

She collected her sodden jeans, dragging them on, then donned her shirt. "When you die this time, Chase, I don't want you to come back."

"What?" He shot to his feet, stabbing his legs into his own pants. "What are you talkin' about? Look at me! Why won't you look at me? Christ, Regin, you're actin' like I'm dead already."

She swiped her forearm over her face. "Because you're as good as."

Declan had never seen her like this. Her eyes were fully silver, but there was no spark in them. She wouldn't look at him. As if she *couldn't*.

Just moments before, he'd felt more centered and

at peace with himself than ever before; now *she* was steeped in misery.

"We need to get to the boat," Regin said distantly. "We're running out of time."

"You don't want me to come back because I'm no' the Aidan you knew?" She'd expected her man to return, to supplant Declan. She'd longed for Aidan for two centuries.

How could she not be devastated? "I don't know why I'm still here. Maybe I did something wrong, fucked up the cycle." Because he was definitely still . . . Declan. "I have Aidan's memories, but they're distant, like the dreams I had." *Somehow, it feels like* I *came first.*

"Exactly, Chase." In a deadened tone, she said, "I don't want you to come back because you're a scarred, fucked-up Celt."

His lips parted. *Never had a shot with her, not as myself.* He ran a palm over his ruined skin, whipped with defeat, wanting to howl his frustration. What to say to her? *I don't want to look like this. Don't want to* be *like this—*

"And I never wanted Aidan," she whispered, "like I want you."

He'd misheard her. "I don't understand, lass." She couldn't have chosen *him* over the perfect Viking.

"I *can't* lose you again. For a thousand years, it's been all about *your* struggle, *your* return! But each time, you leave me as collateral damage. The centuries of waiting, the loneliness, and then that ridiculous flare of hope when I find you again. Though I know how it's going to end—with me shattered." Rain began to pour. "You're going to die, Chase. Soon. There's nothing I can do to prevent it. I know because I've tried over and over. And if you care about me at all, you won't do this to me again. *Don't come back.*"

"Regin, just wait."

"I had it wrong all along. I'm not your doom, Chase. You're *mine—*"

A jet screamed overhead.

They met gazes. *"Move your arse, woman!"* Declan snatched her hand, yanking her along toward the cove.

As they sprinted closer to the shore, they heard Thad yell, "Regin, is that you?"

"We're coming," she cried.

"Uh, don't!"

"What?"

They charged out from under the trees. Natalya, Brandr, and Thad stood before the boat house. But beneath it, the berth was . . . empty.

Natalya's face was pinched. "Somebody gacked our vessel."

Declan shoved his fingers through his hair. "Damn Lothaire! He took it!"

"I'm right here, Blademan." The vampire stood off to one side in the shade of the forest, casually leaning his shoulder against a tree trunk.

"Then who took my fuckin' boat?"

"Your guess is as good as mine. They swooped in while we fought the Pravus."

"No one knew about this place!"

More jets shot past overhead, followed by a distinctive whistling sound. *Payload deployed.*

"Take cover!" Declan tackled Regin back under the

trees, shielding her with his body. Everyone hit the ground, except for Lothaire, who yawned.

Beneath Declan, Regin snapped, "You're covering *me*? You're the mortal—"

Explosions rocked the quiet morning, deafening waves of sound close by. But there was no shaking earth, no trees felled. Instead, ash and grit began to fall, blanketing the beach with the steady downpour. The jets—and their bombs—had blown up in the sky.

Declan lurched to his feet, helping Regin up.

"Chase, what just happened?"

As he and Regin gazed up in bewilderment, he mumbled, "I do no' know—"

A force slammed into his back; unimaginable pain seared through him.

The bite of metal.

He bellowed in agony, shoving Regin from harm's way. . . .

FIFTY-FIVE

Chase's shove sent Regin sprawling to the ground. As she whirled around, her mind struggled to process the wet sound of steel through flesh. She scrambled to her feet, gaping in disbelief.

A blade speared Chase's torso, the tip protruding from his chest. With each beat of his heart, blood streamed out around the jutting tip.

"Nooo!"

Chase's hands clenched the sword point, his body futilely twisting around it. Behind him stood . . . Malkom Slaine.

Regin sprang for the demon, claws bared. *"I'll kill you, Slaine!"*

Brandr was right behind her. But two pulses of energy sent them both flying. *Carrow's* energy?

The witch rushed up beside Slaine. "What is this, Valkyrie? We saved you from the magister!" She motioned for the vemon to withdraw his blade.

Slaine looked deeply troubled. "I've done wrong, *ara*?" As he began pulling his sword out, blood poured from Chase's mouth.

"No, Malkom, of course not!" To Regin, she said,

"You told me to kill the magister after you got vivisected. You *ordered* me to."

When Chase collapsed to his back, Regin dropped to her knees beside him. A sword through his chest, just like before. "Not again," she screamed, "not again!" Tears gathered and spilled as she sobbed, *"No, not again."* Lightning forked out overhead, continuous flashes across the sky.

Chase raised a bloody hand to her face, cupping her cheek. "Sorry 'bout this, lass."

Brandr punched a tree, roaring with grief.

"Don't talk, Chase! We're going to get you fixed."

"You were right. . . . I'm not returnin', Regin."

"No! I-I didn't mean what I said."

"Will no' do this to you again."

"*What?* Shut up! You have to come back. You fucking *have* to."

"I love you . . . too much. Find an immortal male to be with you." He gritted his teeth.

She knew how hard it'd been for him to say that. "I want *you*!" She probably should caress his face lovingly; instead, she clasped his chin and gave his head a rude shake. "I love *you,* dumbass!"

His brows drew together. "You . . . *do.* Christ, you do."

"I'm so sorry, Valkyrie," Carrow said. "I didn't know you'd fallen for him! We heard you yelling, and we've been fighting all morning."

Regin faced her. "You're from the healer caste. Heal him!"

"I can't! I used the last of my juice to blow up fighter

jets and their huge bombs. And you know healing spells take mondo power."

"Then take him to Andoain, and get another witch to."

"Regin, that man probably killed Ruby's mother—my cousin. And he tortured Slaine—my future husband." Slaine dropped his big hand across Carrow's nape, and his shoulders straightened. "No one in the House of Witches will help Chase."

Carrow and Slaine? Can't process that now. "Chase didn't kill your cousin. Please, you're my friend. Help me!"

Carrow surveyed him. "The man's too far gone. The only one who could heal him would be Mariketa, and this operation has tapped her out even more than me. She found this island, a feat in itself, and even devised this." Carrow held up a glowing thumb. "It's a skeleton print key for the torque." She crossed to Regin—with Slaine following protectively—and pressed it to her torque.

The collar that had caused Regin so much frustration dropped to the ground; her panicked mind scarcely registered her freedom. Regin's eyes darted before landing on Malkom Slaine's looming form. "Then I-I need your guy's blood!"

Chase bit out, "Have you . . . lost your goddamned mind?"

Carrow shook her head. "Malkom's an anomaly. We don't know what his blood would do."

Lothaire cleared his throat. "Couldn't help but overhear that you're canvassing for immortal blood."

Regin swung her head around. "Come on, vampire. Let's do this."

"No!" Chase grated. "Don't turn me into one like him."

"It's the only way you'll live," Regin cried. "Can't you see past your hate?"

"Can you?"

"What's that supposed to mean?"

Between blood-tinged breaths, he choked out, "Know about your mother, about all the things vampires . . . have done to you. If I become a vampire . . . I lose you anyway, Regin."

"You'd rather die than lose me?"

"O' course!"

"You tool, nobody's losing anybody! You're taking the blood. I don't care what you are—as long as you're with me." Regin faced Lothaire again. "Please, I need you to do this *now*!"

The vampire examined his black claws. "Must warn you though. I've already drunk from him. If he consumes my blood in turn, there will be unbreakable ties between us. Even more than if I merely became his sire."

"I don't care—do it!"

"For a price."

The leech's three favorite words.

"No!" Declan roared, blood spilling over his lips. "The vampire orchestrated this . . . always knew it'd come to this. Tried to get us together . . . though he knew I'd die. You'll make no vow to him!"

Regin faced Lothaire. "Lemme hip you to some facts.

You're not getting off this island without our help. You do this, and I vow to get my witch friend to remove your torque."

Carrow gasped. "I'm supposed to release one of the most evil vampires in existence—"

"*The* most evil," Lothaire corrected, "if you please, flower."

"—to save one of the most evil mortals?"

"If you don't, Carrow, then your soon-to-be husband will have killed mine."

The witch held up her thumb again. "And we'll be removing Lothaire's torque!"

"Husband?" Chase murmured. But then he shook his head. "I'll fight the turnin'." His lids grew heavy, his face paling.

"Fight all you want, boyo. I'm determined." He'd lost so much blood; it seeped out beneath him, an ever-growing ring in the sand.

Brandr dropped down beside Regin. "Do this, friend. You don't have much longer."

Regin ran her cheek against Chase's hand. "If you love me, you'll make this sacrifice for me. Nothing comes between us, remember?"

"You turned my words . . . against me?" His eyes closed. "Think about what you're doin'. . . ."

When his head lolled, panic set in. She put her ear to his bloody chest, listening for his heart. Still alive. Just unconscious. Over her shoulder, she snapped, "Lothaire!"

The vampire took a knee on Chase's other side, then

bit his own wrist. "Hold his mouth open." Brandr pried his jaws wide so Lothaire could drip a generous stream inside. Then the berserker shoved Chase's mouth shut until he swallowed.

"Now what?" she asked.

The vampire stood, dusting off his hands. "Now you wait. The magister will wake within three days, or he dies—" Lothaire tensed. *"Nïx,"* he hissed.

Regin jerked her head around. Through the rain, she spotted the soothsayer strolling along the beach toward them. Nïx? *She* was the one Regin had sensed?

The soothsayer had white sunblock on her nose, high-heeled flops, a wide-brimmed hat—and Bertil perched on her shoulder. Her T-shirt read: I Lost My Heart on Immortal Island.

"Nïx!" she cried. "Is Chase going to live?"

"Dearling, it's up to fate now."

"Back in New Orleans, you asked me what I would do to break the curse. I said just about anything then. Now I'm saying *anything*! Tell me what to do, Nïx!"

"All that could be done has been. Now as soon as everyone gets here, Malkom will be a dear and trace us off the island." She turned to Carrow. "Until then, good witch, a round of freedom for Regin's friends! And for . . . him." She pointed to Lothaire.

He intoned, "Valkyrie."

"Vampire," she said in greeting. The bat unfurled its wings aggressively.

Regin gathered Chase's head into her lap, frantically smoothing the hair from his cool forehead. When

Brandr's hand covered her shoulder, her tears fell, splatting against Chase's cheek. "Wh-what are you doing here, Nïx?"

"You know how it goes, had some miles about to expire. And it's just like you said. A little vacay was all I needed!"

Her voice thick, Regin asked, "Is Lucia safe? Did she face Cruach without me?"

"Cruach is no more! She and Garreth MacRieve took him out forever."

Cruach's dead. Regin's mind could hardly wrap around the idea.

"The two lovebirds are here on the island," Nïx continued, "hoofing it to get to you."

Lothaire stalked toward Carrow. "Free me, and be quick about it."

"That's right," Nïx said. "You'll want to be at full power before the wolf arrives. Since you broke his female's neck down in the Amazon. Directly after you woke La Dorada."

Regin gaped. "He did *what*?"

"Witch, *now*," he grated.

"Don't get pissy with me, leech." With a glare, Carrow pressed her print to his torque. "Even tapped out, I can still do a love spell to make you fall in love—with the sun."

When the collar dropped to the ground, Lothaire rolled his head on his neck. But instead of disappearing immediately, he traced to stand mere feet from Nïx.

A towering vampire with skin like marble and

chillingly flawless features was staring down a petite Valkyrie with crazed eyes and a cryptic smile.

The tension between the two was palpable. Even on the verge of flipping the fuck out, Regin couldn't look away.

"The Accession grinds on, does it not?" Lothaire said.

"Just like old times." Nïx winked. "Alas, Dorada will come for you once she rises again."

"I'll be ready." He narrowed his red eyes. "You've likely foreseen this moment. Tell me, are we to fight now? As in the past?"

"You defy foresight, Lothaire."

"That's only fair, Phenïx, since you've long defied insight." *Phenïx?*

Nïx canted her head. "What does your Endgame tell you?"

"That white queen will never take black king." He gave her a formal bow. "Until our next match."

"There won't be a next match, vampire."

His brow creased into a frown, the Enemy of Old disappeared.

With a lackadaisical air—as if she just hadn't been toe-to-toe with the Lore's most-feared fiend—Nïx strolled over to Regin. "Tsk, tsk." She gazed down at Chase. "He was such a cute boy. He gave me a hug good-bye that day at the fair, even though he thought I was a fortune-teller crone."

Regin swung her head up. "You *saw* him?"

"Saw who?"

"Nïx!"

"Regin!"

Inhale. Exhale. Pet Chase's forehead. Don't go crazy like her.

Lucia arrived then, hand in hand with Garreth MacRieve. "Regin, thank gods, you're al— who are you holding?"

Out of the corner of her lips, Carrow said, "That's the guy I was telling you about."

Lucia's eyes went wide. "This isn't the man who . . . tortured you?"

"It's complicated, Luce. J-just help me get him back to Val Hall."

"Help *him*?" Garreth growled. "After he tortured my cousin Uilleam? Who, incidentally, is seconds behind us and bent on mauling this mortal."

Freed of his collar, Brandr stepped up. "He'll have to go through me." His eyes glowed, his muscles burgeoning.

Natalya flared her poisonous claws. "And me."

Thad bowed up his chest. "Me, too."

Garreth looked ready to tangle. Lucia plucked her bowstring, her loyalties torn. A howl sounded in the near distance, footfalls crashing closer. . . .

It was Malkom who broke up the tension. "The magister tortured me, as well."

Great, another hater. "You got your revenge, demon! You want more?"

"I have Carrow because of him," Malkom said. "I want no revenge. I seek to repay."

Carrow gazed up at Malkom like a sap. "Let's start by tracing him the hell out of Dodge."

FIFTY-SIX

For two days, Chase lay in her bed at Val Hall, pale, still, his heartbeat so sporadic that at times she thought he'd . . . died.

Brandr had paced a hole in the rug, while Regin struggled to hold on to hope.

No one had any idea what would happen, not even Nïx, who'd only absently said, "Such a sweet little boy."

Now, as another morning broke, Regin rechecked the curtains, ensuring that no light reached him. "Will you stay with him, Brandr? I need to go downstairs for a bit." *To go on a fool's errand.*

"Of course."

She leaned down and kissed Chase's damp forehead. Strapping on her borrowed sword, she marched from her bedroom, down the stairs, and out the front door of Val Hall.

Thad and Natalya were on the porch swing, drinking coffee and holding vigil with Nïx.

Regin's sisters had initially taken issue with a half vamp like Thad and a dark fey like Natalya gaining entry past the wraiths, but Regin had been adamant about their staying.

Thad asked her, "Is DC going to be okay?"

"He's *totally* gonna pull through," Regin said, but even she recognized that she sounded half-hysterical, her words tinged with that out-of-place confidence people had when staring down a gun barrel.

"Don't be long, Regin!" Nïx called. "And if you see Bertil, tell that little scallywag that it's past his bedtime!"

Huh. Nïx is literally *batshit cray-cray.*

Regin tossed her hair toll to the wraiths in order to cross their guard. With their forbidding presence and brute strength, those flying, spectral creatures kept anything out of—or in—the Valkyrie's manor.

But the yard was another matter. Regin cast a murderous look at the crowd gathered along Val Hall's drive. They were like vultures, waiting there either to celebrate Chase's death—or to kill him.

The only thing that kept them from advancing? The recently repaired driveway gate, imbued with Carrow's protection spell.

Regin flipped the crowd off with both hands, bobbling her birds up and down for good measure while mouthing, *Suck it.* Then she headed to the swamp on Val Hall's property.

Near the water's edge she stopped beside a monument, one that looked totally out of place in the bayou: a Norse rune stone, draped with swamp moss, on "indefinite loan" from a Scandinavian museum of natural history.

Taking a deep breath, she knelt in front of it. Clearing her throat, she muttered, "Are you there, Wóden, it's me Regin." She gave a nervous laugh.

"I know you and Freya sleep, and that praying to

you is probably just a big fat waste of time. But I have to try. Seems I'll try anything." Another steadying breath. "So, Wóden, I need you to do me a solid and save the life of Declan Chase, a.k.a. Aidan the Fierce. . . ."

She trailed off. *This is stupid.* She needed to be by Chase's side, not talking to inanimate objects. *What if he . . . dies while I'm gone?* She swallowed. Then he'd still be *gone.* Attention back on the rock, she said, "Look, I know I'm not your favorite daughter, never have been. But I'm still your daughter! If you're punishing Aidan for his hubris, then know that you're punishing me too. No, you're *destroying* me."

Though she tried to bite back the words, out they came: "I've *hated* you for this! How can you do this to me? For a thousand years, I've lived with this curse, when I should have been living with him."

Her voice broke, and embarrassing tears streamed down her face. "P-please . . . please just let me have him this time."

Nothing. Only the sounds of the swamp waking from the night. She hadn't expected lightning to hurl down or anything, but she'd hoped for a glimmer of a sign, anything to give her hope.

Instead, she'd just become deeply aware of how insignificant she was, of how her prayers meant nothing.

Which pissed her off.

She shot to her feet and kicked the stone. That felt good. So she shoved her braids out of her tear-streaked face and kicked it again. "I've never asked you for *anything*!" She drew her borrowed sword, slamming it against the rock so hard her blade and arm vibrated. "Wake—the—hell—up!" Another swing. "I can't lose him again!" She dropped the sword, launching her fist against the rock. Just as Aidan had in ages past.

As sobs racked her body, she pummeled her forearms against the stone. *"L-let me have him."*

A hand rested on her shoulder, and she stilled. Lucia, as silent as ever. "Sister, calm yourself."

Regin turned, unsteady, sucking in a lungful of air.

Lucia's eyes widened at her appearance. "My gods, Regin. You really want him this much? I still don't understand. Carrow said he'd tortured you."

She squared her shoulders. "So our courtship was rocky. When have I ever done anything normally?"

Lucia inclined her head, conceding the point.

"Besides, you're with a *werewolf,* Luce. I don't want to hear it."

"Engaged to him, actually. We were just waiting to find you before we have a grand-scale royal ceremony." For secretive Lucia to be the center of attention that big . . . ? She must truly want MacRieve.

"The wolf was okay with you waiting for me?"

"I explained that I could never do something that important without my wingman."

Regin tried for a smile and failed. "Yeah, well, that's the least you can do since you two ganked Cruach without me." After all these centuries, Lucia was finally freed of her worst nightmare.

"I didn't have a choice, Regin. Since you were tied up with your . . . courtship."

"Did Lothaire really break your neck?"

"Oh, yeah." Lucia unconsciously rubbed her nape. "Garreth went ballistic."

"I can't believe you're going to sacrifice your archery mojo for MacRieve." Lucia would forfeit her fantastical skill with a bow if she was unchaste. "Who am I gonna hang out with when you're a talentless nobody?"

Lucia quirked a brow at that. "I don't have to sacrifice it. Turns out, it's been my own skill for some time."

"Wow. That's great, Luce." Everything was working out for her. "You deserve this happiness after you've waited so long." *But so do I!*

"Now, come on." Lucia reached forward to sweep her thumbs under Regin's eyes. "Things are getting tense around the manor. Even more beings are lining up to take out your man."

"I'll kill them all."

"Though Garreth's cousin Uilleam isn't among that mob, he will seek revenge in the future. Apparently, Chase had him . . . vivisected. What would you do to my fiancé's cousin then?"

Regin tapped her ear. "Hellooo, you got something in your ears? I said, I'll—kill—them—all. Including anyone in your wolf pack, if you don't make with the royal decree and declare my man off-limits."

"Huh." Lucia tilted her head. "I could do that, couldn't I?"

"Yep." As Regin picked up her sword, she gazed at the stone one more time, laying her palm against it. She silently cried, *Please!*

Lucia put her arm around her shoulders. "You know Wóden can't hear you."

"Didn't figure it could hurt."

"Lothaire's blood is strong," Lucia said. "It might still work. But don't depend on our father for this."

Yet as they walked back to Val Hall, a warm breeze blew against Regin's face, almost like a caress.

Declan's eyes flashed open, and he sucked in a deep breath. *Where am I? Where's Regin?* Gaze darting, he shot upright in bed.

Brandr was there. "Easy, friend. You're safe—your woman's safe. She'll return directly." As thunder rumbled the walls, he said, "We're inside Val Hall."

Only then did Declan relax a measure, surveying his surroundings. If he hadn't known he was in Regin's bedroom by her scent, he would have by the decorations.

Concert posters covered the walls, bands from ABBA to Phish. Workout gear and video games abounded. Strands of Christmas lights dangled from the ceiling, only these had strings of vampire fangs wrapped around the cords. Tightly closed tie-dyed drapes blocked out all but a few needle holes of sunlight.

The bedding? *Star Wars* sheets.

"You're healed now," Brandr said. "Your wound's completely mended."

Declan glanced down. There was no new scar to join his others.

All his life, he'd suffered nightmares of that blow, of Regin's screams.

Her grief had hurt him far worse than any cold steel could.

"So I'm a vampire now." Bitter disappointment

settled over him. She might say she wanted him like this, but he could never walk in the sun with her again. And what if his blood-drinking disgusted her?

At the thought of drinking blood, he grew nauseated, still disbelieving that Lothaire's ran through his veins.

"You're an immortal, and that's what matters," Brandr said firmly.

"How long have I been out?"

"Two days. Here"—he tossed him a pair of jeans—"I know you're keen to see Regin."

As Declan rose to dress, he thought he heard someone outside yell his name. "What was that?"

Brandr gave him a rueful look. "There might be a few dozen beings gathered outside. And they might be bent on revenge against you, even for things you didn't do. Apparently, you're the poster boy for the Order, and Loreans want their pound of flesh."

This is what I'm bringin' to the table, Regin.

Brandr continued, "Although there are only about three hundred mortal berserkers left, they are your men to lead, Aidan. Dispatch any of us against your enemies."

"I'm no' Aidan. And I'll clean up my own mess."

"Not Aidan? But you claimed Regin. The curse . . ."

"He's a part of me, but he's long gone. I'm still a scarred and surly Irishman." He reminded himself that he was what Regin wanted. At least, before he'd been turned into a leech.

"You have his memories?"

"Oh, aye, I remember you from before. You were a young smart-arse whose guard was too low." Then he grew serious. "I also remember that you made me a vow ages ago, one you kept for centuries." Holding the man's gaze, Declan said, "I'll protect Regin from now on. I'm releasing you from that oath, Brandr." He cleared his throat. "You've been a true friend. You have my gratitude and always will."

Brandr was looking at him strangely. Not surprising, considering the circumstances, but still . . . Yet he said nothing, just stalked around the room, batting a boxing speedbag, toeing a pink bowling ball on the floor.

Declan exhaled. "Say what's on your mind, berserker."

"Your eyes were just glowing as you spoke. And when you were unconscious, I noticed that—"

"Release the hounds, muthafuckas!" Regin screamed from outside.

Eyes wide, Declan charged toward the sound, with Brandr right behind him. When Declan threw open the bedroom door, it exploded off its hinges. As he stomped down the stairs, he laid his hand on the railing, rendering the wood to splinters.

"Regin!" He stormed out the front door onto the front porch . . . directly into the sun.

FIFTY-SEVEN

"Let us have him!"

"This has nothing to do with you, Valkyrie."

"He'll pay with his life!"

Loreans were out for Chase's blood, which meant Regin was out for theirs.

But at her command, Lucia sighed. "Really, Regin? Release the hounds?" She stood at the gate, her hand on the mystical lever.

"Nut up or shut up, Luce. I'm tired of looking at these assholes, tired of listening to them. Let's do this."

With a roll of her eyes, Lucia said, "I'll be on the porch with Nïx, acting as your spotter." Then she opened the gate.

As beings of all stripes stalked toward Val Hall, Regin choked up on her sword hilt, ready to swing for the fences—

A man's deep voice rang out. *"Regin!"*

"Chase?" Barely daring to believe, she glanced over her shoulder. He was alive!

He and Brandr had come barreling out the front door, but when they tried to make it past the wraiths, those guards hurtled them back.

Lurching to his feet, his face a mask of fury, Declan charged forward again, hitting the barrier like a freight train. The wraiths shrieked. *Never heard them do anything but cackle.*

The third time he charged, he was in full-on berserkrage. Nïx negligently tossed a braid, and the wraiths were all too happy to let him alone speed through.

As he closed in on her, Regin's jaw dropped, and the fracas ground to a halt. Chase was *huge,* and scarred, and he looked *dangerous.* His muscles rippled, his eyes burning with ferocity as his gaze locked on her.

And gods, she was so freaking in love with him.

"Chase!" She ran to him, and he caught her up in his arms, clasping her tight. "You're alive!" She rubbed her cheek against his chest. "And uh, really *strong.*" He loosened his grip on her. She drew back to see him casting her foes a look of such pitiless menace that even the stronger ones backed down.

Then he set her behind him, bowing up his chest, a low growl rumbling from it. *A creature with which one did not fuck.*

Once the beings retreated in a wave—cloistering themselves behind the gates, as if that'd protect them—he turned to her. He took several deep breaths, grappling for control. Finally, he grated, "And what were you doin', Regin?"

She jutted her chin. "About to grease every last one of them."

He cast her a chiding look. "And you did no' tie one hand behind your back? Where's the sport, lass?" Then he wrapped the crook of his arm around her nape. "You're no' goin' to fight my battles. I've done these things, and I'm ready to pay the price."

"The hell! I've finally got you—you think I'm letting you go that easily?"

"We can't run forever. I have to face anyone who'd challenge me."

"Just hear me out. While you were napping, I was busy chatting up our allies. Didn't you know—your woman's a golden-tongued ambassador! My sisters always said I graduated from the shock-and-awe school of diplomacy, but joke 'em if they can't take a fuck, right?"

Chase nodded gravely. "Joke 'em."

"So anyway, we've got some wicked strong allies lined up. These tossers here just missed the memo. The Valkyrie are all on board; a slight against you is a slight against them. All's forgiven with the witches. In fact, Malkom Slaine even feels bad for fileting you! He and Carrow literally shuddered to think what their lives would have been like if you hadn't dispatched Carrow to hell. There was talk of sending you a card at Beltane! So the Valks are down, and the witches are down. Oh, and I talked to Brandr. Get this—"

"The berserkers are down?"

"Way to steal my thunder, Chase."

"Regin, I can't depend on you or any others to fight my battles. I made my own mistakes. That means I must also make sacrifices."

Nïx gave a delicate cough from the porch swing. "No one's sacrificing anything." She called out to any creature who still remained within earshot, "Declan the Fierce is under *my* aegis. If you kill him, you risk my displeasure." Lightning bolts scored the sunny sky like bomb blasts, sending beings scattering. Nïx called after them, "But by all means, smack him around!"

Sunny day? *Sunny*— "What are you *doing*?" Regin shrieked to Chase. "Why aren't you burning? Where are your fangs?"

He rubbed his tongue over his teeth. "Do no' have any."

"So how'd you heal?"

When Nïx rose to enter the house, Regin grabbed Chase's hand and hurried after her. "Whoa, there, soothsayer. How can he go out in the sun?"

Nïx blinked. "Where'd everyone go? What were we talking about?" Her eyes went wide. "I remember! Chase is an immortal now." She gazed at Brandr, Lucia, Natalya, and Thad. "We'll all have an ice-cream cake to celebrate! Except for we don't have a freezer!"

"Nïx, why didn't he turn into a vampire?"

"I suppose because he never died."

Regin turned to him. "I get to *keep* you? You're immortal!"

"Aye, though I don't understand how."

"I believe I do," Brandr said. "While you were unconscious, I looked at your dog tags. The charm on the back of one is the mark of Wóden. You've carried it on a standard, a naval flag, a cavalry crest, and tattooed upon your chest. Your battle with the Pravus might just have been your two hundredth."

Declan's heart started hammering. If this could be true . . .

"I believe you earned ohalla, brother," Brandr said. "The battle count must have been cumulative, the number following the soul, not the body."

"But Wóden wouldn't gift me with it. Not after my deeds in the past."

Regin quickly said, "Let's don't ask too many—or really *any*—questions. You're an immortal, and you're a berserker. That's all we need to know." *Thank you, Wóden, thank you, thank you . . .*

Chase murmured, "An immortal berserker."

Brandr punched him in the arm. Hard. "Took you long enough."

Regin asked Nïx, "Why didn't he turn into Aidan?"

"Chase is too strong. Always will be. And he wants you too badly to ever slink into the background."

Chase frowned at Nïx. "Why did you . . . why would you vouch for me?"

"I've been looking out for you since you were a boy." Imitating an Oirish accent, she said, "Want yer fortune told, me boy? A medallion for luck?"

"*You* gave the charm to me."

"Yes. And before you ask me why I would let everything else happen to you, know this. That misery hardened you, made you grow strong. Without it, your life would've faded to a whisper in Aidan's mind. And Declan Chase suits my sister better." She patted Regin on the head. "Regin doesn't do perfect."

Chase was quiet for long moments, then his lips curled into a breathtaking smile that made Regin's heart flutter. "Then I'm her man."

* * *

Mourne Mountains
One month later

A crackling fire cast light over the cabin's rough-hewn interior. A tray of oyster shells and an empty can of Guinness sat on the table.

Declan and Regin lazed in a big tub before the fireplace, her back to his chest, his arms wrapped tightly around her.

As promised, he'd made love to her more times than she could count. And as she'd told him, they'd been through too much together to ever hold back from one another.

Her tone utterly relaxed, she asked, "So what mayhem are we going to get up to today?"

"Lady's choice. I'm game for anything. But after the mayhem, we should start markin' things off our list. Get married, house-hunt, shop for the new swords I'm keen to buy you. . . ."

Content merely to celebrate a future together, they'd accomplished little. Though before leaving for Ireland, they had gotten Thad and his family settled in New Orleans—into the newly established Lore Relocation Program.

Regin and Nïx had decided the boy should be moved close by so that the Valkyrie could keep him and his family safe from the Order, and to guide him into immortality.

Turned out that young Thad was half vampire, half phantom—one of the rarest Lore mixes ever to live. He'd grow to be a powerful hybrid, with untold abilities. Definitely a key player to have on Team Vertas.

So the Declan Chase Restitution Fund had purchased a *quaint* little mansion in the Garden District for the Brayden family. Regin hadn't quite gotten around to informing Declan that he'd bought it before Thad had loped up to him and walloped him on the back. "DC, I'm really glad you pulled through. And thanks big-time for moving Mom and Gram to New Orleans."

Declan had raised his brows at Regin. "Did I move Mom and Gram to New Orleans?"

Regin had nodded up at him. "The Brayden women about fell out when they saw pics of the place. We're telling them you're a long-lost uncle from the Emerald Isle. . . ."

Unfortunately, some beings couldn't be bought off by the restitution fund. Like Uilleam MacRieve, who'd been out for blood—and nothing less would do.

Anticipating Lucia's interference, the werewolf had come a'calling at Val Hall, but Nïx had taken care of him. As she'd informed Regin, "I simply told Uilleam that one of your offspring was a mate to one of his. He'd never deprive one of his offspring of a mate!"

Regin had been dubious. "Is that even true?"

"Surely? It sounds reasonable. And I didn't specify how many generations."

Still, Lucia's upcoming royal wedding was gonna be *tense*. And Regin and Nïx's bridesmaids' dresses? Hid-e-ous.

When Natalya saw Regin in it, the fey would never let her live it down. Nat and Brandr were both attending. Not together, though. They'd given it one more shot between them, but both zigged again or something, so now they were just friends.

Declan began tracing the backs of his fingers up and down her arm. "What did you and Nïx talk about today?"

"I again tried to get her to explain Lothaire's 'unbreakable ties' comment. But she gave me nothing." Regin hadn't paid much attention to the vamp when he'd warned her of a connection between him and Declan. Now, she was jonesing to know the fine print.

And both she and Declan wondered what Lothaire's open-ended vow would entail.

"I don't feel tied to him," he said. "If I did I might be able to find him—then I could kill him, just to ease your mind. . . ."

The vampire remained a specter in the background, bent on getting that ring, which meant he'd be hunting Commander Webb next. With Declan's memories, the vampire could locate Webb's home, could circumvent every security measure. Though Declan had said nothing, Regin had sensed conflict in him. She'd suggested he call the man and give him a heads-up, and then they'd be even for Webb saving his life.

The conversation had been rife with tension, but in the end Webb had said, "I told the Order that you died on the island. And I'll stick to that, but only if you stand down against our mission."

Declan had replied, "You told me I was either on your side or theirs. You were right. Harm any among my allies, and I'll retaliate."

With that, she'd known he'd shaken away the last of

the brainwashing and had come back into the fold, her born-again Lorean.

Things weren't perfect. But damn, they were getting *close*. . . .

"Did your sister have any update on who stole my bloody boat?"

"None. Nïx just kept calling it the Love Boat. Today she sang that it 'promises something for everyone.' Hey, we didn't need it anyway."

"But they took *my* boat," he grumbled.

Regin gave a laugh. "You are such a . . . a *berserker*." When she turned over on her front to rest her chin on her hands, his shaft pulsed beneath her. "Already?" she murmured with delight.

He grinned down at her, treating her to that breathtaking smile. Over the last month, he'd even begun laughing with her, her own personal captive audience to entertain.

"It's your own fault for being irresistible. And I *am* a berserker through and through, possessive of everything that's mine." His hands trailed down to cup her ass. "Admit it, you've got to be relieved I'm no' a vampire."

She shook her head. "I would've taken you any way I could get you, boyo."

"And if you'd given me leave to, lass, I'd have come back for you a thousand times."

"Luckily"—she leaned up, brushing her lips against his—"the fifth time's a charm. . . ."

EPILOGUE

Hark! Here closes this tale, the legend of Declan the Fierce and Reginleit the Radiant One, a pair of lovers bound and blessed by fate.

It ends, as many legends do, with a destined marriage—this one between a Valkyrie whose long wait was rewarded and a warrior whose yearning was at last fulfilled.

Theirs is a tale of joy and bounty. Be of ease and listen on. . . .

With a consuming love for his lady guiding him heart and soul and Wóden's mark tattooed upon his chest, Declan became a friend to the Lore, a champion of the gods . . . and eventually a doting father.

Filled with hope and a secret certainty that she was Wóden's favorite, Regin became one of the most powerful Valkyrie ever to live, a mistress of her own fate who laughed in the face of adversity . . . and eventually a mother who plagued her children with pranks.

Cherishing Regin endlessly, Declan never left her side again, her immortal match. Perhaps his hubris was forgiven, the Reaper's dark scythe stilled forever.

All he knows is that his Valkyrie's kiss is sweet, their children's laughter a balm to his soul.

Whatever may be the case, to this day, Reginleit runs into his arms.

To this day, Declan clasps her close to his chest, gazing at the sky. In thanks. . . .